She turned to face him and lightning struck.

He swallowed. "Like I mentioned on the phone, I've been out of town for a while." He didn't want her thinking he was a slob.

"No worries. Is there anyplace in particular you'd like me to start?"

"Um, I guess you can start down here, then the bed… r…" Greg's words stuck in his throat. "…pstairs."

S…

"…

t…

"…

"…

h…

"…choice of where to stay and when."

He shrugged, grinned. "It has its perks, I suppose, but it can be exhausting."

"Hmm. Well, I should get started."

"Oh, yeah, sure." He finally stepped from in front of her and suddenly felt like a plug that had been disconnected.

"Kitchen first?"

"Sure." He followed her into the kitchen and rested the mop and broom against the wall. "I'll, uh, get out of your way."

Donna Hill began writing novels in 1990. Since that time she has had more than forty titles published, which include full-length novels and novellas. Two of her novels and one novella were adapted for television. She has won numerous awards for her body of work. She is also the editor of five novels, two of which have been nominated for awards. She easily moves from romance to erotica, horror, comedy and women's fiction. She was the first recipient of the *RT Book Reviews* Trailblazer Award and won the *RT Book Reviews* Career Achievement Award. Donna lives in Brooklyn with her family. Visit her website at https://donnaohill.com.

Books by Donna Hill

Harlequin Kimani Romance

Sultry Nights
Everything Is You
Mistletoe, Baby
The Way You Love Me
My Love at Last
For the Love of You
Surrender to Me
When I'm with You
What the Heart Wants
Forever Mine

Visit the Author Profile page
at Harlequin.com for more titles.

DONNA HILL
and
CAROLYN HECTOR

Forever Mine &
Falling for the Beauty Queen

HARLEQUIN® KIMANI™ ROMANCE

ISBN-13: 978-1-335-45842-1

Forever Mine & Falling for the Beauty Queen

Copyright © 2019 by Harlequin Books S.A.

The publisher acknowledges the copyright holders of the individual works as follows:

Forever Mine
Copyright © 2019 by Donna Hill

Falling for the Beauty Queen
Copyright © 2019 by Carolyn Hall

Recycling programs for this product may not exist in your area.

Printed in U.S.A.

HARLEQUIN®
™ www.Harlequin.com

CONTENTS

This book is dedicated in loving memory to my mom, Dorothy Hill. I'm still trying to move in the world without you. Rest in peace.

FOREVER MINE

Donna Hill

Dear Reader,

I cannot believe that after all these years I'm still birthing these babies! Figuratively, of course, but each and every book is like a child to me, one that I want to show off to the world. With that, I want to introduce you to the gorgeous, sexy, successful chef to the stars and new member of *my* family, Alonzo Grant. You may remember briefly meeting Alonzo in *What the Heart Wants*, which featured his heart-stopping heart surgeon brother Franklin. Now it's Alonzo's turn to bring all his hunkiness to the table.

When I began crafting the Grants of DC series, I wanted to showcase black men in all their glory. The Grant brothers personify everything that is good and honorable about black men.

Alonzo Grant has an enviable lifestyle, but it takes a slight turn when Mikayla Harris literally walks into his house. He has had his pick of women, but none who have enticed him to trade in creating culinary masterpieces for the masses and finally set a table for two.

So, please sit back, perhaps with a glass of wine and your favorite treat, and come along for a journey that will satisfy you in all the right places and hopefully leave you wanting more!

As always, I thank you, my dear friends. Your support has sustained me for an amazing twenty-nine years! I could not have done it without you.

Until next time,

Donna

Chapter 1

Alonzo Grant tugged in an exhausted breath and rotated his tight shoulders. The clang and tingle of pots, china and silverware being gathered by his stellar team punctuated the air that still held the aromas of the five-course meal that he'd created and supervised specifically for tonight.

The last of the high-profile guests finally drifted toward their Porsches, Mercedes, Lexuses and Escalades. Red-jacketed valets moved with gazelle-like grace, speed retrieving cars and presenting them to their owners. The party, or what Academy Award-nominee Kevin Palmer called "an impromptu gathering of a few close friends" at his London townhouse, had mushroomed from dinner for an intimate twenty to a whopping one hundred. So of course, Kevin called on his longtime friend Alonzo to prepare and execute the menu fit for his A-list friends and wannabes. Fortunately for Kevin, chef Alonzo Grant had flown in a week earlier to spend some time with his on-again, off-again lady of the moment, Cheri Lang, while she was on break between filming.

"Lonzo, man, you outdid yourself tonight." Kevin stood in the threshold of the main hall where the party had been held.

Alonzo slowly unbuttoned his signature white jacket with his initials, AG, etched in black letters on the left side of his chest. A shadow of a smile curved his mouth. "Anything for you, Kev. Frat brothers till the end." He clapped him on the arm. "But next time," he said, pointing a long finger in his friend's direction, "try to get the head count earlier than the morning of your event." He shook his head in wry amusement.

"I know. I know." Kevin held up his hands in subjugation. "Totally apologize. Everything was all last-minute. Who knew I was gonna get an Academy Award nod, and that you would be in town?" He grinned, snatched a bottle of champagne from the ice bucket, filled a flute for himself and one for Alonzo. "The stars were aligned—no pun intended."

"Helluva performance in *Dreamers*." He tipped his glass toward Kevin, then took a sip. "You deserve it."

"Thanks, man. Still can't believe it." Kevin took a long swallow from his glass. "No sooner than the nomination came in, my phone starts ringing with offers."

Alonzo chuckled. "You always did walk under that lucky charm."

"I do have *some* talent," he quipped. He rested his

weight against the wall. "One of the calls came from none other than Ryan Carrington."

Alonzo's brow lifted. "*The* Ryan Carrington, that directed Fishburne and Jackson in *Interboro*?"

Kevin flashed his money-winning smile. "The one and only."

Alonzo bobbed his head in approval and raised his hand for a fist bump. "Making friends in high places."

Kevin tapped his fist against Alonzo's. "He wants me to come in and see him, said he has a project he's working on and thinks I'll be perfect." His grin made his brown eyes crinkle in the corners.

"Now that's news. Congrats. No matter how it shakes out, you made an impression on him."

"You've met Ryan, haven't you?"

"Yeah, a few times at different parties that I catered. I did a small one for him about a year ago. Doing something bigger for his upcoming birthday."

"We're all done, Mr. Grant."

Alonzo glanced toward the door. Jasmine Cole, his head chef and right hand, untied her apron. "'Scuse me a minute, Kev." He crossed the room to where Jasmine waited. "Couldn't have pulled this off without you," he said and smiled down at her. "You're a miracle worker."

"You know how to put a great team together, Zo. And in a hurry, at that."

"With you as my wingwoman," he said, winking, "can't go wrong." Because of all his travels and his connections, he'd built a stellar team of cooks and servers that specialized in everything from delicate patisserie to down-south soul food, dinner for two or two hundred and everything in between. At a moment's notice he could gather some of the best in the business to pull off an event. Of course, he had his core team that—when it wasn't an out-of-the-country emergency—were his go-to crew, with Jasmine as the lead.

He took a thick envelope out of his pocket. "Everyone's check is inside. I added a little something extra for all the last-minute craziness."

"I know they'll appreciate that." She took the envelope.

"What time is your flight back to the States?"

"Eleven. Can't wait. A full week to do absolutely nothing. As a matter of fact, I think I'll order in every day!"

They laughed.

Alonzo leaned in and lightly kissed her cheek. "Rest well and safe travels."

"When are you returning?"

"I thought I'd stay in London another week. See some sights."

She gave him the side-eye. "You and Cheri?"

"A gentleman never tells. Good night, Jasmine."

She squeezed his bicep. "See you when you get back. Try to stay out of trouble and out of the headlines." She turned and walked toward the door.

He pressed his hand to his chest. "You wound me," he called out to her retreating back. She waved a hand in dismissal.

Time out of the spotlight would do him good. His brothers, Montgomery and Franklin, ragged him constantly about his status as a ladies' man, which was almost on par with his culinary skills. His face had landed on the cover of every food magazine worth its salt and pepper, right along with *Entertainment Weekly*, *People* and *Us* magazines. The fact that he basked in the spotlight and there wasn't a camera that didn't love him only added to his aura. But in a million years he would have never guessed that his childhood love for cooking would one day find him as master chef for actors, athletes and entertainers all over the globe.

Alonzo returned to where Kevin was finishing off his drink. "I'm gonna head back to my hotel."

"Sure, sure. I'll walk you out." He draped his arm across Alonzo's broad shoulders as they walked to the front door. "I can't thank you enough, man."

"Don't mention it." He tipped his head and lowered his voice. "Seriously, don't mention it. I don't need word getting out that folks can treat me any old way," he chuckled. "Mess up my MO."

"The secret is safe with me."

They shared a hard handshake and pulled in for the one-arm brother hug. "Take it easy, man, and congrats again."

"I'll probably see you in a month or so, for Ryan's birthday bash. He invited me." Kevin grinned.

Alonzo chuckled and shook his head in amusement. "See you then." He jogged down the four steps and walked along the pathway that led to his rented car.

It was nearly midnight. He'd been on his feet since before eight, and tired didn't begin to describe how he felt. It took all his concentration to remember to stay on the correct side of the road. The drive from Kevin's townhouse was barely twenty minutes to the Crowne Plaza where he was staying, but it already felt like hours.

He considered calling Cheri, have her spend the night in his room instead of hers, work out the kinks, but he didn't have anything left in the tank. Cheri Lang was an up-and-coming actress who had a few small parts to her credit. Her current film role as an FBI agent—that brought her to London—could be her breakout role. At least that's what she kept saying when she sweet-talked him into coming to London, promising that during her downtime they would get together. It really wasn't a heavy lift to convince him. England was one of his favorite places and getting to spend time with Cheri was a plus.

But right now, what he really needed was sustenance. As crazy as it was, he was starving. With all the food for the party, he didn't actually eat a full meal but only taste tested each of the dishes for quality. He made a quick left and drove in the direction of his favorite all-night restaurant. Warren Hobbs, a classmate of his, had packed his US bags, relocated to merry old England and opened the best Italian restaurant outside of Italy. They'd met when they were both students at the Castello di Vicarello in Tuscany, having already begun to build reputations as top chefs after their intense training at the International Culinary Institute in California. Anytime he visited England, he made it a point to stop in and check on his friend.

By the time he arrived, all he could think about was Warren's signature dish, tortelli with ricotta and spinach, a recipe he'd mastered in Tuscany and then put his own special spin on it; the secret to which Alonzo was determined to uncover.

He eased into a vacant spot two doors down from

the restaurant, cut the engine and hopped out. When he reached the glass front of Hobbs he stopped short. Seated just beyond the plate-glass window was Cheri with Dominic Logan, her leading man. For a moment he stood there in disbelief, watching. Unless they were role-playing as a couple that couldn't keep their hands off each other, they were definitely more than two actors out for a nightcap.

He should have walked away, but walking away wasn't in his nature and hadn't been since he was five and his kindergarten teacher told him to let Stevie have the last toy in the basket, even though Stevie had pushed him out of the way. At five he couldn't put into words the dynamics of what was happening, or give voice to the twist that knotted in the pit of his stomach. He remembered looking at Stevie's pink cheeks and blue eyes, eyes that matched Ms. Holly's. He said no, snatched the toy, held it to his chest and marched back to his place on the brown-and-orange rug. Ms. Holly actually tried to pry the toy from his hand. He remembered biting her hand. She yelled and called him a dirty little nigger. He didn't know what *nigger* meant, but in his child's mind, it was connected to being small and dirty, and the look of red fury on Ms. Holly's face only confirmed that it was something awful, that *he* was something awful. After his father and mother paid Ms. Holly a visit the following day, the thought of walking away from anything or anyone never entered his mind.

Alonzo pulled the door open and walked inside. Cheri had her back to him and was practically lip to lip with Dominic. He casually strolled over.

"Cheri, hey!" He placed his hand on the back of her chair.

Her head snapped up. Her hazel eyes widened. "Zo! Hi, uh…"

He waved a hand dismissively. "Just wanted to say hello. You're Dominic Logan, right?" He turned on his smile.

"Yes." Dominic stuck out his hand.

"Alonzo Grant." He shook Dominic's hand. "Nice to meet you in person."

"How do you know Cheri?"

"Oh, Cheri and I go way back. Right?" He grinned down into her stricken face. He stealthily stroked the back of her neck with the pad of his thumb. All those acting lessons weren't doing her much good.

"Yes, we do," she said softly.

"Hey, I just stopped in to grab a bite. Don't let me hold you two up. Nice seeing you, Cheri—and meeting you," he said to Dominic.

Without another word he turned away, half amused, half annoyed, his order for tortelli forgotten. He didn't even bother to find out if Warren was working. The upside of this made-for-TV moment was that at least he and Cheri would never have to engage in the "it wasn't me" conversation. He pushed open the door, stepped out into the mist-filled night and returned to his car.

Once in his hotel room he poured himself a shot of bourbon and began to peel out of his clothes. On the ride to his hotel he replayed the scene at the restaurant. It was almost funny, complete with clichés. He tossed his white shirt across the chair. Cheri was sexy, great company and probably as noncommittal as he was. They got together whenever they were in the same city, had plenty of laughs and fabulous sex. There had been times when they'd awkwardly danced around the idea of going exclusive. Those conversations generally devolved into a romp in bed.

Knowing all that, there was still that male-ego part of him that was totally pissed off. Clearly, Dominic had no clue that anything was going on with him and Cheri, but *she* knew and that's what stung—a little.

He tossed back his drink. If he was honest, although he'd never committed, he cared about Cheri. He'd cleared the decks for her—sort of, or at least he gave their relationship more attention than any of the others he engaged in from time to time. That meant something.

In the morning, he'd have to call the airline. They'd flown from LAX together and had first-class tickets to return. That would be awkward. He chuckled. In the meantime he'd chalk this one up to a learning experience. The lesson—hmm, he was still learning.

Chapter 2

Alonzo all but dragged himself out of the Uber that dropped him off in front of his two-story Beverly Hills vista. The grueling eleven-hour flight was made more difficult by a teething toddler that, he swore, cried for the entire eleven hours—including layover. His ears still rang and he was pretty sure that high-pitched screech would haunt his dreams for weeks.

He shrugged the thick leather strap of the duffel bag off his shoulder and dropped it onto the foyer floor next to the matching carry-on. As he rolled his stiff shoulders, his gaze quickly scanned the open space that showcased the contemporary living room, dining room and, of course, the chef's kitchen. From his vantage point he could see straight out to the back patio and pool.

"Home sweet home." He walked through the living

room and into the kitchen. Even a first-class flight had its limitations when it came to cuisine—at least cuisine that rose to his high standards. He pulled open the double-door stainless steel fridge and groaned, which seemed to echo in the cavernous space of the near-empty vessel. Withered vegetables, imported water, a half loaf of French bread and a plastic container of assorted cheeses.

"Got to be kidding," he grumbled. He'd been so focused on his packed schedule that the last thing on his mind before leaving was stocking the fridge.

He'd been gone for nearly six weeks. Before arriving with Cheri in London, he'd had a gig in Atlanta for the grand opening of Terrance Paul's expansion to his state-of-the-art movie studio. After that he was off to Tokyo, then back to the States again to Colorado for a major fund-raiser for Alison Francis, who was running for senate. He'd taken some downtime in Saint Kitts just to refuel and be catered to for a week. Then it was a stop in New York to cater for the crew of *Power* in celebration of the upcoming season.

He'd actually been looking forward to spending time with Cheri and doing nothing but chilling and making love. Of course there was the last-minute gig for Kevin, but after that it should have been all play.

Humph. He shut the door, drew in a contemplative breath, then sniffed the air. Stale. The whole place needed airing out and a good cleaning.

Since he planned to stay in LA for a little while, he was going to have to get stocked and have someone from the cleaning service come by pronto. First things first. He needed to wash the eleven-hour trip out of his pores.

* * *

Mildly refreshed, but now truly ravenous, he toasted two pieces of French bread and added a slice of Jersey Blue cheese accompanied by a glass of wine. Seated at the island counter, he scrolled through his phone, found the number and called the cleaning service, only to hear that the number was no longer in service. Sure that he'd dialed wrong, he called again. Same message.

He finished his wine, frowned, poured another glass. Damn, he hadn't been gone that long. Now what? His mother would tell him to clean his own house, the same way she'd insisted that he clean his disaster of a room. Ellen Grant stayed on him about his room. She could not fathom how he could exist in the chaos that he created and chided him daily to pick up and put away, 'cause no one was going to do it for him. He chuckled. Of the three brothers' rooms, his was always the one that looked as if an explosion had happened. He'd gotten better over the years, but housekeeping was not his strong suit. In fact, he'd grown a bit anal about how his place looked. So having his house cleaned twice per month was not a big deal—no matter what his mother said!

He squinted at the screen of his phone while he searched for a cleaning service that was relatively local, and ready to come today. After two strikes he tried one more: At Your Service. It was a bit out of the way but he was getting desperate.

The call was answered on the second ring.

"At Your Service. How can I help you today?"

The voice, full-bodied and potent like an imported wine, made him thirsty. "Hello. My name is Alonzo Grant, and I'm really hoping that you can help me. I've been out of town for nearly six weeks. Just got in today and, well…you can imagine."

She laughed, rich and throaty.

"I completely understand, Mr. Grant. Let me get some information."

"I'm in Beverly Hills on Lago Vista Drive."

"Oh…"

"Is that a problem?"

"Um, no, not at all. What is the address?"

Alonzo gave her his address.

"And the number that came up on my screen—is that home or cell?"

"Both, really," he said with a chuckle.

"Me too." She cleared her throat. "I can have someone to you in two hours. Does that work for you?"

"Works fine. I think I can hang on until then."

"Great. And thank you for contacting At Your Service." He started to hang up. "Oh, wait."

"Yes?"

"What's your name…in case of…anything?"

"Oh, I'm sorry. Mikayla."

"Thanks, Mikayla." He disconnected the call.

The next calls were to the food delivery service and the local Italian restaurant that he swore by, where he placed a huge order for all his favorites, then refilled his wineglass and waited.

Chapter 3

Mikayla jumped up from the chair at her kitchen table—her home office—and did her version of the happy dance. On her shoestring budget she'd put together a pretty decent website, bought a stack of business cards and had been handing out flyers in her East LA neighborhood announcing her house-cleaning services. It had been nearly two months without an ounce of interest until today. And in Beverly Hills! She let out a whoop of joy.

Would she accidentally on purpose run into any celebrities? No time for wishful thinking. She checked the time on her cell phone. Wow, she promised to be there in two hours. The drive was a solid forty-five minutes to an hour, on a good day, and she had to stop off and check on her mother first.

She darted into her junior bedroom and pulled her At Your Service polo shirt from the closet. The black short-sleeved top hugged her a bit close but she'd gotten a half dozen at a discount and had no intention of sending them back. She tugged off her jeans and traded them for a pair of black khakis, then put on her black sneakers.

All the cleaning supplies were in the hall closet. She collected the bucket that held the cleaners, sponges and rubber gloves, tucked the mop and broom under her arm, grabbed her jacket and headed over to the rehabilitation and treatment facility.

Rehab and *mother* were two words she would never have thought to put together. Now they were interchangeable. Throughout her childhood, her mom, Stella, had been the Energizer Bunny, full of health and vitality. She was at every recital, volleyball game, school play, graduation. It had been just the two of them all of Mikayla's life. Her mom wasn't just her mother; she was her best friend. When her mom started forgetting things like her keys or if she'd bought detergent, Mikayla didn't think much of it. People forgot stuff, right? But then the forgetfulness grew more pronounced, like on the day they were to meet for lunch in Harlem and her mother showed up at the restaurant but was surprised to see her daughter waiting for her.

One of the best facilities in the country for early-onset Alzheimer's was in California. Mikayla didn't think twice. She packed up her apartment and her mother and made the trip across the country.

She pulled in front of Greenwood Rehabilitation Center. For a moment she sat, staring at the words of the facility carved into the stone edifice. Her eyes stung. The ache of what was happening to her mother twisted inside her like a soaked towel being wrung dry of every drop of water.

The past six months had drained her emotionally, physically and financially—hence At Your Service. Her dream of the big or little screen took a back seat to taking care of her mother. Whatever she needed to do, it would be done. She drew in a long breath, pressed her lips together in resolve and got out of the car.

Today would be a good day. She would will it into existence. She pulled open the glass-and-chrome door and stepped inside.

Having faith and belief in powers greater than yourself remained Mikayla's mantra. She wasn't a particularly religious person, at least not one that frequented church services. She was more of a spiritual believer and practitioner. She believed in the power of positive energy and positive thought. Today was one of those days when the positive thoughts that she wrapped herself in as she walked into the facility came to fruition.

The weight that occupied space in the center of her stomach eased after she saw her mom, who was fully engaged in the present and had Mikayla in scandalous stitches about how she had her eye on one of the male staff members and she just may fake some ailment or the other to get his undivided attention. That was the Stella Harris that Mikayla knew. It may be short-lived but she'd take it.

At least now she could concentrate all of her attention on knocking the socks off her very first client and hope that he would be so blown away that he'd recommend her to all his Beverly Hills friends. She put the positive vibe out into the atmosphere as she exited the highway and entered the rarified air of Beverly Hills.

Mikayla inched down the tree-lined streets that shaded the gated properties. The few cars that were parked on the spotless streets were the who's who and what's what of luxury vehicles.

"Damn." Her heart thumped along with the slight rattle of her Honda. She eased to a tentative stop in front of an eight-foot gate with Alonzo Grant's address in chrome lettering. She pulled up to the box and pressed the talk button. She could hear a ringing.

"Yeah. Hello?"

That voice. "Hello. I'm here from At Your Service."

"Great. Come on in."

Soundlessly the gates opened inward.

Geez, her thighs were shaking. She eased the car down the short drive and pulled up in front of the two-story French provincial house. *Nice*. She cut off the engine just as the front door opened.

Oh. My. Lord. Please don't let this be the *Alonzo Grant?* The one she'd drooled over on a Food Network special, the one who reminded her of Kevin Atwater on her fave TV show, *Chicago P.D.*

He stood framed in the doorway.

Yep. It was him all right. She'd dreamed about those lips and wondered if the abs outlined under his white chef jacket were real. *Don't just sit here. Get out, silly woman.* She willed her heart to stop racing, popped the trunk, got out and collected her supplies.

On wobbly legs she walked to the entrance.

"Hi. I'm Mikayla Harris from At Your Service. Mr. Grant?" She put on her best smile.

Those eyes. That skin. This was the embodiment of the voice on the phone. Damn. His last housekeeper was a stout Polish woman who did a helluva job but had slowed down after her knee surgery. Mikayla Harris needed to be on the cover of a magazine.

It took him a minute to find his voice. "Thanks for coming on such short notice," he finally managed. "Let me help you," he said, scrambling for his manners. It would have never occurred to him to offer assistance to Mrs. Kowalski, who looked as if she could bench-press him and his two brothers without breaking a sweat. He relieved her of the mop and broom and led the way inside.

She turned to face him and lightning struck.

He swallowed. "Like I mentioned on the phone, I've been out of town for a while." He didn't want her thinking he was a slob.

"No worries. Is there any place in particular you'd like me to start?"

"Um, I guess you can start down here, then the bed... rooms." The word got stuck in his throat. "Upstairs."

She nodded. "You have a very nice place."

"Thanks. I'm really not here much. A few months out of the year."

"Must be nice."

"Nice?" He loved the way her lips moved and the way her honey-colored eyes picked up the light.

"I mean it must be nice to be able to travel. Have your choice of where to stay and when."

He shrugged, grinned. "It has its perks, I suppose, but it can be exhausting."

"Hmm. Well, I should get started."

"Oh, yeah, sure." He finally stepped from in front of her and suddenly felt like a plug that had been disconnected.

"Kitchen first?"

"Sure." He followed her into the kitchen and rested the mop and broom against the wall. "I'll, uh, get out of your way."

He went into the living room, then decided it would be best to leave altogether. He crossed through to the sliding glass doors and went out on the patio. The farther away he was from Mikayla Harris the better. He could easily see himself saying or doing something totally out of order. She was there to clean his house, not get hit on by the person who hired her.

Chapter 4

Mikayla could barely think over the pounding of her heart. Alonzo Grant should have been an old, fat retiree. Far from it. She viciously scrubbed the counters. How in the world could she concentrate on cleaning his house when that gorgeous specimen of a man was mere feet away? And damn if he didn't smell good, too.

She got the oven cleaner and sprayed the eight-burner, double-oven range, opened the cabinets and placed all the dishware on the island counter. The kitchen was bigger than her entire apartment and loaded with every kind of shiny gadget imaginable. The cost of everything in the kitchen alone had to be astronomical. *Does he live here with someone?* Gleaming pots and pans hung from ceiling hooks. *Does he cook for her?* The massive double-door stainless steel refrigerator was as beautiful as it was intimidating. She pulled open one door and was stunned to find it virtually empty. *Hmm.* If a woman was around, she wouldn't have an empty fridge.

There was a wine cooler that stood as tall as the fridge and was lined from top to bottom with bottles of what she knew would be top-of-the-line spirits.

She sprayed the inside of the oven. Was he watching her? She dared not turn around. She closed the oven to give the cleaner time to work, then turned her attention to wiping down the cabinets. She used a stainless steel spray on the fridge and sink until everything gleamed. After returning the dishes to the cabinet, she finished working on the oven.

He hadn't reappeared since she began working, yet she felt his presence as if he were only a step behind her. Her skin tingled, the fine hairs on her arms stood on end. She swallowed over the dry knot in her throat. How could a barely there meeting turn her inside out? Sure, it had been a minute since she'd been sexually involved with anyone or even remotely interested. Between trying to keep her head above water, running to auditions and looking after her mom, she didn't have the energy or the time. Alonzo Grant, however, had awakened her sleeping libido in epic fashion.

She pushed out a breath, wiped at her damp forehead with the back of her wrist, took a look around. The kitchen was spotless. Stella Harris would be proud. Gathering up her things, she left the kitchen with the intention of working on the living room before heading upstairs, but she came to a dead stop when she crossed into the open space.

Alonzo came in from the back porch, and with the blaze of the sun setting behind him, he appeared momentarily surreal, something out of a dream. Air stuck in her chest.

The doorbell chimed and broke the spell. She breathed in and out.

"Hungry?" he asked while walking toward the door. *What?*

He pulled the door open, engaged in friendly banter with the delivery person, then returned with two large shopping bags. He held them up and grinned. "I'm starving. And I'm sure you've noticed the cupboards are pretty bare. Join me?"

"Um, Mr. Grant, I don't think—"

"Don't think about it. Come on." He cocked his head in the direction of the living room. "Take a break for a minute."

She swallowed. "Mr. Grant…"

He flashed her a smile that lit her up from the inside out. "There's no way I can eat all this food by myself."

Her eyes skipped from one large bag to the other. The aroma of sauce and something spicy trailed in the air. The last meal she'd had was dinner the night before. Her stomach squawked. "Okay," she finally conceded. "Let me wash my hands."

"Great."

Alonzo turned toward the living room while she went to the kitchen sink. This was beyond a bad idea. She turned on the water and soaped her hands. It broke every kind of rule she had for herself and her business, but she couldn't stop herself. She turned the water off, dried her hands and joined Alonzo.

* * *

While Mikayla was in the kitchen, Alonzo took the containers out of the bags and set them on the smoked-glass living room table. What was he doing, inviting the help to join him for dinner? There really wasn't anything wrong with asking someone that worked for him to have a bite to eat. He'd done it countless times—just not in his house.

He glanced up and Mikayla was in front of him. His insides vibrated. It was akin to being hit with a jolt of electricity, or at least what he imagined it would feel like. Second time in one day.

"Hope you like Italian."

"I do, actually."

"Make yourself comfortable. I'll get some plates. I like takeout, but I can't do plastic and Styrofoam." He pushed up from his seat and strode into the kitchen. The distance would give him a moment to get his head together.

Damn, he could barely see straight when he looked at her. What the hell was wrong with him? She was just a pretty woman. He'd seen and been with countless pretty women. What was it about her?

He tugged open the overhead cabinets and took out two plates, grabbed forks and knives, took a deep breath and returned.

"Here we go." He put a plate in front of her and set the flatware in the center of the table.

"This smells incredible."

Alonzo grinned. He snapped the plastic cover off one of the food trays, revealing deep-dish lasagna. The second container held veal Parmesan, the next linguine with oyster sauce and the last was a garden salad. There was also a loaf of warm Italian bread already sliced.

"Take your pick. Have some of each. I guarantee you won't be disappointed."

She hesitated, then reached for the lasagna.

"My personal favorite," he said with a smile.

They filled their plates, sampling a bit of everything.

"Buon appetito," Alonzo said as he lifted a forkful of lasagna to his lips. He took a mouthful and chewed slowly. His eyes closed and he hummed with appreciation.

Mikayla giggled. "I guess you really like the food."

Alonzo flashed her a smile. "How can you tell? Oh!" He put down his fork. "What's Italian cuisine without wine?" He jumped up and went out to the wine cooler and returned with a bottle of white and red each and two glasses. He held them up alternately.

"Red," Mikayla finally said.

"Red it is." He filled a glass and gave it to her.

"Thank you."

He poured for himself, then lifted his glass. "To… new things."

"New things," she echoed and touched her glass to his.

Several minutes of silence passed between them, the ting of silver against china the only conversation.

"It was you that answered the phone when I called?" Alonzo abruptly asked.

Mikayla peeked up from beneath her lashes. "Yes. It was."

He frowned slightly. "So you handle the phones *and* the jobs?"

Mikayla put her fork down. She looked him solidly in the eye. "Yes. I do. I hope that's not a problem."

The instant her words bounced off his chest, he knew he'd crossed some invisible line that he shouldn't have crossed, and wouldn't have if he'd seen it. The words were simple enough, expressed in that same throaty, moth-to-a-flame voice that drew him in, but it was the look of defiance in her eyes that told a different story. This was not a woman to be trifled with. She would layer her words with honey and sting when you came in for a taste. He knew a woman just like her—Ellen Grant.

Alonzo cleared his throat. "Not a problem at all. Just curious. I didn't mean to pry."

Mikayla lifted her chin. "You have every right to know who's in your house, Mr. Grant."

"Hey, no pun intended, but we're breaking bread together. You can call me Alonzo."

She pinched her lips together in a semblance of a smile.

"So, how long have you been in business?"

She drew in a breath, and wiped her mouth with the paper napkin. "Six months."

His brows rose. "Really? Just getting started. How has it been?"

"Great!" she squeaked. She reached for her glass and took a sip of wine.

"You must be the one that put my regular service out of business," he joked.

Mikayla didn't comment.

There were a million questions he wanted to ask— *How is a beautiful woman like you cleaning houses?*

*Is it a stepping stone for something else, or a family
business? What do you do in your spare time? Are you
seeing anyone? How long should I wait before I ask
you to come back?*

"You mentioned that you'd been traveling."

He grinned. "Yes, a little too much, actually. But
it's cool. I get to do what I love. Cook." He chuckled.
"Although you'd never know it from the looks of my
refrigerator."

Mikayla bit back a smile. "I wasn't going to mention
that, but..." She tugged on her bottom lip for a moment.
"I don't want to sound like some fangirl, but I was really rooting for you on *Top Chef.*"

It was the first indication that he'd gotten that she
knew who he was. He wasn't sure how he felt about that.

"Yeah, that was a tough competition to lose."

"But it was the platform that you needed. Right?"

He slowly nodded his head. "Yeah, it was, actually.
The recognition opened doors that might not have been
possible otherwise." She seemed to study him. He liked
the look of exploration in her eyes. "We all have to start
somewhere in pursuit of what we want. Sometimes it's
a direct flight," he said, shrugging, "sometimes you
gotta make connections."

"True. Did you always enjoy cooking?"

"Hmm, probably so. I mean for as long as I can remember I was 'experimenting,' as my mother would
say," he added with a laugh. "Mixing stuff intrigued
me, and then when it actually turned out to be edible,
I was hooked.

"What about you—did you always want to be an

entrepreneur?" He slowly chewed his salad. There was that look again, as if she didn't quite trust his questions.

She cleared her throat. "Not exactly." She drew in a breath. "This is going to sound so Hollywood cliché."

"What?"

She hesitated a beat. "I want to act."

"Do you have an agent?"

"I did when I was in New York, but when I got out here...things didn't work out." She turned her focus to her plate.

He had friends that could easily point her in the right direction. He could probably pull some favors and get her an interview with an agent, but offering a meal was a far cry from offering to help "the help" with their career. That would totally be out of bounds. He wanted to see her again, but not because he was pulling strings.

"Are you any good?" he asked with a smile.

Mikayla tipped her head to the side. "Yes. I am. But I'm biased."

He nodded and pointed his fork in her direction. "That's what it takes to make it out here—anywhere, actually—belief in yourself."

She wiped her mouth, took one last sip of wine. "I really should get back to work." She stood. "Thank you so much for this." She ran her hands down her hips. "I really don't want you to think that I make it a habit to—"

He held up his hand to cut her off. "Please. Don't even think about it. I enjoyed the company. I should be apologizing to you for taking you away from your work."

"I'll take care of all this and get started in here," she said.

"Sure. Of course."

He closed containers and started to collect the dishes.

"Please, Mr. Grant. I'll do it. This is what you're paying me for."

He stopped, put the dish back on the table and straightened to his full height.

Mikayla's gaze rose to meet his.

He held up his hands in surrender. "Okay. I'll totally get out of your way."

"Thank you," she said with a whisper of a smile.

Alonzo took the bottle of wine and his glass, then returned to his lounging spot on the back patio. He could have spent the rest of the evening listening to her talk, watching her eyes and the expressions on her face. But she wasn't here for any of that, and in her way, she made that pretty clear. What he needed to do was to stop making this woman the would-be salve for his bruised ego. She made it clear that she was there only to do what he'd hired her to do.

He set the bottle and glass down on the circular white iron table, then lowered himself onto the cushioned chaise lounge.

The sun had fully set and the high temperatures of earlier settled to a comforting warmth, the air laden with the scents of yellow poppy, pink and red sugar bush and purple nightshade, which spread across the hilltops and valleys like a nature-made quilt. It hit him how much he actually missed all this, the serenity, the beauty, time to simply be quiet and reflect. This was his oasis. Although his roots were in DC, nothing could compare to this, not even the silhouette of the Lincoln Memorial pressed against the skyline.

He glanced over his shoulder. The living room was empty. *She must be upstairs—in the bedrooms.* He reached for his wineglass. That was a vision he didn't want to get stuck in his head.

Mikayla could barely concentrate on cleaning and dusting the living room, vacuuming the floors and fluffing pillows. She struggled to ignore that Alonzo Grant was barely twenty feet away, that she'd spent the past half hour sitting opposite him, watching his smile, his eyes, listening to his voice. She still quaked inside as if she'd developed a nervous condition. If it wasn't for the rubber grip of the gloves, she would have dropped everything she picked up.

When she reached the top of the stairs, she turned right at the landing and started with the bathroom that was right out of her imagination.

"Well just damn," she whispered in awe. This wasn't a bathroom—it was a mini spa. She snapped on her rubber gloves, organized her cleaning supplies and got to work. The space gleamed when she was done. Now to the bedrooms.

She turned the knob and opened the door closest to the stairs. It was clearly a guest room. Although nicely decorated, it didn't have a personal feel to it. She checked the hall closet. It was lined with linen. She took out two sets of sheets and got to work on the guest bedroom.

For several moments she stood frozen in front of what she knew was his bedroom. She peeked over the railing to see if he'd come back into the house. From her vantage spot she could see the entire ground floor.

Alonzo was nowhere in sight. She dragged in a breath and opened the door.

Even though the house had been unoccupied for nearly six weeks, there was no doubt that this was Alonzo's bedroom. The air hinted at his scent, something intoxicating, but elusive. She flipped on the light and the room was bathed in soft white, showcasing the contemporary furnishings from the overhead recessed fixtures.

The king-size bed dominated the room. In the corner by the window that opened onto a small terrace and overlooked the backyard and pool was an overstuffed lounge chair. The furnishings were a deep onyx that sat in sharp contrast to the white area rug that covered the center of the hardwood floor.

She set down her supplies, opened the terrace doors to air out the room, then got to work. There wasn't much to do beyond changing the linen and dusting. How many women had spent the night in that bed? She shook her head to dispel the image. None of her business. No reason for her to care one way or the other.

She moved pieces around on the dresser and nightstands, dusted, polished and gingerly returned everything to their exact spots. She took a final look around, hoped this wouldn't be her last time, gathered up her things and went back downstairs.

Chapter 5

The sliding door opened behind him. He sat up, turned. That crazy lightning strike hit him again. He threw his long legs over the side and stood.

"All done," Mikayla said from the doorway.

"Great. I can't thank you enough for doing this on such short notice."

"Not a problem. At your service," she quipped. She handed him the bill.

He barely looked at it. "Um, I, uh…since my regular service is 'out of service,' I was hoping that you'd be willing…" He felt like a nerdy teen asking the prom queen out on a date.

"I'm sure we can work something out." She took a card out of her pocket and handed it to him. "Give me a call. When you're ready."

"Sure. Thanks. So…cash, check, credit card?" He smiled.

"Whatever works for you."

"I rarely keep cash around. Let me get my wallet." He eased by her in the doorway and his arm brushed against hers.

Their gazes collided, then darted away.

"Be right back," he murmured.

Mikayla's heart banged in her chest. For an instant she experienced light-headedness. The skin-to-skin contact short-circuited her brain and rooted her to the spot. As much as she needed the work, being in Alonzo Grant's presence was totally unnerving. She was a wreck. It was a miracle that she hadn't broken everything she touched.

"Hope you take American Express," he said, coming up behind her and holding up the card.

She turned, her breath caught. God, he was gorgeous. Those lips. She cleared her throat, forced a smile. "Absolutely." She took a small, square white plastic card reader from her pocket and connected it to her cell phone. She slid the card through the slit and Alonzo Grant's information showed up on her screen. She typed in the cost, showed it to Alonzo for his approval and signature, then processed the payment.

"If you give me your email address, I can email your receipt."

"Sure." He gave her his email address.

She hit Send on the screen. "All done. Thank you so much for choosing At Your Service."

"I'm sure it won't be the last time." The air hung between them. "Let me take those," he said and relieved her of her bucket of supplies. "I'll walk you out."

They walked to her car. She had the crazy sensation of being on a first date, and when they reached her car, he would lean in, tell her to drive safely, then kiss her goodbye.

She popped her trunk and Alonzo deposited her equipment.

"Thank you." She walked to the driver's door and opened it.

He held the door for her while she slid in. He leaned down. "Drive safely."

He was so close. She couldn't breathe. Then he shut the door and stepped back.

She channeled all her mental energies on getting the key in the ignition and turning on her car. She pressed the button in the armrest and the window lowered. "Have a good evening and thanks again for the great meal."

"Next time I'll fix it myself." His look was direct, unwavering.

She swallowed. "O-kay," she managed.

He tapped the roof of the car. "I'll call you…to set up another visit."

"Great." She put the car in Drive and prayed that she didn't hit something on her way out.

Somehow, she managed to get back to her tiny apartment in one piece. When she walked through the door, the stark contrast between her life and Alonzo Grant hit her like a gale-force wind. Her entire apartment could fit in his bathroom. Suddenly her comfy apartment that she'd struggled to make feel like home looked shabby.

Her cell phone vibrated in her pocket. She pulled it out. Traci's name showed on the face.

"Hey, girl," Mikayla greeted.

"Hey yourself. How did it go?"

Mikayla blew out a breath. "T, I don't even know where to begin."

"Sounds like a convo deserving of drinks. Want to meet me at Jack's?"

"I'm beat. Can you come here?"

"Don't have to ask me twice. See you in about an hour. What should I bring?"

"Whatever you want to eat and drink," she said, laughing at their inside joke. Mikayla was notorious for buying bargain brands, wasn't the greatest cook in the world and rarely had more than green tea and water to drink. Needless to say, Traci had champagne tastes.

"See you in a few."

Mikayla disconnected the call and tossed the phone on top of her secondhand couch. The tan-colored twill fabric had seen better days, but the frame was sturdy and the colorful throw pillows helped to camouflage the frayed areas.

Traci said an hour, and that didn't include her pit stop to Whole Foods or some artisan eatery that she'd discovered. That would give Mikayla time to take a hot shower to wash off her day and get her mind right so that she could explain how meeting Alonzo Grant had turned her inside out.

"*The* Alonzo Grant that you drooled over during *my* favorite show, *Top Chef*?" Traci curled her bare feet beneath her on the couch. Where Mikayla was a die-hard *Law and Order* and *Chicago P.D.* fan, Traci was devoted to every cooking show in existence, even the ones with kids. She acted as if she were on a first-name basis with the hosts.

"Girl, yes."

"Stop lying." Traci leaned forward to the table laden with a full-course Mexican meal and loaded a nacho chip with freshly ground guacamole and salsa.

"I'm telling you I was so rocked I couldn't think straight and then he invited me to eat with him!"

"Say what?" A dribble of guac slid down her chin. She swiped it with her finger and sucked it off.

"Yes." Mikayla took a bite of her chicken burrito. She slowly shook her head in amazement. "That's not all."

"There's more?"

"He walked me to my car, and after I thanked him again for the meal, he said, 'Next time I'll fix it myself.'"

Traci's mouth dropped open. She folded her arms, leaned back and tilted her head to the side, lips pursed. She started looking around. "Okay, where are the cameras, 'cause I know I'm being punked."

Mikayla sputtered laughter over her mouthful of food. She reached for a napkin. "T, you are crazy."

"Let me see if I got all this straight. You just started your house-cleaning business. Ain't had nary a client since you started. But the first damn client you land is a freaking fine-ass celebrity chef living *la vida loca* in Beverly Hills no less…and I think he wants you to do more than dust his knickknacks."

Mikayla burst out laughing; she laughed so hard and long that tears sprouted from the corners of her eyes.

She struggled to catch her breath, but Traci wasn't finished.

"Like who does that happen to? What are the odds? It's like some page out of a bodice ripper." Her eyes widened in cartoonish fashion. "He didn't try to rip your bodice, did he?"

"Traci!" Mikayla's laughter slowly dribbled down to giggles.

"Anyway, chalk this up to an amazing day. Clearly he has manners, but what is he like?" She rested her forearms on her thighs and leaned in. "Does he smell as good as he looks?"

A slow smile moved across Mikayla's mouth. "Yes, he does," she said dreamily, dragging out the words. "He's funny, has a sexy smile. Much taller than he appears on television—at least six three, four. His eyes are kinda cinnamon color and crinkle in the corners when he laughs. He seemed really interested in me wanting to act. He even tried to help me do my job." She reached out and covered Traci's hand with her own. She lowered her voice. "Every time he got near me, the hairs would stand up on the back of my neck, my stomach fluttered and the pulse would pound so loudly in my ears I couldn't focus." She shook her head. "Crazy, right?"

Traci stared at her for a moment. "You sure you didn't dust his knickknack?"

"Girl, if you don't stop with your craziness…pass me the wine."

"Well, hopefully Chef Grant will call again," Traci said as they cleaned up the containers and glasses.

Mikayla dragged in a breath. "Hmm, maybe."

Traci lightly nudged her with her elbow. "He really made an impression, huh? You have this faraway look in your eyes."

"I can't explain it." Her brow tightened. "I've never been so unanchored by a man. I'm still trying to get my balance back. And it isn't some starstruck reaction. I mean, yeah, it was surreal to walk into the home of the man I'd daydreamed about, but that wasn't it." She turned toward Traci. "It was a connection." She shook her head. "Crazy."

Traci's eyes widened in sincerity. "Maybe not," she said softly and gave her a wink.

Mikayla chuckled. There was one thing that she could always rely on with Traci, and it was her support. Her ride-or-die friend. Since their early days at New York University's drama school, working late into the night together practicing for auditions, sipping wine over broken hearts and dreams, and cheering on success, Traci was there. And she had no idea what she would have done if she hadn't had Traci when her mom got ill.

It was Traci—who two years earlier picked up stakes, after having her heart broken, and took her dreams of acting to California—that found the facility for her mom. She was the one who did the relentless research on new treatments, and she was the one who opened the doors to her small home and her arms when Mikayla arrived and needed a place to stay. She was the shoulder that Mikayla cried and leaned on. So it was just like Traci to suggest that maybe what happened between her and Alonzo wasn't so crazy after all.

* * *

Alonzo turned out the lights on the back patio, collected the almost-empty bottle of wine and his glass and went inside. He drew in a deep breath and glanced around.

The air was totally different. Fresh, with a hint of something intangible. He knew it was Mikayla's scent. *Torture me.* He half smiled as he moved slowly from room to room examining her handiwork. Everything gleamed, from dresser tops to the floors. He could see his reflection on the refrigerator. She really was good at her job, but he couldn't imagine her doing it for long and wondered why cleaning houses was her go-to option. Most aspiring actors had some kind of side gig until they got a part in something that would pay the bills. It was usually restaurant work. But there was nothing usual about Mikayla Harris. He could easily see her face on the screen, and he was sure that all she needed was a break—to meet the right person.

He put his glass in the dishwasher, turned out the kitchen lights and went back to the living room with the intention of watching a movie or catching a game on ESPN. He plopped down on the couch and reached for the remote. The small black-and-white card caught his eye. It was Mikayla's business card. He picked it up and ran his thumb lightly across the embossed letters. The echo of her throaty voice played in his head. He smiled, then shook his head. *You are really letting this woman get under your skin.*

He pressed the power button and the wall-mounted television bloomed to life just as his cell phone vibrated in his pocket. He rolled to the side and dug out his phone. *Faith Dawson*. He grinned.

"Faith. How are you?" he greeted.

"Better now that I finally hear your voice," she said. "I've been trying to reach you for weeks. Where you been and why didn't you return my calls?"

"Hey, sorry, doll. I've been out of town, actually out of the country. As a matter of fact, I just got in today."

"Perfect timing. You can make it up to me. I'm having some people over tonight. Nothing big. But it wouldn't be a party without you. And you don't have to cook, be famous or talk shop. Just enjoy yourself for a change." She paused a beat. "And when I send everyone home, we can...catch up."

He rested his head against the cushion of the couch. It wasn't his plan to go out, and definitely not spend it around a lot of people. He'd done that for the past six weeks—nonstop. But he and Faith had a special relationship—quid pro quo—with benefits. "Okay. What time?"

"Folks should start arriving around nineish. So whenever you get here. And don't worry about a toothbrush, I have extra," she said with a laugh.

Alonzo chuckled. "See you later, Faith." He disconnected the call and checked the time on his watch. 7:15. He had time to at least unwind with a mindless movie, then he'd get dressed and head out, to arrive late enough so that the party was up and running and his arrival would go unnoticed, and early enough not to be rude.

Spending the night with Faith may be just the tonic he needed.

He pointed the remote at the television and began scrolling.

* * *

The drive to Faith's home took a little more than a half hour. Spring in California can be fickle, shifting from steamy to cool in a matter of hours. Tonight was perfect. He'd made the half-hour drive with the top down on his vintage black Mustang. By the time he eased down Faith's winding driveway, it was 10:30. A young brother decked in a short black jacket, white shirt and black slacks darted to his side of the car.

"I'll park your car, sir," he said, his eyes wide in admiration of the ride.

"Not a problem." He put the car in Park and got out. "Be careful with her," he advised the young man, who ogled the car like a man in heat.

"I will. I will."

Alonzo threw him a side-eye before walking along the pathway to the entrance of the ranch-style house.

He and Faith went back several years. When he first arrived in California to help cater a party—as an apprentice—he'd met Faith while he was serving trays of appetizers. She'd taken a canapé and whispered to meet her by the pool. He had no idea who she was, only that someone had spray-painted her into her dress.

It was a couple of hours before he could break away from his duties. She told him she was an agent and he had the perfect look for the camera. "Not my thing. Next time you see me, I'll be *the* chef, not the server," he'd told her. He'd kept his word and had Faith's connections to thank for some of that. Her client base was deep, a who's who of Hollywood. When opportunity arose, she'd make a connection for him to cater a party or a dinner. His reputation for exotic twists on everything from fish to oxtails, along with his unique flair for presentation, grew, and so did that on-again, off-again thing between him and Faith.

"You made it." She sashayed up to him, cupped his chin in her palm and pressed her peach-tinted lips against his. "Missed you," she whispered before stepping back.

The right corner of his mouth lifted. "Looking fabulous as always, Faith." Tonight her signature strawberry blond hair fell in waves around her bare shoulders and the hip-high, low-cut silver sheath showcased the smooth cocoa-brown skin.

She linked her arm through his and guided him into the center of the gathering. The room was full. At least fifty people. Music, wine and food flowed.

"What's the occasion?" he asked, swiping a flute of champagne off the tray of a passing waiter.

"Networking. Nothing special. How have you been?"

"Busy." He took a swallow of champagne. "Traveling a lot. Just glad to be home to chill for a while."

"You've come a long way baby, as the saying goes."

"True. True." He nodded his head in agreement. "So, why am I here. Really?"

She turned to him, looked into his eyes. "Sometimes you just want someone that's real." The flirtatious tone was gone, replaced by sincerity. "Someone to block out all the noise. Know what I mean?"

"I think so."

She pressed her lips tightly together. "You're probably the realist person I know. Not bad in all the other departments, either," she added with a wink. She kissed his cheek. "I'm going to mingle a little. Everyone should start wandering out in another hour or so," she added with innuendo filtering through her voice. She kissed his cheek and flitted away before he could protest.

He moved around the fringes of the room and didn't notice any familiar faces, and thankfully none of his clients or anyone that he'd had after-hours encounters with. Generally, Faith's gatherings overflowed with A-listers. Not tonight. He was relieved. After taking a small plate of finger foods, he strolled out to the deck, leaned on the railing and became mesmerized by the majestic view of the mountains etched against the purple sky.

He felt an arm slide around his waist. He angled his head.

"The last of the guests are gone," Faith said.

He glanced over his shoulder, looked through the glass doors. Waiters were cleaning up.

"Nice turnout. Was it what you expected?"

She shrugged lightly. "I've been doing these small networking events for a couple of months. Great opportunity to meet and mingle on a social level, build a support system, cull potential clients."

Alonzo slowly nodded. "You never were one to miss an opportunity."

"One of my many attributes," she murmured and moved closer. She pressed her hand against his chest.

Alonzo covered her hand, held it in place. He leaned in and kissed her forehead. "I'm going to head out. It's been a helluva long day."

Her eyes moved slowly over his face. "Wow. The forehead kiss. Who is she?" she asked.

He frowned. "She?"

"*Coy* is not one of your attributes, Zo. We've known each other for, what, five, six years. If we're nothing else, we're honest with each other, and this would be a first that you've turned me down." She feigned a pout. "So…who is it?"

He snorted a laugh. "What do you have stronger than champagne and I'll tell you all about it."

She cocked her head to the side. "Whatever you want." She linked her arm through his and they went back inside.

By the time he pulled in to his driveway it was after ten in the morning. It made sense to just crash at Faith's place, since they'd talked long into the night and jet lag had gained its grip. But once he confessed about Mikayla Harris, and his inexplicable attraction, they both agreed sleeping in the same bed was out of the question. Faith was remarkably cool about the whole thing and advised him to take his time and be careful. With all the outcry about bosses coming on to workers, she didn't want to read about him in the tabloids.

He'd spent the night in the guest bedroom for the first time in their relationship, but before he left, he whipped up breakfast for them both as a way of making it up to her. When he'd left her standing in the arch of her doorway, they both understood that their relationship had taken a new turn, and it was okay.

When he returned home, there was one thing that was high on his priority list and that was stocking his fridge and cabinets. With all the home delivery services available, shopping was no more than a few clicks away on the computer. But being beyond particular when it came to food and ingredients, he deigned to do it himself. Food shopping was his guilty pleasure. Holding something in your hand, stroking a fruit for firmness and texture, sniffing spices for freshness could never be accomplished on the internet. For him, selecting the perfect cut of Kobe steak and collecting ingredients for freshly made pasta and sauces or stumbling upon a delicacy was a sensual experience for him. He took pleasure in working with his hands, with bringing out the inner essence of what he created. That love, that desire to woo with a scent, a taste or a presentation flowed into his relationships, whether short- or long-term. He catered to the women he was involved with on every level. Making them feel as if they were one of a kind, a delicacy, was as much his mark as a consummate lover as it was as a connoisseur of cuisine.

One of his favorite spots when he was on the West Coast was Gelson's Market on West Santa Monica Boulevard in West Hollywood. It carried pretty much everything he needed, from prime meats, imported cheeses, fresh fish and excellent baked goods to a full wine cellar. For his spices and some specialty vegetables he always went to the Korean market.

After a quick shower, he changed into his run-around clothes, Nikes, gray sweats and a T-shirt. Wallet, car keys and phone and he was ready and out the door.

It was yet another perfect day for driving with the top down. The sun was high in the sky, temperatures were in the upper seventies and the breeze off the Pacific ocean leveled out the air. Although the drive was only about fifteen minutes, he enjoyed every minute of it.

The only downside to his excursions to Gelson's was that he invariably ran into someone who recognized him from *Top Chef* or one of his guest spots on the Food Network. It never failed that someone would insist that it would take him only sixty seconds or less to detail one of his recipes, or make a suggestion for an intimate dinner. It was both amusing and invasive, but he'd grown used to it. The moments of television star recognition had slowed considerably over the past couple of years as his capital as celebrity chef to the stars had risen exponentially. When he was recognized now, more often than not it was by someone from an event he'd catered or a satisfied client.

He was in the vegetable aisle examining a bushel of greens.

"Hi. I know you get this all the time, but you're Alonzo Grant, right?"

The voice. He turned with a smile already in place. "Hey." His grin was in full bloom.

Mikayla giggled. "What are the odds? Up until yesterday I've never seen you before in my life except on television. Meet you once and then here you are again."

"Fate." He took a peek into her cart. "Salmon. Capers." He nodded slowly. "What are you fixing with it?"

She held up her hand. "Trust me. This is not for me. My friend Traci is the cooking queen. She's having a friend over for dinner but she couldn't get away to shop. Audition or something. So…" She held up the list and waved it. "Here I am."

His gaze moved over her face. "Seems like you have everything under control." He leaned in. "I would suggest a lemon sauce for the salmon. A sure hit for her friend." He watched the pulse flutter at the base of her throat and felt that same flutter in his belly. "I, uh, guess I should let you get to it."

She ran the tip of her tongue across her bottom lip. "I would guess you'll be here for a while. Stocking up."

"Yes." He shrugged. "I actually enjoy it, though."

"Really? Food shopping?"

"Yeah, nerdy but true."

"I can think of so many things I'd rather do. Don't get me wrong. I love a good meal with the best of them, but when it comes to picking stuff and fixing, I'm real basic."

He rested his forearms on the handle of the cart. "Takes practice. But, I'd be happy to show you some tips. I'll put a list together for you the next time you come to the house. I'm thinking in another two weeks or so the house will definitely need your amazing touch."

"Um, sure. That would be great. I think," she said with a laugh.

"It won't be anything complicated. Something simple, but tasty and easy to prepare, just to get your feet wet."

She seemed to study him as if looking for a story beneath the surface. He straightened. "I'll call you in a couple of weeks."

She bobbed her head. "Sure. Absolutely."

"Take care." He pushed off.

"You too," she said, moving in the opposite direction.

Damn if that crazy Traci wasn't right. When she'd told Traci that he'd ordered takeout because his fridge was bare, Traci said she knew that wouldn't last long, and if she remembered correctly from one of the cooking shows, he frequented Gelson's and mentioned that it was one of his favorite emporiums. As a matter of fact, she'd added, one of the episodes on the Food Network was filmed there.

But Mikayla didn't actually think she'd see him. She stole a glance over her shoulder. He was gone, but she still felt warm and giddy. When she spotted him in the vegetable aisle she became so lightheaded she thought she would faint. It was a small miracle, along with her acting abilities, that allowed her to walk up to him as if running into the man of her dreams was an everyday occurrence.

When Traci asked her to help out with her shopping errand, it was last on her list of things she wanted to do, until Traci sweetened the pot with the tidbit about a possible Alonzo sighting. She pretended to reluctantly agree.

She felt about as out of place in Gelson's as if she'd walked into a male-only sauna. Walking through the enormous aisles laden with products she'd never heard of before was overwhelming to say the least. It took her nearly an hour just to find the capers after purchasing the Alaskan salmon. She'd been wandering up and down the aisles when she did a double take. She must have surreptitiously watched him for a good five minutes before she dragged up the nerve to walk over and speak to him.

Mindlessly she moved down the checkout line. She placed the items on the rolling belt, paid with the cash Traci had given her, since her own cards were maxed out, offered a vague smile of thanks to the cashier and walked out into the early afternoon sunshine.

She slid on her shades and furtively scanned the parking lot in the hopes of spotting Alonzo again. *But for what, silly woman? It's not like he's going to ask to carry your bags like a high school jock wanting to make an impression on one of the cool girls.* She picked up her pace and zigzagged in and out of the lanes of parked cars until she reached her ten-year-old Honda.

What she needed to do was to stop fantasizing that Alonzo was being anything more than nice to someone he hired to clean his house. She opened her trunk and put the packages inside. The sooner she accepted that reality the better. She got in behind the wheel, took a last hopeful look around, then put the car in gear. But before she pulled off, she tapped Traci's number on her cell phone. Traci answered on the second ring.

"Hello?"

"You were right."

Chapter 6

Alonzo pushed his loaded shopping cart out to his car. His haul filled his trunk, the back seat and floor, and the passenger seat. He should have asked to have his purchases delivered, but he was so messed up in the head after running into Mikayla that he didn't even think to mention it.

Damn, what were the odds of that? He eased out of his parking lane and headed for the exit. He'd turned down what would have been a spectacular night with Faith because some weird place in his soul had shifted after one meeting with Mikayla. It's not that he was some bed-hopping, womanizing creep. If anything, he was pretty much the opposite. Although he was a bit of a full commitmentphobe, he always treated every woman in his life with honesty and respect. He was transparent. There was no woman that dealt with him that didn't know where he was coming from. The life he led—the constant travel, the company that he kept—simply didn't lend itself to permanence.

Now he was in some odd headspace, some weird fork in the road. He couldn't approach Mikayla the way he normally would any other woman, and at the same time he suddenly wasn't interested in pursuing anyone else.

Maybe he could have at least asked her for a late lunch or coffee or something. He eased onto the exit ramp and pulled into traffic. No. The last thing he needed was to have her think anything crazy. These days celebrities and politicians were going down like bowling pins, being accused of everything from saying something sideways to out-and-out physical attacks. He had no intention of falling into any of those categories. So he hoped that when he'd blurted out that he'd fix the next meal that she didn't take it the wrong way.

Going forward, no matter how much he may want it to be otherwise, it had to be strictly business. After her next visit he would make it his business to secure a different cleaning service. Hopefully, he'd get another Mrs. Kowalski.

Alonzo was in the middle of unpacking groceries when his cell phone rang. It was his buddy Harrison.

"Hey, man."

"Hey yourself. You back in town?"

"Got back yesterday, as a matter of fact. Just came in from Gelson's."

Harrison chuckled. "Of course. What are you doing later?"

"No plans. What's up?"

"You know Pierce Jackman, from my office, head of the camera crew?"

"Hmm, yeah, yeah. Why?"

"He's getting hitched. Some of the guys are getting together at Junior's Lounge tonight for drinks. You know everybody. You should swing by."

"Maybe I will." It would get his mind off Mikayla. "What time?"

"Around eight. Seven thirty if you want to order dinner."

"I'll let you know."

"Cool. So, how was London?"

"Started off great. Ended with a bit of a fizzle."

"Meaning?"

"You know me and Cheri were supposed to be… hanging out."

"Yeah…"

"Well, she decided she'd rather hang with her leading man Dominic Logan."

"Damn, bruh. For real?"

"Yeah. But I'm good. I think my ego was more hurt than anything."

"Even more reason to come out tonight. Soothe the wounded soul," he said with a chuckle.

Alonzo hummed deep in his throat. If only his wounded soul had something to do with Cheri, he'd be over it by now. "I'll holla at you and let you know."

"Cool."

"Lata." He disconnected the call and slid the phone back into his pocket. He put the last of the groceries away, leaned his hip against the counter. What he really wanted to do was call Mikayla and find out what *she* was doing later and if he could join her.

"Didn't I tell you? I told you!" Traci squealed as she unpacked the bags that Mikayla dropped off. "I'm in the wrong line of business. I need to be a damned fortune teller."

Mikayla snickered. "Whatever, girl."

"Anyway, you saw him again. Still the same tingle and tickle?"

"Yes," she said on a breath. "Maybe worse. First time, I could chalk it up to the surrealness of meeting this gorgeous celebrity. But today…whatever that flutter was in my stomach is still there today. And it's not nerves."

"So what are you gonna do, girl? Not like you can pretend to be someone else to get with him, like J.Lo did in that movie *Maid in Manhattan*," Traci quipped.

"Yeah, right. Hey," she sighed, "not much I can do. Hopefully, he'll call again. Main thing right now is I need the work. I'm hoping that at the very least he'll recommend me to some of his friends."

"Kayla, I told you, instead of struggling you could stay here, rent free. I know things are tight. Insurance is only going to take care of so much." She rested her elbows on the table and leaned forward. "At least rent and utilities would be off your plate and whatever you make can fill the gaps with the rehab center."

Mikayla lowered her head, slowly shook it. "I can't do that, T. I appreciate everything that you've done for me and mom. But the best way to ruin a friendship is to move in with your best friend. The first couple of months, staying here, that was cool, but I have to do this."

Traci sighed. "Fine. But don't let your pride get in your way."

"Promise." She pushed to her feet. "I'm outta here." She walked around the table and kissed Traci's cheek. "Have fun tonight."

"Oh, I intend to." She walked Mikayla to the door. "Drive safe." She paused, shoving her hands into the back pockets of her jeans. "I have a callback in the morning for that part we tried out for," she said almost apologetically.

Mikayla smiled and pressed her hand on Traci's shoulder. "Congratulations, T. And look, you don't have to hold back on good things that happen when it comes to all this acting stuff. We both know how random some things can be. I'm happy for you. What's for me is for me, and what's for you is for you. No worries." She leaned in and kissed her cheek. "Break a leg."

"Thanks, girl. For real."

"You got this."

"I'll call you tomorrow."

"You better."

Mikayla walked down the three steps and across to her car. Before she left New York to come to California, her acting opportunities were beginning to pick up steam. She'd had a couple of walk-ons, a Target commercial—which was still paying residuals—and a small role in a sitcom pilot that unfortunately didn't make it to television. But at least she was in the mix. She was getting calls and she was making the rounds. She'd worked with a temp agency that sent her out for office work to answer phones and type. Those jobs paid the bills while she pursued her dream. When her mom got sick, everything changed. Her priorities shifted and what she wanted was no longer important.

She stopped at the red light. This whole new life took getting used to, and the reality was, her dream seemed further out of reach. Not because she didn't have talent, but she no longer had the fire in her stomach. You needed that to succeed in this business. She pulled across the intersection, then made a left onto the entry ramp of the freeway.

In the meantime, she would put the same energy into building up her business, securing a reliable income so that whatever her mother needed she would be able to make it happen. That was the only thing that mattered.

Now if only she could figure out a way for Alonzo Grant not to see her as only his housekeeper.

Alonzo pulled open the door to Junior's and was greeted with the welcome crooning of classic Marvin Gaye. The bar as usual was filled from end to end with an assortment of dressed-up and dressed-down grown folks. What he always enjoyed about Junior's Lounge was that he didn't have to concern himself with young hot-heads and underage sistahs with fake IDs.

Junior Evans, the owner, made his mark by catering to an adult crowd, with the music, real liquor—nothing with umbrellas—and the overflowing plates of slap-yo'-mama meals. The back room had three full-size pool tables, and upstairs was set up for pure chilling on the soft tan leather couches and love seats.

Once his eyes adjusted to the dim lights, he made his

way around the circular tables and the ebb and flow of bodies in search of Harrison and the crew. He spotted them at a table in the rear of the lounge.

"You made it," Harrison greeted.

They gave each other the brother handshake and chest hug.

"What's up, fellas?" Alonzo said to Mark, Felix and Pierce. "Congrats, Pierce." He clapped him on the back. "Does the poor woman know what she's signing up for?" he teased. He pulled out a chair and sat.

"Hey, man," Pierce said, "that secret stays at this table. Don't want her running off before the I dos."

The group laughed.

"We just ordered drinks," Harrison said.

"Cool." Alonzo swiveled in his seat, spotted the waitress and signaled her. "First round on me, in honor of our soon to be departed from bachelorhood friend."

"Bring 'em on!" Mark said.

The group rolled into their usual ragging on their sports teams and new management at the production studio. After a good stiff drink their attention zeroed in on Pierce.

"So you really ready, man?" Harrison asked.

Pierce slowly nodded his head. "Yeah." He glanced around at his friends and a slow smile curved his lips. "She's the one."

Alonzo sat back and studied the expression of certainty on Pierce's face and the assurance in his voice. His older brother, Franklin, had that same look and sounded the same way about Dina. Franklin, the family had sworn, would forever be single because nothing seemed to be more important than his work—until

Dr. Dina Hamilton. Would Alonzo ever feel the same? "How did you know?" he blurted out.

All eyes turned toward Alonzo, then settled on Pierce. They seemed to simultaneously lean in as if waiting for the wisdom of the world to come down from on high.

Pierce took a sip from his drink, then set the glass down. He pushed out a breath. "This is gonna sound all kinds of corny." He paused for a moment. "When I see her, talk to her, hear her laughter—nothing else matters. I think of ways to make her smile. Check it…if Janice was to call me right now and say to come home, I would leave y'all's ashy elbows with the quickness. And not feel bad!"

They all laughed.

"Damn man, you got it bad," Harrison joked.

"Mark my word, my brother, there's someone out there for you. And when she finds you—you're done. Nothing you can do about it." He finished off his drink just as the second round of buffalo wings arrived.

Alonzo took it all in, even as he listened to the jokes and taunting that bounced around the table. He didn't have much to compare to the crazy feeling he had for Mikayla. The women he'd dealt with were bright, sexy, fun to be with, but they didn't fog his brain or stay in his thoughts beyond them parting ways in the morning. Was that what Pierce experienced with Janice, or Franklin with Dina?

After a round of congratulatory drinks, wings and coleslaw, the guys began peeling off one by one, needing to get in for an early call in the morning. Alonzo and Harrison were the last.

"Glad you came out, man. It's been a minute," Harrison said before picking up a stick of celery and dunking it in blue cheese dressing.

"Yeah, me too. I've been on the run for months. It was good to not be the one in the kitchen!"

"I hear ya. So what are your plans now that you're back on the coast?" He chewed slowly.

"Relax. There's Ryan Carrington's affair coming up in a few weeks, but other than that I'm not taking on any new clients for at least a month."

"Oh yeah, Carrington." He nodded his head. "I'll probably see you there for that. I got the invite a couple of weeks ago. Didn't RSVP yet. You working that one night?"

"Yes, which is why I don't want to take on anything else until then. Ryan isn't the easiest person to work for. He must have changed his mind at least five times already."

"I feel for you. But you'll pull it off. You always do. You're not the celebrity chef to the stars for nothing," he teased.

Alonzo chuckled.

"So with Cheri out of the picture, any new prospects?"

"Me and Cheri were never serious. I kinda thought I might be heading in that direction, but obviously we weren't on the same page." He shrugged. "I did meet this woman, though."

Harrison reached for the last wing. "Yeah. Cool. Who is she?"

Alonzo lowered his voice. "She, uh, is the house-keeper. I mean she runs a housekeeping service and we met."

Harrison stared at Alonzo with his mouth partially open. "Say what again? The housekeeper or the owner of the housekeeping service? What happened to Ms. Kowindowsky?"

"Kowalski," he corrected.

"Whatever. What are you talking about? 'Cause now I'm interested."

Alonzo ran a hand over his face, then rested his fore-arms on the table. "Well…"

When Alonzo wrapped up his story of meeting Mi-kayla and fireworks going off, and running into her at Gelson's and not being able to stop thinking about her, Harrison for several moments stared at his friend in disbelief.

"This really happened?" he finally said, his brows knitted tightly together as if trying to get Alonzo into focus.

"Yeah, what…you think I don't have anything else to do but make up shit to tell you?"

"Naw, I'm just saying it sounds like one of those Hallmark movies."

"Thanks, man."

"No, I'm sorry. It's just that I've known you for years. We been through some things and I have never, I mean never, heard you talk about a woman the way you just talked about her. Never. This is an epic moment." He sig-naled for the waiter and ordered two glasses of Hennessy.

Harrison lifted his glass. "Like the great Arsenio Hall pontificated—*things that make you go, hmm*."

Alonzo chuckled and tapped his glass against Harrison's.

"So, what are you going to do, man? You can't cross that line with her working in your house. That's a TMZ moment waiting to happen."

"Yeah, I know." He sipped his drink. "I actually thought about just not asking her to come back and then call to ask her out. But that would be pretty foul and I get the impression that she needs the work until the whole acting thing kicks in."

"Hmm. Hey, I'm sure you'll figure it out. Just be careful. You don't want anything that you say or do to be taken the wrong way."

"Exactly."

As Alonzo lay in bed that night staring up at the ceiling, Pierce's words of warning wisdom replayed in his head—*When she finds you, you're done.* He turned on his side and switched out the light. Had he been found?

Mikayla spent her morning washing the few feet of linoleum in her tiny kitchen, emptying out her fridge and banishing dust bunnies. Several times in between she checked her website to see if there were any new inquiries for her services. According to the site, there were three new searches but no requests for an appointment. The time on her computer read 9:15. She had forty-five minutes to get ready for the audition that Traci hooked up for her. It was a small one-line walk-on for an indie project, but whether she got the part or not, at least she would have the chance to put her face and skills in front of folks that mattered.

She powered down her computer, put away her cleaning stuff and headed off to take a shower.

Refreshed and dressed, she dropped her keys and phone into her tote, made sure she had a copy of the script and headed out, just as her cell phone vibrated. She opened the door, then shut it behind her while she dug in her bag for her phone.

The name and number on the face of the phone stopped her cold. Her heart thumped. She drew in a breath and pressed the green phone icon.

"Hello?"

"Good morning, Ms. Harris. This is Dr. Simpson from Greenwood."

"Yes, yes. Is something wrong? Is my mother okay?"

"That's why I'm calling. She had a very bad episode this morning. Bad enough that we had to give her a mild sedative."

"What!"

"I assure you, it was necessary, Ms. Harris. We didn't want her to hurt herself."

The muscles in her throat grew so tight she couldn't swallow. Her eyes burned. "Hurt herself! Oh my God. I'm on my way."

"She will be in and out of sleep for a couple of hours. But it would be good if she can see you when she is fully awake."

A tear slid down her cheek. She blinked back the sting in her eyes. "I'm on my way."

"I'll have the head nurse come and get me when you arrive."

"Thank you," she whispered and disconnected the call. She slumped against the frame of the door, squeezed her eyes shut for a moment and dragged in a breath to steady herself.

She opened her eyes and strode to her car.

On the entire thirty-minute drive all she could think about was what her mother was going through and how utterly helpless she felt in not being able to make it better. After her dad died when she was only four, her mom became everything—mother, father, best friend, counselor and provider. There was never a time in all her growing-up years that her mom had not been a central, active part of it. She couldn't recall ever seeing her mother break down or appear weak. She never saw her mother cry, not when her husband died, not even when she'd sat in the third row and watched her daughter walk across the stage to get her degree from NYU. Stella Harris was the strongest woman she knew.

Knowing all that, living all that, and to see her mom now was more devastating than anything she could have ever imagined. It was the worst of ironies. Stella Harris was a teacher and a writer. She worked all her life enlightening others in the classroom and out. She could explain theory, debate religion and politics, could read anyone under the table, and now…some days she didn't know her own daughter. Mikayla cried enough for the both of them.

The road in front of her blurred. She sniffed hard and wiped her eyes, made the turn onto the winding lane that led to the gated facility.

Greenwood was rated as the top rehabilitation center in the country. Their doctors were renowned for cutting-edge physical and psychological therapy, and advanced technology in a setting that was straight out of the future. Indoor pools and terrariums, state-of-the-art workout rooms, art and music classes, and top-of-the-line meals in a dining room that easily rivaled a five-star restaurant. The entire staff were highly trained and certified. Even the maintenance staff were required to take classes in how to deal with the client base to ensure that should they ever be caught in an episode they would immediately know what to do. Hence the hefty cost. Health insurance didn't make a dent.

She parked in the visitors' parking lot and went inside. She stopped at the front desk, which resembled the check-in counter at a hotel.

"Good morning."

The on-duty clerk looked up from whatever she was writing and smiled. "Good morning, Ms. Harris." She closed the folder. "Dr. Simpson is expecting you."

"Thank you."

The clerk made a call. "He'll be right out," she said, setting the phone back on the hook. "Please have a seat. Can I get you anything?"

"No. I'm fine, thank you." Mikayla adjusted her tote on her shoulder and glanced around. The waiting area resembled a lounge in a five-star hotel; plush white leather seating surrounded low wood tables—fastened securely to the floor—with potted plants and the latest magazines strategically displayed. In the far corner were urns of coffee, tea, lemon-flavored water and cookies. Muzak floated butterfly soft in the air. The rooms, or rather the minisuites, were located on the second and third levels, with all the medical offices and treatment rooms on the main level.

"Ms. Harris."

She turned toward the familiar voice. "Dr. Simpson."

He walked toward her, his thin, pale hand extended. It was hard to gauge his age. His thick shock of steel-gray hair belied the light and fire in his green eyes and the smooth unlined face.

"Thank you for coming so quickly." He patted her hand in a fatherly way, which once again threw off her age radar. "Why don't we go to my office first and talk before you see your mother."

Mikayla wanted to protest. What she wanted to do was see her mother now! She pressed her lips tightly together and walked alongside Dr. Simpson to his office at the end of the quiet corridor.

He opened the door and stepped aside to let her pass. "Please, have a seat."

He walked behind his desk, extracted a pair of wire-framed glasses and slipped them on before turning to his computer screen. He spent a few minutes looking at the screen. Mikayla wanted to shake him.

He cleared his throat, took off his glasses and turned his attention to Mikayla. "Your mother has been here for almost four months. She has made some progress since she was admitted, between the diet, physical and psychological therapy, along with medication. Last night, however, set her back weeks, if not months. She had a full-blown break with reality and became physical with the nurses on duty. We had to sedate her."

Mikayla linked her fingers together so tight they

began to lose circulation. She bit down on her lip to keep it from quivering.

"We are going to run some tests, a brain scan, MRI, blood, et cetera. But in the meantime, until we can get a handle on what went wrong, she will have to be monitored at all times. We'll keep her lightly medicated, but not enough so that she cannot function."

"Is she just…getting worse?" she whispered, her voice breaking up between the words. She blinked rapidly to keep from crying.

Dr. Simpson linked his fingers together and leaned forward. "Alzheimer's is an insidious, tricky disease. Every day we make progress and then take two steps back. Will she be cured?" He drew in a breath. "Probably not. But what we are hoping is that we can stop the progression."

She knuckled away an errant tear. "How long is she going to be medicated?"

"A day or two."

Mikayla nodded. "Can I see her?"

"Of course. She may be a bit more disoriented than what you are used to."

"I understand."

"Okay, then." He pushed back from his seat and stood. "I'll take you to see her."

Mikayla held her breath for the short one-floor ride on the elevator. She walked in silence next to Dr. Simpson, who intermittently spoke to or nodded at staff along the way. Finally they reached her mother's room. There was a nurse seated inside.

"Why don't you take a break, Carol," Dr. Simpson said.

The nurse walked out while Mikayla slowly approached her mother's bed. Her heart stopped when she saw the restraints on her wrists. She whirled toward Dr. Simpson, her eyes wild with outrage. "Get those off of her! Now." She was shaking all over.

Dr. Simpson placed a gentle hand on her shoulder. "I know it looks frightening. But it's for her own safety. Until she is fully awake and can be assessed, we don't want her to wake up agitated. She attacked a nurse last night," he said softly.

She pulled up a chair and sat, took her mother's hand and gently stroked it. "Mom, I'm here," she softly said.

Stella's lids fluttered, but she didn't wake.

"How long is she going to be asleep?"

"A little hard to say." He came to stand beside her. "An hour, maybe two. I'd thought she would be awakening by now."

Mikayla's head snapped up. "What does that mean? Is something wrong? Is that why she's not awake?"

"Please relax," he said gently. "Everyone reacts to sedation differently. She had a stronger dose last evening and a milder one at the start of shift this morning. Our hope is that with the lessening of medication she will gradually awake."

"I'm going to sit here until she does."

"Of course. I'll be back to check on you both after rounds."

Mikayla nodded, then turned her attention to her mother.

It was nearly noon. The nurses had come in and out several times to check Stella's vitals and to check on Mikayla.

Mikayla was in the middle of a makeshift prayer when she felt her mother's fingers tighten around her hand. She jumped up and leaned over Stella.

"Mom. Mom." She stroked her cheek.

Stella's lashes fluttered. Her lids lifted, descended, lifted again. Her gaze was unfocused, then she smiled.

"Kay," she whispered. "My baby."

Mikayla's throat was so tight she could barely get words out. "Hey, Mom." She sniffed. "I'm here. You had a really good sleep," she said, trying to make light of things.

Stella frowned as she tried to raise her hand and realized she couldn't. Her eyes widened, fearful.

"It's okay, Mom. They didn't want you to hurt yourself. Nurse. Please take these off."

"I need to get Dr. Simpson's approval."

"Then please get it, or I'll take them off myself."

She picked up the wall-mounted phone. "Yes. Please page Dr. Simpson. Let him know that Ms. Harris is awake and her daughter wants the restraints removed. Thank you."

"It's okay, Mom. We're going to get these off."

"I'm sure it will only be a few minutes," the nurse said.

The wall phone rang. The nurse answered. "Yes. Of course. Thank you." She turned to Mikayla. "Dr. Simpson is with a patient. However, he said that it would be fine for me to take off the restraints." She smiled at Mikayla.

"Thank you," she whispered.

The nurse came over and spoke in cooing tones as she unbuckled the restraints on each wrist, tenderly massaging them. She patted Stella's hand, offered a tight-lipped smile to Mikayla and returned to her unobtrusive spot on the other side of the room.

"Oh, that's better," Stella said, flexing her wrists. She angled her head toward her daughter. "What time is it?"

"A little after two."

"In the morning?"

"No. Afternoon."

"Oh my, and I'm still in bed!" She struggled to sit up. Mikayla helped her.

"Easy."

"I missed lunch."

"I'm sure we can get you something." She turned toward he nurse.

"The menu is in the top drawer," she said to Mikayla. Then to her mom, "Whatever you want, Ms. Harris."

Mikayla opened the nightstand next to the double bed. "Do you want to look it over or do you want me to choose?"

Stella frowned for a moment. Her lips parted. Her gaze darted away, then back to Mikayla. She smiled as if seeing her for the first time. "My baby."

Mikayla's heart raced. "Mom," she said with a hitch in her voice. She studied her mother's expression, the light and dark in her eyes waiting for that painful moment when her gaze clouded over and the here and now descended to some unreachable place. But it didn't come this time.

"I think I'd love some grilled salmon and that yellow rice. It's always so fluffy. Never could get my rice like that."

Mikayla audibly sighed in relief, let out a giggle. "Whatever you want, Ma."

"And that sherbet that I like for dessert."

Mikayla leaned down and kissed her cheek. "Whatever you want." She picked up the bedside phone, called the kitchen and put in her mother's meal order.

"While we wait, why don't I help you get up and dressed, Ma."

Stella slowly shrunk away. She looked at Mikayla from the corner of her eyes. Her bottom lip quivered. "Where's Carol?" Her voice rose. Panic lit her eyes. She gripped the sheet in her fist.

"Mom," Mikayla said gently.

The nurse came to the bedside. "Everything is fine, Ms. Harris. I'm right here and so is your daughter, Mikayla."

The tight lines that pulled her brows together slowly eased. A smile curved her mouth and that wild expression receded.

"Kay, are you losing weight? You're looking thin."

Mikayla grinned. "No, Ma. I wish. Let's get you up and dressed before your food arrives."

Stella had her blood drawn, then went for her CAT scan before lunch, with the MRI scheduled for the following morning. After lunch she and Mikayla walked and talked, laughed and watched a couple of Stella's favorite shows. For those few hours her mom was the woman that she'd known and loved all her life. There were a few foggy moments, but for the most part she had a good day. Mikayla stayed until after dinner.

While her mother was undergoing her CAT scan, Mikayla sat with Dr. Simpson, who explained that for now it appeared that the incident from the night before was isolated. What he planned to do was to evaluate every inch of everything that she'd eaten, who she'd seen, her activities, sleeping patterns over the past week to see if they could identify any external factors that may have contributed to the episode. He promised to let her know as soon as all of the test results came back.

By the time she walked back to her car, she was physically and mentally exhausted. The strain of what was happening to her mother was taking a toll on her and she was crumbling under the financial weight of her mother's care. The money they got for the house was going to run out soon. Her business was not going to cut it. She got into her car, rested her head on the steering wheel and let the tears she fought to keep at bay finally flow.

Gradually she pulled herself together. She dug in her tote for a tissue and wiped her eyes, then saw the light of her cell phone deep in her bag. She pulled it out. Six voice messages and an equal amount of texts. The first two calls were from the studio, along with two text messages. The rest were all from Traci.

She squeezed her eyes shut and sputtered an expletive. The audition! She'd all but forgotten about it and never even called. Traci was going to flip. She'd used her connections to get her in. She didn't have the energy to call and explain. She turned the key in the ignition and drove off.

Chapter 7

Alonzo parked his car in the driveway of Ryan Carrington's Beverly Hills estate. The past five, six years that he'd been building his business and his brand he'd seen his share of palatial estates. He'd prepared spreads for heads of corporations and heads of state. His favorites were always the television and movie clients. They were the least enamored of themselves and simply wanted to have a good time around people who understood what it was like to not be able to go to the grocery store short of wearing a disguise. He'd made not only contacts at those gatherings but friends, as well. And word of mouth was his greatest advertiser.

A gray Honda pulled up behind him. It was Jasmine. He got out of his car and waited.

"Hi. Sorry I'm late," she said and squeezed his upper arm.

"Not late at all. I just got here myself."

They walked toward the front entrance that was straight out of *Gone with the Wind*.

"So how have you been since London?" Jasmine asked.

"Can't complain. Relaxing. You?"

"Catching up with friends, hanging out with my sister. Did Cheri come back with you, or is she still shooting?"

"Uh, no."

She glanced at his profile. "Doesn't sound good."

"Let's just say Cheri has moved on to other things."

"Oh… You okay with that?"

"Yeah. It is what it is."

They reached the front door. Alonzo pressed the bell, slid his hands into his pockets.

"You were too good for her anyway," she whispered as the door was opened by the housekeeper.

Alonzo shot her a look and chuckled. He turned to the middle-aged woman at the door. "Hello. Alonzo Grant. Jasmine Cole. We have an appointment to see Mr. Carrington."

"Yes, of course. Mr. Carrington is expecting you. Follow me. He's out back."

"I met someone," he said, not sure why he was confessing to Jasmine, other than she was always telling him he needed to slow down and find a good woman.

"Really?" She elbowed him in the side. "Who?"

"You wouldn't believe it if I told you."

The housekeeper opened the sliding doors to the backyard that seemed to go on for miles, complete with an Olympic-sized swimming pool, tennis and basketball court, and at least an acre of grass and trees for doing whatever.

Ryan turned from his reclining spot on the striped lounge. "Hey, Zo." He threw his longs legs over the side and stood. He extended his hand. "Thanks for coming by."

"Good to see you again, Ryan. This is Jasmine Cole, my head chef."

"Ms. Cole. Pleasure."

"Beautiful home," she said.

He chuckled. "Thanks." He turned to Alonzo. "So let's talk. I have some ideas, but of course I want your input."

"Of course," Alonzo echoed and gave Jasmine a side-eye, to which she bit back a grin.

After more than two hours of talking, suggesting, cajoling, laughing, Alonzo walked out with a tentative menu for three hundred guests, and a deposit check for ten thousand dollars.

"That was intense," Jasmine said as they walked to their cars.

"Ya think?" He chuckled.

"I love watching you mold and guide the client, getting them to realize what they want is what *you* want to do for them."

"Hmm." He stopped in front of her car door.

Jasmine propped her hands on her hips and looked up at him. "So...who is this person that I wouldn't believe?" She angled her head to the side.

He grinned. "She's, um, the owner of the cleaning

service. She came to clean my house when I got back from London."

"Get out! For real."

"Look, nothing is going on. Nothing." He held up his hand.

"So then I'm confused. What is going on?" She folded her arms and leaned against the side of her car.

Alonzo pushed out a breath and told her what happened from the moment he met Mikayla Harris.

"Damn," she murmured when he was done. "This is a first for you, Zo. I've been with you from the early days and I have never heard what I'm hearing in your voice. But…she works for you. That's… I don't know… sticky."

"Yeah. I'm open to suggestions."

"Me. I'm all about honesty. You can't go wrong. Be up-front." She shrugged. "You won't know how she feels if you don't open the door. She certainly can't."

"True. She can't."

"Guess you have your answer." She patted his shoulder and opened her door. "Good luck." She got in. "She must be special."

Alonzo grinned. "Yes, she is."

She shut her car door and rolled down the window. "I'll start putting in the orders for the items that need to be shipped in. I'll give you an update at the end of the week."

"Thanks. Drive safe."

He stepped back, walked to his car and pulled out of the winding driveway with Jasmine close behind. When they finally exited the property onto the roadway, Jasmine honked her horn and turned left. Alonzo waved and turned right. Faith, Harrison and now Jasmine all pretty much said the same thing: *Go for it*. It was starting to sound better and better.

Mikayla pressed her head against her palm, eyes closed as she talked to Traci.

"I know I blew it, Trace. I'm sorry, but I didn't have a choice. When I got that call…"

"Kayla, I know. I do. If it was me I would have done the same thing. I get it. But there's no way I can go back to that well for you—or even for me. And as big as this town is, it's small. Word travels fast."

Her stomach knotted. "I know," she whispered.

"If it was the basic open call, it would be different. But this was set up for you."

"I'm sorry, especially if I messed up anything for you."

"I'll be fine. Enough about this BS. What's going on with your mom?"

Mikayla was beyond burned-out by the time she got off the phone with Traci. She'd screwed up big-time by not calling to cancel or reschedule. Totally unprofessional. What she was most upset about is that she may have messed up Traci's good name in the process.

She ran a hot bubble bath with the intention of soaking until she turned into a Raisinet, and that's just what she did.

Feeling almost like herself, she generously lotioned her body, slipped on her nightgown and crawled into bed. Her whole body sighed with pleasure. She turned onto her side and reached for the nightlight, and that was the last thing she remembered before the sun rose the following morning.

Mikayla sat at her kitchen table, going over her bills, when her cell phone rang. Her heart raced. Greenwood was her first thought until she saw that it was her business phone. She exhaled a sigh of relief.

"At Your Service."

"Good morning. This is Alonzo Grant."

Her heart thumped and tumbled in her chest. "Good morning, Mr. Grant."

"Sorry to call so early, but I was hoping you could come by later today. If you're not booked."

"Uh, can you hold on? Let me check the schedule." She put the phone on mute, jumped up and did a three-sixty around her kitchen table. This is just what she needed after the day she'd had yesterday. She dragged in a breath and unmuted the phone. "I have an opening at noon. Will that work for you?"

"Perfect. Will you be coming again?"

She paused a beat. "Yes. Is that a problem?"

"Not at all."

Was that relief she heard in his voice? "I'll be there at noon."

"Great. See you then."

Mikayla put down the phone and allowed herself to breathe. It was a business call, she mentally repeated. She did a good job. He wanted her to come back. Nothing more. She smiled as she floated around her tiny apartment. It might be only a business call, but she was going to see Alonzo Grant again. That made all the difference in the world.

* * *

She knew she was being silly. Other than being a gentleman, Alonzo Grant hadn't given her any indication that he was interested in anything more than her cleaning skills. However, even though she was in uniform, it didn't stop her from putting on her favorite oil, ensuring that her twisted hairstyle was vibrant and popping, and her makeup was subtle yet appealing, with just enough tinted lip gloss and strokes of eyeliner to highlight her two best features, her pillowy lips and wide brown eyes.

She gave herself a last once-over in the full-length mirror that hung on the back of the bathroom door. Satisfied, she gathered up her supplies and headed out to her car.

The instant Mikayla said yes, Alonzo went straight to work on preparing the perfect early afternoon treat. He knew the way to just about anyone with a beating heart was through the stomach. He planned to put the old adage to work today.

His trip to Gelson's was definitely paying off. He had everything he needed to present an assortment of treats from appetizers to a full meal. He didn't want to come off too crazy, but for some reason he wanted her to be impressed with his skills or maybe his culinary powers of seduction.

In an attempt at nonchalance he placed the spread along the kitchen island counter, like a sampling station at a restaurant. The mix of aromas, the bursts of colors on display lifted his lips with pride. Hopefully, Mikayla would be enticed and not overwhelmed. He took one last look, then darted upstairs to take a quick shower and change. Mikayla would arrive in about forty minutes and the last impression he wanted to make was greeting her at the door with a towel around his waist.

Mikayla pulled to a stop on the driveway of Alonzo's house and glanced up at the front door. She felt her insides flutter that way a leaf blows in the wind. She pressed her hand to her stomach, dragged in a breath and got out. Rounding the car, she opened the trunk and got out her supplies. Before she could reach the front door, it swung inward. Alonzo appeared in the doorway. He jogged down the three steps and strode to her car.

"Hi. Let me help you with those." He took the carrying tray of supplies from her. "How was the ride over?"

"Fine. Traffic was pretty light."

He held the door open for her. "Really appreciate you coming by on such short notice."

"Not a problem at all."

He shut the door behind them.

She subtly sniffed the air. "Something smells good."

"Oh," he said, hoping he sounded casual. "I was trying out some recipes for a party I'm doing in a few weeks. Come on. Love to get your opinion." He led the way to the kitchen.

"Whoa," she exclaimed when she walked into the kitchen. "You've been busy." She laughed.

"Yeah," he chuckled, "just a little."

She slowly strolled along the length of the counter. "What is everything?"

He took a plate from the cabinet and handed it to

her. "Take some of everything. You'll be my official taste tester."

She glanced at him with skepticism but did as asked. "So tell me what I'm eating."

"Okay. So this—" he pointed to the first tray "—is mushroom, leeks and fontina frittata."

"Hmm," she hummed deep in her throat. She lifted the triangular slice and placed it on her plate. "And this?"

"This is a vegetarian enchiladas verdes."

"Yum. And this?"

"Salmon Nicoise."

"Fancy," she teased and added it to her plate. "Shrimp and grits," she said with delight at the last tray.

"Yep. With my special twist." He winked. "Have a seat."

While Mikayla sat down, Alonzo added a little of everything to a plate of his own and then sat down next to her.

"I do want your honest opinion," he said.

Mikayla settled herself in the padded chair. She put down her fork and angled her body toward him. "Mr. Grant—"

"Alonzo."

She ran her tongue across her lips. "As much as this is absolutely wonderful…and… I don't feel right."

He immediately got up from his seat and took a step back. "Please, I have no intention of making you uncomfortable." He held up his hands, palms facing her. He swallowed. "I did all this because I wanted to impress you."

She frowned for a moment. Her head jerked back. "Impress me?"

"From the moment I heard your voice on the phone and then you showed up on my doorstep I haven't been able to stop thinking about you. I've been making myself crazy trying to figure out if or when I could cross the line and tell you that the only reason I asked you to come back wasn't because I wanted you to clean my house, but because I wanted to see you again."

The only sound in the room was the chirping of the birds outside the kitchen window.

"I'm sorry." He lowered his head and shook it. "That was totally out of line. I—"

Mikayla got up. She stood in front of him. "Me too," she admitted.

A slow smile of relieved happiness sparkled in his eyes. "You too," he said with a hint of awe in his voice. He took her hand, and when she didn't pull away, he said, "You're fired."

Her eyes widened, her lips parted to speak but he cut her off.

"I can't date someone that's working for me." His thumb stroked the back of her hand. "Is that okay with you?"

Mikayla blinked several times.

"I can recommend you to all of my friends if you're worried about work," he said, reading her thoughts. "You'll have as much as you can handle."

Slowly she lowered back onto her chair. "I don't think I've ever been fired before," she finally said, with a smile that broke the tightrope of tension.

Alonzo chuckled and plopped down in his chair.

"There's a first time for everything." He forked a piece of frittata and brought it toward her mouth. "I want to have many firsts with you." He leaned just a breath closer. "Try this," he said barely above a raw whisper.

Mikayla's lips parted but she couldn't tear her eyes away from his. The burst of flavor, the perfect temperature and texture, exploded in her mouth. Her eyelids fluttered closed. She sighed.

"I love that sound of satisfaction," he said.

Mikayla's eyes opened. She swallowed the lighter-than-air frittata. She leaned toward him. "What happens if I want more?" she practically purred. "Are you up for that?"

The corner of his mouth lifted to a grin. "Always."

"Wow, just wow," Mikayla sighed. She glanced at the row of half-eaten trays of food. "I'm glad you fired me before we ate, because you would have definitely had to fire me after. No way I'd be able to work. That was…beyond incredible."

Alonzo tossed his head back and laughed. "All this—" he ran a finger along her jaw "—was only an appetizer."

He watched the pulse quiver at the base of her throat. It took all of his willpower not to press his lips there, to feel the vibration of her against his mouth. He drew in a deep breath of resolve.

"Since it seems like neither one of us is in the mood to work, why don't we go out back. I made a pitcher of mimosas."

Mikayla gave him the side-eye, then broke into laughter. "Of course you did."

He pressed his hand to his chest. "Madame, are you insinuating that I had nefarious intent?"

"Uh, yeah." She hopped down from her seat. "Let's see if your mimosas can match your appetizers."

"What's Ryan Carrington like in real life?"

He chuckled and refilled her glass. "In real life?"

She made a face. "You know what I mean. When all the cameras are off. What's he like?"

"He's a decent guy. Treats people well. Good sense of humor."

"What's it like being around famous people all the time?"

He gave a slight shrug. "Not always. They're regular people. I mean some of them have a big head, but for the most part, at least the people that I've met and dealt with are pretty cool."

She sipped her drink and pushed out a sigh. "At one point I thought that would be my life." Her gaze drifted off to the distance.

"What changed? You never actually said."

"You don't need to hear my sad story."

"I wouldn't have asked if I didn't want to know."

She pressed her lips together. He didn't need to know that she'd given up everything—her home, her career, her finances, everything—to care for her mother. She didn't want him to see her as someone to feel sorry for, or some martyr.

"I came out here to try my luck and…well, things didn't work out. I have to keep a roof over my head and I always wanted to have my own business, so I decided on housekeeping. I figured with everyone owning homes there would be plenty of business."

"Is there?"

"It's slow. But I'm going to stick with it."

He was quiet for a moment. "What about your acting? On the back burner?"

"For now."

Alonzo studied her profile. "Would you go back if you had the chance? To acting. I mean if an opportunity presented itself."

The fiasco with her audition the day before flashed in front of her. "I don't know. Maybe."

"Come with me to Ryan Carrington's birthday party."

"What?"

"As my guest...my date."

She gulped, put down her glass and sat up straighter. "A date?"

"Yes. You get all dressed up, I come and get you and take you to the party. I would have to leave you on your own for a lot of the time. I have to work the party, but you can rub elbows." He grinned.

She laved her bottom lip. Attending a party for Ryan Carrington would be a dream come true. She would exhaust her imagination thinking of all the A-listers that would be in attendance. The opportunity was golden, but this was happening too fast. She didn't want Alonzo to think that she was an out-of-work-actress opportunist. If they were going to be a thing, it had to be with no strings attached, no favors owed.

"That's a big ask for a first date. I don't think we're there yet." As soon as the words left her mouth, she regretted it. One thing her mother always stood by—don't question your blessings.

Alonzo leaned back on the lounge chair, slid on his sunglasses and linked his fingers across his stomach. "Fair enough. Then we start small. Brunch. Dinner. A movie. Walks along the beach…" He turned his head and peered at her above the rim of his shades. "How does that sound?"

She tucked in her smile. "Sounds like something I can get behind."

"Good. Then we'll start tonight. We already did the brunch thing. So dinner."

"Tonight?" she squeaked.

"Do you have plans?"

"Um, no, not really."

"Good." He turned toward her, lowered his shades. "I have just the place I'd like you to experience."

"Dress up or dress down?"

"Hmm, casual. Pretty relaxed atmosphere, but the food and music is five-star."

She put down her empty glass. "In that case, I probably should get home." She swung her legs over the side of the lounge chair and stood.

Alonzo did the same. He was right in front of her, so close that she had to glance up just a bit to look him in the eyes. And then his fingers were threaded through the wiry twists of her hair, pulling her to him. The world disappeared and she fell into the dark pools of his eyes as he lowered his head to capture her lips.

She gasped when the surge of electricity zipped through her veins. His mouth gently covered hers, soft, sweet, firm all at once. So tender that she nearly wept.

Alonzo slowly broke the kiss and she felt as if her anchor had been lifted and she was drifting away from the shore. The sound of his voice brought her back.

"The way I imagined," he said, his voice slightly raw. He dragged his thumb across her cheekbone. "I'll walk you to your car."

The pulse pounded so loud in her ears she only imagined what he said, and figured it out when he guided her back through the house to collect her supplies, then out to her car.

"Seven work for you?" he asked when she got behind the wheel.

What was he saying? "Sorry?"

"Seven. Is that enough time for you?"

"Oh." She laughed from nerves. "Sure. That's plenty of time."

"Good. Text me your address when you get home. I'll pick you up."

Before she could respond, he turned and headed back to the house.

She turned on the car and slowly followed the path out to the front gate. Was this actually happening? She'd never been so thrilled to be fired from a job.

"Say what!" Traci squealed through the phone.

"Yes, all that. Everything. For real, for real. Oh my God, T, when he kissed me, I swore I was gonna freaking faint!" She laughed and flipped through the skimpy selection of outfits that hung in her narrow closet.

"Girl, I told you something was brewing. But I am so glad that he came at you the way he did. A gentleman. I like him even more now."

"Me too," she said wistfully. She frowned at her less-than-appealing choices. "I don't have anything to wear! Damn, I actually said that."

Traci snickered. "I got you. Listen, I have one stop to make, then I'll run by my house and bring—"

Then it hit her. "No." She couldn't have Alonzo pick her up from her apartment. "I'll come to you. It'll be easier. He can just pick me up from your place."

"Not a problem. I'll be home in about a half hour."

"Okay. So I'll see you around four thirty."

"You still have your key. If you get there before me just go on in. *Mi casa, su casa.*"

"Thanks, sis. I'll see you later."

"Later."

Alonzo was gathering up the remnants of their brunch when the front gate buzzed. His first thought was that it must be Mikayla. He answered the intercom only to find out that it wasn't Mikayla but Jasmine.

"Hey, Jazz, come on down." He buzzed the gate. Jasmine didn't make it a habit to simply drop in. Generally they got together to plan events or test out new recipes. Unless he was missing something, he had no clue why she was here.

The front doorbell chimed. He crossed the foyer and pulled the door open.

"Hey." He leaned in and buzzed her cheek. "Come on in. Everything cool?"

She stepped inside. "Yes. Fine. Sorry to just pop up without calling."

"No problem." He walked ahead of her into the living room. "What can I get for you?"

She sat on the couch. "You had company." She lifted her head toward the two glasses and empty mimosa carafe.

"Oh, yeah." He smiled. "The woman I told you I met. Actually have a date tonight." He sat on the love seat opposite Jasmine. "So, what's up? Problem with the shipment?"

"No. Everything is in the works." She crossed and uncrossed her legs.

"So…what's going on, Jazz?" His brow creased. He rested his forearms on his thighs.

"Um…we've known each other for a while, right?"

"Yeah. Of course."

She dragged in a breath, stole a quick glance at him, then focused on her sandaled feet. "I've totally enjoyed working with you, traveling, getting to know so many extraordinary people and learning from you."

"Wait." He slowly rose to his feet. "You're not quitting? Someone else wants you to work with them?"

"After this party I think it would be best if I moved on."

He ran his hand across his head. "I don't understand. What. Is. Going. On? Talk to me, Jazz. Whatever it is we can work it out."

"No. We can't. That's obvious. Maybe not to you, but it's obvious to me."

"What are you talking about?" His voice rose in frustration. "Jazz." He took a step toward her.

She held up her hand and stood. "It's just business," she said softly. She got up. "I wanted you to know about my decision as soon as possible."

Alonzo shook his head as if it would somehow reorganize the pieces of this conversation so that it would make sense.

"I'll keep you posted on the deliveries. I have my end taken care of and I'll get the team together in about a week for a run-through." She forced a half-baked smile. "I'm sorry, Zo." She turned and walked out.

Alonzo stood in the middle of his living room floor—stunned. Words escaped him. What had transpired was so out of left field he never in his wildest imaginings saw it coming.

He crossed the room to the bar and poured a shot of bourbon. Jasmine had been by his side from the beginning. He tossed back the drink, closed his eyes against the burn. None of this made sense. Had she been wooed away by another chef the way he'd done when they'd met in DC, nearly a decade ago? The moment he'd tasted the risotto, cooked to perfection alongside the expertly grilled and seasoned salmon, and the exquisite arrangement of the meal on the gleaming white china plate, he knew he had to meet the chef. When she arrived at his table, she was nothing like what he imagined. He'd expected someone older, more than likely a man. Jasmine Cole was none of those things. If anything, if you took off her chef jacket, she could easily sit at the head of a corporate boardroom. Her petite stature belied the assertiveness in her eyes and the confidence in her voice when she responded to his questions about her meal prep, and she was not fazed by his budding reputation. He liked her—from day one—and quietly shared with her his plan. He left his card and encouraged her to contact him if she was interested in being a partner in his venture. They'd been together ever since, building a business that was unmatched. This made no sense.

Was she planning to strike out on her own? But even

if either of those scenarios were true, there was no reason for the cloak-and-dagger delivery of her decision. He sighed heavily, started to refill his glass but changed his mind. He needed a clear head. The plan was to spend the evening getting to really know Mikayla Harris, test the waters to see if the mutual attraction was real. For now he would have to put this whole Jasmine debacle on the back burner and put his entire focus on Mikayla. The tightness across his brow and the heaviness of Jasmine's news on his chest eased, simply by thinking about Mikayla. That had to mean something.

"I think you should put your hair up," Traci said from her perch on the side of her bed.

Slowly turning left, right, Mikayla peered over her shoulder to check out how she looked in the borrowed dress. "You don't think it's too suggestive?" she asked, gingerly running her hands along her hips. The navy wrap dress was threaded with Lycra, which allowed for freedom of movement while curving to every inch of the body. She adjusted the deep opening in front of the dress and the tie at the waist.

"Isn't that the point?" Traci teased.

Mikayla made a face, which Traci ignored. "I don't want him thinking that—"

"That what?" she asked, cutting Mikayla off. "That you think he's hot. That you like him. That you want to see where things go. That you can't stop thinking what it would be like to make love to him. Those *thats*?" She flopped back onto the bed and put her hands under her head.

Mikayla faced the full-length mirror. "Since you put it that way."

They both broke out laughing.

She sat down next to Traci. "It's been a while for me," she said softly.

"I know." Traci placed a hand on Mikayla's arm. "Drake Morris was an asshole. He was the one that screwed up. His loss, not yours."

Mikayla lowered her head and sighed. "I still think about him, what we had or what I thought we had."

"Only natural. You gave him almost three years of your life. You lived under the same roof." She flipped onto her side, propped her head up on her palm. "I know he's a big part of the reason why you lost your passion for acting, and then everything that happened with your mom." She sighed. "Sucked the life out of you. But you have the chance to start over, right here. Put your life in New York in the rearview along with Drake."

"I know you're right. But it doesn't help that I have to see his face on some commercial every other time I turn around."

"Girl, please. C-level commercials at best. Besides, he's always in the background. Just like in real life—in the background."

Mikayla snorted a laugh.

"Anyway, enough about him." Traci hopped up from the bed. "You need accessories and a bag. And you need to get your mind right for date night with one of the most eligible bachelors, like, anywhere!"

"He should be here any minute," Mikayla murmured while she sat, stood, paced.

"You need to chill. He's the same guy he was earlier."

The sound of a car door closing froze them both in place.

Mikayla threw a look of terrified expectation at Traci.

"Breathe." She got up ready to answer the door. She whirled toward Mikayla. "Quick, go in the bedroom. You can make an entrance," she said with a mischievous grin. "Plus you don't want to have him thinking that you were pacing yourself crazy waiting for him."

"Right. Right." Mikayla darted to the back bedroom just as the front doorbell chimed.

Traci walked to the door and pulled it open. "Hi," she beamed. "I'm Traci. Mikayla is in back."

Alonzo smiled in response. "Alonzo Grant."

"Please come in, have a seat. I'll let her know you're here."

"Thanks."

He slung his hands into the pockets of his black slacks and strolled into the living space. He casually looked around, trying to get a sense of Mikayla from the room. Her distinctive scent lingered lightly in the air but there was nothing in the space that reflected anything personal about her that he could connect with his impressions of her.

The room was totally LA—smooth sight lines, low furniture in light colors. Minimalist. That's not what he envisioned as Mikayla's space. For whatever reason he saw cozy, warm, bursts of color, comfy pillows, eclectic art, books. This was a magazine-cover-ready home.

"Hi."

He turned toward that voice and the flame licked at

his belly. He felt the smile tug the corners of his mouth. "Hey. You look great."

"Thank you." She crossed the room to where he stood. "Sorry to keep you waiting."

"Totally worth it," he said, his gaze skimming across her surface. He reached for her hand and she stepped closer. He ran his finger across her knuckles. "I hope you like Japanese."

"I do."

"Excellent." He dragged in a breath. "Ready?"

"Yep. Traci!" she called out. "Leaving."

Traci reemerged from wherever she'd been. "Enjoy. I'm probably going to head out in a bit myself." She crossed the room barefoot. "Nice to meet you, Alonzo. I'm a big fan."

He grinned. "Thanks. 'Preciate that."

"Maybe one evening you could whip up one of your *Top Chef* meals over here—for us."

Mikayla bug-eyed her friend. "Trace."

Alonzo chuckled. "Not a problem. I'd like that." He shot Mikayla a questioning look.

Mikayla sighed. "Sure." She gave Traci a playful shove. "Let's get out of here before she talks you into something else." She looped her arm through his and ushered him out.

"Nice place," he said while he opened the passenger door for her. She slid into her seat. "But it didn't feel like you." He shut the door and rounded the front of the Mercedes coup and got in.

"What do you mean?" she asked once he was in and settled.

He gave a slight shrug of his left shoulder. "I don't

know. It feels like a place to live, but it's not home. It's beautiful, don't get me wrong," he quickly qualified. "But—" he turned to her for a moment "—it didn't feel like *you*." He turned the key in the ignition, checked the mirrors and pulled off.

"And what do I feel like to you?" she softly asked.

His eyes cinched at the corners. "Warm. Inviting. Vibrant." He looked at her. "Desirable."

Mikayla's breath hitched.

"Too soon?" he asked.

She tugged on her bottom lip with her teeth. "No," she finally said on a breath.

He pulled the car to the curb, and in one uninterrupted motion unsnapped his seat belt and hers, leaned in and gathered her in his arms. His mouth pressed against her until her lips parted ever so slightly. Her sigh mingled with his groan when his tongue brushed her lips, then dipped inside. His arms tightened around her, pressing as much of her body against his that space and gravity would allow.

His hand trailed down her back. He felt her shudder beneath his fingertips. His pulse raced. From a single kiss he had a full-blown erection that he desperately wanted to relieve. With a moan he pulled back. His gaze raked across her face, her pouting lips. "Been thinking about that all day." He put the car back in Drive and pulled off.

"Me too."

Matsuhi was one of Alonzo's favorite spots and not because he knew and revered the owner, Nico Matsuhi, but because the cuisine was unparalleled. Wherever he traveled, he was sure to find a Matsuhi with its forty locations on five continents, and he made it a point to always stop in. The artistry and presentation of every item was part of the restaurant's signature and almost too beautiful to eat. The items on the extensive menu had been photographed for every food magazine of note. Nico had built a brand that was unsurpassed and a legacy that would inspire generations of chefs. Alonzo strived to walk in Nico's footsteps.

He pulled the door open. "You're going to love this."

"Mr. Grant, welcome," the hostess greeted. She offered a slight bow and Alonzo returned the greeting.

"Good to see you, Sikura. Is Nico here tonight?"

"I'll let him know you have arrived. A waitress will seat you and your guest."

"Thank you."

Sikura lifted her hand and a young woman in a stark white blouse and black skirt appeared silently next to them.

"Follow me, please."

She led them down the row of tables to a private booth in the back with a view of the mountains in the distance.

She turned over the teacups and poured tea, then placed a menu in front of each of them. "I will return shortly for your order. Can I get you anything from the bar in the meantime?"

Alonzo looked to Mikayla.

"White wine, please."

"Make that two," Alonzo added.

"Are you on first-name basis with staff in all the restaurants?" she asked.

Alonzo chuckled. "Not every restaurant, but a few. The owner is somewhat of a mentor of mine."

"Really?" Her brows rose with interest.

He told her about how he'd met Nico when he was studying at the Culinary Institute. "Nico was a guest instructor. I got to talk with him after the session and told him what I wanted to do. He was impressed and said that if I ever needed any assistance, he would be happy to help. And he did. Introduced me to other restaurateurs, chefs, potential clients. He's been in my corner every step of the way."

"Lucky guy."

"Maybe, but hard work and vision are my guides."

The waitress arrived with their wine. "Do you need more time to order?"

"Yes, just a few minutes," Alonzo said.

She turned over their wineglasses, opened the bottle and poured for each of them.

"Thank you."

Alonzo lifted his glass. "To new beginnings."

Mikayla touched her glass to his. "To the future."

Alonzo grinned, took a swallow, then put down his glass. "I like that—the future." He paused a beat. "We probably should order."

Mikayla picked up her menu. "Suggestions?"

"I would start us off with nameko miso soup, and shrimp tempura. For the main course either the lobster broiled in butter and wasabi pepper, or the salmon fillet teriyaki with wasabi pepper. Or both." He grinned. "Oh. You have to try the jumbo clams with anticucho sauce." He brought his fingers to his lips and kissed them. "Perfection."

Mikayla laughed. "Everything sounds incredible."

Alonzo signaled for the waitress and placed their orders, then turned all his attention on Mikayla.

"Tell me about you, about your life in New York. Family, friends..."

She wrapped her slender fingers around the bowl of her glass. "Hmm, I was actually born in Barbados. My mom went into labor three weeks early while she was there visiting her cousin."

His eyes widened. "Wow. An auspicious arrival."

She laughed. "Yes, it was."

"So are you a dual citizen?"

She nodded. "Yep."

"Do you get to 'go home' often?"

"I haven't been back in about four years. Me and my mother used to go once a year for vacation."

"Hmm. Why'd you stop?"

The waitress arrived with the miso soup and the shrimp tempura. The presentation of their appetizers was a work of art.

"This looks too beautiful to touch," Mikayla said with awe.

"Wait until you taste it." He snapped open the white linen napkin and placed it on his lap. "You were telling me why you stopped going to Barbados." He dipped his spoon into the soup and took a sip. His eyes closed with satisfaction. "Mmm, excellent," he murmured.

"Yes, it is."

"So, you were telling me about why you stopped going to Barbados."

She tried to shrug it off. "Life got in the way, I guess."

"Happens. What about now? Is life lining up the way you want?"

"Little by little. I'm getting the business off the ground. Although I did lose a client today." She gave him a pointed look. "But I'm confident."

"Listen, if it's business that you're looking for, I know I can help with that. Do you only cater to homes? What about offices?"

"I'm open."

He nodded. "I'll keep that in mind." He finished off his soup. "Are you planning to get back to your acting?"

Mikayla glanced away, took a bite of the shrimp tempura. "Oh my goodness. Delish."

"Told ya."

She chewed slowly, took a sip of wine. She didn't really want to have the acting conversation. It would open the door to other areas of her life that she wasn't quite ready to divulge. But a part of her felt that she could trust Alonzo with her truths—just not yet.

"You don't have to talk about it if you don't want to." He shrugged, offered a smile. "We can talk about whatever you want. You can recite the alphabet if you want. I just love hearing your voice."

Mikayla laughed. "Right." She tipped her head to the side, tugged in a breath. "I moved out here because my mom got progressively ill." She swallowed over the knot growing in her throat. "Traci—who you met—did some research and helped me find this facility that is doing revolutionary treatment. So, I packed us up, closed shop in New York and came out here." She reached for her glass and found it empty. Alonzo refilled it.

"That must have been tough," he said gently. "I know

what it's like when a parent isn't well. I nearly lost both my mother and father in one fell swoop about a year ago."

Her brows lifted.

"Mom was driving. Dad was the passenger. She had a heart attack and crashed."

"Oh my God."

"Thankfully, they both pulled through. My brother Franklin and his wife, Dina, are both cardiothoracic surgeons. That helped."

"Wow. How are they now?"

"Living life in DC, and planning on a cruise at the end of the year."

Her gaze drifted off, the soft smile slowly faded. What she would give to be able to say that about her mom. Stella Harris wouldn't be going on any cruises or planning out her life, at least not a life that she'd ever envisioned.

"So, you and Traci are roommates?"

She swallowed. "Yes." Maybe not at the moment, but they had been. It was only a partial lie.

The main course arrived and commanded all of their attention as the waitress detailed how everything was prepared especially for them by Chef Nico.

"Anything for Chef Grant and his guest."

Alonzo glanced behind him and his expression bloomed in delight. He pushed up from his seat. "Nico!"

The two men hugged like the old friends that they were.

"When I heard you were here, I knew I had to sprinkle my magic on your meal."

"Ha!" Alonzo put his arm around Nico's shoulder. "This is Mikayla Harris."

Mikayla stretched out her hand.

Nico brought her hand to his lips. "Welcome." He gave a slight bow. "Anything you want on the menu is yours."

"Thank you."

He turned to Alonzo. "How long are you in town?"

"A few weeks. Month. I have an event in a couple of weeks."

"Be sure to stop in before you fly off again." He clapped Alonzo on the back.

"I will."

Nico turned to Mikayla. "Pleasure." He walked off.

Alonzo sat back down.

"You should see your face," she commented.

His brows tightened in question.

"You have that look when someone is stunned to run into their idol."

Alonzo chuckled. "That bad, huh?"

"I think it's endearing."

"Endearing?"

"Yes. It makes you real. Humble. With someone that has so much and can go and come as they please, rub elbows with folks that most of us only read about—to see him awed by someone else is…endearing."

"Never thought about it. I come from a belief system that views everyone as added value to your life and therefore they have value. We all have something to offer, even if it's as simple as listening."

"And what is my added value?"

"I want to take my time and find out. If you'll let

me." He reached across the table and covered her hand. "Will you?"

"I'd like that."

They oohed and aahed throughout their meal while they touched on music, travel, friends. Mikayla kept her part of the conversation limited. She wasn't ready to tell him about her financial situation or about where she lived. She didn't offer a lot of details, but she offered her ear to listen. Alonzo saw the world in brilliant Technicolor and there was no challenge that he wasn't up to meeting. He'd started out mixing messes in his mother's kitchen to be one of the most sought-after chefs in the country. He was beyond successful, but he was still totally real and down-to-earth. He would stop in the middle of one of his stories to listen to what she thought or to ask a question to keep her involved in the conversation. Then there were the little touches on her hand, her arm, the simmering looks that flashed in his eyes. His voice soothed and aroused her and with every passing moment; every shared laugh or look only stoked the flames that had been lit the moment she'd walked through his door. A few weeks, a month. That may be all the time she had with him to make something or not. But she'd take it, even if it was for a little while.

Whatever thin veil that may have blurred the space between them was gone by the time they walked out with Alonzo's arm wrapped tightly around her waist.

"I don't think I want to take you home."

She glanced up at his profile. "What do you plan to do instead?"

He stopped, spun her toward him until she was pressed flush against his body. "I plan to spend the rest of the night exploring your body the way you explored my mind. I plan to make crazy love to you until we are both unable to move. I plan to wake up in the morning and find you curled beside me. And then I plan to fix breakfast and make love to you some more. That's my plan." His eyes moved over her face. "What do you think about that plan?"

She looped her arms around his neck. "I think we shouldn't waste any more time talking about the plan." A smile curved her mouth a moment before her lips locked with his.

Chapter 8

The drive from the restaurant to Alonzo's home seemed to take forever. While he kept one hand on the wheel and the other on her thigh, she struggled to stop thinking about how tight her nipples felt pressed against her bra or how damp she was between her legs. She wanted him to pull over so that she could straddle him, put out the fire at least for a little while. Instead, she bit down on her lip to keep from screaming with desire.

She envisioned reaching his door and the two of them turning into television-show lovers, him kicking the door open, their mouths slamming against each other, clothes being ripped off as they hungrily grabbed and spun each other around the room. She always marveled at how the on-set lovers didn't hurt themselves.

That's not the scene that played out.

Mikayla heard the door click shut behind her. Alonzo's palm settled on the small of her back.

"Can I get you anything? Glass of wine?"

"Sure. Thanks."

"Turn on some music if you want. Plenty to choose from," he said while going into the kitchen to get a bottle of wine from the wine cooler.

Mikayla wandered over to the sound system that came complete with a turntable and rows of actual vinyl records. Slowly she flipped through, finding that his taste was very similar to hers. He was clearly a hardcore R & B and jazz fan, and his collection—some of them collector's items—included *Songs in the Key of Life*, *Who Is Jill Scott?*, D'Angelo, Anita Baker, Phyllis Hyman, Luther, and the Temptations greatest hits albums; Ella Fitzgerald, Nancy Wilson, Miles, Monk and Dizzy were all represented.

She slid D'Angelo's *Brown Sugar* out of its sleeve and placed it on the turntable. The sultry beat and seductive voice floated in the air.

"Great choice," Alonzo said, coming up behind her.

She turned toward him and her heart leaped in her chest. Was it going to be like this every time she saw him or heard his voice, or when he touched her?

He extended the glass of wine.

"Thanks." She concentrated on keeping her hand from shaking. "You have an incredible collection. I can tell that most of these are the originals."

He chuckled. "Guess you can tell by the wear and tear, huh?"

She took a sip of her wine. "Just a little," she teased, while glancing at him over the rim of her glass.

"Song fits you perfectly."

A slow heat spread from the bottom of her feet to the top of her head. Her lips parted.

Alonzo snipped the glass from her hand, reached smoothly around her and placed it on the shelf of the wall unit. He slid his arm around her waist and eased her close.

"Dance with me," he whispered in her ear and sent a shiver down her spine.

She moved into his arms and felt herself melt and meld along the hard contours of his body. She rested her head on his shoulder, closed her eyes and inhaled the scent of him as they swayed to D'Angelo.

He tenderly kissed her forehead. She sighed. They swayed. She floated. He anchored her. He arched his head back. Her eyes fluttered open. He titled up her chin with the tip of his finger. She held her breath.

The sweet warmth of his mouth covered hers and she gave in, submitted to the pleasure of his lips, the exploration of his tongue, the stroke of his hands down the curve of her back.

His low groan vibrated deep in her belly and spiraled outward. Her temples pounded when his fingers drifted to her waist and untied the sash. She hitched in a breath. With little effort and no resistance he parted the folds of the slinky dress and whipped the sides of it behind her so that her exposed brown-sugar skin taunted him to taste it.

His lips trailed down the column of her neck, lingering for a moment at the tiny beat at the base of her throat, before dipping down into the valley of her breasts, barely encased in black lace.

"I want you." He kissed the rise of her breasts. His thumbs pressed against her pelvis, slid down beneath the elastic band of her panties, tugged them off.

Desire fluttered through her limbs and pulsed between her thighs. Her knees weakened but it was Alonzo's firm hold at her hips that kept her upright.

The song ended, but the dance continued. He peeled the dress off her shoulders and down her arms until it surrendered and fluttered to the floor.

Her breath hitched in concert with the snap of her bra coming undone. Alonzo groaned. He eased the frilly lace away with his teeth until the sweet fruit of her breasts were displayed for his sampling. He teased and suckled, bringing her nipples to hardened peaks that he flicked and laved with his tongue. Then without warning he scooped her up in his arms, to her startled laughter, and carried her up to his bedroom.

Alonzo lowered her to the bed, stood above her, his gaze slow and hungry as it slid across her nearly naked body. "Beyond beautiful."

Mikayla extended her arms out to him.

Alonzo unbuckled his belt, unzipped and stepped out of his slacks. Mikayla's eyes widened at the erection that threatened to split his boxers in half. He stepped out of his boxers, stretched out on the bed next to her, then turned onto his side. She did the same and draped her leg over his.

Alonzo caressed the curve of her hip, kissed her collarbone. She pressed closer. His erection throbbed against the dip in her stomach. He lowered his head and took her breast in his mouth. Her back arched as the air caught in her throat. Rivers of pleasure scuttled through her. She locked her fingers behind his head, binding her to him. He eased her onto her back.

Her lids fluttered open. He reached over to the nightstand, rifled around and pulled out a condom. Rising up onto his knees, he tore the package open. Mikayla took it from him.

"Let me." She sat up against the fluff of the thick down pillows. She took him in her hand, wrapped her fingers around his thickness, stroked him until he groaned and gripped her shoulders, before she finally teased the condom down along his length.

Alonzo's jaw tightened. Mikayla eased back, slid her body beneath his. He slid his arms beneath her thighs, lifting them until they were high and wide. Her position left her unable to move and totally at his mercy. He pressed against her slick opening. She gasped. He pushed. Stars popped behind her eyes. Her fingertips dug into his back as he moved inside of her by tantalizing degrees until she was filled and breathless.

Alonzo lowered is head and covered her mouth with his, swallowing her soft cries as he moved in and out of her until the sounds shifted to ragged moans.

Wave upon wave of pleasure roared through her. Every move, every thrust sent her closer and closer to the edge. Whatever she might have imagined being with Alonzo would be like was eclipsed by the reality. He was perfection—the way his touch sent her head spinning, the tenderness of his kisses, the way he fit perfectly with every inch of her body outside and in.

The crazy longing that fueled the rise and fall of her hips, commanded her tongue to dance with his, insisted that her hands memorize every inch of his body intensified with every stroke, every thrust, every rotation of his hips and slap of skin against skin.

She couldn't breathe. Her limbs were on fire. A tingle began at the bottom of her feet. His pace kicked up a notch. She cried out. The tingle climbed higher, grew more intense.

Alonzo gripped a handful of her hair. "Don't want this to end," he groaned. "So good…so good. Ahhh."

"Zo!" Her insides gripped him. The power of her orgasm shot out from her center to the tip of her limbs and sent Alonzo hurtling to a shuddering release that rocked them both and set off a second wave that shook them until they were weak and limp.

Alonzo flopped over onto his back and threw his arm across his face. "Damn" was all he could manage.

Mikayla laughed weakly. "Understatement."

She turned onto her side to face him. He angled his head toward her. She reached out to stroke his cheek. "Wow," she whispered with a smile.

"I second that." He dragged in a breath, then slid his arm under her shoulders and eased her against him. "Hmm. That's better."

Mikayla listened to the steady beat of his heart and realized that she couldn't hear her own because it matched his beat for beat. A wave of joy swept through her and her vision clouded. It had been so long since she felt happy. Just plain old happy. Every day for the past few months were filled with worry, angst, more worry, sadness and fear. But not tonight. Not since she met Alonzo. She saw the sun again, felt hopeful, dared to dream. Maybe this might not last beyond tonight, this moment—but even if it didn't, she'd had her night with him and she would cherish it forever.

Alonzo wiped a tear from her cheek with his thumb. "You okay?"

She nodded vigorously. "Yes." She sniffed. "Fine."

He lifted her chin so that he could look into her eyes. "Sure?"

"Positive. Happy. That's all."

"Hope I figure into the mix. I want to make you happy."

"You might have a small—" she made a tiny space between her thumb and forefinger "—part to play."

"That small, huh?"

She giggled.

He moved to brace himself above her. "I'm gonna have to work on my happiness game." He leaned down and kissed her slow and deep.

She wrapped her arms and legs around him. Yes, she could get used to this brand of happy.

"Hmm." Alonzo stretched. "I'm going down to the kitchen. What can I get for you? Hungry?"

She scrunched up her nose. "Actually, I'm starved."

Alonzo chuckled. He sat up, threw his legs across the side of the bed and stood. "I got you. Want to watch me work some predawn magic or would you prefer to lie here like the queen you are and be served?"

"Well, sir…since you put it like that…" She paused dramatically, then tossed the sheet aside. "No. I'd prefer to watch you work." The truth—she wasn't ready to not be in the same space with him. *Silly girl.*

"Blame it on my overblown ego but I love an audi-

ence. Come on, I'll whip us up an omelet and croissants."

She giggled. "But of course."

He found his boxers and put them on. "Let me get
you a robe or something." He went to the closet and
took out one of his shirts and held it up for her approval.

"Perfect. Thanks." She crossed the room and took
the shirt from him.

Alonzo clasped her wrist. "Wait. Let me look at you
before you cover up all that lusciousness." His eyes
did a slow stroll up and down her body. "Humph." He
took a step toward her. "I'd rather have you for breakfast." He brought his mouth to hers, kissed her, then
stepped back.

Mikayla grew hot all over again. Damn. Damn.
Damn. She would jump back in bed with him in a heartbeat. Instead she followed him downstairs and into the
kitchen.

"Got plans for today?" Alonzo asked while he
whipped the egg whites.

"Actually, I have a client later this afternoon," she
said and didn't know why she lied.

"Oh, that's great." He took a quick glance at her over
his shoulder. "And after that?"

"Not sure. What about you?"

"I have a meeting and I want to look at a potential
space. I'm thinking of opening a small restaurant."

"Wow. That's major. Where?"

"In the valley." He half shrugged. "I need to see how
much work needs to be done. It might be more than I'm
willing to take on. And I have to consider the time that

I'm on the road and who will run things." Jasmine's impending departure colored everything he'd do with the business going forward. "How is your mother doing?" he asked, shifting gears.

She linked her fingers together on the countertop. "She had a bad episode the other day."

He stopped what he was doing and turned to her. "Oh, wow. I'm sorry. What can I do to help?"

Her brow lifted in question. "Help?"

"Yeah. Whatever you need."

Her heart tumbled in her chest. She blinked back the hot rush that threatened to spill from her eyes. "Thanks. But I'm good. Handling things." She glanced away.

Alonzo wiped his hands on a dish towel and came to sit next to her. "Look. I know we're—" he shrugged a bit "—getting started on this thing we have going on between us." He took her hand. "But one thing you need to understand about me—when I'm in, really in, I'm in one hundred. I don't do anything halfway. You want to talk, we talk. You want to cry, we cry. You want to get couples massage, we do it." That made her smile. "You need to come here just to chill, you can. Whatever it is." He paused a beat. "I understand what it's like to have a sick parent. I know you have your friend Traci, but now you have me, too." His gaze settled on her face. "Cool?"

Her lips tightened. She nodded her head.

He leaned in and kissed her. "Now, back to work. Hey, you want some juice?"

"Sure."

"Help yourself. Whatever you want." He returned to preparing breakfast. He kneaded the pre-made dough for the croissants and prepped the cooking tray, cut the dough into triangles and gently rolled them before popping them into the oven.

Shortly after, the room became infused with the comforting scent of baking bread and she was back in her mother's kitchen. Maybe she was eight or nine. She could see herself standing next to her mother while she floured and kneaded the dough. Her mom was talking softly to her, explaining what she was doing and why. She even let Mikayla stick her fingers in the dough and squeeze. The sun was streaming in the window and cast a halo around her mother while she worked. She thought at that moment that her mom was the most beautiful, kindest, smartest woman in the whole world.

She closed the refrigerator.

Alonzo stopped chopping and turned to her.

"My mom has advanced Alzheimer's. Very aggressive." Her voice cracked. "Came out here because Greenwood is doing great work, experimental treatments. Left everything behind in New York." Her nostrils flared as she sucked in air. "It's so hard…to see her like that." She turned her face away.

Alonzo sat down next to her. "I know it is. I'm not gonna blow a lot of sunshine at you. There's nothing like seeing our parents hurt or suffering. But you are doing what you can. That matters."

Her eyes widened with pain. "Some days she doesn't even know me. She looks right through me." Her breathing escalated. "It hurts so bad some days that I can't think straight."

"She's getting great care, right?"

Mikayla nodded.

"Are they making any progress—with the treatment?"

"That's just it." Her voice cracked. "They were, and then she had a major setback." She wiped away a wayward tear.

"What happened?"

She swallowed, hesitated, then slowly told him what happened—the call from the facility, and even how she never showed up for her audition that Traci set up. She'd screwed up her best friend's contact and blackened her own name on top of everything else.

He put a comforting hand on her shoulder. "Aw, babe. I'm sorry. Really." He pulled her into his arms and held her. He kissed the top of her head. "The doctors are gonna take care of your mom, and there will be other parts. You need to believe that."

"The rational part of me knows that. It's the emotional part that doesn't."

"I get it. Maybe I can at least help with the emotional part. Be here to listen or whatever you need. Okay?"

She stared at him, doubt and questions in her eyes. "Why do you care so much?"

"Because I care about you and the things that matter to you. Give me a chance to be there for you." A mischievous grin tugged his lips. "I really want more than great sex."

Her gaze rose to meet his. She tugged on her bottom lip with her teeth. "Oh, so it *was* great sex."

He threaded his fingers through her hair. "What do you think?"

"I think…that after you feed me, I want some verification."

Alonzo tossed his head back and laughed. "I'm sure that can be arranged."

* * *

After an amazing breakfast of the lightest omelet she'd ever eaten and the fluffiest croissants accompanied by fresh fruit, juice and fresh ground coffee, Mikayla was treated to a deep soak in Alonzo's Jacuzzi tub complete with soft lights and the hint of music from some unseen source. By the time she finally dragged herself out of heaven and padded into his bedroom, she was as weak and soft as a brand-new baby.

Alonzo had changed the sheets, closed the blinds and drawn the curtains. "Rest," he said and pulled back the sheets.

She didn't have the energy to protest. She crawled into the bed and curled into a fetal position. Alonzo gently covered her with the sheet, leaned down and lightly kissed her forehead. "Rest."

When she awoke, she was completely disoriented. The room was dark. Where was she? What time was it? She tried to move but found herself weighted down. Slowly her foggy brain cleared.

Alonzo's arm and leg were draped across her body. The warmth of his breath fluttered against the back of her neck. By degrees the previous night and well into the morning drifted back. It wasn't a dream. She'd actually had the most incredible night of her life with this man right here. She covered his hand that was casually—if not on purpose—cupping her breast. He moaned softly.

It was still hard for her to fully accept that a man like Alonzo Grant was all in, especially with a woman like her and the baggage she came with. Traci'd told her time and again that she needed to get Drake and his trifling ways of out her head and get back in the game. He'd done a serious number on her sense of self and she had not fully recovered. Her ability to trust was fractured; her willingness to open herself up to another was on serious hold. She was still amazed that she'd confessed as much as she did to Alonzo about her mom.

She sighed softly. Maybe this time would be different, but she still struggled to see how long Alonzo Grant would be interested in a washed-up, would-be actress-housekeeper, especially considering the kind of life he lived and the circles that he traveled in. Where could she possibly fit in?

"Are you sure you don't want me to go with you?"

"No. I'll be fine." She kept her back to him while she dressed, inexplicably needing to create some distance.

He came around to stand in front of her and angled his head to the side to look at her. "What is it? You've been silent as a monk since we got up."

She lowered her head, shook it slowly. "Nothing." She sucked in a breath, put on a smile and looked at him. "Just…getting used to the newness."

Alonzo waited a beat. He cupped her chin. "That's all it is?"

"That's it."

He studied her for a moment. "All right," he conceded. "Let me tie up a couple of things and I'll drop you at home."

Her stomach jumped. "Um, I can take an Uber."

"Yeah, I know you can. But I'm going to drive you." He widened his eyes,

"Okay," she said on a breath.

"I'll be ready in about fifteen minutes." He walked into the bathroom. Moments later she could hear the shower.

She tied the sash on her dress and went downstairs to the living room. She turned on the television in time to catch *The View*. The ladies were in the middle of interviewing Cheri Lang about her new movie. But what caught Mikayla's attention was the mention of Alonzo's name. She sat straighter and turned up the volume.

"Alonzo and I—" she smiled demurely "—will always find our way to each other. We both have busy lives. I'm traveling for work. And he does, as well."

"How can you make that kind of relationship work?" one of hosts asked.

"Mutual agreement."

The ladies laughed.

"I read recently that things had soured between you two when you were filming in London. Any truth to the stories?"

Cheri shifted slightly in her seat. "As with every relationship there are bumps in the road. We hit a bump." She shrugged. "Nothing more."

"So will we be seeing you two together as the awards season starts heating up?"

"Keep your eyes peeled."

"Speaking of awards season," one of the hosts jumped in. "You will be starring in the upcoming film *Betrayal*. That's what you were filming in London. Tell us about it."

Mikayla reached for the remote and turned off the television, just as Alonzo reentered the room.

"Ready?"

"Sure," she mumbled and grabbed her purse from the spot beside her on the couch. She walked to the door and out without another word.

Throughout the trip back to Mikayla's stand-in apartment, she remained quiet, her face turned to her window, staring at nothing. The interview played over and over in her head. Why was he any different from Drake? He wasn't. He just pretended to be. She'd been the "side piece" once before and for far too long. She didn't travel halfway across the country to get twisted up in another no-win scenario. It was a role she had no interest in playing.

Alonzo pulled up in front of what he believed to be Mikayla's home. He cut the engine, unsnapped his seat belt and turned to her. "Now do you want to tell me what's wrong?"

She fiddled with her belt and finally got it undone. "Nothing. I told you late."

"Can you please look at me and tell me that?"

She pressed her lips into a tight line and snapped her head toward him, but when she knocked into the look of pure concern and sincerity in his eyes, her resolve faltered. Her lips parted.

"Talk to me," he urged.

"While you were in the shower, Cheri Lang was interviewed on *The View*." She watched his expression tense. His jaw flexed. "She gave the impression that there was a relationship between you, ongoing and current." She lifted her chin, daring him to dispute what she'd said and at the same time hoping that he wouldn't.

He squeezed his eyes shut and raised his head upward. "Listen." He turned all his focus on Mikayla. He draped his arm along the back of her seat. "This is not a two-minute conversation. I will tell you everything you want to know. But not right now. What I will tell you now is that Cheri is way off base and I'm pretty sure that her performance was for my benefit."

"We're real early in this thing between us. Rather than get all caught up in drama and explanations and whatever else—maybe we should just chalk this up to a remarkable time and move on." She unlocked her door. "Thanks for everything." She opened her door.

"Mikayla! Wait." He jumped out of the car and stopped her. "We need to talk. Please. Don't walk away. We...there's something here between us. Something real. I know it and so do you. Are you really willing to just toss it aside? Give me the chance to explain everything. After you hear me out, if you still want to walk, I won't stand in your way." He held up his hands. "I swear."

She drew in a breath. She tucked her lips in, thinking it over. "When are we having this talk?" she finally said.

"I can swing by here later this evening. You have a client and I have business, as well. Tell me a time and I'll be here."

"Fine. Eight o'clock."

"I'll be here."

"Fine."

Chapter 9

Mikayla used the spare key to Traci's apartment and let herself in. She heard humming coming from the back room. She dropped her bag onto the paisley padded chair in the kitchen.

"Trace!" she called out. She walked toward the sound of humming.

A door opened along the short hall. Traci stuck her head out. "Hey. Getting dressed. I'll be out in a sec."

"Sure." She walked back to the kitchen and sat down. She checked her work phone, hoping to get a message about a job. No luck. What was she doing wrong? There had to be a way to break into the business, or maybe this wasn't for her. She needed a job. She needed a steady income. The money from the sale of the house in New York was almost gone. Her savings was on life support.

She pressed her palm against her forehead. Starting tomorrow, she would hit the pavement.

"Hey, sis." Traci burst into the room, walked to the counter and poured a cup of coffee. She plopped down in a chair opposite Mikayla. "You still have on the outfit from last night. That's always a dead giveaway." She winked and took a sip of coffee. "Girl, didn't I tell you to keep your legs closed?"

"Um, nope."

"In that case, how the hell was it?"

Mikayla lowered her head and chuckled. She got up and fixed a cup of coffee as well and returned to the table. She peeked at Traci over the rim of her coffee mug. "Fan-tas-tic!" She beamed.

"Now that's what I'm talking about. You needed to get rid of those cobwebs. It's been a minute for you, and damn if you didn't find Prince Charming." She sipped her coffee.

"I wouldn't exactly call him Prince Charming."

Traci's exuberant expression sobered. Slowly Mikayla put down her cup. "Everything was beyond wonderful." She told Traci about their night out and their night in. And then seeing Cheri Lang.

"Whoa." Traci frowned in concentration. "I seem to remember reading something about the two of them, but it was nothing serious. That was a while ago."

"Apparently it's still going on. They were together in London."

"There are always two sides to a story and then there is the truth. She has her version. If you feel like it can be something between you and Alonzo, then you owe it to him and yourself to hear what he has to say. Besides, why would he bother to go through any hoops if he wasn't really interested in you?"

Mikayla shook her head. "I don't know."

"But you are going to see him later and hear him out."

"Yeah."

"Take it from there. See what he has to say. Every man isn't a piece of crap like Drake."

Mikayla's nostrils flared. The sting of what he'd done, how he'd humiliated her lingered right beneath the surface. Their relationship was a series of fireworks that thrilled them both. What she didn't know was that Drake was also thrilling other women in the process, their mutual director in particular. She dragged in a breath.

"I have to get going," Traci said. "Are you staying?"

"Um, I'm going home, but I'll be back. Alonzo is going to pick me up here at eight."

Traci paused, puckering her lips. "Look, I have no problem with you being here. You know that. But I think you know better than anyone that dodging the truth in any relationship is the death knell. And definitely no way to start things off." Her expression softened. "If he's the one, he will accept who you are, where you live and how much money you have in your bank account." She grabbed her keys from the countertop. "See you later."

Mikayla watched Traci walk out. She knew the advice was right, but it didn't make it any easier to swallow. Her phone vibrated in her purse. She dug inside. It was the company cell phone.

"At Your Service, Mikayla speaking."

"Hello. This is Stacy Fleming. I was referred to you by Alonzo Grant. He said he was very impressed with your work and I am looking to replace my current service. I was wondering if you have time in your schedule to stop by."

"Let me check. Hold on a moment." She did a happy chair dance and squeezed her lips together to keep from screaming. She took a breath, composed her expression. "Hi. I have an opening. I can come by in an hour."

"Excellent. Let me give you the address."

Mikayla put the information in her phone. Stacy Fleming's home was in Lago Vista, the same high-end community as Alonzo. It was already one. She needed to go home, change, get her supplies and get back over to meet her potential new client.

She pushed up from the chair and went into the spare bedroom to retrieve the clothes she'd left the day before. She changed and hung up Traci's dress, then hurried out.

So, he'd been good to his word when he said he'd recommend her to friends. She turned the key in the ignition. That didn't erase the issue about Cheri Lang, but it was a start.

Alonzo circled the block several times in search of a parking space, but also to get a sense of the neighborhood and the foot traffic. The space that he was considering for the restaurant was located in East LA, not the best of neighborhoods, but it had the potential for revitalization minus gentrification. It was a concept that he and Jasmine had discussed and planned for. Part of what he wanted to do was to host cooking classes once per month and package meals, as a kind of give-back to the community. Although the dream was still there, some of the air had been let out of his sail.

He parked and walked down the block toward the building but slowed for a moment when he spotted a car near the corner with a driver behind the wheel that looked a helluva lot like Mikayla. But before he could really focus, the car turned the corner and was gone. She had totally gotten into his head. Now he was seeing things. He kept walking.

The building was located along with a strip of struggling small businesses that ranged from coffee and bagels and fried chicken spots to laundromats. He was scheduled to meet up with the Realtor, get a tour and discuss possible terms.

Richard Epstein, the Realtor, stood out front. "Mr. Grant." He extended his hand. "Thank you for coming."

Epstein had unusually large hands for such a small man. He barely came up to Alonzo's chest, which made it difficult for him to ignore the big shiny bald spot with the strawberry birthmark on the top of his head. Epstein made some more small talk that Alonzo wasn't paying much attention to. Epstein used his code, disengaged the lockbox and opened the front door. He switched on the lights.

Alonzo slung his hands into his pockets and strolled through, trying to look at the space with clear eyes. Would it serve his purpose? Was he up to all the work it was going to take to get this new venture up and operational? And how in the hell was he going to pull it off without Jasmine? He was still wrestling with her abrupt announcement. It made no sense.

"So, what are your thoughts, Mr. Grant?"

Alonzo blinked Epstein back into view. "I think it can work. But before I can make a final decision, I'm going to have to reassess some things on my end."

Epstein gave a short nod. "I totally understand. Do you have some idea of when you will make your decision?"

"Maybe a week, two at the most."

"I can't guarantee that I can keep it off the market that long. If a viable offer comes in…"

"Of course." He extended his hand. "Thanks. I'll be in touch." He walked out. This project was a dream he'd had for years. Building his brand nationally and internationally made what he wanted to do next in his career possible. But he'd laid out the plan with Jasmine in mind. She would be the face of the new location while he continued to travel.

He opened his car door. He'd figure it out. In the meantime he needed to get his mind right to talk with Mikayla later. He pulled off from the curb and into late-afternoon traffic. Why in the hell was he stressing over this woman, anyway. So what if she'd sprinkled some kind of lose-your-mind dust on him and had him willing and ready to change his wandering ways? Maybe Mikayla seeing Cheri on television was meant to be—a sign that he wasn't ready for something truly stable. Well, whatever it was, he needed to put together a game plan before he went to see Mikayla.

His phone rang as he made the entrance onto the freeway. He pressed a button on the dash. The disembodied voice floated through the speakers.

"Zo, it's Stacy Fleming."

"Hey, Stacy."

"Your referral is quite wonderful. She just left. I think she'll work out fine. Thank you."

"Not a problem."

"I won't keep you. I'm sure I'll see you around."

"Absolutely. Thanks again, Stacy." He disconnected the call. At least that was one thing that went right today. He headed home.

Once inside, he fixed a drink and went into his home office. He turned on the computer and pulled up the plans that he'd developed for the restaurant, going over more of the community service elements of the plan than the restaurant itself. It was definitely a big idea. It had the potential to not only engage the community but provide training for jobs and offer nutritious meals to struggling families.

He'd have to find a way to make it work.

Mikayla glanced once over her shoulder before turning the key in her door. Her heart still raced. She'd thought that red light would never change. She unlocked the door and quickly shut it behind her.

When she drove by Alonzo on the street, she thought, at first, that she was imagining things. But when she checked her rearview mirror, she was certain. She'd know that body, that smooth chocolate skin with her eyes closed.

What was he doing over here? A better question, did he see her? She didn't have time to dwell on it. She needed to shower, change and get back over to Traci's.

She flopped down on the worn-out couch. This was crazy. Why was she going through all these hoops to impress a man? Was it really that important that he believe she wasn't as bad off as she actually was? This was her life. She was broke and struggling. This was where she lived. It wasn't a fancy mansion in Beverly Hills but it was hers. She had nothing to be ashamed of. But since tonight would probably be the last time they saw each other, she could keep her secret intact and hold on to the shreds of her dignity. She checked the time on her phone. If she hurried, she could stop in to see her mom before heading over to Traci's to meet Alonzo.

The sunroom at Greenwood could easily double as an oasis. There was a mini waterfall that resembled something right out of the tropics. Soft music was pumped in. Tables that lined the walls held trays of snacks and urns of water, iced tea, lemonade, coffee and tea. There was an area for watching television or playing a game of checkers. Overstuffed chairs and couches were strategically placed to afford intimacy if needed or for a small group gathering.

Mikayla looped her mother's arm through hers as they navigated around the staff and residents to find a seat near the windows that looked out onto the valley.

"Heard you had a great day today, Ma." She helped her mother into a side chair.

Stella smiled at her daughter. "Yes, they had me in the exercise room today." She laughed. "The instructor is really handsome," she confessed. "Too young for me, but perfect for you."

"Ma." Mikayla laughed.

"What is his name again? I keep forgetting." She frowned in concentration.

Mikayla knew exactly whom she meant. "Drake. His name is Drake. But remember, we broke up."

Stella blinked in confusion, then her expression cleared. "Oh, yes. Shame. I think I liked him. Did I?"

Mikayla took her mother's hand. "Yes. You did."

"Good." She glanced around. "I wonder what's for dinner. Are you staying for dinner?"

"Not tonight, Ma. Maybe another night. Okay?"

Stella leaned toward her daughter. "I want you to be happy. I need to know that you are happy."

"I am. I promise."

"Good." She leaned back. "It's not so bad here, you know. I don't want you to worry about me."

Mikayla's throat clenched. "It's my job to worry about you," she said, in an attempt to make light of what her mother said.

"I want you to have someone in your life. Someone else for you to look after and for them to look after you. I won't be around forever."

"Ma. Don't say that."

Stella looked at her daughter, curious almost. "I wonder what's for dinner."

"Do you want to look at the menu?"

"Menu?"

"Yes, you know there is a menu for all the meals. You can choose what you want."

"I didn't see any waiters. What kind of restaurant is this?"

Mikayla drew in a breath. She moved closer to her mother and tried to get her to focus on her. "They don't really have waiters here, Ma. The staff serves the meals." She watched her mother's slender fingers dig into the cushioned arms of the chair, the same fingers that braided her hair, soothed her cuts and scrapes, wrote poetry and shopping lists. Her heart ached to see the vibrant woman she grew up with now a shadow of who she once was—there but not quite.

"I...want to go to my room and wait for my daughter." She peered at Mikayla. "You look so much like my daughter."

Mikayla offered a tight smile. "Thank you." She took her mother's hand and led her back to her room.

"I wish there was something I could do, sweetie," Traci said.

Mikayla wiped the tears from her eyes. "It's just so damn hard, you know."

"I know. I know."

Mikayla dragged in a breath and sat up straighter. She sniffed back the last of her tears. "I just have to hold on to the good days. The memories. For both of us." She linked her fingers together on the table. "Anyway, I should get ready. He said he would be here by eight."

"I'm going to say this because I'm your friend."

Mikayla lifted her eyes to meet Traci's.

"Be honest with him. He seems like a decent guy. Clearly it doesn't matter to him that you clean houses for a living. None of the other stuff should matter, either."

"I don't want him feeling sorry for me."

"I don't think he will."

"You don't know that."

"Neither do you, and you won't if you don't give him a chance. Building any kind of relationship on lies and deceit is a no-win situation. Drake is a perfect example."

Mikayla groaned in agreement. "I ran into him today. Well, almost."

"Who? Drake?"

"Gosh, no. Alonzo. I was on my way home from the job he set me up with and I saw him on the street."

"Apparently he didn't see you."

"No. I don't think so."

"See, that's exactly what I'm talking about, Kayla. You can't be playing cloak-and-dagger. What if he had recognized you? What would you have said? Lie?"

"All right. All right. I get it."

"Good." She got up. "Wash your face and freshen your makeup and decide what you're going to do about Alonzo Grant."

The doorbell rang at precisely eight. Traci darted into her bedroom with a final whispered warning to come clean.

Mikayla went to the door and pulled it open, and just like every time she saw Alonzo, her heart did that extra thump and her stomach danced.

"Hi."

"Hi yourself."

She moved aside and held the door open. "Come in."

He stepped in, stopped just beyond the entrance and turned to her. She closed the door. He moved toward her. She held her breath. He leaned down and kissed her. Heat popped in her veins. His arms wrapped around her, pulled her close. His tongue teased her lips open. She moaned and leaned into him, weak with wanting.

"Whatever it takes," he murmured against her mouth before releasing her. "Whatever it takes to make it right." He stared down into her eyes. "All I ask is that you hear me out."

She nodded her head. "Okay." She swallowed. "I have some things to talk with you about, too." There, she'd said it. No turning back now.

"I have a cooler in the trunk. Let's drive out to Venice Beach. It's a beautiful night."

"I'll get my things."

As Alonzo said, it was a beautiful night. The windows were down, the sunroof open and the night breeze was perfect. Alonzo turned on the radio to the local R & B station that kept them company along the thirty-minute drive.

"Thank you for the recommendation," Mikayla said. She snatched a look in his direction.

"Glad it worked out. Stacy is the wife of a buddy of mine. They own a couple of day spas in Santa Monica."

"Wow. Nice."

"Maybe you'd like to go sometime. I can make a call."

"Maybe." She fiddled with her fingers. "Alonzo, I appreciate the reference, the invitation to the party and the offer for the spa."

"But…" he said for her.

"But I'm used to taking care of myself. I don't want to feel like I'm indebted to anyone."

"Is that really how you feel? That you're going to owe me?"

"Well…yes."

He made a noise in his throat. "Why don't you feel that you deserve to have things done for you? Did you even think that maybe I offer because I want to, not that I'm looking for something in return?"

She studied her fingers. "It's...hard for me."

He slowed the car and turned in to the parking area of the beach and shut off the engine. He unbuckled his belt and angled his body toward her. "Kayla," he said gently. "I realize this is all new. It's new for me, too. And we probably have a lot of kinks to work out. But one thing you can be certain of is that I'm not in this for points or to make you feel less than the amazing woman you are." He pushed out a breath. "Let's find a spot and talk."

Alonzo got out, came around and helped Mikayla out of the car, then retrieved the cooler from the trunk. He took Mikayla's hand and they walked along the board-walk.

"How about over there. Empty cabana."

"Lucked out," Mikayla said.

They took two rolled beach towels from the rack on the boardwalk, then went to claim the cabana.

Alonzo set up the cooler that, when opened, doubled as a serving table that was loaded with canapés, rolled prosciutto and imported cheese, wafer-thin crackers and pâté, red grapes and chilled wine.

"Wow." Mikayla laughed with delight. "This is definitely no regular picnic cooler."

"I think you'll find that I don't do *regular*." He spread some pâté onto a cracker and lifted it toward her mouth. "Taste."

She opened her mouth and took a bite, chewed, hummed in delight. "Oh. My. Goodness."

"Like?"

"Yes." She finished off the cracker, then reached for the skewered prosciutto and mozzarella with melon.

"Try it with this." He uncovered a small dish with triangular slices of focaccia bread.

They tasted each of the offerings, oohing and murmuring with satisfaction, as the warm night breeze and the intoxicating scent of the ocean wrapped around them.

"You know it was my friend Traci that insisted how wonderful you were. Her enthusiasm made me start watching you on *Top Chef*."

He took a swallow of wine. "And what do you think of me now?"

She drew in a breath and slowly released it. "I'm figuring it out."

"Fair enough." He paused, leaned back on the lounge chair. "Maybe this will help." He turned his head toward her. "What you saw and heard the other day from Cheri is not true, at least not anymore." He told her about their on-again, off-again romance and what happened in London.

"I'm sorry," she said softly.

He waved his hand in dismissal. "Don't be. If it was real, what went down would have never happened." He popped a grape into his mouth. "I won't lie—I've had my share of relationships, some more serious than others, but I've always been honest about who I am, what I want and what I'm willing to give. I thought that maybe Cheri and I could be more than ships in the night and headlines in the tabloids. Humph. But Cheri is about what someone can do for her. She made that clear."

"So, I'm on the rebound."

Alonzo sat up, turned fully toward her, planted his feet in the sand. "You have got to be kidding. Hell no. Listen, when I walked in on Cheri at the restaurant, I wasn't even hurt, maybe my ego but definitely not my feelings." His brow tightened. "That told me something—that what we'd been doing was playing at being in a relationship. When I first heard your voice on the phone—man, something hit me. Then when you showed up at my house... I was done." He chuckled. "But I get it. You have your doubts. That's cool. I get it. As long as you let me prove you wrong."

Mikayla turned onto her side. "Seems like we have a lot in common."

He frowned in question.

"His name is Drake. We were together when I was in New York. He's an actor." She sputtered a derisive laugh. "Anyway, we were together for two years, almost three. He was everything to me. We were in the long haul together. At least I thought we were." She blinked away the images.

"Hey," he said gently. "You don't have to tell me. It's okay. I get it."

"No." She shook her head. "I...need to say it out loud." She hesitated a moment. "I'd auditioned for a small walk-on for a film and got the part. Instead of being happy for me, it was like he resented me for it. Drake started auditioning like crazy and finally seemed perfect for a role in a major film. He was hell-bent on getting the part. Swore up and down that it would be the part to set his career on track. He was obsessive about it. He got it. Then rehearsals started and he would come home later and later or not at all. We barely saw each other. While he was gone, I worked on my own writing. Screenplay I'd been dabbling with for ages." She gazed off into the distance. "Everybody knew except me. He was screwing the director. Finally came home one night and told me he was leaving me for her."

Alonzo muttered a curse.

"I guess the upside is the movie never got made."

They shared a light chuckle.

"So I guess I'm on the rebound," he teased, mimicking her words.

She cut her eyes in his direction. "I haven't quite bounced back yet." She looked into his eyes. "But I'm working on it."

He leaned closer. "I'm here to help with the process." He plucked the bottle of wine from the cooler and refilled their glasses. He lifted his glass. "To our new beginnings. Together."

Alonzo held Mikayla's hand while they walked along the beach right up to the edge of the water that slid in and out and tickled their toes. The more he listened to what she'd given up to make sure that her mother had the best care possible the more he was into her. She reminded him of the commitment that his own family had for one another and how he and his brothers would move heaven and earth for their parents.

"I've always taken care of myself. I'm not one to depend on anyone. And the last thing I want is someone feeling sorry for me or that I'm some kind of charity case. Because I'm not!"

He squeezed her hand and stopped walking. "Look at me." She grudgingly did as he asked. "I know all about what it means to build your own success, not beholden to anyone. To have that rush of pride that you jumped over the obstacles. You've had a helluva couple of years. I get it. But sometimes the burdens aren't as heavy when someone is willing to share the weight." He flexed his muscles. "I've been told I have great shoulders," he added with a smile.

Mikayla bit back a smile.

"Look, I'm not saying turn your life over to me. It's not what I want and I know you don't, either. Besides, I got plenty to do." He gave her a lopsided grin. "All I'm saying is that I'm here and I have means and I have friends and if you think I can help in some way I will. But I'm not going to shove any of that at you. Just know that I'm around because I want to be."

She cupped his jaw in her hands, looked into his eyes. She was scared. Afraid of being betrayed again, of not being able to hold it together for her mother, of failing, of not measuring up. She leaned in and kissed him hard, giving herself over to the wave of emotions that Alonzo stirred inside her. It would be so easy to let go, but she wasn't quite ready. Not yet.

"Between the sea air, the food, the wine—" Mikayla stretched and yawned "—I could sleep for a week."

Alonzo chuckled. "I know the feeling." He turned the key in the ignition. "Stay with me tonight."

She shot a look at him and tugged on her bottom lip with her teeth. "Hmm, only if you promise to make that fabulous omelet and croissants again."

"That's easy. But I want to introduce you to the rest of my morning repertoire."

She tipped her head to the side. "What's on the menu?"

"You."

Her heart bumped in her chest. "Is that right?"

"As a matter of fact, I usually plan my menus in advance. Thought I'd start tonight."

"I always admired a man with a plan."

"Then I'm your guy."

They'd barely crossed the threshold of Alonzo's home before they were entwined, starved for the taste and feel of each other. Clothing fell away, leaving a trail of cotton, denim and lace from the door to the bedroom.

They tumbled onto the plush down of his bed.

"God I want you," he groaned into her ear. His hands roamed her curves, taunting and teasing, caressing, making her squirm with pleasure. His fingers trailed between the heat of her thighs up to the slick folds. His thumb teased the swollen bud until her body shivered and her soft whimpers invited him in.

"That was…it was…crazy," Alonzo said, breathing hard. "Damn." He flopped back onto the pillow.

Mikayla's joyous giggles fluttered in between her gulps for air. "Certifiable," she managed.

"Come here." He slid his arm beneath her and pulled her close. He kissed the top of her head. "I'm going to be up-front," he began slowly, choosing his words, as he felt her flinch. "My work, what I do, is part of who I am. I love my life. This life takes me all over the world sometimes for weeks or months at a time. But it's not the ideal situation when you have someone in your life.

I guess that's why it's always been easy for me to deal with women that weren't really into commitment."

She shrugged away from his hold and angled her head to look at him. "So what are you saying—that as much as 'this is crazy' that you're just passing through? All that stuff you were spouting at the beach was just BS?"

"No." He turned onto his side and held her shoulder. "No," he repeated. "What I'm trying to say, and apparently not very well, is that I want you in my life. I know it will get difficult at times. I can guarantee that, and I can get obsessed with a new recipe or a demanding client, but I don't want you to think that you will stop being important." He tugged in a breath. "Look, I guess what I'm asking is that I need you to trust me. I need you to trust that I won't hurt you or betray you, whether I'm right here or half a continent away." His eyes moved languidly over her face. "It's new for me, too, but I want to give it a shot. Together."

She pouted, then draped her leg across his hip. "So basically you're telling me don't believe the hype when I see it or hear it, 'cause you're coming back to me."

He grinned, leaned in and kissed her puckered lips. "Exactly."

The next morning, as promised, Alonzo laid out a feast.

"I'm going to be big as a house if you keep this up," Mikayla said even as she had her second helping of fruit whipped into some kind of confection that was out of this world.

"That's why I have a pool and an indoor gym to use

when I can't get to my trainer." He winked. "At your disposal." He leaned across the table and wiped a dot of cream from the corner of her mouth. "Tell you what, I promise that every morning that we wake up together I'll create something new—just for you."

She clasped his hand and pressed it to her cheek. "Every morning?"

"Every morning. I'll even teach you a few culinary tricks."

She snickered. "You will definitely have your hands full. Trust and believe me, kitchen magic is not my strong suit. Now, if you wanted me to *write* about the adventures of a woman who is culinarily compromised, then I'm your girl," she joked.

"Hmm, maybe that's not a bad idea. You said you wanted to write scripts."

Her expression wrinkled at the idea. "Yeah, but… I don't know…"

"Hey, something to think about." He braced himself above her. "In the meantime, let me demonstrate the other items on the menu."

Mikayla took a peek at Alonzo's furrowed brow and how he rocked his jaw when he was working out a detail on the party, and realized that she was happy, happier than she'd been in ages. In the weeks since the night at the beach, the night of emotional cleansing had given her a pathway to a destination of joy and fulfillment. Zo was right on point when he said that his work often consumed him. It was clear in his tunnel-vision focus in preparing for Ryan Carrington's party. But what was also true was that as focused as he was, his attention to her and her needs never fell short. He'd hold her when she cried about her mother's setbacks and rejoiced with her on the good days. He fed her delicacies while she read a scene from the screenplay that she'd begun. When he made love to her, he made her believe true happiness was hers for the taking. Her business, thanks to Alonzo's early referral, was beginning to pick up, and if the pace continued, she was going to have to actually hire someone to help out.

So when she came to him at night, achy and exhausted, he never gave a second thought to running a bath for her, rubbing her feet or massaging her back. It seemed too good to be true, and every now and again she felt her old demons of doubt creep between them and try to wrestle her away.

For nearly three years she was with a man that she believed she loved. They had the same goals and desires. She gave her heart to him. Committed to him. Trusted him. But when opportunity presented itself, he discarded her and everything they'd built without a backward glance. There was a part of her that expected Alonzo would eventually do the same thing.

The experience, the humiliation, gouged a hole in her spirit and left her doubting her sense of self, and then her mom got sick and sicker and what was left of her life spiraled out of control. So there were days lying next to him, listening to his heartbeat, or sitting in the kitchen watching him work and listening to his very bad singing, when she waited for the other shoe to fall, for him to suddenly realize that this ordinary woman with tons of baggage was heavier than he wanted to carry. She closed her notebook and took a sip from her cup of herbal tea.

"If I don't actually kill Ryan, I think the party will be a major hit," Alonzo joked while he put additional information onto the spreadsheet of his computer.

She laughed. As much as Alonzo may gripe about Ryan's party, she saw how he thrived and rose to the challenge. He actually enjoyed all the craziness. "Right. You love this stuff and you know it."

He looked up and beamed a smile at her. "True." He chuckled. "But when this is over, I have a job in New York and then New Orleans. Both short. I'll be gone about two weeks, tops. But when I get back, I want us to take a trip, anywhere you want to go."

"Won't you be exhausted after all that traveling?"

"Exactly. That's why I want to find someplace and wind down. Just us."

"Anywhere?"

"Yep."

She rested her arms on the counter. "Thanks to you and your introduction to Stacy, my business is picking up. I can't leave my clients in the lurch."

"Maybe it's time you hired someone. You've been hinting at it. Just do it. Look, when I started out, I was a one-man band, too. I wanted to do it all. But the better I got, the more demanding the work became, and I had to get help if I wanted my dream to survive. So I put together the best team I could find." He shrugged. "Now here I am, doing what I want when I want. I can pick and choose my assignments. You can do the same thing. Plus, hiring someone will free you up to write and spend time with your mother."

She sighed heavily. "It's a big step, Zo. Being your only employee is easy, but being responsible for someone else's livelihood is another story."

"Yeah. But the benefits are worth it. Think about it. I can help you…if you want me to," he quickly added.

"I'll think about it. Seriously."

"That's a start." He closed the cover of his laptop, stretched. "I'm gonna take a shower, then turn in. Crazy day tomorrow." He pushed to his feet. "Join me?"

She giggled. "Showering together seems to always turn into more than soap and water."

He frowned in mock confusion. "That's the point, isn't it?" He extended his hand.

Chapter 10

"Girl, you need to go to that party."

"I won't know anyone and he has to work."

"He said you can bring a friend. *Moi!* So what is wrong with you?" Traci picked up the dishes from the table and put them in the sink.

"Trace…" she puffed. "It's not that simple."

"Why the hell not? The man invited you more than once, and don't tell me it's 'cause you don't have anything to wear."

"Well, I don't."

She wagged a finger at Mikayla. "That can be fixed. Next excuse."

Mikayla rolled her eyes. "He… Alonzo's world is totally different from mine."

"And? He's been asking you to be a part of it."

"It's just that when it's the two of us, in our little co-coon, I can handle that. There's a fantasy quality to it." She gazed off into the distance, smiled. She dragged in a breath and turned to Traci. "But the minute we step out of the fantasy into his world, then everything gets real."

"Is that what you're afraid of, that you may have to stop *playing* house and get serious?"

"Maybe."

"Seems like, at least from what you've been telling me, Alonzo is already serious. So whatchu gon' do?" she challenged while rocking her neck. "Get in the game or sit on the bench?"

Mikayla bit back a smirk. "I think I'm going to let you go shopping with me for a dress for this party."

"'Bout damned time! Let me finish up and we can go, like, right now."

"You sure you'll be okay coming on your own? I can send a car for you and Traci later," Alonzo said in an absent rush as he got dressed.

"I'll be fine, babe. Don't worry about me."

He stopped buttoning his white shirt and turned to her, gathered her close. "It's my job to worry about you," he said, his voice dipping down to her center. "You're gonna have to get used to that." He lowered his head, kissed her slow and deep. She looped her arms around his neck and curved her body to his. A groan rumbled in his throat. He eased back. "Keep this up and I won't get out of here."

She stroked his cheek with the tip of her finger.

"I love you, Kayla."

Mikayla's eyes flashed. Her lips parted ever so slightly. "Zo," she whispered.

"Yeah," he said over a shaky chuckle, "surprised me, too." He stepped back, studied her face. He ran his thumb along her bottom lip before giving her a light kiss. "Gotta run. See you later. We'll talk tonight."

All she could do was nod her head and watch him walk out. Love *me*? He loved *me*? Her heart raced so fast she got light-headed. She sat down on the side of the bed just as that crazy, giddy, tickling feeling started in her stomach and grew and spread until it exploded in uncontrolled joyous laughter.

"Look at you!" Traci said, when Mikayla answered the door. "Damn, sis."

"Thank you, thank you." She gave a little curtsy.

"Told you the teal was the right choice." She walked inside. "OMG," she said on a breath as she took in the space, looking around like a tourist. She dropped her clutch on a striped accent chair and walked fully inside with her mouth open and her eyes wide, taking in every inch.

She swung toward Mikayla and planted her hands on her hips. "And you don't want to play house for real? Girl."

Mikayla grinned. "I may not have much of a choice after tonight," she said, stringing out the tease.

"And what does that mean? What's going to happen after tonight, besides me meeting someone that is going to kick my career into high gear."

"He told me he loves me."

"Whoa. For real? When? What did you say?"

"Yes, for real." She sat down on the couch. "A few hours ago, just before he left."

"And what did you say?"

"I didn't say anything. I was too shocked."

"Why shocked?"

"I don't know." She frowned, looked away. "I wasn't expecting it. I didn't think he was that serious."

"Serious about the relationship or about you?"

"Both, I guess."

"Why, Kayla? The man is crazy about you. Bends over backward. Even goes with you to visit your mom. Meanwhile you still have him thinking you live with me. What's holding you back?"

"I'm working on it."

"Do that, or you'll wake up one morning and wish that you had, but it'll be too late."

Traci pulled her Lexus in the line of cars to be parked. The night was illuminated with spotlights that crisscrossed in front of the two-story Spanish colonial.

"Whoa," Traci murmured, peeking at the breathtaking spread. "I've seen this place in my dreams."

Arches and pillars buttressed the grand opening. Towering trees stood as sentinels on either side of the paved walkway. The sound of live music floated across the sea-brushed air.

A red-vested valet opened the car door and handed Traci a ticket. Mikayla and Traci got out and made their way to the entrance. The massive front lawn was dotted with circular linen-draped tables beneath white canopies. Waiters with trays of hors d'oeuvres moved seamlessly through the dressed-to-kill gathering.

Mikayla spotted several familiar faces from Alonzo's team. As much as she wanted to see him, she knew he had his hands full managing this crowd.

"Is that Viola?" Traci whispered in a harsh hiss.

"Oh my goodness. Yes." She snatched two flutes of champagne from a passing waitress and handed one to Traci. "Jesse Williams, two o'clock," she said over the rim of her glass.

They both giggled.

"Might as well get used to it. We'll be doing this all night," Traci said, "and we haven't even gotten inside yet."

Mikayla raised her glass. "Cheers to a helluva night." They strutted inside.

"I heard the house was designed by Marc Appleton," a vibrant blonde woman was saying to her companion as Mikayla and Traci walked by.

Mikayla forced herself not to gape at the high ceilings in the living room and the glass doors that lead out to the pool and spa.

Tinkling laughter danced around the room, in concert with the sparkle of diamonds that caught the light on delicate wrists and long throats. Everywhere they looked, there was another familiar face.

"We're probably the least famous two people in this place," Mikayla joked. "Everybody is somebody."

Traci looped her arm through Mikayla's and leaned in close. "And I plan to meet a somebody before the night is over."

Mikayla giggled. "I wonder where Alonzo is." She peeked between bodies and over heads.

"Working, like he said. Come on, let's sample some of his handiwork."

They continued through the main entrance. On either side of the massive room were rows of covered tables, weighted down by tray upon tray of food, from simple appetizers to entrées. White-jacketed waitstaff served the line of partygoers buffet-style.

"This is fabulous," Traci said, getting a bit of everything on her plate.

"Yes, Alonzo definitely did his job."

"Hi. You must be Mikayla." A petite woman in a white coat stood in front of her. Her dark wavy hair was pulled back into a tight bun at the nape of her neck.

Mikayla tilted her head to the side. "Yes. Do I know you?"

The woman smiled. "I'm sorry. I'm Jasmine. I work with Alonzo."

"Oh! Jasmine. Yes, Alonzo told me so much about you, how important you are to him. He's said he wouldn't have been able to do all this without you." She stuck out her hand. "Nice to finally meet you. We're both sorry that you're leaving. I know Zo is taking it pretty hard."

"There comes a time when you have to move on. I'm sure Alonzo will do just fine."

Mikayla turned to Traci. "Um, this is my friend Traci Foster."

"Nice to meet you. Well, I'll be running around, but if you need anything, you can ask for me."

"Of course. Thank you. Um, did you know where Alonzo is? I wanted to let him know I was here."

Jasmine's lips tightened. "Pretty sure he's busy in the kitchen. I'll tell him."

"Thanks."

Jasmine nodded and walked away.

"I got a shady vibe from her," Traci said. "I don't like how she looked at you when you asked about Alonzo."

"Hmm, I thought it was my imagination."

"Nope. Don't think so. What I do think is Ms. Girl has a thing for your man."

Mikayla was quiet for a moment. "Now it makes sense."

"What does?"

"Zo told me that she said she was leaving the business. Out of the blue. Really rocked him. They've been together from the beginning."

"Then you came along."

Mikayla threw her friend a side-eye. "I'm pretty sure that she's seen plenty in the years that she's worked with Zo. I wouldn't be the first."

"No, but apparently you're the only one that made a difference and she knows it."

"Hey, baby," came a rugged whisper from behind her.

That familiar tingle fluttered through her. She turned and her body heated at the sight of him. "Hey yourself."

He took her shoulders and kissed her lightly on the mouth. "You look absolutely incredible. Damn." He came close to her ear. "Can't wait to get you home. Don't you dare take off this dress until I get there. I want the pleasure." He took her hand, then turned his attention to Traci. "Good to see you again, Traci. Glad you could come."

"Thanks for the invitation. This place is fabulous."

"As soon as I get a minute, I'll introduce you both to Ryan. I think he's out back by the pool. Listen, baby, I need to do my thing, mix and mingle, keep everything flowing."

"Sure. Hey, I met Jasmine a few minutes ago."

"Yeah." His expression tightened. "This is our last rodeo." He forced a half smile, then gave her a quick kiss on the cheek. "Enjoy yourselves." He moved into the crowd.

Mikayla watched him from a distance, how he glided from one guest to the next, knew when to stop for a few words or a handshake or a kiss. He laughed, he cajoled, he offered samples of his cuisine. Everyone that she noticed seemed to know Alonzo to some degree, and the women all but lifted their skirts for him. He was as much a star of this party as the host, and she wasn't quite sure how she felt about that.

As the evening moved on, the level of celebrity only seemed to grow, from barely recognizable faces to the biggest names and faces in entertainment, sports and even politics. The party was in full force, with the band rocking in back, free-flowing drinks, sit-down meals and buffet for those who wanted to keep moving.

Mikayla and Traci found their way to the back and nearly fell over each other when they saw John and his wife Chrissy chilling by the pool.

"If he sings, I will faint. I'm just warning you," Mikayla said.

"They'll have to scrape us both up off the floor."

They bent their heads together in laughter.

"Come on, let's mingle," Mikayla said.

They moved in and out of several gatherings, introducing themselves, listening in, adding tidbits to conversations. Even though both of them were "in the industry," they were really on the edges. They'd gotten small parts here and there, a commercial or two, but nothing major and nothing at this scale. This was a whole other level.

"There he is," Traci whispered.

Ryan Carrington was crossing on the other side of the pool and Alonzo was with him. Alonzo noticed her, lifted his chin. He said something to Ryan and they started walking toward them.

"Ryan," said Alonzo, with his hand on Ryan's shoulder, "this is the young lady I was telling you about, Mikayla Harris, and this is her friend Traci Foster."

"Pleasure to meet you both. Zo tells me you act."

"I need to check on a few things," Alonzo interrupted. "I'm sure you all can take it from here." He clapped Ryan on the back and turned in the opposite direction.

"Your glasses are empty," Ryan said. He signaled for a waiter and the empty glasses were soon a thing of the past. "So tell me what you've done." He steered them toward an empty table.

"Nothing major," Traci offered. "Some walk-ons. I just landed a part in an upcoming television series. We'll see what happens after they shoot the pilot."

"Good luck with that. Hope it works out. What about you?" He lasered in on Mikayla.

She swallowed. "I haven't worked since I left New York. A few auditions, but nothing has panned out. I've started working on a script, actually."

"Are you any good?"

"At acting or script writing?"

He grinned, flashing a deep dimple in his left cheek. "You pick."

"I think I am."

"One thing I've learned is that if you want to make it in this business, you can't be shy about your talent. Don't *think* that you're good, *know* that you are. Showing confidence is half the battle."

"I'll remember that."

"Remember that when you come to see me. I'm casting for an upcoming film and I'd like to see what you can do with the role. Small part, a few lines. You have a phone?"

She could barely process what was happening. "Um, yes."

"I'm going to give you the info for the casting."

"Oh, sure, yes." She opened her purse and took out her phone. Ryan gave her the address, day and time.

He stood. "Ask for my assistant, Cherise, when you get there."

"Thank you so much. I'll be there."

He gave a brief nod and walked off.

Mikayla spun her chair toward Traci, eyes wide in amazement. "Did you hear that? Oh my goodness. He asked me to come to a casting call for his movie. Ryan freaking Carrington."

"See! And you didn't want to come. Hot damn. This is the break you needed. Now all you have to do is go in there and nail it."

"I'm shaking," she said and stuck her phone back into her purse. "Now I need a real drink."

They both hopped up from their seats.

"I can drink to that," Traci said.

* * *

The rest of the evening was a whirlwind of music,
laughter and rubbing elbows. Mikayla watched with a
combination of pride and a bit of jealousy as Alonzo
moved through the gathering, collecting accolades for
his fabulous spread, being touched and cuddled by
women, taking pictures and seducing new business.
Even Ryan took a moment out of the festivities to have
the throng raise their glasses in a touch to the chef and
his team.

"Your man is pretty amazing," Traci said as they
slow-walked to retrieve her car.

"Yeah, he is," she murmured, still wrestling with all
that his notoriety entailed.

"Something wrong?"

They stopped at the end of the walkway and the valet
hurried over to retrieve their ticket.

"No. Well, I don't know. I mean, you saw how
Alonzo was out there. How he flirts and teases, practically enticing women with 'samples' of his work. He
loves it. It's like a turn-on for him."

"Do you hear yourself?"

Mikayla folded her arms, pursed her lips.

"You knew that about him from the moment you
met."

"Exactly! That's what he did to me."

"And who is he with? You. He told you he loves you,
Kayla. Why can't you accept that and stop looking for
the boogeyman?"

She pushed out a breath. "You're right. I know that.
It's just hard seeing him like that with other women.
Dredges up old wounds."

"I get it. But you're either going to trust him or you need to move on. Otherwise you'll make yourself crazy. Especially when he's out of town."

The valet pulled up with the car.

"He's leaving day after tomorrow for New York, then New Orleans," she said.

Traci looked at Mikayla across the roof of the car. "And you will be just fine until he gets back."

Mikayla stepped out of her heels the instant she crossed the threshold. What a night. She should be tired but the adrenaline rush of the night was still humming in her veins. She still could not believe that she'd been sitting at a table with Jamie Foxx, listening to him recount some of the crazy bloopers on his last film, or when she and Traci got a selfie with Kerry Washington, who'd been chatting it up with Jada and Will.

Of course the major highlight of the evening was meeting the host and actually being invited to audition. Her head was still spinning over that. She knew that part of the reason was Alonzo's connection, and maybe that's the only reason why he extended the invite to her. But whatever the reason, she would go in there and prove that she was more than someone being done a favor, but that she had real talent.

She padded barefoot into the kitchen and got a bottle of spring water from the fridge. It was nearly two in the morning. She had no idea how much longer it would be before Alonzo got in. She curved herself into the corner of the couch, tucked her feet under her and took a long swallow of water. A smile eased across her mouth. *What a night.*

The next thing she knew was a sensation of being cuddled and lifted. Her eyes fluttered open.

"Hey, baby," Alonzo whispered as he carried her up the stairs.

"Hmm, hi." She looped her arms around his neck and pressed her head against him. "I'm sorry…fell asleep."

He kissed her softly and pushed open the bedroom door. "It's okay." He tossed the covers aside and laid her down, then sat next to her. "Do you know how beautiful you are?"

She touched his face. He curved his mouth to kiss the inside of her palm.

"You promised to help me out of my dress." She watched his eyes darken.

"I did, didn't I."

She sat up. He reached around her for the zipper and dropped a hot kiss on her collarbone. She drew in a sharp breath. His finger trailed down the column of her spine as the silky fabric parted. His mouth traveled up her neck, nibbled the lobe of her ear. Her limbs tingled. He slid the strapless dress down to her waist to reveal that swell of her breasts barely contained in the silk-and-lace covering.

Alonzo drew in air from between his teeth before dipping his head into the warm valley to nuzzle and taste.

"Ohhh." She arched her back, offering herself to him.

He latched on to a ripening nipple, sucked and teased it with his teeth and tongue until it peaked and stiffened, leaving Mikayla sighing for more.

He stood and tugged off clothes, tossing them to the floor. He pulled her from the bed and finished getting her out of her dress until it pooled at her feet. His fingers slipped beneath the thin elastic of her panties and made quick work of discarding them, as well. Barely a breath separated them.

Mikayla reached down between them and took his stiff penis into her hand, without taking her eyes off his, and began to stroke him. He clasped her shoulders, his strong fingers pressing into her flesh as she continued to taunt him with pleasure. She rose up on her toes and slid him back and forth along her wet slit.

"Ahh," he groaned and tried to push up inside her but she wouldn't let him.

"Not yet," she cautioned. She grinned as she kept stroking and sliding him across her folds, even going so far as to let the swollen head dip inside her walls for an instant, which nearly sent him over the edge.

"You're a very bad girl," he said in a ragged whisper. "I'll have to do something about that." He grabbed her hand and eased her back down onto the bed.

She flopped back on the pillows.

"Open for me."

Her nostrils flared. She bent her knees and spread her legs.

Alonzo kissed her legs, up her inner thighs until he felt them tremble. His thumb played with her slit until it was wet with her juices. He lowered his head between her legs and sampled the offerings.

She gasped, gripping the sheets in her fists as her hips instinctively rose. He expertly prepared her for him with the same care and attention that he did for his most delicate recipes.

In that instant when he entered her, the connection

shot beyond the physical. In that moment they realized it. Awareness sparked in their eyes and he sank deeper and she gathered him to her and in her while the rest of the world disappeared.

The next day went by far too quickly and the night even more so. Before she was ready, Alonzo had his bags at the door and was waiting on his Uber to the airport.

"I could have driven you," Mikayla said. She rested her head on his chest while he teased a strand of hair between his fingers.

"Naw. Traffic this time of day to LAX is crazy and you wanted to see your mom and you have your own stuff to do. You have two clients today, right?"

"True," she conceded. Her day was already full and she hadn't left the house.

A horn blew out front.

"There's my ride."

They untangled themselves and Alonzo got up. Mikayla walked with him to the door.

"I'll call you tonight after I get settled."

She turned into his arms, pressing herself against him, and a sudden overwhelming sensation bubbled up inside her, spilling from her lips. "I love you, Zo," she said, and the words like a valve opening freed her. "I love you," she repeated and sealed her vow with a long, soul-stirring kiss that left them both shaken.

Alonzo stepped back and looked into the light in her eyes. "Love you, too," he said softly. He kissed her lightly one last time, then hurried to the waiting car.

Mikayla slowly closed the door and went back inside.

She felt the tug of a smile and the unsteady beat of her pulse. Saying the words, hearing them, altered everything, but more important it awakened the realization that whatever she thought she'd felt in the past was not this. Before was merely pieces that didn't quite fit. Now all the scattered parts fit perfectly, and she felt whole, complete in a way that she had not experienced before.

She wrapped her arms around herself and squeezed. Getting fired from a job had never felt this incredible.

"You got this, girl," Traci was saying over the phone.

"I know." She put the phone down and switched to speaker while she finished getting dressed. "I'll call you as soon as I'm done."

"You better. Break a leg."

"Thanks. Later."

No sooner had she disconnected the phone than it rang with a call from Alonzo.

Her heart skipped a beat. "Hey, babe."

"Hey yourself. You about ready? The time difference messed with me. Thought I might have missed you."

"No. You're right on time. I'm heading out in about ten minutes. How was the event last night?"

"Went off without a hitch. Definitely not as big as Ryan's but it still took its toll. Totally beat."

"Wish I was there to soothe it all away."

"Hmm, me too." He yawned, chuckled. "Sorry. Listen, babe, you go in there and knock 'em dead. Call me later."

"I will."

"Love you."

"And I love hearing you say it. Love you back."

"Bye for now."

"Bye."

She momentarily held the phone to her chest and sighed. Damn, she was really happy, and it sure felt good.

The studio was located in downtown Hollywood. She'd been to her share of studios and this was typical. It was housed on the entire level of the fourth floor, several offices and a waiting area with the actual studio located down a long corridor.

"Hi. My name is Mikayla Harris. Mr. Carrington said I should ask for Cherise," she said to the young man behind the desk.

"If you could sign in, please." He handed her a clipboard with a list of names already filling the sheet.

Mikayla took the clipboard and filled in the required information and handed it back.

"Thank you." He pushed his glasses farther up on his nose. "I'll let Ms. Weathers know that you're here. You can have a seat."

"Thanks."

Mikayla walked over to the row of about a dozen seats, half of which were occupied, and sat down. An interesting assortment of people, she noticed, and began playing a game in her head, creating little scenarios about them. Like the man at the end with the full gray beard and shiny bald head. She cast him as the priest being investigated in a scandal with a nun. Or the young woman chewing very hard on a wad of gum, who looked to be in her early twenties, could easily be cast as the wise-talking older daughter of an incumbent congressman.

"Ms. Harris."

Mikayla stood, draped her jacket over her arm and walked toward the woman who'd called her.

"Hi. I'm Cherise Weathers. You can come with me."

She walked alongside Cherise down the hallway.

"How do you know Ryan?"

The question threw her for a minute. "I don't. Not really. We met at his party."

"Oh. He's said such great things about you. Gave me the impression that you knew each other."

Mikayla's face tightened a bit with uncertainty. "Not at all."

"Well, you obviously made a great impression." She turned to Mikayla with a tight smile and opened the door. "Go right in. Good luck," she added.

"Thanks." She stepped into the room with two cameras, a white drop screen and a table behind which sat four people, one of whom was Ryan Carrington. Several microphones were set up, as well.

A young woman with her hair held in place with a baseball cap hurried over to her with a set of papers. "Everything that's highlighted is you."

"You can take a few minutes to look that over," Ryan called out.

Mikayla looked up from the sea of words. He was smiling at her. She nodded, walked over to one of the high-boy chairs and sat. As best she could, she scanned the copy, trying to get a sense of what the story line was. Basically she was playing a waitress at a local bar in Brooklyn who witnessed an assault but was too afraid to tell what she knew. She drew in a breath and straightened her shoulders. "Ready."

The same baseball-cap-wearing young woman walked over. "Your mark is right there." She pointed to a square on the floor.

Mikayla took her mark.

"The scene is at the bar following a shooting," Ryan said. "You saw what happened when you'd stepped out for a smoke. You recognized the shooter and have no intention of saying anything to the cop."

"Got it." Her pulse was pounding in her temples.

The woman in the baseball cap fed Mikayla her lines, taking on the role of the officer.

They ran the lines together three times.

"Okay. Now let's see what it looks like on film." Ryan signaled the camera operator.

Mikayla took her mark. They did several takes from various angles.

Ryan got up and went to check the playback. "Looks good. Thank you, Ms. Harris. We'll be in touch."

Mikayla blew out a breath of relief. "Thank you."

"You can go out this way," the woman said, indicating a door she hadn't noticed before.

Once back on the street and behind the wheel of her car she actually took stock of what had transpired. It was not what she expected. That was a full-blown audition, minus rehearsal. Wow. She replayed her performance over and over in her head. She did the best she could. Now it was up to Ryan.

She put her car in gear and headed toward Greenwood. Hopefully it would be a good day and she could share her news with her mom.

* * *

Mikayla lay in Alonzo's king-size bed wishing he were next to her while she told him about her day, the excitement of the audition and the great time she'd had with her mom, instead of him being hundreds of miles away. She never imagined that she would feel this way, a longing and desire to be wrapped around another person and the emptiness of their absence. Her relationship with Drake was a far cry from what she and Alonzo had, even though being with Drake was years in the process. Something had been missing, and she never knew what it was until she found it with Alonzo—an all-encompassing willingness to make the other happy.

"I knew you would knock it out of the park," Alonzo was saying. "How do you feel about it?"

"Good. I think under the right circumstances I did great."

"Anyone else auditioning?"

"Hard to tell. Based on the folks sitting in the waiting room, I can't see them in the role. But who knows who came before me or after."

"You got this."

"You sound so sure."

"I am."

"Why?"

"What do you mean, why?"

"Why are you so sure? Are you sure because you really believe in my talent or because he's doing you a favor?"

"What? You can't be serious."

"Why can't I be serious, Zo? I mean, let's look at the facts. Ryan is a friend of yours. You introduce me after you pull off one of the major gatherings in LA that people will be talking about for months. He not only invites me to a casting call, but I get special treatment when I arrive."

"Stop. Okay. Just stop. I made an introduction. Period. End of story. I did it because I want you to have every opportunity *if* you want it, and if I can help make that happen, then so be it. Believe me, I didn't have my hand up his back moving his mouth or making decisions. But if you honestly feel that way, you don't have to worry about anything like that every again."

"Zo…"

"Hey, I gotta run. I'll call you tomorrow after I land in New Orleans. Have a good night."

"Love you," she managed, but he'd already hung up. She squeezed her eyes shut. "Damn it! Kayla, what is wrong with you?" She flopped back on the bed. "Aargh Do you really want to mess this up?"

She turned onto her side and pulled her knees close to her chest. *Get rid of him before he gets rid of you. Is that the plan?* She sighed. Alonzo Grant was a dream come true. He was kind, generous, sexy, smart, loving and he wanted her. What was she so afraid of?

Mikayla and Traci sat out on Alonzo's back deck watching the sun descend over the mountaintops. The horizon was a magnificent display of orange and gold with streaks of purple.

"When you look at all of that," Traci said, "you can believe that anything is possible." She lifted her glass of iced tea and sipped through the straw. "And because I choose to believe that anything is possible—" she angled her body toward Mikayla "——I choose to believe that it is possible for you to finally have a relationship that is deserving of you, despite your efforts to sabotage it."

Mikayla made a face.

"Alonzo didn't do anything wrong. He didn't grease anyone's palm or kick an old lady to the curb to make room for you. All he did was make an introduction. The rest was on you. Not to mention you don't even know if you got the part."

Mikayla sipped her iced tea.

"At some point you are going to have to trust him if you want it to work. You can't sit around waiting for him to screw you over. He's not Drake."

"I know," she conceded. "I don't think I realized how much what Drake did affected me."

"Yeah, like relationship PTSD."

Mikayla sputtered into her glass. "I'm working on it."

"Well, don't run the man away in the meantime." She picked up her phone from the table. "I should get out of here."

"There's plenty of room. Stay. It's late. Go home in the morning."

"Pajama party?" She grinned mischievously.

"Sure."

"But only if I can try out that Jacuzzi tub."

Mikayla laughed. "Enjoy. I'm going to call Alonzo— make peace."

"Good idea."

"I get it," Alonzo said.

"I'm working on the whole trust thing. I'm going to

slip up from time to time, but it doesn't mean that it's anything you've done. It's my issues. But I promise I'll do better."

"I'm going to hold you to that. But just remember when those doubts creep into your head that I love you and I wouldn't do anything to hurt you, betray you or diminish you in any way. Understood?"

She sniffed. "Understood."

"Now…tell me how much you miss me and what you plan for my triumphant return!"

The following morning Mikayla was in Alonzo's home office going over her schedule for the week. She was going to have to hire someone, especially if she got the part. There would be no way for her to handle rehearsals, keep up with her mother and her treatments and manage the growing list of clients.

Her personal cell rang. She didn't recognize the number.

"Hello?"

"This is Ryan Carrington's assistant, Cherise Weathers."

"Oh, hello." Her pulse kicked up a notch.

"I'm calling because Mr. Carrington would like you to come to the office this afternoon, at five, to discuss the part and get you a script."

Oh my God! "Sure. I can do that."

"Great. If you have a pen, I'll give you the address."

Her hand shook as she scribbled down the address. "Got it. Thank you. I'll be there at five."

"Have a nice day."

Mikayla leaped up from the chair and did a happy

dance, barely able to contain her squeals of excitement. Ryan Carrington wanted to see her. She got the part!

She called Alonzo but got his voice mail; Traci, the same thing. Well, her bubble would not be busted. Off to find something to wear.

Mikayla found a parking space a block away from Ryan's office that was located on Hollywood Boulevard. The street was lined with shops, restaurants and office buildings. His office was on the sixth floor of the last building on the corner of West Street.

She pushed through the revolving doors, checked with security and was instructed to go to the sixth floor.

The elevator doors opened directly onto the suite of offices. She pushed open the glass door and nearly sank into the plush off-white carpet. She felt like she should take off her shoes.

A young blonde woman was at a glass desk. "May I help you?"

"Mikayla Harris. I'm here to see Mr. Carrington."

The woman gave her a quick once-over. "One moment." She pressed a button on the phone. "Ms. Harris here to see Mr. Carrington. Sure." She glanced at Mikayla. "Ms. Weathers will be right out."

"Thank you."

"Ms. Harris."

Mikayla turned. Cherise was walking toward her.

"Thanks for coming." She turned her focus on the woman at the desk. "Denise, we're done for the day. You can go. Follow me," she said to Mikayla. They started off down the hall. "Congratulations. You really impressed Mr. Carrington. It usually takes him a while to settle on someone. He's very particular." She pushed open a door. "Ryan. She's here."

Ryan came from behind a massive desk. "Ms. Harris." His camera-ready smile was on full display.

Ryan Carrington was average in the looks department, but there was something charismatic about him. He reminded her of a young Bill Clinton. Where he shined, however, was his cinematic vision. He had two Academy Awards under his belt and this third nomination would put him in an exclusive class of directors.

He crossed the room with his hand extended. "Thank you for coming on such short notice. Please come in and have a seat." He addressed Cherise. "Thanks, Cherise."

She closed the door behind her.

"I was very impressed with your reading."

"Thank you." She set her purse down beside her.

"I'm thinking after seeing you read that you may be more suited to a larger role." He leaned against his desk, folded his arms and crossed his feet at the ankle.

Her brows rose. "Really?"

He pushed away from the desk, reached behind him and lifted a sheaf of papers and handed them to Mikayla. "The part I'm thinking of for you is the detective."

"That's a lead."

"Supporting. But a step up from the waitress." He smiled.

"I… Thank you. I'll read it over."

"Good. Do that. I'll have you come back in for a table read in about a week."

She dragged in a breath. "Thank you."

"I told you, confidence is half the battle. You came

into that audition and owned the part. That's what I like to see." He walked toward the door and opened it. "Thank you for coming in. Cherise will be in touch with a day and time."

Mikayla picked up her purse and walked to the door, the script tucked under her arm. "Thank you again."

She started to move past the narrow opening he'd allowed between himself and the door.

"Words can be so hollow without action behind them."

Her eyes widened. A wave of panic shook her. "Excuse me. I need to leave."

His hand was on her shoulder. "Don't you want to be a star?"

"Please." She had to get out of the door.

"You are quite beautiful." His other hand was at her waist. He pushed her against the frame of the door. The metal bit into her back. "I can see your face gracing the screen."

He went to kiss her. She twisted her face away. He grabbed her face in a grip so tight it felt like he would dislocate her jaw before he forced her mouth on his. He was heavy, heavier than he appeared, and all of his weight was pressed against her, pinned to the wall. She couldn't breathe. Paralyzing fear gripped her. She could feel his hands on her, trying to pull up her skirt. He was between her legs, tugging her panties aside, fumbling with his zipper.

She went totally limp, stopped resisting, and he lost his grip, giving her just enough room to knee him with all her might.

He howled like an animal, went down on a knee, and

she ran blindly down the hall, turning the wrong way, then going back and finding the exit.

The halls and offices were empty. The receptionist was gone. Cherise was gone. She ran to the elevator, punched and punched the button. Any second he was going to come around that corner.

The doors slid open and she got on, pressing herself against the wall. She was shaking so hard she thought her legs would give out.

When the doors opened in the lobby, she ran out, down the street to her car. She got in and locked the doors. The terrifying sensation that he was right behind her held her in a vise grip.

She leaped in her seat from a knock on her window.

"Coming out?" the man mouthed from the other side of the glass.

Her heart thundered. It took her a moment to realize that it wasn't Ryan Carrington. She managed to nod her head. With shaky fingers she got the key into the ignition, turned on the car and pulled out of the parking space.

Chapter 11

By some miracle she made it home without getting into a major accident. She didn't realize until she pulled to a stop that she'd gone back to her East LA apartment and not Alonzo's home. She put the key in the door, but something stopped her, froze her in place. Like a shadow, the terror of what happened to her floated right above her shoulder, creeping, keeping pace with every move she made.

What if he was inside? What if he'd found out where she lived? Her temples pounded and she started to shake. She tugged the key out, ran back to her car and locked the doors. She sat there, holding herself, rocking back and forth, replaying every moment over in her head. She couldn't sit here all night, and she wouldn't go inside. Not alone.

She dug in her purse and pulled out her phone. She called Traci.

* * *

"Here, drink this," Traci said and handed Mikayla a cup of herbal tea. "Can you tell me what happened?" She sat next to Mikayla on the couch.

Mikayla gripped the cup in two hands, stared off into space. "I don't know. It was like an out-of-body experience, like it was happening to someone else and I was outside of myself watching. I…froze."

Traci gently stroked her back. "Did he…"

"No!" She shook her head vigorously. Her jaw still ached from the pressure of his grip. "He tried. He would have." Her voice cracked. "I kicked him and I ran."

"Did you see anyone, tell anyone?"

"No. The office was empty. Everyone was gone." She swallowed, frowned. "Like he planned it that way."

Traci sputtered an expletive. "You have to go to the police."

"No."

"What? Why the hell not? That man attacked you!"

"That's Ryan Carrington. He's a big name. I don't want my life dragged through the mud. You know what happens to women that come forward." She shook her head. "I won't do that to myself." She curled into a tighter ball.

"Are you listening to yourself? How many times have we heard these stories years after the fact and wonder why the woman never said anything? Meanwhile the bastard is free to do it to someone else."

"She never said anything because she knew what would happen to her if she did!"

Traci pushed out a breath of frustration. "I know I can't make you do anything. But I really need you to think about this. I don't want you to wake up years from now and wish that you would have said something. You need to tell Alonzo."

"Absolutely not. He'll blame himself for introducing us in the first place and there's no telling what he might do."

"So freaking what. That's your man. He loves you. He deserves to know."

"I just want to forget this happened."

"But you can't. And you won't."

"Honey, I'm home!" Alonzo called out the instant his foot crossed the threshold. He dropped his travel bag in the hall and walked inside. "Kayla, you here?"

The door from upstairs opened. "Hey," she called out and descended the stairs and walked straight into his arms. Damn, he felt good, and she felt safe for the first time in days.

"I missed you," he said in a ragged breath before kissing her as if their lives depended on it.

Mikayla sank into him, clung to him. Now that he was back, his presence would shove all the boogeymen away that popped out of corners and lurked in the dark, invaded her dreams.

"What's wrong? You're shaking." He held her at arm's length and scrubbed her face with his gaze.

She forced herself to smile. "Just glad to see you." She tried to kiss him again but he stopped her.

"I know you well enough to know when something is wrong." He frowned. "Did something happen with your mom? You haven't been sleeping. You have dark circles under your eyes."

She lowered her head. "Mom is okay."

"The audition? No callback?"

She flinched.

"Kayla…look at me. Talk to me. What's wrong?"

And then the tears that she hadn't shed streamed from her eyes. Her face twisted as she tried to contain the sounds of agony that crawled up her throat and spilled across her lip. Her body shook as the sobs rocked her to her core.

Alonzo held her as tight as space would allow, taking on and absorbing her pain. "Whatever it is, you can tell me, baby," he cooed as he held and rocked her in his arms. "It'll be okay. I promise. Talk to me." He led her over to the couch and sat down.

She bowed her head and rested it against his chest, letting her tears flow until she was drained and weak.

"Don't move." He got up, went to the bar and fixed them both a drink. "I know you don't like Hennessy, but it will make you feel better." He held the glass to her lips. She took a sip and shuddered from the heat of the heady liquid. He tried to get her to take another sip, but she held up her hand to block him.

"That's enough," she croaked, her voice hoarse from crying.

He moved a wayward lock of hair away from her face. "Talk to me," he softly whispered.

Alonzo listened, and with every word that Mikayla spoke, his fury mounted. It took all of his self-control not to leap up, go find that sorry excuse for a man and beat him into oblivion. He slowly stood and paced the floor, seething with rage. He didn't know what he expected when Mikayla finally decided to speak. He was sure that it was something about her mother that she was worried about or that the business was falling apart. Never did it cross his mind that Ryan Carrington, a man he thought he knew and admired, was no better than scum. The realization that it had been his doing that put them together only added salt to the wound. He thought he was helping. He looked at Mikayla, shaken and spent. That was the result of his helping. His stomach knotted. He'd put this all into motion and he was the one who had to stop it.

Chapter 12

Alonzo held Mikayla close against him throughout the night, holding on to her as if believing he could love away her hurt, as if the strength of his heartbeat would strengthen hers. They'd talked long into the night. In lieu of music talking, listening to Mikayla's voice especially soothed him. He needed soothing, something, anything to keep him from doing something crazy. And she needed to go somewhere else, other than revisit that room. So he listened to the sound of her voice, held on to it, and she took the trip with him.

He heard for the first time what it was like for Mikayla growing up without her dad and could not imagine how hard that must have been, knowing the role and importance that his own father had in the lives of his family. But it explained so much about her conflicted personality, the independent side versus the one with self-doubt.

"My dad was our everything."

He could feel her smile in the darkness. "Tell me about him."

She sighed. "Daddy worked for the post office. Never missed a day of work or getting home in time for dinner, never missed a school event. I was Daddy's little girl." She half laughed. "Just not his only one."

Her words startled him and then she was quiet for so long he thought she'd drifted off to sleep.

"I had a sister. A year younger than me," she finally said, her voice floating and hollow. "She died in the same car crash that killed my father and her mother. He was driving. I was four."

He stroked her hair. Listened to her breathe. Felt her body stiffen against his.

"Had a whole other life, another family. If he hadn't died, we might have never known. The betrayal was so total, so sweeping that it sucked the life out of my mother. I didn't understand what had happened. All I knew was that my dad was gone and my mom wouldn't stop crying. I found out the truth by accident. I overheard my mom and my aunt talking about my dad's *other family* and how my mother never knew. They used words like *liar, adulterer, cheater, bastard.* I'll never forgive him, my mother said." She dragged in a shaky breath. "Funny, now when I talk to her, if she brings him up, it's in glowing terms, all the happy times. I guess part of her mind has forgiven him."

He listened and tried to imagine what that kind of discovery would have done to him and his brothers, their mother. Now he understood Mikayla's reluctance to trust herself, and to trust men in particular. What happened with her father, the first man she'd loved, had eroded everything she believed in. And now this crap with Ryan resurrected and maybe even reinforced the doubts and insecurities. All the more reason why he needed to make sure that it never happened again.

Alonzo awoke to a light chill in the air and overcast skies that threatened to open up at any moment. He eased out of bed and tiptoed into the bathroom, quietly shutting the door behind him. He didn't want to wake Mikayla, who'd drifted off into a deep sleep only shortly before the sun rose.

His eyes felt gritty and his reflection in the bathroom mirror only confirmed his lack of sleep. Dark half-moons outlined his slightly reddened eyes. He turned on the faucets and splashed cold water on his face. He gripped the edges of the sink and stared into the mirror. Everything Mikayla said replayed in his head. He couldn't see her hurt, he wouldn't, and he'd be less than a man if he didn't do something about it. What happened with her father—there was nothing he could do about that beyond working like hell to make her feel that she could trust him and trust herself with him. Ryan Carrington was another story. He understood her not wanting to involve the police, even though he didn't agree. Him handling Ryan Carrington man-to-man was a given. He turned on the shower full blast.

Mikayla padded into the kitchen just as Alonzo was finishing up fixing breakfast. "There she is," he greeted. "Mornin', baby. Finally got some sleep, huh?" He poured a mug of coffee and handed it to her.

She took the mug and hummed in gratitude. She slid onto the stool, rubbed her eyes and yawned. "I guess I did," she said with a slight frown of confusion. "Don't remember drifting off."

He chuckled. "It was pretty late, almost daybreak."

"What time is it?"

"After eleven. Do you have clients today?"

"No. I'm going to visit my mother. Maybe stay with her for dinner."

"Yeah, I think you should."

She shot him a curious look, took a sip of coffee.

He set a platter on the table that was covered with fresh fruit, Canadian bacon and a feta cheese omelet.

"Sorry for the meager spread but I have to take care of some things today and I need to get going."

"Meager spread. You are funny." She pulled the platter toward her. "What's on the agenda?" She glanced up.

He turned to the stove to remove pans and put them in the sink. "Need to talk to the owner of the space I want to rent. Still some sticking points that I want ironed out before I decide."

"Oh. Okay." She spooned some eggs onto a plate and added strawberries and bacon. "Figure out what you're going to do about Jasmine leaving?"

"Another thing on the agenda. Still can't wrap my head around why she would do this."

"Hopefully she'll eventually tell you."

"Yeah, but in the meantime I have a business to run." He rinsed the pots and pans, then put them in the dishwasher. He came around to her side of the counter, threaded his fingers through the back of her hair and eased her close. "I'll see you this evening," he said against her mouth before kissing strawberry-sweet lips. He ran his tongue along her bottom lip. "Hmm." He kissed her again. "Gotta go."

Mikayla sat at the counter for a long while after Alonzo left. The events in Ryan's office were still raw but didn't sting quite as badly. She'd been reluctant to say anything to Alonzo about what happened but was glad she did. Alonzo had a way of soothing her, making her believe that everything would be all right; he made her feel safe and loved, the way her father once did.

She'd never shared that story with anyone, not even Traci, with whom she shared some of her most private thoughts and secrets. She wasn't sure what she'd expected his response to be, but for the first time that heavy cloud that she'd carried in heart lifted. Alonzo assured her that what happened with her father in no way reflected his love for her, but rather decisions her father made that they may never know or understand. What she needed to remember was that her father never treated her in any way other than with love. She needed that to be true.

Alonzo circled the block several times before he finally found a metered parking spot a half block away. Each step he took toward the entrance fueled him. Images of what Ryan had done and attempted to do to Mikayla burned lava-like through his veins.

He pulled open the glass-and-chrome door and strode in, stopped at security and was directed to the sixth floor. When the elevator doors swished open, he went straight to the receptionist.

"Good afternoon." Recognition kicked in. "Oh, Mr.

Grant. How may I help you? Is Mr. Carrington expecting you?"

"No, but I need to see him." His jaw tightened.

"Of course. Everyone is still talking about that party." She beamed, then punched in a number on the phone. "Yes. Mr. Grant is here to see Mr. Carrington. Sure." She hung up the phone. "Cherise will be right out." She linked her fingers together and smiled demurely. "You must get to meet so many interesting people."

"Hmm."

"Have you ever worked for Beyoncé? I'm dying to meet her."

"Mr. Grant." Cherise came from around the corner, effectively cutting off his response. "Ryan wasn't expecting you. He has someone in his office, but he'll be with you shortly. You can come with me. I'll set you up in the conference room. Can I get you anything?"

"No. Thanks." His temples pounded.

She pushed through a glass door at the end of the hall, then opened a heavy wood door on the right. "Sure I can't get you anything?" she asked again, standing to the side to let him pass.

"I'm fine. Thank you."

She offered a tight-lipped smile. "Hopefully, Ryan won't be too long." She closed the door behind her.

Alonzo slowly took in the room that screamed money and power—the massive oak desk, paneled walls, crystal vases and glassware lining the built-in shelves, and framed photos of his Academy Award-winning movies and images or of Ryan posed with the who's who of Hollywood. There was even a picture of Ryan and Cheri during some red-carpet event. He snorted his annoyance.

"Zo! Hey."

He turned, and the instant he set eyes on the smiling face, the lava that had been bubbling since Mikayla told him what happened burst to the surface. His nostrils flared. He came from around the table. "You lowlife son of a bitch!"

"Whaaat? I—"

Before Ryan could get the words out of his mouth, Alonzo's right hook slammed him back up against the door, dazing and knocking him to the floor. Alonzo leaped on top of him and delivered another blow to his face. He grabbed him by the collar. Blood dripped from Ryan's lip and nose and dribbled onto his stark white shirt.

"That's for Mikayla. Consider yourself lucky," he said, breathing hard. He pushed him aside like a sack of laundry, stepped over him and walked out.

He strode out, didn't look left or right, ignored the goodbyes from the receptionist. When he got outside, it was pouring. By the time he got to his car, he was soaked, and in his car he finally took a moment to consider what he'd done. He shook off the pain in his fist and sat there for a few moments as water rolled down his face. The moment his fist connected with Ryan's nose and the crunching sound replayed in his head. He turned on the car. The wipers swished back and forth, providing intermittent clarity against the driving rain. Some of the rage he'd felt eased but didn't go away. He'd bury the rest and move on, and today's little beatdown would remain between him and Ryan.

Chapter 13

"After I get things settled with the new space, I want us to take a trip somewhere," Alonzo said as he stepped out of the shower. "Next month maybe. I have a couple of events to handle and that will give you time to finish looking for an assistant." He wrapped a towel around his waist. "And I think it's time you give up your place. Don't you? Crazy to pay rent for somewhere that you don't stay. Then Traci can find a new roommate." He used a second towel to dry his hair.

Mikayla stepped out of the shower behind him. One thing she'd discovered in the months that she'd been with Alonzo was that he was definitely a morning person. He was at one hundred while she was still putting the key in the ignition. In one breath he'd just lobbed at least a half dozen things for her to process. She pulled a towel from the rack and wrapped it around her body. "I don't even know what you just said," she remarked, partly in jest. "Why do you even talk to me before two cups of coffee?"

He looked at her in the mirror and laughed. "True. I'm a work in progress." He turned around and swept her up against him. He leaned in and kissed her damp skin and inhaled deeply. "Hmm." He pulled her towel away.

"Zo!" she said, feigning shock.

"Damn, I can't get enough of you," he groaned, tugging away his own towel. He took his time worshipping her body, spurred on by her soft moans, the sweet scent of her freshly bathed body and shaky sighs. He turned her around so they both faced the mirror.

Mikayla bent over and gripped the edge of the sink. Alonzo wrapped an arm tightly around her waist and entered her in one stiff stroke.

After a second shower, Alonzo went to his office to check his email and review his work schedule for the coming month—something that Jasmine used to do—to figure out the best time for their getaway. His head jerked back, then he peered closer at the email. "What the…"

Alonzo,
Wanted to let you know that we won't need your services for the party.

Morgan

He went to the next.

Mr. Grant,
After some consideration we have decided to use another service.

Jamie

   And the next.

Mr. Grant,
I will no longer need you to cater for the Bahama trip.

Celine

   He rocked back in his seat, stunned into disbelief. One cancellation maybe, but three. These were all people he'd worked with before. There'd never been a problem. If anything, catering their events brought on more business.

   He read the emails again. They'd all been sent within the past hour. He leaned forward and typed responses to all three clients, thanking them for the heads-up and inquiring as to their change of heart.

   He slammed the cover of the laptop closed, fuming. This made no sense. In the years that he'd worked independently and established his reputation and brand, nothing like this had ever happened. Why, was the question.

   "Hey, babe." She stopped. "What's wrong?" She stepped fully into the room.

   "Every client for the next month canceled."

"What?" She pulled up a chair and sat next to him. "Why?"

"Very vague reasons. Change of mind." The tight expression drew his thick brows together.

Mikayla covered his hand with hers. "Maybe it's just a crazy coincidence, babe. Or fate telling you to slow down and take a break."

"Yeah, maybe," he said, totally unconvinced. He pushed out a breath. "I responded to them all. I'll see if they answer me."

"I'm sure there's a good explanation. Please don't worry."

He shot her a look. "Going out?"

"Yes. To interview my potential new employee, remember? I'd already canceled once after…" She let the rest hang in the air. Her expression tightened. "Anyway, I didn't want to put it off any longer."

"Where are you meeting?"

"At the Starbucks."

"You could have done it here. I don't see why you have to meet in some café when you can use my office."

"We talked about this. I appreciate the offer, but I want to do this on my own."

"Hey, whatever. I'm only trying to help. Clearly you don't need it."

She flinched. "What is wrong with you?"

"Not a thing, Kayla. Go. Do your interview."

She started to kiss him goodbye but changed her mind. "I'll see you later."

Alonzo waited an hour, checking and rechecking his email. No response. He didn't tell her about the phone call earlier in the week from the network saying they might not be using him as a guest judge for the upcoming season of *Top Chef* program. He pushed away from the desk, swept a stack of folders onto the floor and stormed out. Maybe a swim would help calm him down.

He swam until his limbs burned. He pulled himself out of the pool and stretched out on the lounge chair on the back deck. He still couldn't wrap his head around the cancellations and he didn't want his thoughts to go where they'd been trying to go all morning. Hopefully, it was no more than what Mikayla said, a crazy coincidence. As long as it was a coincidence and not some ugly turn of fortune, he would push through with the purchase of the space. He tucked his hands behind his head. The other matter to handle was finding a replacement for Jasmine. That would be harder than anything.

Mikayla found Alonzo relaxing on the couch upon her return home. She dropped her tote onto the side chair and came to sit next to him. She didn't do well with men and their male egos, which Traci reminded her of when she'd called to tell her about how Alonzo was acting.

"What do you expect?" she'd said. "That's the man's livelihood. Here you are, building your little empire, and his is crumbling. He's no longer the knight in shining armor coming to your rescue. Give him some slack."

"Any news?" Mikayla asked, coming to sit next to him.

"Not a word."

Her eyebrow rose. "Wow." She curled next to him.

"I'm sorry, babe." She stroked the back of his neck. "So, what's the plan and what can I do to help?"

He half grinned and pecked her lips with a light kiss. "'Preciate the offer but there's not much you can do."

She rested her head on his chest. "I hired her."

He reared back and looked at her with a grin on his face, their tiff of earlier apparently all forgotten. "Congratulations, baby. You are officially an employer."

"And it's petrifying."

"You'll be fine. I'll help you with whatever you need. No worries." He kissed her forehead. "When is she going to start?"

"Tomorrow, actually. I have two jobs in Santa Monica and one in the valley. I'll take her with me. I want to see her work and we can get finished faster."

"Business is really picking up, huh?"

"Yes. I can hardly believe it." A few months ago she was struggling to keep a roof over her head. She raised her shoulders and lowered them. "You must be my lucky charm." She cupped his chin and kissed him.

He wasn't feeling particularly lucky.

A week went by with no response to his email inquiries, and when he called, all he got was voice mail.

Mikayla poked her head into Alonzo's office. "Hey, you've been in here all morning." She crossed the room. "What's going on?"

He pushed out a breath. "Nothing, that's the problem."

She sat down on the edge of the desk. "Still no response from your clients?"

"Nope. And if I didn't know better, I'd think someone was intentionally trying to ruin my business."

"But why? And who? I mean it's not like what you do is so easy to duplicate."

"I don't want to think who it might be."

"What do you mean?"

"The only person that I can think who would have anything to gain is Jasmine."

"Whoa. Jasmine? Do you really think she would do that?"

"I don't know what I believe anymore. What I do know is that something's up. I just don't know what it is."

"Why don't you talk to her? Face-to-face. Not to mention that she needs to give you the real reason why she left."

He sidestepped a reply. "Where are you off to?"

"Visit my mom."

He nodded. "No jobs today?"

"Lena is working. I'm managing." She smiled. "If the work keeps coming in, I might have to bring on another person. Wouldn't that be something?"

"Hmm. Booming business."

Her eyes narrowed at the sarcastic tone. She wasn't going to step into that minefield. "Guess I'll see you later."

"Yep. See you later."

He rocked his chair back and put his feet up on the desk while he waited on a call from his brother Montgomery. Monty was firmly entrenched in real estate and property management in DC, and knew a worthwhile piece of property with his eyes closed. He'd bought several B and Bs, a small boutique hotel and several residential buildings—all of which were doing extremely well, and he was always in the market for a profitable real estate venture.

Alonzo had sent Monty the specs for the restaurant space, along with pictures. Monty promised to look them over as well as check out if there were any violations or liens on the property. He was looking forward to talking with his younger brother. He'd been so wrapped up in his own life and the whirlwind relationship with Mikayla that he'd been remiss in keeping in touch with his family.

It had been a while since he'd been home to DC, and he was missing hanging with his brothers for basketball night at his brother Franklin's crib. Maybe the trip he and Mikayla should take would be to DC.

The idea gave him pause. Bringing a woman home to meet the family—even indirectly—was a leap he'd never taken before, at least not as an adult. His lifestyle didn't lend itself to much stability, and his mother was forever getting on his case about having "a port in every storm." Bringing Mikayla home to meet the family might signal something he wasn't certain he was ready for, especially now. Why wasn't he?

The sudden uncertainty made him uncharacteristically anxious. One thing he'd always prided himself on was his ability to make clear-headed decisions. But everything about their relationship happened like a lightning strike—swift and blinding—stunning them both. He'd never actually made a decision about what they would be to each other; it just happened. The pieces fell into place. Now here they were. But where was that?

The buzzing from the intercom at the front gate pulled him back from the twist of his thoughts. He got up from the desk and walked over to the wall mount by the office door. He pressed the buzzer and was stunned to see his brother Montgomery parked in a rented Audi.

"Monty? What the hell…"

"Open up, man. Figured I bring the Monty to Mohammad."

Alonzo chuckled and pressed the release button to open the gate.

"Man, what are you doing here?" Alonzo greeted his brother with a bear hug. He dropped his arm around his shoulder and ushered him inside.

"Hey, I haven't been out to the 'left coast' in a minute. Figured I get some vacation time in, see my big brother and check out this property of yours up close." He took off his shades and stuck them in the pocket of his shirt.

"How long are you in town for?"

"Few days. Week at most." He looked around the space in admiration. "Living large, bruh. That whole cooking thing you do really paid off," he joked.

"Hmm."

"I say something wrong?" He plopped down on a side chair and crossed one right foot over his knee.

"Naw. Few setbacks, but nothing serious."

"What kind of setbacks?"

"Want a drink?" he asked instead of answering.

"Sure. Then you can tell me about the setback."

Alonzo walked over to the bar and fixed two glasses of bourbon. He handed Montgomery his glass.

Montgomery raised his glass. "To brothers."

"To brothers."

They tossed back a deep swallow.

"How're the folks?"

"Doing well. Dad is running Mom crazy, but that's the usual. She swears she wants him to get a job so he won't be underfoot all day, as she puts it."

Alonzo chuckled. His parents had been married for fifty-one years. The prior year they'd celebrated their fiftieth anniversary and he and his brothers threw them a fabulous party at Monty's hotel. Not too long after the party, his parents were driving home from a day on the town and his mother suffered a heart attack and drove the car off the road. She required surgery. His dad was pretty banged up but okay. Through both of their recoveries their only concern was each other. His parents had the kind of relationship that he eventually wanted, which was probably why it had been hard for him to even consider settling down. He couldn't see "forever" with the women who traveled in his circles. Then came Mikayla.

"So, what's the deal? Not like you to have setbacks."

Alonzo leaned back against the plush cushions of the couch. He took another swallow of his drink and ran his hand across his close-cropped hair. "You know my business has its foundation on word of mouth, recommendations."

"Yeah."

"At least half of my client base are returns."

"Okay. I'm sold. Now tell me what the hell is going on."

"Over the past couple of weeks, all of my scheduled client events were canceled."

Montgomery frowned and uncrossed his leg. "Why?"

"That's what I don't know. If it was one cancellation I could understand that. But it's four in total. At least a hundred thousand dollars gone. And no one is telling me why or returning my calls."

"Wow." He rested his forearms on his thighs. "Okay, you can tell me. Whose wife or girlfriend did you seduce and piss someone off?"

"Humph, at least if it was that—which it's not—I could understand it." He shook his head. "This I don't get."

"What does Jasmine have to say?"

His brow knitted. "She quit."

"Say what?"

"Yeah. Quit. The gig we did a couple of weeks ago was her last."

"Why? You two have been a team from the beginning."

"Same question I've been asking myself."

"Well, you need to stop asking yourself and talk to her."

"Same thing Mikayla said."

"Who? Who's Mikayla?"

Alonzo pushed up from his seat, crossed the room and fixed another drink. He turned to his brother. "She was my housekeeper..."

"Damn, man, leave you alone for a couple of months and all hell breaks loose," Montgomery said after listening to Alonzo lay out the events of the past few months.

"Looks that way."

"So there's been no blowback with this Carrington dude?"

"He wouldn't dare. Too much of his rep would be at risk if he came at me. It would come out why I was there in the first place."

"I hope your lady appreciates what you did. You could be in jail instead of here."

"She doesn't know."

"Aw, man. Really?"

"She wanted to let it go. I couldn't."

"She doesn't want to report it?"

"No."

"You're cool with that?"

"Not at all, which led to me having a 'conversation' with Carrington." He pushed out a breath.

"I'm not one to get involved in other folks' relationships, but from where I'm standing, if you two can't be honest with each other..."

"Yeah. Things have been a little strained between us this past week. I offer my help," he shrugged, "but she doesn't need it."

Monty paused a beat. "I might be off but it kinda feels like since she's making her own way and you're having this bad patch—you have nothing to fix or save. She was a project. A recipe that you were trying to perfect."

"What?"

"If you're honest with yourself, you'll admit that it's true."

"You're staying here, right?" he said instead.

"I'd planned to but you have your lady staying here. I can get a hotel."

"I have plenty of space. Besides, the hotel will never feed you the way I can."

Montgomery pointed a finger at his brother and grinned. "You're right about that."

"Then it's settled."

"Cool. I'll get my bag from the car. We can talk about this property that you want to purchase. I brought some paperwork with me."

While Montgomery went to his car to get his bag, Alonzo headed into the kitchen to see what he could whip up for dinner. He was looking forward to Monty meeting Mikayla. It wasn't exactly bringing your girlfriend home to meet the folks, but it was a blueprint. He wanted Monty to like her. For the first time it was important. But what Monty had warned about honesty, and looking at Mikayla as a project, put a bit of a damper on his enthusiasm. He'd handle it. He always did.

Chapter 14

"Your brother is really nice," Mikayla said in a pseudowhisper while they stacked the dishwasher. "He'd be perfect for Traci."

Alonzo laughed. "Monty! My brother is too busy building an empire to focus on a relationship."

She rested her hip against the sink. "Same thing you thought," she teased.

He shut the door of the dishwasher and turned to her. "Is that right?"

She lifted up on her toes and kissed him. "Yep."

She was right. The prospect of settling in with one woman was far from his mind until he met her, and there were still parts of him that fought against the inevitable. He slid an arm around her waist. "Something I need to talk with you about."

"Okay." She wiped her hands on a dish towel. "Listening."

He cleared his throat. "I know that you wanted me to stay out of dealing with Carrington."

Her body stiffened. She stood straighter.

Alonzo lightly braced her arms. "I went to his office."

"Zo..."

"Let's just say he was on the wrong end of a hard right."

Her eyes widened. "What? Oh my God. You didn't."

"Look, I would be less than a man, less than *your* man, if I let what he did go unchecked. I respect the fact that you want to keep this private. I don't agree, but I respect your wishes. But baby, no way I could turn the other cheek. Not when it comes to you. It makes me crazy just thinking that he put his hands on you. Couldn't let it go." He shook his head. "Couldn't do it."

Her look of alarm slowly softened as her eyes scanned his face. She cupped his cheeks in her palms and brought her lips to meet his in a slow, deep kiss.

"Thank you," she whispered against his mouth.

"Anything for you." He caressed her cheek. "My brother made me realize that if we're going to make this work, we had to be honest with each other. Even if it wasn't pleasant."

She took a step back, lowered her head.

"What? What is it?"

She looked into his eyes. "I... I don't actually live with Traci."

"I don't understand."

"I haven't lived with Traci for nearly a year. I, um, have a place in East LA."

"What am I missing here? I've picked you up and dropped you off."

"I know." She pulled in a breath. "I didn't want you to know where I lived, how I was living. I didn't want you to feel sorry for me. And after I saw how you lived, the life you lived…"

"Kayla, did you really believe that would make a difference to me? That's what you think of me, that I would judge you because of where you lived?"

"I didn't know. And the longer I didn't say anything, the harder it got to tell you."

He pulled her into his arms. "Woman. Get your bag."

She leaned back and looked at him. "What?"

"Get your bag. I'm taking you home."

Mikayla's heart thudded in her chest as she turned the key in the lock. All during the ride over, she stole glances at Alonzo to gauge his reaction to the rapidly changing landscape. His expression didn't change.

She eased the door open. "Home," she said with a hitch in her voice.

Alonzo walked in. To Mikayla it felt as if his physical presence took up what little space there was. He strolled into the center of the main room that doubled as living room, dining room and kitchen.

Mikayla bit down on her bottom lip, waiting for the verdict.

He swung toward her. "This feels like a home. Warm, filled with color, intimate. Like you," he added, then went to sit on the couch. He patted the space next to him. She came and sat down. He put an arm around her shoulder. "You'll have to do better than this if you want to run me away." He stretched and yawned. "It's getting late." He stood and took her hand. "Show me your bedroom."

"Takes a while for the water to get hot," Mikayla called out from the curled position on her double bed.

"Okay." He turned the shower on full blast, then went back to sit next to Mikayla. He planted a hand on her round hip. "I kinda like sleeping close."

She gave him a half grin. "Not much choice."

"I still like it."

"Enough to give up your pillow-top king-size bed?"

"Hmm." He leaned over and pecked her lips with a kiss. "If I can spend it with you."

"You sure know what to say to charm a girl."

"Come join me in the shower, then I'm going to do what I promised. For every morning that we wake up together, I'll fix breakfast."

"Well, you will have to pull all of your magic out of the hat. I don't cook—as you know—and I don't shop."

He tossed his head back and laughed. "Let's get showered." His thumb stroked her bottom lip. "We'll figure out the rest."

She looped her arms around his neck. "Yes, I think we will."

"I'm going to take Monty over to the restaurant site later today," Alonzo said.

"When are you going to talk to Jasmine?"

He shot her a look. "Today. I'm going to call her

today. I promise. As a matter of fact, I'm going to ask her to meet me at the restaurant."

"Good." She patted his hand. "You'll feel better moving into this new venture knowing the truth."

He nodded. "You're right. And speaking of new ventures...now that I know your deep, dark secret." He winked. "If you want to keep your place, I'm cool with that. I get it that you need to do things your way without relying on anyone. This is yours and it's yours for as long as you want to keep it. Just remember that my home is yours, too, for whenever you want it."

Her eyes glistened with gratitude. "Thank you. But since there is no way that fab Jacuzzi of yours can fit in here, and you have opened my taste buds and groomed an aversion to takeout in little white boxes, you'll be seeing a lot of me."

He tossed his head back and laughed. "Anytime, baby, anytime."

Chapter 15

"I see why you're a little bit crazy about Mikayla," Montgomery said as they pulled to a stop in front of the restaurant space.

Alonzo shot him a questioning look. "Meaning?"

"She's special. And you can't buy the way she looks at you when you aren't paying attention. I've never seen you like that with a woman. They've all been—" he shrugged as he searched for the word "—placeholders, until you found the right one. I think she's it."

The corner of Alonzo's mouth lifted to a grin. "I love her. I'm in love with her," he said quietly. "All I want to do is make her happy, make her smile, take care of her." He shook his head in wonder. "Never felt like that before. Like, never."

Montgomery chuckled and cupped his hands around

his mouth. "Two Grant brothers down in aisle six," he teased.

Alonzo gave him a brotherly shove.

"Only one left standing. I gotta hold it down, bruh."

"Hey, a friend of mine told me, 'When the right one comes along, there's nothing you can do about it.'"

They got out of the car.

"In the meantime, before I get got, I'm going to enjoy myself. Now—" he took off his shades "—let's see what you have here."

The real estate agent was waiting out front.

"This is my brother, Montgomery Grant. He's an agent in DC."

"Ah, second opinion! Very good." He pressed the code into the lockbox and opened the door.

The trio stepped inside.

Montgomery was quietly observant as the agent went through his spiel about the space and its potential. Then they talked comps and the rehabilitation of the neighborhood. Alonzo stepped back and listened with pride at his brother. It was eye-opening to watch him do his thing, be in his element. Sure he'd built a real estate empire in DC, and he was very well-off. People came from far and wide to stay in his hotel and B and Bs. He'd established a brand of high quality and knew how to hire the best people to run it. Alonzo knew all of that but now he saw how the magic happened. His little brother was the truth.

The two men shook hands. Montgomery walked over to Alonzo. "It's pretty much what I figured, only better. If this is the next level for you, then you should step up. It's a good spot. The building has great bones. In another couple of years you won't be able to afford to get in this area."

Alonzo nodded in agreement as he listened. He clapped Montgomery on the back. "Thanks, man." He walked over to the agent. "I'll sign the bill of sale and get it over to your office this week."

"Wonderful." He vigorously shook Alonzo's hand. "Congratulations."

"I thought you asked Jasmine to meet us here," Montgomery said before getting back in the car.

"I did. Well, I left her a voice message. I'd hoped she would show up." A twinge of concern hit him. No matter the issues between them, Jasmine always returned his calls. "Hey, I'm going to drop you back off at the crib and swing by her place."

"You sure? I can get an Uber."

"Naw. It's on the way."

When he pulled up in front of Jasmine's ranch-style home, he was at least relieved to see her car and her SUV parked in front of the garage, a good sign that she was home. Hopefully, she hadn't gone out of town and had simply taken another mode of transportation. He pulled up behind the vehicles and parked. He wasn't sure what he was going to say to her but he needed to get her to explain her decision. There were too many years, good times and what he thought was an unbreakable friendship between them to simply toss it away without explanation. It bothered him more than he let on.

He rang the bell and waited. He heard movement and moments later the door opened.

"What are you doing here, Zo?"

She looked even smaller in her T-shirt and shorts, more like a college coed rather than a seasoned woman.

"Can I come in?" From the look of barely controlled annoyance on her face he actually thought she was going to say no.

Finally she stepped aside. "Come in. But don't get comfortable."

"Can I at least sit down?"

"Fine." She shut the door and stomped inside, leading the way down a short foyer. She stopped in the living room and turned to him with her arms folded. "So, what is it? Why are you here?"

"I need you to talk to me, Jazz. Tell me what's really going on."

"I already told you." Her lips tightened as if trying to keep any more words from coming out.

"No. You didn't. Did I do something, say something?"

"Why does it have to be about you?" she snapped. "It's always about you."

His eyes cinched. "What?"

Her chest rose and fell. "It's always about you. *Your* recipes. *Your* face on the cover of the magazines. *Your* interviews. *Your* television appearances. You! What about me, Zo? When is the light going to shine on me? You probably wouldn't be where you are without me, without me holding it down."

He could barely process what he was hearing. "Are you serious?"

Tears glistened in her eyes. "Hell yes, I'm serious, Zo." She sniffed hard.

"Listen, there has never been a day that we have

worked together when I haven't made sure that you know and that everyone in our presence knows that you are the backbone of the business. You run the entire team. You sit with me into crazy hours of the morning coming up with new recipes and new presentations. Every article that has ever been written about me I make sure to talk about you, and you know that." He dragged in a breath. "But let's be real honest here, Jazz, I'm a chef. I brought you onto my vision. You learned from me as much as I learned from you. My weaknesses are your strengths and vice versa. I'm broken in half without you, but if you really feel that way, that I somehow have slighted you, held you back instead of up…then I guess it's best if we part ways. I'm sorry." He held her gaze for one short moment, then turned toward the door.

"Wait."

He stopped with his hand on the knob and turned back around.

Her lip trembled. "None of what I said is true." She paused. "I…didn't know how to tell you. Because I know you, damn it, and you would try to fix it."

He shut the door. "What are you talking about? Fix what?"

She sighed in resignation. "Come and sit. I'll explain."

"I was diagnosed about six months ago, sarcoidosis," she was saying. "I'd been so tired and achy. Headaches, blurred vision. Some days I would wake up and all my joints were swollen. These swollen knots would appear on my legs."

"Why didn't you tell me?"

"I didn't want you to worry, to get off your game. We had so much going on."

"Jazz, I could have—"

She cut him off. "Helped. I know. Tried to fix it. Take on my troubles, 'cause that's what you do. But I needed to handle it on my own. Find my own way."

"I'm freaking surrounded by stubborn, independent women!"

It was the first time she smiled. "And I knew that you'd finally found someone to take care of you and I could take a step back and take care of me."

He sighed heavily. "What does that entail—the taking care of you part?"

"Rest. Eight hours sleep per night. Good nutrition. Exercise. Keep my stress level manageable. Take medication when I have a flare-up. The doctors say since I'm young and it hasn't affected any organs, it may very well go away on its own eventually, but I need to be vigilant."

He nodded in understanding. "I know you don't want me to do anything or to help so… I won't, but I have a proposition. You don't have to say yes now, but at least think about it. I'm buying the building. And who better to run it than you. It's what you love. You wouldn't have to travel. Build your team. Go home and sleep in your own bed every night. You'd be the face of the business and it will do so much for the community." He pushed to his feet. "Thank you for telling me. For trusting me."

She wrapped her arms around him and rested her head on his chest. "Thank you for being you, Zo."

He kissed the top of her head. "Think about it."

"I don't have to."

He froze in a moment of alarm.

"I'll do it."

He swept her up off the ground and spun her in a circle. "The band is back together again," he shouted over her laughter.

Yes, yes, yes. The enthusiasm he had for this new project was back in full force. The missing piece had been Jasmine. He would have pulled it off. He would have found someone to step in, but they never would have filled Jasmine's shoes. If he could sing, he would. He turned the radio on instead at the same moment that a phone call came through the car speakers.

Cheri's name showed on the dial. He started not to answer, but he was feeling so good that nothing Cheri would say could change that. He pressed the talk button on the dash. "What can I do for you, Cheri?"

"Are you alone?"

"Why?"

"Because this is only for you to hear."

He pulled over to the curb and parked. "What might that be?"

"I know I screwed up with us. I'm sorry and you probably never wanted to hear from or see me again and I don't blame you. You're one of the last good guys. It was a real crappy move on my part."

"If this is what you called about, forget it. I'm over it. I've moved on."

"Ryan Carrington is blackballing you in the industry, every which way but loose," she blurted out.

"What?"

"Word on the street is that he's in everyone's ear that if they ever intend to get any favors from him or anyone he knows, they need to kick you to the curb. Said you had underhanded business practices. All kinds of non-sense. He's a powerful man, Zo, and he intends to ruin you. I've had my dealings with him. He's a sleaze, and there isn't a day that goes by that I wish—"

"What? Wish what?"

"That I'd told someone." Her voice broke as the words tumbled out of her mouth about the afternoon that changed her life nearly five years earlier.

Alonzo sputtered a string of expletives. "He has to be stopped. Who knows how many other women he's assaulted."

"I'm just one voice, Zo. It won't matter and then he'll come after me…"

"No, you're not. And no, he damn well won't."

Chapter 16

Mikayla sat on the edge of the club chair with her fingers laced tightly together. "So he abuses women and can't take a punch," she said with utter disgust. "The fact that he would go after you! Hell no." She shook her head vigorously. "I can't let that happen. You worked too hard. He's not going to ruin that."

"If we do this, if we go public, they're going to come after us—after you."

"I don't care about any of that anymore." She stared into his eyes. "You were right. I should have gone to the police when it happened. Who knows how many others he's done this to?" She swallowed and smiled softly. "Besides, I've got my knight in shining armor and it's past time that I let him do his knight thing."

His eyes sparkled. "I love you, woman."

"I love you."

"We're going to handle this, and no matter what happens on the other end, we have each other."

Alonzo had done an anniversary party for Natalie Durban, one of the editors at the *L.A. Times*, a few years earlier. If Carrington hadn't poisoned that well yet, maybe Alonzo could get her interested in exposing him. He made the call and was beyond relieved to know that not only would she be interested in writing the piece, but she had time in her day and wanted to get started by getting Mikayla's story right away. The one thing that she did suggest was for Mikayla to immediately go to the police so that the assault would be on record and would boost the validity of the article. "And get a good lawyer," she'd added. "You'll need one."

Barely a week later, in the entertainment section of the *L.A. Times*, the headline read, "Movie Mogul and Academy Award-Winning Director Ryan Carrington Accused of Sexual Assault." The article was explosive and alluded to the fact that his staff was knowledgeable about what he'd been accused of and complicit in securing the women.

The fallout was fast and furious. Reporters were camped out in front of Alonzo's door wanting to interview Mikayla, having put together, somehow, that she was staying there. They were finally able to sneak out one night from the back and go hide out at Mikayla's apartment for some privacy.

"This little place came in handy after all," Mikayla giggled as they tumbled onto her bed.

"Definitely. Those reporters are relentless."

"I don't know what I expected." She turned onto her side. He curled up behind her. "But no matter what, I know we did the right thing."

"You did this. It's your words, your determination that is going to end his ugly journey. And because you stood up, others will, too."

Every talk show and television entertainment outlet buzzed about the story. Anchors from all the major news outlets wanted to interview Mikayla. The only television interview that she agreed to was with Rachel on MSNBC. Telling her story on a national stage was terrifying, but liberating. She was reclaiming her voice and hopefully speaking out for all those women who felt voiceless.

"Girl, you're famous," Traci teased as they watched her interview on television.

"Never expected it to happen this way."

"Yeah, I know. But what you're doing makes a difference." She covered her hand with her own. "I'm proud of you. And ya look good on TV, too."

They laughed.

"Where's that fine man of yours?"

"At the restaurant with Jasmine going over plans, and working with the contractors."

"Glad that worked out."

"Yeah. Me too. Sometimes we women try to be too strong and don't know when to ask for help. Want to do it on our own, sometimes to our own detriment."

"Am I hearing a new Mikayla Harris?"

"Yes. I think so. New and improved." She grinned.

"Do you think Monty will come back for the opening?" Traci asked coyly.

Mikayla slid her a knowing look. "Cute, isn't he?"

She sighed. "For real." She glanced at the television. "Whoa. Look. Isn't that Cheri Lang?"

Cheri was standing in front of a bank of microphones on the steps of what looked like a courthouse.

"I should have come forward a long time ago," she began, her big brown eyes scanning the gathering. "But I was afraid. Afraid that my name and my career would be ruined by Ryan Carrington." She lifted her chin. "It was because of the courage of Mikayla Harris that gave me the courage to come forward to tell the world that Ryan Carrington sexually assaulted me and I know he's done it to others. I stand here today to implore any woman out there that has been violated by Ryan Carrington or any man to share your story. Don't be afraid. You are not alone." She looked directly into the camera. "Thank you, Mikayla, for giving me back my voice."

"OMG," Traci sputtered.

Mikayla flopped back against the cushions of the couch. "Wow."

"Now you're really famous."

They looked at each other and high-fived.

In the days that followed, nearly a dozen women came forward. The district attorney brought formal charges against Ryan Carrington and every newspaper had his face plastered on the front page, handcuffed while being walked into court. In the months to come, it would be hard when it came time for her to testify, but she was ready.

Mikayla had truly become a household name and a symbol of resistance. Once word got out that she was actually the owner of At Your Service, she could barely keep up with requests for all those who wanted to make sure they supported her and women in general. She'd had to hire six more workers and lease vans to accommodate the expansion. She had enough of a solid income that she no longer worried about the expense of her mother's care. Whatever it took and for however long, she'd be able to handle it. But the best part of it all was being in love and being loved by Alonzo.

Alonzo's business was back on solid footing, supported by real friends and true clients. He took the apologies in stride, determined to move on bigger and better than before. With Jasmine by his side again, they moved full steam ahead to get the space open and operational. But she said if he asked her one more time if she was feeling okay, she would quit. And he swore he would drag her back kicking and screaming if she did. At the very least she'd better not quit before the grand opening.

Chapter 17

Three Months Later

The news services were out in full force and everybody who was anybody walked the red carpet to the grand opening of Grant's.

"This is like being at the Academy Awards," Traci said close to Mikayla's ear.

"I know! Everywhere I look, there's another famous face. I'm so happy for him. This is Zo's dream."

"There you are, baby." Alonzo came up beside her and slid his arm around her waist. "I want you right next to me tonight. This is our night." He kissed her cheek. "I want you to meet my folks. They just got here. And, uh, I think there's someone that wants to see you," he said to Traci.

Her eyes widened in delight. "Lead the way."

"Ms. Harris, Mr. Grant. Can I get a few words?" a reporter asked, shoving a cell phone in their direction. "How have you been since the trial?"

"We've been great," Alonzo said and hugged Mikayla closer.

"You and Ms. Harris have been an item for a while. Any big plans that you might want to share?"

He looked at Mikayla and grinned. "Maybe. But I guarantee you *won't* be the first to know. If you'll excuse us, I have to mingle." He took Mikayla by the hand and led her around the tables to the private room in the back where his family was gathered.

"Everyone, this is Mikayla," he said, looking at her with love and wonder in his eyes. "And her best friend, Traci. You both know Monty and of course Jasmine. This is my mom and dad, Ellen and Louis Grant."

"I'm so glad to meet you. I feel like I know you already," Mikayla said and walked over to embrace them both.

"I've heard all about you." Ellen took Mikayla's hand and pulled her close to whisper in her ear. "I hope you know how much you mean to him."

"I think I do," she whispered over the sudden knot in her throat.

"And this is the other dynamic duo, my older brother, Franklin, and his wife, Dina."

"If you got my brother to slow down, you have got to be part of the family," Franklin said and kissed her cheek.

"Takes a special kind of woman to land a Grant

man," Ellen said, looking from her husband to her sons with unwavering love and pride.

"Yes, it does," Alonzo said. He cleared his throat. "I don't think I realized what special was until I met Mikayla, or how unfulfilled my life was. I traveled the world, met dignitaries and superstars, but none of them could hold a candle to her." He looked into her eyes. "You make me a better version of myself and I want to spend the rest of my days getting better and better for you—with you at my side. The world is ours for the taking, baby. Let me show it to you every day for the rest of our lives. Let me love you morning, noon and night. I want to sit across the table from you for the rest of my life. Marry me."

He reached into his pocket and slowly got down on one knee. He opened the box to display a dazzling diamond.

Tears of utter joy streamed down her face. Her entire body trembled, and as much as she knew she was in a room full of people, all she could see was Alonzo, see today with him, tomorrow, the future.

"Yes. Yes," she cried.

The room burst into applause.

Alonzo slipped the ring onto her finger and rose from his knees. He took her in his arms, lowered his head and covered her mouth in a smoldering kiss that had the room humming in appreciation.

When he finally let her go and looked into her eyes, she said, "Who knew that getting fired would lead to this?"

They laughed, they hugged and they laughed some more.

* * * * *

Charlotte turned to face the window to avoid her cousin's questioning stare. She made eye contact with Richard, who was standing outside with the other parents on the sidewalk, spying on their girls while shielding themselves from the rain with umbrellas. He flashed a heart-fluttering smile.

He loved her.

Though the words hadn't left her lips, Charlotte knew she loved him. Was it even possible in such a short amount of time? Charlotte looked away but only caught her cousin staring at her.

"I stand corrected. Say who?"

"What?" Charlotte blinked innocently.

"What's going on with you and Richard Swayne?"

He loves me, Charlotte wanted to say in a giddy outburst, as if that answer explained everything. What she felt for Richard was unlike anything she'd ever experienced before in her life. She couldn't wait to spend more time with him and Bailey.

"I don't know what you're talking about."

"Right," said Lexi. "I've never seen Richard flirt with another woman like what I've just seen. Not even with…"

Having your story read out loud as a teen by your brother in Julia Child's voice might scare some folks from ever sharing their work. But **Carolyn Hector** rose above her fear. She currently resides in Tallahassee, Florida, where there is never a dull moment. School functions, politics, football, Southern charm and sizzling heat help fuel her knack for putting a romantic spin on everything she comes across. Find out what she's up to on Twitter, @WriteOnCarolyn.

Books by Carolyn Hector

Harlequin Kimani Romance

The Magic of Mistletoe
The Bachelor and the Beauty Queen
His Southern Sweetheart
The Beauty and the CEO
A Tiara Under the Tree
Tempting the Beauty Queen
Southern Seduction
Falling for the Beauty Queen

Visit the Author Profile page
at Harlequin.com for more titles.

FALLING FOR
THE BEAUTY QUEEN

Carolyn Hector

I'd like to dedicate this book to Shirley McDonald…
best mom ever. I'm glad my bestie, Amy,
shares her with me.

Acknowledgments

To my husband, who keeps wowing me with his
parenting skills and keeps me sane. And once again,
I'd like to acknowledge my dad, Dr. Henry J. Hector,
because without him, I wouldn't know
what a great dad looked like growing up.

Dear Reader,

Welcome to Black Wolf Creek! This vacation destination, not far from Southwood, is the perfect spot for a runway coach to hide away from the rest of the world.

Meet Richard Swayne, a devoted former teen dad dedicated to raising his daughter as a single father. He is also the most unattainable bachelor in Southwood. All Richard wants to do is spend some quality time with his daughter before she heads off to college in the spring and leaves him with an empty nest. When his daughter learns there's a professional runway coach— *the* runway coach—vacationing right next door, their plans change.

I'm a reality show junkie hooked on Bravo, TLC and, of course, MTV. I've been watching *Teen Mom* since it was *16 and Pregnant*. I love the moms but also wonder about the dads. *Falling for the Beauty Queen* is my interpretation of a good dad.

All the best,

Carolyn

Chapter 1

I heard Idris Elba is single.

Charlotte Pendergrass's eyes left the road for a brief moment as the blue letters scrolled across the screen on the dashboard of her BMW. Just as the words began to register in her head, a long wayward branch, trailing down from the pine trees lining the windy gravel-and-red clay road, practically jumped out at her. A horrific screech came out of her mouth as branches almost scraped the passenger's side of the car. Charlotte gripped the fuzzy cream-colored steering wheel cover to keep the car steady and cursed, hitting the talk button just as the sender of her text called in on the phone.

"Girl," Charlotte gasped, "you almost made me wreck with your text."

She felt the lack of sincerity in the apology her cousin gave through the dashboard. Lexi Pendergrass Reyes laughed. "Don't do that, I haven't had a chance to hug your neck yet."

"I'm going to try," said Charlotte, trying not think about the damage she might have done to the car. "Seriously, Lexi, I swear no one has been up here since the '90s."

"You're exaggerating," replied Lexi. "The roads have been paved, at least."

A rock on the path scraped the bottom of the vehicle and jolted her in her camel-colored leather seat. The fall weather had stripped the trees of their leaves but not their dangerous branches, which slapped the windshield. A few more fake ghosts and some budding young horror actors and this would be the perfect spot for a spooky Halloween trail in a few days. "Are you sure about that?"

"It's been a few years since we brought the kids, but I'm pretty sure they paved the road from Magnolia Drive."

"You mean Gardenia Drive," Charlotte corrected. Silence from her cousin had Charlotte rethinking the directions. "You know what?"

"You went the wrong way?"

Nodding, Charlotte sighed. "Am I lost?"

"No, we used to get to the cabin through Gardenia, so you'll just come in on the other side of the house. We had that road closed because of the coyote dens, which reminds me—don't forget to lock up the garbage cans, Charlotte."

"I can't do that, Lexi," Charlotte said sweetly, "unless I get there."

"Just follow the path."

"Great," said Charlotte. She looked forward to the peace and quiet over the next few days. She needed a place to think about her life and what direction she needed to take now that her career as a pageant runway coach was over and her divorce from Denny O'Malley was finalized. The clincher was losing the company, CEO Runway—what she'd thought was cute and was short for Charlotte Elizabeth O'Malley—which now belonged to Denny. It didn't matter that it was her expertise as a former beauty queen that built the coaching company up from a college hobby to a world-renowned business. What an expensive way to learn to read the fine print. Charlotte planned on using this time away from the world to grieve her baby she'd raised from a small idea to a full-blown, successful agency.

"Anyway, did you like my flash fiction about Idris?" Lexi asked, clearly trying to avoid letting Charlotte slip back into the dark hole she'd been in since losing her studio. "It's a thing—make up a story in a few words."

"Damn." Charlotte shook her head. "You had to go with a fictional one?"

Lexi's chuckle crackled through the speakers. "Y'all will be on the same page one of these days. Besides, you don't want him to be the rebound guy right after your divorce."

Just because the ink had dried on the paperwork last week didn't mean Charlotte's marriage to Denny O'Malley had ended then. Thanks to his infidelity, they'd been separated for the last two years, but their lawyers hashing out their assets had prolonged things. Denny had moved on and was dating. Hell, he'd never stopped, even after they married. Charlotte kicked herself for having wasted so much time with Denny, believing he'd wanted to start a family with her when the time was right. When they'd finally officially split, Charlotte went out more often in hopes of finding the right man who shared her dreams of raising children together. There'd been a few dates, but most of them were frogs. The bar hadn't been set that high. She wanted someone who didn't humiliate her by cheating on her, someone who treated her with respect and, most of all, someone who wouldn't use her for her money or what material things she brought to the relationship. Charlotte was already past her self-appointed deadline at being a mother by thirty. She didn't want to wait another ten years.

"Hey, you still there?" Lexi asked over the sound of a finger snap. Now that could have been her cousin warning her three children before they got into trouble.

"I am," answered Charlotte. "I think I see the roof of the house up ahead."

"Oh, great. You're going to be amazed at how good you'll feel after a few days of solitude. You don't need everyone in your business."

Charlotte maneuvered her car to the side of the house. She had to use the restroom. "Speaking of privacy," she began, turning off the car, "you didn't tell my folks what's going on now, did you? I don't want to hear their we-warned-you-so's, at least not yet."

"What? You mean about you being in town or the divorce or the studio?"

"They know about the divorce," she said drily. "I believe they had celebratory sex over it." Charlotte paused to laugh at Lexi's *ew*. "They don't know I lost the company."

"I haven't said a word to anyone," Lexi swore.

The only people who knew about Charlotte losing her training studio were Denny, his lawyers, Charlotte's and Lexi. Rumors swirled in the pageant industry but there hadn't been a public announcement of the change. The only reason Lexi knew more details was because after consuming an entire bottle of wine after the hearing, Charlotte had broken down and called her cousin. Lexi was the only person who understood the importance of getting ready for a beauty pageant, which meant having the perfect walk. Charlotte had built her name and career as the most sought-after runway coach in the country. She readied ladies for Miss America, Miss Universe, Miss Sweetheart and, as of late, Miss World.

Now, due to not having paid enough attention to the paperwork she filled out while registering her business, Charlotte had lost everything to Denny O'Malley. When they'd left college, he'd put up the money for her trademark registration for her business. Blinded by love and determined to prove her disapproving parents wrong, Charlotte hadn't listened to anyone's advice and warnings about making sure her name was on the paperwork. And now here she stood outside her family's cabin thirty miles away from Southwood, in Black Wolf Creek, mourning the loss of her business, her baby. Loneliness seeped in. This place used to give her joy and now it saddened her with the painful reminder that she was truly alone.

Charlotte pushed her loss out of her mind and got out of the car. Her red-bottomed, stiletto heels sank into the dying grass and Georgia clay. When she'd run CEO, Charlotte had preached to girls about living in their heels, and she practiced what she preached. "Where's the key again?" she asked Lexi.

"Are you at the screen door?"

After climbing the four steps and crossing the wide, wraparound porch, Charlotte nodded, despite her cousin not being on FaceTime. Sweat beaded at the nape of her neck, and a swarm of gnats unnecessarily greeted her at the door. Charlotte swatted around her face. "Good Lord, I'm being attacked."

"Mosquitoes?"

"Gnats," Charlotte said with a frown.

"Blah. The key is on top of the door on the frame."

Not too original, Charlotte thought, but then again, nothing bad ever happened in Black Wolf Creek other than the occasional sightings of coyotes. Just to be careful, Charlotte cast a glance over her shoulder. Bright orange, red and yellow leaves flittered in the wind, proudly announcing the fall season. Rivulets of water bounced off the smooth rocks under the river's surface danced in the air. The trickling sound reminded her she needed to hurry up inside. Following the directions, Charlotte found the single key on a plastic triangle key ring and let herself in. Rays of sun broke through the window and exposed the flakes of dust floating like fairies. She sneezed.

Lexi laughed. "I'm guessing you're inside now. I'll let you go so you can settle in for the week. Don't forget that I expect you to come over for at least one Sunday dinner a month. And if you wait until the end of the month, I'll bring dinner to you. All of us."

Charlotte needed to reinvent herself. The new change meant moving away from home she shared with Denny in Mantoloking, New Jersey, when they weren't traveling during the year. She spent the summer packing her belongings and memories and made plans to set down roots in Southwood, Georgia. It was better than returning home to her parents in Peachville. Once the movers arrived with her furniture next week, she planned on staying at the condo Lexi still kept in downtown Southwood until she found something else. Lexi and her husband lived in the suburbs. They had room in their two-story home, but Charlotte didn't want her blues to bring them down.

As the cousins said their goodbyes on the phone, Charlotte ran back outside to get the three bags she'd brought with her. Once again mud caked her heels, which she stomped off at the butterfly welcome mat at the front door.

Inside the cabin a white sheet covered an L-shaped beige couch, which surrounded a square coffee table facing the stone fireplace, a chimney reaching the vaulted ceiling. Two full-length windows flanked the large glass French doors, which looked out over the porch onto the creek and the forest beyond. A set of wooden staircases led to the three bedrooms upstairs, where the kids used to sleep when they visited. Two master bedrooms were built under the loft. In hindsight, and a lot too late, Charlotte realized how her parents must have known when their children were still up and awake in the middle of the night. *This place was magical—still is*, she thought.

Old family photos in gold frames cluttered the oak table behind the couch. Her great-grandparents' faces greeted her, frozen smiles from the day they married as they cut their cake. There were also baby pictures of her and her cousins and now their own children. Without thinking, Charlotte pressed her hand against the flat of her stomach. Was she ever going to contribute her baby pictures to this growing collection? If things had gone the way she wanted, Charlotte would be here with her own children. Inhaling deeply, she shook the pain and irritation out of her mind.

One good thing about being the only adult in the cabin meant she'd graduated from the upstairs bedrooms. Charlotte looked forward for her first night in the king-size bed. She brought her suitcases into the bedroom, which appeared bigger than she remembered. What better way to celebrate than taking a nap? She opened the door with a sheepish grin. The long drive had done her in, and the emotions of the divorce had taken their toll on her. Sleep called her name.

But the sudden loud booming of music stopped any chance of rest.

Richard Swayne pulled his black pickup truck into the circular driveway of his family's cabin. Thankfully, turning off the engine stopped the obnoxious sound that his daughter considered music pouring out of his speakers. Since she liked it, though, he tolerated it. Out of curiosity, he observed his surroundings. Black Wolf Creek wasn't named that for nothing. Folklore claimed the cooler months brought out the creatures, though he'd never seen one in all the summers he'd come up here with his parents and sisters. He hoped bringing his daughter out here wouldn't be the occasion of the first sighting. The slam of the passenger's side door caught his attention.

The setting sun graced his beloved Bailey with a halo, resting above her mop of red hair, inherited from him, piled on top of her head. Pride swelled in his heart.

"Don't make being up here a big thing, Dad," Bailey said, ruining the moment with her nonchalant attitude.

In a few weeks, she'd be heading off to college— she'd already deferred once to go on a gap year to travel in the beauty pageant circuit around Georgia. After her mother left when Bailey was a year and a half, it had just been the two of them. Richard's sisters helped out as well as their parents, but Richard didn't want to have to lean on anyone for help. While his family understood, the ladies in his hometown of Southwood did not stop trying to offer their support. It had been a hard lesson to learn early on, but after a few bad relationships, Richard had eventually learned to keep his mind closed to the idea of a healthy one. Richard realized most women were interested in his legacy at Swayne Pecans rather than being a part of a ready-made family. And that was fine with him. He and Bailey got along without help from anyone else.

"You want me to act like you're not leaving your dear old dad soon?" Wounded, Richard clutched his heart and pretended to sway.

The reaction he received was classic Bailey—an eye roll. "What was that I heard you say to Aunt Kenzie's brother-in-law? One and done?" Bailey returned the dramatic heartache and took a few unsteady steps. "I bet you're turning my room into a man space."

"It's called a man cave, thank you very much," Richard teased. "C'mon, let's get inside and start our daddy-daughter bonding time."

Bailey sighed, but at least she came around to the front of the house. Both of them stopped before the first step onto the porch. Last week's rain had uprooted the grass he'd planted the previous summer. He wanted the next week to be about them spending quality time together rather than putting the house back together again. Once she was out of the house, Richard didn't know what he was going to do. It had been just the two of them for just about her entire life. Bailey was his world. Work would keep him busy during the day but what would he do in the evening if he was not helping her with her homework, listening to the highs and lows of her day or staring at the front door, waiting for her to come in by curfew? The idea of dating and filling the house with someone else's voice didn't sound appealing right now. Which was why he needed to make the most of their time now.

Filled with excitement, Richard took one giant step and rushed the door. The screen door welcomed them with a squeak. Bailey responded with another one of her epic eye rolls.

"This place is so old, Dad."

"It's rustic," he corrected her. "Don't you remember coming here as a little girl?"

"No," Bailey answered, "but I do remember Aunt

Maggie saying she'd come here to unplug from the world. Is that true?"

Richard opened the lock on the wooden door and gave it a shove with his shoulder. "What scares you more, being out here in the wild without Wi-Fi?"

Her eyes widened. "Seriously, there's no Wi-Fi?" Bailey began to wave her phone in the air. "Where's the nearest cell tower?"

"Don't worry," Richard laughed, "Aunt Maggie could never live without being connected to the internet one way or another." The truth about the internet clearly pleased his daughter. Bailey's sigh of relief came through loud and clear. Richard laughed to himself and led them into through the entrance.

While every Swayne in the generations before Richard's worked with the family farm in some form or fashion, his sisters had managed to bypass getting dirty on occasion. Richard carried on the family tradition. Maggie loved being in the spotlight, becoming an internet sensation, while their youngest sister, Mackenzie, took to recording Southwood history. Both girls kept up the tradition of being beauty queens, Kenzie a bit longer, and they'd talked Bailey into trying out for the Miss Southwood Beauty Pageant last year.

When Richard was younger, his father had fitted a floor-to-ceiling glass wall on two sides of the great room, allowing sunlight to enter and minimizing the use of electricity. The afternoon light spilled over the rosewood table. When he told his sisters his plans to come here with Bailey, they'd sent over a cleaning crew to touch up the place ahead of time. A crisp, lemon-fresh scent came off the black countertops in the kitchen and filled the air.

As he'd expected, Bailey's memories eventually came back to her. She tossed her purse on the dark brown leather couch and headed up the stairs. "I call the loft," she said. The stairs leading to the second story were off to the left, through the great room.

It was fine with him. Richard looked forward to waking up in the master bedroom in time to watch the sun rise off the tops of the points of the pine trees. While Bailey connected with her friends on her cell phone, Richard went on to get the rest of their belongings. Their plan was to stay for at least a week, although Richard had brought enough food for two. Since it was fall, the water was too cool for a swim, but they could fish out on the lake.

When Richard had put the last of the groceries away, he headed down toward the concrete landing where he and his father, Mitchell, had installed a stone grill when he was fifteen. A small fire pit, surrounded by five beach chairs, sat empty. This was where he'd had reunions with the Swaynes and his mother's family, the Hairstons. Richard remembered being a teen and waiting for his dad to finish grilling while he, his siblings and their cousins dried off in the sun and how they transitioned from eating outside by the pit to making s'mores. A few years after that, Richard went from being a preteen waterskiing on the lake to becoming a teenaged father. He and his then girlfriend, Octavia, had been surprised to find themselves expecting a child at sixteen. The timing was off, but Richard had been ready for the challenge. He'd looked forward to raising a child and having someone depend on him. Richard still lived for the moments to make Bailey proud to have him as a father. Needless to say, their parents were disappointed with them. Mitchell insisted Richard attend college and work. He did. It wasn't easy, but he spent his freshman year working to send money to Octavia, who allegedly stayed home with her parents and took care of Bailey. It had been hugs from Bailey that got him through the semesters. The pictures of her sleeping in her crib or holding a sign each month to mark her growth made him set aside all things most kids his age did.

Richard picked up the stray branches scattered around the pit, broke them in half and tossed them into the pit as he thought about Octavia and how she'd changed their plans. It still burned him up inside with anger at the way she'd betrayed him. While Richard worked hard and studied harder, Octavia had made plans for her future with one of Southwood's privileged elites. Richard was okay with Octavia's plans to break up with him to date other guys, but the fact she no longer wanted to be a mother to Bailey angered him. Money, immediate money, meant more to Octavia than her own child. It had broken his heart, listening to Bailey cry at night for her mother. His fierce love and protection of his daughter made him vow early on to never let another person hurt her. Richard's parents stepped in and took care of Bailey until Richard graduated with his MS in agribusiness. Since then, he'd put his degree to use, boosting the company to a nationally competitive level, which resulted in wealth that would transcend Swayne Pecans for generations. Octavia recognized her mistakes far too late to come back into their lives. She'd shown her gold-digging cards early on.

Richard crunched the twigs in his hands, the sound sending a flock of birds fleeing from their nests. From the windows of the loft, Richard could hear the music start up again. He shook his head and chuckled. It wouldn't be the first time he'd have to bang on an eighteen-year-old's door and tell them to turn down the radio.

Higher education was a key to Richard's success. His parents insisted on him going forward with his MA. He'd wanted to take Bailey with him but would not have been able to study, work and care for his daughter like she needed. He reluctantly let them take care of her during the week while he worked and went to school. One of the jobs Richard took when he started his master's program was as a resident assistant of Gillum Hall. The dormitory had been named after Tallahassee's youngest city commissioner, who was not only a gubernatorial candidate but a fellow alum of Florida A&M. He'd been able to save money on an apartment by living in the dorms. Though he'd hadn't been much older than members of the seventeen- and eighteen-year-old incoming freshmen class, Richard used the skills he'd developed as an older brother to maintain his authority.

Just as Richard turned to go up the stairs to head back to the cabin, he caught the scent of freshly baked cookies. He sniffed the air. Someone was in the Pendergrass house. Since he hadn't seen any kids at the lake, he didn't think Lexi Pendergrass Reyes was here. That meant Lexie's older sister, Lisbeth, might be visiting.

Richard didn't look forward to running into her

again. She, like many of the women he'd met in his life, had seen Richard as a meal ticket. Like the Swaynes, the Pendergrasses had strong ties to Southwood's early beginnings. Lisbeth had felt they belonged together because of their similar financial backgrounds. Most people found Lisbeth a darling. Richard did not. After the breakup from Octavia, Lisbeth came around again, hinting at her unhappiness in her marriage. Richard had realized after a few weeks of talking to Lisbeth that she was not the one, especially when she suggested he make future plans send Bailey to boarding school with her daughter, Jolene, who was a few year older. He'd run into Lisbeth last summer, and she'd again made her intentions known. The whole town had buzzed after Bailey graduated. Women he'd put off with the reasons of focusing on Bailey had come out the woodwork to offer comfort in anticipation of his empty nest. Lisbeth was no different.

Anger consumed him at the thought that Lisbeth or whoever would come up here and intrude on his time with Bailey. Richard dropped the rest of the wood down into the pit, then wiped his hands on the back of his jeans.

His tan Timberlands stomped the bit of grass between the two homes. The Pendergrass house sat west of the Swaynes'. A rumbling creek acted as a fence between the two structures. In one long stride, he crossed the water and stormed to the front door. He wasn't sure what he'd say, but he was surely going to make sure the Pendergrasses stayed the hell away from them this week. With a heavy hand, Richard banged on the door frame, rattling it on its hinges.

The door flew open with a quick yank. Richard stared at outrageously high leopard-print heels, then moved up the shapely golden thighs, barely covered by a red romper. The outfit tapered at the waist and opened at the neck, giving a peek at the firm breasts beneath. A gold necklace circled a slender neck. When he looked into the woman's face, a surprised feeling slammed against his chest. He'd expected to find a Pendergrass on the other side of the door. Just not this one.

"Charlotte?"

Five minutes ago, Charlotte had found herself spying out her bedroom at the cabin next door to hers. She was woman enough to admit she'd been ogling the hottie in the fitted jeans, boots and skintight long-sleeve white shirt. Had she realized it was her former RA at Florida A&M University, though, she might not have looked so hard.

A hurricane had flooded the boys' dorm the summer before Charlotte's freshman year, and so the school had scrambled to create living spaces for everyone. Richard Swayne had been the RA in the new coed dorm and kept law and order. All the girls on her floor had a crush on him. Not like she blamed him. Richard's reddish-brown hair, green eyes and six-foot-five height caught everyone's attention. Time had only made him finer.

"Richard Swayne, really?"

Richard took a step backward and crossed his muscular arms over his chest. "Well, damn," he sighed.

The last time Charlotte had remembered having a heart-to-heart talk with him was when he called her into his office and tried to talk her out of leaving college. How dumb had she been back then?

"So, you *are* a Swayne," Charlotte had said the first time she asked him if he belonged to the famous family in Southwood. The red hair was a dead giveaway, but Richard had kept her at bay back then. But it wasn't their first encounter that stuck with her most. The painful memory of their last interaction came back so clearly. No one had ever rejected her with such a disappointed look before. Richard had been the first person she admitted to about leaving school when he called her into his office to confront her about the rumors. When he'd brought her into his office to try to talk her out of dropping out, she'd rebelled against him and his examples of instances when Denny scammed other students. Her friends and roommates had tried to point out Denny's wandering eye. She'd rebelled against everyone, determined to prove to the world that her then boyfriend, Denny O'Malley, was not the evil mastermind everyone thought he was. Pushing the memories aside, she inhaled deeply and fought against the heated shame threatening to attack her cheeks.

"I never said I wasn't from the Swayne family," Richard said now. "I just didn't appreciate the way you looked down on me for coming from a farming family."

Gaping, Charlotte clutched her chest in genuine surprise. "I think we're remembering things different."

"No, we aren't," he replied with the same dismissive look on his handsome face.

"Correct me if I'm wrong," Charlotte began, "but you were the one who approached me after that three-on-three basketball game."

"The one where *you* were giving *me* the look?" Richard raised his left brow. "The one where only everyone twenty-one and over was allowed to attend?"

Like an age limit was going to stop me back then, she thought with a devilish chuckle. Charlotte had used her cousin's ID in order to get into the club. She didn't attend just to drink; Charlotte had always desired to be in the know on everything. Freshmen her age were limited to what they could do. Everyone twenty-one and older looked like they had more fun. She didn't want to be left out.

The first time Richard recalled them meeting might not have the first time Charlotte did. She'd been on campus two weeks before school started and stayed at the apartment Lexi kept for business purposes. Since Charlotte had helped out Lexi with runway coaching even back then, she felt entitled to stay there and help herself to Lexi's things, including an old ID.

At the game, Richard had caught everyone's eye. He was talented on the court and aloof with the ladies—and that only made them want him more. If only they could see him now. Charlotte shivered and focused on the man before her.

"We're not going to rehash old stuff." Charlotte waved him off with the flick of her wrist. "Tell me what you're doing at my door."

"I thought…" He paused then shrugged his shoulders. "I thought I smelled someone cooking up here."

"This isn't Gillum Hall, Richard," teased Charlotte. "We're allowed to have hot plates here."

"You're funny," said Richard, "but try not to burn the forest down."

"As long as you keep your booming music down, we'll be just fine." Charlotte crossed her arms over her chest. The longer she stared at him, the more reasons she needed to come up with to keep this man at bay. A little cabin tryst sounded great. She could easily imagine her legs wrapped around his tapered waist or running her fingers through his silky-looking beard. Charlotte tightened her fists and crammed them under her arms.

"I'm not sure how long you guys plan on being here." Richard cocked his head to the side and looked beyond her and the doorway.

Charlotte let out a laugh. "Oh, you think I'm here with someone?"

"The last time we spoke, Charlotte, you were turning in your key and leaving school to marry Denny O'Malley."

Charlotte tossed her head so her hair was off her shoulders. Richard and Denny had been fraternity brothers, but even Richard had spoken out against Denny. Charlotte should have learned her lesson then. "Yeah, well, we're history."

"Sorry to hear that," Richard replied. She felt the sincerity in his deep green eyes.

Charlotte blinked and looked away. "It's really okay. And I'll be here for maybe two weeks."

"Let me guess," said Richard before the silence between them could become awkward, "you're here to get over a broken heart. There's no better place than the lake at Black Wolf Creek."

"Not quite the broken heart like you think." Charlotte laughed and said, "I used to come here when I was a kid."

"Me, too," Richard said, leaning against the railing of the porch. "Maybe we just missed each other."

Boy, did we ever, she thought. "I'm here for the peace and quiet." Charlotte nodded in the direction of his cabin, where the music boomed—just as her smoke detector suddenly decided to go off.

"Sorry about that," Richard said through a grin. "I'll take care of the noise on my end if you do the same here."

"My dinner!" Charlotte exclaimed as she realized she'd forgotten about her food. She spun around and headed into the kitchen as thick, gray smoke billowed from the oven. Thinking quickly, she grabbed the oven mitts from the table and pulled the tray out. "Not too bad," she said out loud. *Had I not been spying out the window*, she thought, grimacing. Thankfully there was more cookie dough left in the tube she'd found in the freezer. Charlotte had remembered to bring all her heels but not to stop and pick up food for tonight.

"Your dinner cannot be cookies from a tube."

Though she'd left Richard on the porch, she hadn't expected him to follow her inside. He moved to open the lock on top of the French doors to air out the downstairs. *My hero*, she thought for a second and then remembered this was partially his fault for distracting her. Charlotte fanned the tray of burned cookies.

"Dessert first," Charlotte quipped.

"I insist you come over for dinner."

"I don't need—" The moment she opened her mouth,

Charlotte's stomach growled loud enough to drown out her stubbornness.

Judging from the grin across Richard's face, he'd heard it, too. "I'm firing up the grill at six—dinner's at seven. We'll see you then."

We? Before she got the chance to ask, Richard disappeared in the smoke, fleeing the cabin. Her stomach protested once more. Great. Now she was going to spend the evening with Richard and whoever his girlfriend was. Oh well—it wasn't like she had any pride left.

Chapter 2

Richard wasn't sure what he was doing on the internet, but he found himself at the Facebook search page for Charlotte Pendergrass. There were twenty-one Charlotte Pendergrasses out there. Half of them had posted a cartoon character for a profile picture, and another looked close to Bailey's age. Richard scrolled farther down on the See All selection where the Charlotte Pendergrass without a photo stated she was "In a Relationship with the Air-Conditioning." He smiled to himself, recalling the one day when the power had gone out in the residence hall and Charlotte had been the most vocal in complaints. Even this afternoon, he had thoroughly felt the arctic air coming from her opened door.

Richard clicked on the profile again. Most of the comments and posts were from friends. There was one image of Charlotte at a dinner with a group. He inhaled deeply at the sight of her in a little black dress and a pair of spiked heels—as he began to realize was her signature. He sank into the overstuffed chair, balanced the laptop on his knees and sat back farther to view Charlotte's stunning beauty.

"Ew, gross, Dad," Bailey squealed when she bounced down the stairs into the living room and saw her father. She'd made her first outfit change of their vacation. Tonight's attire consisted of a pair of dark jeans, a white T-shirt and a flannel shirt wrapped around her waist in case the temperature dropped later while they ate by the fire.

"What did I do this time?"

"I don't want to know what's causing such a smile on your face," Bailey said with a sigh, "but you need to take that into your bedroom."

Richard shut the laptop tight. "I'm going to curb the amount of time you spend with Aunt Maggie."

"I'm an adult now, Dad," replied Bailey. "You can't tell me what to do." Bailey followed up her comment with a giggle.

Richard shook his head and laughed as well. He didn't have to order Bailey around. Even though he worried about her going off to school, deep down she was a good kid. Richard set the laptop on the coffee table, then tailed Bailey into the kitchen.

"There are three steaks." Bailey pointed to the marinated meat in the glass dish by the stove. "Are we having company? Because you know you do not need to eat two of these Fred Flintstone steaks."

Richard barely heard her. The smell of old charcoal filled his nostrils as he covered his face with his hands. After leaving the Pendergrass cabin, Richard had cleaned off the grill in order to prepare for dinner tonight. He didn't know why, but he wanted things to go perfectly. Maybe the discovery of Charlotte's pain concerned him. Denny and Richard had pledged the same year. They were supposed to be brothers, but truthfully, Richard had never cared for him. The man was boisterous and reckless. Anytime Denny threw a party, the police came, which diminished the reputation of the fraternity.

When Richard first met Charlotte, they'd hit it off—until he mentioned he'd worked the summer as a farmer. A chill ran down his spine with the memory of the frosty greeting. The way she turned her nose up so quickly at him, it was no wonder how she ended up with a man like Denny, who had money to spare. Most of the college women he came across were like Charlotte and completely uninterested in a farmer. She saw the potential of that man rather than the dirty one in front of her. Or at least she had. *Who knew now?* It wasn't until later when he connected her last name with the Pendergrasses of his town he realized why she'd been drawn to Denny. She came from a banking family. Denny flashed a lot of money around. At that point, Richard had started working at the coed dorms and learned Charlotte, as his resident, was hands off in more ways than one.

The refrigerator slammed shut, breaking Richard from his trance. Bailey faced him with her hands on her hips. "Are you even listening to me?"

"Sorry," Richard answered with honesty.

Bailey raised her right brow at him. "You seem distracted. Is it over whoever getting the third steak?" Not sure how to answer, Richard blinked a few times, which evoked a groan from Bailey. "Dear God, don't tell me you're becoming one of *those* men."

"You'll have to refresh my memory on what 'those men' means," said Richard, using air quotes over her term. "And then you can follow it up with how you know one of these men."

"I'm talking about the secretive kind who don't answer questions flat out and avoid the topic."

In jest, Richard cast a glance out the window over his shoulder to where the red coals glowed in the evening light. "Oh look, it's time to put on the steaks. Honey, will you make a salad?"

"Daddy." Bailey stomped her foot in a joking protest, then grinned, her large eyes becoming saucer sized.

Chuckling, Richard shook his head. "It turns out we have a neighbor, and I invited her—"

"Her?" Bailey chirped up.

"—over for dinner." Richard folded his arms across his chest. "Are you okay with that?"

With a shrug, Bailey opened the fridge again and took out the romaine lettuce they'd brought. "I don't mind at all. The more, the merrier."

He couldn't help but wonder if she meant the more she didn't have to share her with him. Richard reminded himself they were here to spend time together. Quality father-daughter bonding. That's why they were here, right? Richard's eyes averted from Bailey and toward the path leading to the Pendergrass cabin.

"Do I know this mystery guest?"

"I doubt it," Richard said, turning back to his daughter. "She's from Peachville, not Southwood." Then he thought about his answer and scratched his chin.

Bailey's brows cocked upward with curiosity. "So, you *know* her, know her?"

Before his daughter's mind went into overdrive, Richard waved his hands in surrender. "Don't."

"What?" Bailey asked, tacking on an innocent high pitch at the end of her question. "Who is over there? Lexi? Kimber? No, Kimber's still at school. I'm intrigued. Is this mystery relative Lexi's sister? What was her name?"

"Lisbeth," he answered flatly, "and no, it is not her. Now before your head explodes, wash off a few cherry tomatoes."

"Okay, okay." Bailey went on as if ready to drop the conversation, but Richard knew his daughter like the back of his hand. She wouldn't let it go. Where most girls attended tea parties, dance recitals and other such things with their mothers, Bailey had gone with her aunts or her grandmother, and never complained or compared herself to her friends. What she did do often was try to set him up with the single mothers of her friends. She'd never focused on having a mother for herself. In fact, Bailey had adjusted fine to not having one around. Richard always made sure to stay attentive to his daughter, taking her to movies, trips or shopping sprees, especially when Octavia came in to town.

"Don't get any crazy ideas," said Richard, stamping down the matchmaking excitement he spotted churning in her light hazel eyes. "We're just being neighborly."

Bailey began opening and closing the cabinets before she found what she was looking for—a large bowl.

Richard turned to gaze out the window, where the steps led beyond the pit to the river's edge. A few years ago, he and his dad had placed a cement bench by the water, where they could sit and fish. His eyes followed the drizzling creek toward the Pendergrass house again.

He wondered what Charlotte was doing right now. Was she going through her outfits, trying to find what to wear to dinner? Judging from all the pictures he went through, she'd more than likely a pair of heels would be a part of her ensemble. Who wore heels around here? *Charlotte*, Richard answered himself with a grin.

Charlotte's heels clicked on the wooden floors and echoed off the high vaulted ceilings as she paced through her cabin. She stopped several times at the screen of her opened laptop on the kitchen counter. The face of her former best friend, Mitzi Cabrera, cluttered the homepage of her former business. The one Denny had stolen from her.

After Denny gained the company in the divorce, Charlotte had wondered what he planned on doing with it. It wasn't like he would teach budding pageant queens to strut the catwalk. He liked the travel, parties, glitz and red-carpet treatment, but he'd hated the long hours Charlotte spent with each beauty queen. When push came to shove, Denny wouldn't be able to do her job. But Mitzi could. Charlotte's onetime best friend had represented CEO from coast to coast while Charlotte was abroad at one of the big four pageants. Since the divorce, Mitzi had kept up working with the local clients, keeping them happy—and satisfying Denny as well.

Charlotte shrugged her shoulders and pivoted in the

kitchen. She didn't want the man. She wanted her business back. But as stated in their divorce decree, Denny had paid for everything at the beginning. He'd started the company with Charlotte as the face and name. But it was Charlotte's sweat and tears that kept the customers coming. If only she hadn't blindly followed Denny and his advice. How foolish had she been to believe they were in this together? Denny had carved himself a safety net in case the marriage failed. It wasn't just the infidelities that broke the proverbial camel's back. It was the fact enough rumors had spread about Denny getting another woman pregnant. Charlotte then came to her senses, realizing he put their lives in jeopardy without protecting himself. She'd learned the hard way to value herself over a man.

The heel of Charlotte's stiletto snagged on a piece of raised wood, nearly causing her to slip. Instead of falling, Charlotte caught herself, but a painful twinge raced down her back in the process. The pain reminded her of her rapidly increasing age. Soon she'd be thirty, divorced, with no children in sight.

A shrill of laughter cracked through the silence. Charlotte snapped out of her pity party and shook her head. She'd forgotten that Richard had invited her to dinner. Somehow a chipper evening with him and his company no longer appealed to her, regardless of her rumbling stomach. She hasn't meant to spend this time away hiding and stewing over the loss of CEO, but this Mitzi news—that she'd stayed with the company—was brutal. Betrayal called for a tub of chocolate chip frosting and submergence into a romance book courtesy of The Cupcakery and the latest Brenda Jackson novel.

A whining howl coursed through the heavy pipes in the bathroom when Charlotte turned the brass handles. She half expected to see liquid rust pouring from the waterfall showerhead. Lexi had mentioned something in an email about the cabin's need for a makeover. As long as the air-conditioning worked, Charlotte was fine. Charlotte did not plan on being here forever, just long enough to figure her next business move, since she no longer owned CEO Runway.

Accompanied by a mound of bubbles, Charlotte sank into the tub once the water rose to the right height. Her mind started to wander. This had to be the first time she'd ever stayed here alone. Lisbeth used to beg their parents to let her spend the weekend alone in the cabin, but her parents never went for it. They always invited Charlotte to come along, sure she would tattle. The parties never happened. Charlotte had been too scared to stay in the room upstairs by herself.

Funny how she wasn't frightened now, especially with Richard, ever the resident assistant, next door; Charlotte knew if a serious problem arrived, she could count on him. A growl rumbled in her stomach. She could be at his place eating whatever that delicious scent was wafting through the window of her bedroom into her house from his grill. But hunger was not a reason to head over there…regardless of the way his perfectly white and straight teeth had bitten down on the side of his bottom lip when he looked at her. Charlotte sank farther into the bubbles and tried to push Richard out of her mind. He was here with a guest.

After a long soak and four straight chapters, Charlotte dried off and changed into a pair of purple silk pajama bottoms and a cotton camisole to curl up in a chair front of the bare fireplace downstairs. The bright yellow glow of the rising moon reflected off the rippling creek. Fortunately, with the way the trees lined between the properties, Charlotte still had her privacy. If she'd wanted to traipse around naked, she could, but why tempt things, knowing someone occupied the cabin next door? Richard Swayne.

A slow smile spread across her face as she imagined herself walking across the living room in front of the floor-to-ceiling windows, bare naked, at the precise moment Richard waded through the river waters for some night fishing. Combined with the desire to tease him and the heavy romance in her book, Charlotte was feeling a little on the naughty side. Richard still looked good as hell. But she remembered one important fact.

"Idris Elba might be single," Charlotte said to herself as she changed lounging positions to let her long legs dangle on the other side of the arm of the chair, "but Richard isn't."

Before closing her book again, Charlotte pulled out the white envelope with the word *options* written on the front. She'd stuffed it with future ideas for herself before she left New Jersey. Her options in life. Inside she had a few brochures on dating after divorce, how to fall in love, adoption and then in-vitro fertilization. All items ended with an important goal: *To have a baby.*

Ever since she could remember, Charlotte had wanted to be a mother. Sure, pageantry and coaching took over her life but she felt destined to raise a child of her own. Charlotte admired her mother and in some ways she wanted to be like her, but with more children. The more, the merrier. Denny had known this when they married but laughed every time she said she wanted a house full of kids. She guessed he didn't take her seriously enough. Charlotte's arms ached with emptiness whenever she saw a mother with her new-born. Traveling the world and helping budding beauty queens helped fill a void, but not enough. There was no one to come home to at night.

Charlotte pulled herself out of the comfy chair, set envelope next to the book on the coffee table and grabbed the tub of frosting before heading into the kitchen. She dipped her index finger into the fluffy goodness and snagged a chocolate chip. Just as she filled her mouth with a scoop, someone knocked at the door. Still not alarmed, Charlotte shuffled to answer it. The motion sensor indicated her visitor, and her heart leaped into her chest as she opened the door.

"Richard," Charlotte mumbled through a mouthful of frosting. She stuck her finger in her mouth to clean off the sweetness, which took a few moments longer than expected. Richard's well-developed biceps flexed as he held a foil package in his large hands. "What are you doing here?"

"You were missed at dinner," Richard began before his eyes narrowed on tub of frosting in her hand. "Are you eating frosting as a meal?"

"That I am," Charlotte answered. "What are you doing here away from your company?" She prayed the sudden burst of jealousy did not reveal in her tone or her face.

"Company, as in my daughter?"

Again, Charlotte hoped her face did not give away

her feeling of relief. Of course he'd be here with his daughter. As far back as she could remember, Richard had been a devoted dad. All the girls on her floor had thought it was sweet, the way he worked so hard to send money home back to his family. It dawned on her he'd mentioned only the daughter. Charlotte's eyes scanned his left hand.

"I'm sorry," said Charlotte with a curt nod. "I didn't mean to stand you up."

"It's fine. I get you came out here to get away."

How much did he know? Was he going to be a part of the pack of friends and family wanted to remind her of the fact they'd warned Charlotte about Denny? Last year, when Charlotte had announced her divorce, Charlotte's parents, Iris and Arthur Pendergrass, had made it a point to pull out an old letter they wrote together on the day Charlotte and Denny eloped but had never mailed. They'd mended their relationship over the years, but Charlotte knew Iris would go ballistic over the news of her lost company.

"We came out here to get some peace and quiet, too," Richard went on.

"I could hear," she said, nodding. "Was that Lil Wayne I heard?"

Richard chuckled. "Drake, to be exact."

"It's all noise to me." Charlotte shrugged. Her stomach growled in an embarrassing fashion just as his laughter died down.

"Sorry," said Richard. "I came over here to bring you the dinner you missed this evening." With that, he pushed the plate into Charlotte's outstretched hands while she felt the heat of her blush burning her cheeks.

Richard noticed. "Don't be 'shamed," he teased. "My meat has been known to make mouths water."

Charlotte widened her eyes as if she hadn't heard him right. Instead of the apologetic grin she expected her former RA to give, Richard stood there with a cocky lopsided grin and a twinkle in his green eyes.

"Well, all right, then," Charlotte responded, fanning her face with her free hand as she turned from the door and took the plate from his hands. Steam piped out from beneath a corner of the foil. Immediately her stomach begged for a taste. The sexy nature of his remark didn't dawn on her until she left Richard at the entrance and she heard the door close, with him inside. His flirtatious words replayed in her head. What were all the reasons why she couldn't seduce him? Because he wasn't single? "Can I offer you anything to eat?" Charlotte asked.

"Like frosting?"

"It's from The Cupcakery." Charlotte grabbed a spoon and fork from the drawer in the kitchen's island and set them on the wooden top next to the three containers. Charlotte had chocolate, chocolate chip and peanut butter cream frostings with her.

No one could resist a morsel from Southwood's infamous bakery. The seasonal cupcakes were known to bring people together. Some folks flew in for the summer for their lemon or peach cupcakes, while others lingered longer over the holidays for their double chocolate cupcakes rimmed with crushed candy canes and their decadent white champagne cupcakes to ring in the New Year. In lieu of flowers, some men knew the best way to make up with a woman was to send an arrangement of the tasty treats. Charlotte didn't mind traveling down County Road 17 for an extra twenty minutes from Peachville just for the flavor of the month. This month the featured cupcake was pumpkin. Charlotte was sure she was the only person left on earth who didn't crave the root vegetable like the rest of the world.

"Well, if it's from The Cupcakery." Richard followed Charlotte into the kitchen. She stood on one side of the island bar across from him. Richard picked up the one of the containers she'd left out and chose chocolate. "This wasn't your dinner?"

Giving him a half shrug and head nod after debating for a few seconds how to answer his question, Charlotte sighed. "I planned on making a sandwich, but I burned the cookies."

"A cookie sandwich is not a proper meal," said Richard.

"We aren't in the dorms anymore, Richard," Charlotte reminded him as she opened the wrapped plate. A juicy steak, string beans sprinkled with pepper and a fluffy potato slathered in sour cream and butter greeted her. Charlotte's mouth watered. "Dear Lord, I've died and gone to heaven."

"Not heaven, just the common sense of a well-balanced meal."

"Proteins and veggies," Charlotte noted. "And for a treat, carbs. I shouldn't, but I am." She scooped up a bite of the potato.

"Said the woman who was about to eat a cookie sandwich for dinner."

"I planned on having milk with it."

"Really?"

"No," Charlotte confessed with a laugh.

Richard grinned and opened the container of frosting. "This is going to cost me a couple of extra miles."

"Are you still running?" Charlotte grabbed a knife and cut into the perfect medium-rare steak.

Patting his flat abs, Richard nodded.

"My room had the best view of the track. When all the girls on the floor wanted to watch you, guess where they came?" Charlotte watched with a tight smile the way Richard tried not to blush. How modest of him. He gave his head a quick shake.

"Whatever."

"Aw, that's so cute," cooed Charlotte. "You had no idea how everyone wanted the hot dad."

"Yeah, let's change the subject," said Richard. He nodded toward something behind her. "Is that the reason you didn't come over for dinner?"

Charlotte followed his glance. The screen was open to an internet article about Mitzi and Denny's new business. It was a photograph of Mitzi seated at the desk Charlotte had picked out, with her long legs draped over the side. The headline stood out in bold letters.

"'There's a new CEO in town,'" Richard read aloud. "Weren't you the *C* in CEO?"

"According to Denny's lawyers, that *C*, *E* and *O* are up for interpretation." Charlotte pushed the plate away from herself. "I was too stupid to investigate."

"Hey," Richard began, reaching across the space between them and covered her hand with his. "Denny is a slick one."

"Said the man who introduced us," Charlotte blurted out with a double eye roll. One was for the mention of Denny being slick, and the other was for herself. This wasn't Richard's fault. "Sorry, I'm still a bit angry about the article."

"It's okay." Richard brushed off her snark and went on. "You came to school as a beauty queen and sprinkled your good-luck glitter on everything. I can recall all the work you did at the step shows on campus and with the modeling troupes, and I read up on you this afternoon. When you left school, you took that experience and made a powerhouse. You've worked hard creating a brand."

The walk down memory lane made Charlotte's heart flutter. She wiggled her brows. "You did your research on me?"

Richard shrugged his broad shoulders. "Why not? I needed to have something to talk about with you over dinner, had you shown up."

"Sorry." Charlotte glanced down.

"It's excused this time, but you won't have any excuses tomorrow."

The flutter in Charlotte's heart traveled down to her stomach. "We're having dinner now." She pulled the plate closer and cut a piece of meat.

"I'm having dessert," Richard clarified. "And for the record, I didn't push Denny on you like you think."

Straightening, Charlotte tapped her chin. "You grabbed him by the arm as he walked by after we'd been eye flirting all afternoon and finally got the chance to talk."

The return of the dazzling smile was followed by the raise of Richard's index finger. "Let's go back that moment."

"We don't have to," Charlotte said, jutting out her chin.

"First of all, you represented yourself as older than what you were," Richard began. "You weren't twenty-one."

Humiliation set in once again at the memory of the talk Richard gave her once he discovered she was underage and living in his dorm. "We don't need to rehash that."

"Okay, the only reason I introduced you to Denny was because of the way you acted when you found out I was a farmer from Southwood. I thought you were like the rest of the ladies I met, you know, dismissive of me for farming over the summer. If I could take it back, I would."

Charlotte narrowed her eyes. "You know, you mentioned that earlier, and I've come to an important conclusion."

"Oh yeah?" Richard said, holding back a grin while his eyes crinkled at the corners. A few gray hairs at his temple, ones she hadn't noticed earlier, popped out under the kitchen light. Because her marriage had ended so long ago, Charlotte had been able to go through the emotions to prepare her to move on, even going through a few bad dates. Richard might be the only man to ignite a passion in her blood since Denny.

"You're losing your memory in your old age. If I frowned, it was because you were from Southwood, where my cousins lived, and they would have told you I was eighteen."

"And yet once you moved into the dorms, I found out." Richard tilted his head to the side. "I think you look like you."

"Thanks," she said, beaming, then inquired, "So, you know my cousin Lisbeth?" She raised a brow.

As if to avoid answering, Richard scooped some frosting in his mouth. Tight-lipped as well, Charlotte shook her head. Nothing had ever happened between herself and Richard, but when it came to her cousin, a sudden surge of possessiveness toward him came over Charlotte. It would be just like Lisbeth to make a move on Richard. Besides being in her age range, he was good-looking, and she was a sucker for a pretty face. Charlotte had her answer. There'd been an age difference between Charlotte and Richard, and a five-year age difference between her and Lisbeth. Charlotte being younger than him now didn't seem such a big deal as it had been when she was a freshman.

"What is your next move for your company?"

Charlotte half shook her head and focused on his question. "I'm sorry, what?"

"Well—" Richard pointed his index finger at the monitor "—you're not going to take that lying down, are you?"

"Denny received the company unfair and square," Charlotte explained, "so there isn't much I can do."

Richard stepped back and leaned against the opposite counter. "Correct me if I'm wrong, but isn't your cousin a talent scout or something?"

"Pageant coach," she answered, puffing out her chest. "She inspired me to coach runway."

"And my sister runs the Southern Style Glitz Pageant. Small pageant world, isn't it?"

The news of Maggie becoming the new host and president of the prestigious event had spread like wildfire, thanks to the *Pageant Press Gazette*. Kenzie, Richard's younger sister, ran in the same pageant circles as Charlotte. It broke Charlotte's heart to not be able to

RSVP to Kenzie's wedding last summer, but she'd been in Vegas, helping over fifty women perfect their runway walks for the judges at the Miss Universe pageant.

"I'm hanging up my stilettos," Charlotte sighed.

Richard cocked his head to the side again. She'd swear he licked his lips as his green eyes trailed down her legs and landed on her fuzzy upper part of her heels. "Retired, huh? Those shoes say something different."

"Old habits die hard." Charlotte shrugged her shoulders. "I saw a sign at the bait and tackle shop. They need help."

Chuckling, Richard folded his arms across his chest. "I would pay to see that. You counting out worms?"

"You have me confused with someone else," she laughed and then wondered who he would be thinking of. Lisbeth? "I can not only pick up a worm, but I can bait my own hook. And to let you in on a little secret—I've eaten worms when I worked in Asia."

"What?"

"I did," Charlotte boasted. "I promised this pageant squad that I would eat ten worms if they made it to the preliminaries. Sure, they were candied, but I ate them nonetheless."

"Well, I stand corrected." As if he was impressed, the corners of Richard's mouth turned upward. "I guess that means I'll see you around this week?"

Charlotte hid her shiver from the idea of having to work at the bait and tackle shop. It wasn't like she never worked. As an ultimate supreme queen at the age of five, Charlotte earned her first five hundred dollars. She remembered the previous year's winner fanning her face with hundred-dollar bills. All she cared about at the time was the sparkling Swarovski crystal crown, which was half her size. As she got older, the tiaras grew smaller but the purses became larger. Being a pageant runway coach was a lucrative career. "I've got to get the job first." Charlotte flashed him a smile. "There were a lot of more qualified people interviewing as well."

When Richard set the frosting down on the counter and moved toward her, Charlotte's heart swelled with an uncertain anticipation. "If you need help, I know the owner."

"You're not my RA anymore, Richard," said Charlotte. "You can't fix everything."

As his eyes searched her face, Charlotte licked her lips. The memory of the butterflies that had flittered around in her belly the first time they met flooded her mind. It was so easy to get lost in his green eyes. The kitchen light highlighted the red in his close-cropped cut.

"You're right about one thing, Charlotte." Richard lowered his face toward hers.

Finally, her mind screamed; they were on the right page at the right time. Charlotte tilted her head up. Their mouths were just inches apart.

"Dad!"

The voice broke through the sexual tension as it echoed through the woods.

"Hey, Dad, where'd you go?"

Richard straightened. "And that would be my daughter, Bailey."

Who needed a cold shower to cut through the thick cloud of sexual tension when there was a teenager around? Charlotte thought, praying the heat would subside.

Chapter 3

The next morning, Richard sat up in the bed thanks to Bailey's shrill scream followed by a series of oh-my-god-oh-my-god-oh-my-gods. Her tone indicated no danger. Richard learned had to distinguish the differences between when she saw a bug, and when she was excited for her favorite celebrity. Coverless, he turned from his side and lay flat on his back. Somewhere in the middle of the night, his comfortable blue plaid sheets and blanket had fallen to the ground. The noise stopped and then started up again. Clearly awake, Bailey ambled down the stairs, rattling the beads dangling from the antlers of the buck he'd shot and posted on the bedroom wall.

It was too early in the morning. He needed coffee. An image popped into his mind of what else he needed—Charlotte Pendergrass. The sweet scent wafting from her dark locks, a mixture of ink and silk, still lingered when she'd turned her face from his—right before he'd almost kissed her. *What was he thinking?* Richard took his time getting involved with women. But just as he had the first moment he'd ever laid eyes on her, he was mature enough to admit the initial attraction to himself.

The sounds of clanging pots and the water blasting from the kitchen sink worried Richard right now. Back in the day he recalled hearing these familiar sounds. The only time his mother got back to basics was out here. Paula Hairston Swayne preferred to make reservations rather than cook, but she made a mean stack of flapjacks and bacon. Even with all the time spent at his parents', Bailey was not known for her finesse in the kitchen. The last thing he wanted was a fire in the woods.

"Hold up," Richard hollered, slinging his legs over the side of the bed so he could reach down and grab a pair of gray sweatpants from the floor.

The warmth of the material made him aware of the temperature dropping through the night. Though they were still in south Georgia, Richard had started to believe the area never received the memo about the change of seasons. As a farmer, he couldn't complain about the dream weather. Business at Swayne Pecans was booming in this quarter alone. His hard work had helped the family company hit a record high this year. This was the South. The Thanksgiving holidays weren't complete without a pecan dish in some form or fashion gracing the table. Richard had moved out of the agriculture sector years ago and found his niche with the business side. The deal he'd secured with Charmant Cocoa and their new baking line of brownies and mixes, chocolate pecans and candy bars, was sure to set up the Swayne family for life. Swayne Pecans would be in nearly every premade, refrigerated and box mix this coming year. This new venture already had him traveling. He told himself he was fine with being away from home so much now that Bailey was grown up. Richard looked forward to more traveling. Coming home to an empty house bothered him. He wondered if he'd ever have anyone to greet him when he came home in the future every day or after a long trip.

In the kitchen Richard found Bailey standing with her hip against the counter and two pots in her hands. The smell from last night's grill lingered in the air, and most importantly, the pans were void of coffee or bacon.

"I thought that might get you up," Bailey said smugly.

Richard couldn't believe he'd fallen for that old trick. Nothing had gotten him out of bed quicker than hearing a five-year-old Bailey in the kitchen messing around with things. He'd been afraid she'd turn on the stove and hurt herself somehow. Bailey had long ago learned the art of faking like she was going to cook in order to get him up.

"I'll miss these moments when you go off to school."

"About that," Bailey said. "I'm not sure if you heard me yell or not, but there may be a change of plans."

Sighing, Richard steadied himself for whatever adventure Bailey had planned for him. With two sisters more different than night and day and two controlling parents, Richard had learned early on not to hover over Bailey, but there were days she needed guidance. "You already took a gap year, Bail."

"I'm still going to go to school," said Bailey. She stepped aside and handed him the pot he used for grits.

"As long as we're clear on the issue." Richard started to pour water without using a measuring cup. Grits were his specialty.

Bailey sighed heavily. "Gosh, Dad, really? Here I am, coming up with plans to pay for my own education."

Richard turned off the water to hear this plan better. "I'm listening."

While she spoke, he pulled out the thick-cut bacon and the carton of eggs. First he set the bacon in the cast iron skillet and then went to scramble the eggs. Bailey always had funding set aside for college but he liked the idea of Bailey not relying on family money and earning her own way in life.

"There's a regional pageant. The Royal Regional Contest is a road to Miss America."

The word *pageant* made him cringe. Growing up with two sisters, aunts and a mother who reveled in that world had been a pain. Who wanted to see their best friends ogle the women in his life? Miss America, whatever they wanted to call it now, contest or competition: it was still a pageant. Yes, he knew the good of a pageant outweighed the bad but still, she'd be on display. It was one thing to deal with his sisters in pageants but something different when it was his daughter. His baby girl. It seemed like he couldn't get away from them. "How does the pageant help you get *back* into Florida A&M next semester? I thought you were already enrolled."

"I am. But you wouldn't have to pay a dime if I entered and won."

The "and won" part was a no-brainer. Richard had the most beautiful daughter in the world, if he did say so himself. "I have money to pay for college. You have a trust fund to help you. And if there was any reason why the funds might not work, your grandparents have a plan for you."

"Remember how excited you were for Aunt Maggie when she became independent?"

That social butterfly sister of his had been content on living off their family's fortune. At one point last year their father, Mitch, set a plan in motion for Maggie to get off social media and become a working woman. Getting a real-life job was hard for Maggie, but she'd managed to make it work.

"I don't think you can enter the Southern Style Glitz Pageant," said Richard. "Nepotism."

"This is a new, smaller contest, Dad," said Bailey. "I was just reading up on it. They want to have young professional girls. Future business leaders of the world."

"And the swimsuit portion?" Richard anticipated her answer with a cringe.

"There isn't one. This contest is based on my volunteer hours and my work experience. I'm going to do my community service at the Elder Care Center and then my summer job working at Shenanigans. I'll leave off the work at the family business, though."

"And your talent portion?"

Talented in everything, Bailey puffed out her chest. "I may do a bit from a play, maybe a little song and dance from *Hamilton*. I did practice a number last year for the Miss Southwood Pageant."

"Isn't *Hamilton* old?"

Bailey's voice cracked as she gaped. "*Hamilton* will never be old."

"Okay, if you want to do another pageant, that's fine with me. Even better if there isn't a bikini involved and you're going to earn tuition."

Richard continued to make breakfast and listened to Bailey spout off all the things she'd need for this upcoming pageant. It sounded to him like all the bonding time they were supposed to spend together was going to be taken up by pageant preparation. Over breakfast Bailey continued to go on about needing to get a dress from Lexi. The mention of a Pendergrass brought his thoughts back to Charlotte. Was she awake? Had she eaten breakfast—a proper one, at that? And if she didn't, like he expected, would she want another plate brought over?

If he did head up to the cabin, Richard wasn't sure he'd be able to keep his hands to himself. He recalled Charlotte had been the first woman to put the ideas of love at first sight and happily-ever-after in his head after his break-up with Octavia. Leaving her place left him with that same potential feeling of happiness. Richard had learned from his parents what a healthy relationship and a family man looked like and he'd wanted that for himself. Having a past with Charlotte's cousin complicate things. He worried over his past loose relationship with Lisbeth, who'd not only been his first sexual encounter in high school. They'd also had a series of hookups after he broke up with Octavia until she'd suggested he think about sending Bailey off to school.

Last night had Charlotte asked about her. What was he supposed to say? He and Charlotte weren't at any point in their friendship for him to give her details like that, though lust simmered between them. Right now, Richard had no plans to kiss and tell.

"Do you want to get in some fishing today?" Bailey asked, scraping her spoon against her blue-and-white-patterned bowl.

"You don't need to go shopping for a dress?"

Bailey grinned. "I'll send Lexi a text."

"You can't assume she's going to make a dress for you."

"Yes, I can," Bailey said with a bright smile. "I'll run upstairs and send her a text, then we can go out onto the water if you'd like. I'll even let you bait my hook for me."

He'd like that very much. Richard sat back in his chair with the last piece of bacon on his plate. Of course Lexi would make a dress for Bailey. Maggie still used a lot of her clients in her pageant in Savannah. So, if the Southern Style Glitz Beauty Pageant wasn't putting on this pageant, who was this new group?

"The next blind date dinner at the Dragon Room is coming up; let me know if you want me to fill out a profile for you."

The sound of a robotic computer voice came from an app on Charlotte's cell phone, startling her out of her nap. She didn't need to look at her notifications as she got up. It was from Lexi, still trying to make Charlotte laugh. The surprisingly warm afternoon sun drained the last bit of energy left in Charlotte. Or at least she believed it was the last. A flutter of excitement coursed through her veins as she looked out of the window at the sight of Richard in a boat speeding down on the lake. A light-haired girl stood in the front with her arms in the air, screaming she was flying. Charlotte pulled her oversize black sunglasses down her nose for a better glimpse and a chuckle at the *Titanic* reference. Her eyes went to the man behind the wheel.

Taking advantage of the Indian summer, Richard wore a tank top, probably to keep cool, but to Charlotte, it showed off his muscles. The curves of his biceps and forearms were delectable. A pair of well-developed calves poked out from the knee-length board shorts. The sun highlighted the coppery red of his sun-kissed skin. She licked her lips and cocked her head to the side. This attraction was no different than her freshman year in college. But now she didn't have to share the view with a dozen other girls. It was just her.

"Hey!" The cheery person at the helm of the boat turned and waved in Charlotte's direction. "Hey, neighbor!"

The girl's greeting gave Richard a reason to turn in her direction. His aviators reflected the sun back on Charlotte. With her left hand, she shielded her eyes while waving with the other. "Hi, neighbors."

Richard turned the boat to the Pendergrass dock, which stuck out farther from the pebbled shore. Charlotte adjusted her maxidress over her legs and fitted her feet in her heeled sandals. The hem of the dress floated over the three shapely pumpkins she'd placed along the pier to make the cabin a bit more festive for this time of year. She walked down the stone pier like a pro. She wondered if this was where she'd gotten her love for the runway.

"Hi," Charlotte said, making it toward the end of the pier. "It's great seeing someone out on the water."

"We didn't disturb you," Richard asked, "did we?"

"No, I actually was getting a little freaked out about how quiet it is out here in the woods," said Charlotte. The young girl, clearly Richard's daughter, beamed as she watched the two of them talking. She remembered seeing pictures on his door back in college. She was adorable then and even more so now. "You must be Bailey."

"I am," answered Bailey. "And you're Charlotte O'Malley."

"Pendergrass," Charlotte and Richard chorused. Their unison evoked a raised brow from Bailey.

"And how do the two of you know each other?"

Since it took Richard a moment to answer, Charlotte spoke up. "Your dad was the resident assistant in my dorm."

"What?" Bailey looked back at her dad. "You never told me," she said to him, then looked back at Charlotte. "You went to school with my dad. We need to talk. I need to know all about my dad when he was younger. You'd swear he was born a grown man."

She wasn't lying, Charlotte agreed inwardly. "I can tell you your dad loved you very much even back then."

Bailey curtseyed. "Well, I was an adorable baby."

"And modest, too," said Richard. "Can you tell which aunt she takes after?"

"I'm going to tell Aunt Maggie you said that."

"See—" Richard wagged his finger at his daughter "—I never said which one."

Rolling her eyes, Bailey stepped off the boat and

approached Charlotte, ignoring Richard's warning to not intrude.

"I'm not," said Bailey. "Miss Charlotte just said she was getting freaked out about it being so dead out here."

Those weren't her exact words, but Charlotte agreed with her. "I was about to go inside and get some lemonade. Would the two of you care to join me?"

Before answering, Bailey half turned to her father. Richard gave a pinched smile that Charlotte guessed was a nonverbal approval. Charlotte liked this Richard. He was still in control, just as he had been as an RA. Someone else signed his paychecks there. Here, Bailey was clearly the boss.

Once the engine died on the boat, Bailey tethered them to the dock. "Walk this way," Charlotte instructed them. "The little rocks over there are not as tight as they used to be—I'd hate for you to fall."

"Are you wearing heels?" Bailey asked.

"I am." Charlotte lifted the hem of her dress to show off the jeweled sandals. "I got them in India."

"When you were training contestants for Miss Universe?" Bailey asked.

Charlotte stopped walking for a moment for Bailey to catch up. "You certainly know your pageants."

"You're only the most sought-after runway coach in literally the world."

"Retired," Richard corrected from behind her.

Bailey gave the two of them a questioning stare. "What?"

"I am no longer with CEO," Charlotte explained. They headed across the patio into the side entrance leading right into the open living room.

Still close to her, Bailey gasped. "Why would you give that up?"

"Bailey," Richard said with a warning tone. This time it was more serious than on the dock. "Stop with all the personal questions."

The quick pout across Bailey's flawless face disappeared in seconds. "I'm sorry. I'm just so excited to meet you and get to talk to you. This is like fate."

Fate for what? Charlotte wondered. Fate for her was the fact she and Richard were reunited and at this time they were both equally single. Judging from the near kiss last night—and the fact that Charlotte had later used her battery-operated boyfriend in the nightstand— there was a definite spark between the two of them. Charlotte opened the refrigerator and silently thanked God for the cool air to chill the heat threatening to expose her feelings.

"I'm going to enter a beauty contest in a few weeks," announced Bailey. "I'm going to win and pay for my own college. I won Miss Southwood last summer."

"That's wonderful, another Swayne in the pageant world," Charlotte cooed over Richard's groan. "What? Oh, don't tell me you're one of those people who thinks pageants are just about the beauty. Everyone forgets how much money goes into your education. She's smart," she added to Richard.

"She gets that from me." Richard stood at a six-top table and there was a good distance between them, but she could still see how his face still beamed with pride.

After pulling out the pitcher of the powdered lemonade drink Charlotte had stirred together this morning, she grabbed three glasses from the cupboard. "Let's sit here." She motioned toward the table.

Bailey helped Charlotte with the glasses. She was helpful, too. Charlotte was impressed. She envied Richard for having a daughter. In another world, she'd have a house full of kids. With a child in college, Richard must be glad to be an empty nester soon. This fate that brought them together for this week just drew a line in the sand. Richard couldn't be looking to start all over again.

"What do you have in mind for a dress?" Charlotte asked, "You know my cousin is…"

"Lexi Pendergrass Reyes," Bailey provided. "And she makes the best OOAK—one-of-a-kind—dresses in the world."

Nodding, Charlotte smiled, proud of her cousin, who had been making dresses since her clients were her dolls. "I couldn't agree more."

"I already sent her an email to request a fitting with her."

"An email?" Charlotte rolled her eyes. "Hang on." She tiptoed outside to where'd she left her phone and came back in dialing Lexi's number. "Lexi," she said.

"Hey, cuz." Lexi's cheerful voice came over the speakerphone. "Have you decided to let me fill out your profile for Mrs. Li's blind date service? I sent you a text. It's cool, you'll love it," she went on without taking a breath. Charlotte smiled apologetically and tried to fight the horrific embarrassment of needing to be set up on a blind date. Why did it bother her that Richard stared at her with a comical grin across his chiseled face? "She gets your profile and sets up a date. You sit down at a table with a curtain for a partition. Then everyone pulls the screen back and meets her perfect mate. She matched my former dance instructor, Chantal, remember?"

"Okay, so, no," Charlotte said slowly. "I was calling to see if you were free. I have Bailey Swayne in here. There's a new pageant coming up."

"Really? Where?"

Charlotte glanced at Bailey, who twisted her lips trying to remember. She imagined the girl was surprised Charlotte had made the call. "I'm not sure, but she's going to be needing a dress."

Bailey wiggled in her seat. A feeling of pleasure washed over Charlotte at the idea of making someone happy with such a simple deed. Within seconds she'd set up a fitting later on this afternoon.

Bailey squealed in delight. "I've got to tell my friends. Dad, can I borrow the car?"

Richard lifted his hands in the air. "If I say no, I'd be a monster."

"Probably," Charlotte and Bailey chorused.

Now it was Richard's turn to toss an inquisitive glance between the two of them. "It appears I am outnumbered."

Taking that as her blessing, Bailey scrambled out of her seat, hugged her father and Charlotte, and ran off to get ready. Left alone in the kitchen with Richard, Charlotte rolled her glass between her hands. Its condensation only made more noticeable the heat growing between them.

"I am sorry," Charlotte finally said. "You two were supposed to be here bonding, right?"

"I just like seeing her happy," said Richard. "It used to be hanging out with me made her happy, but the older she gets, the more she's learned that other things make her happy as well."

"Pageants, though?" Charlotte asked. "It really is in the Swayne blood, isn't it?"

"And Hairston," Richard said, probably thinking of his beauty queen mother and maternal cousins.

"We aren't that different. My mother was Miss Peachville, placed in the top fifteen in Miss Georgia and was the runner-up in Miss Sweetheart. Lexi's mom caught the bug, too. I think Lexi went farther in the circuit than me, I was always runner-up or in the top five in the runoff for Miss Georgia USA."

"Excuse me, but what did my daughter call you? Queen of the runway?"

"I'm better behind the scenes."

Richard shrugged his shoulders. "I distinctly remember you on the homecoming court float in the parade after winning Miss Gillum Hall. You turned quite a few heads."

Not yours, she thought. "That was a long time ago, Richard."

"And now." Richard lifted his drink to his luscious lips. "I can admit you've got my head turning."

Charlotte pressed her lips together, not sure how to answer. "So you're just going to put that out there like that?"

"What? That I agree with Bailey on one thing. I think fate brought us here together at this exact moment in our lives."

Funny, she'd had the same thought in her head. "Richard, I don't know what to say."

"Don't say anything. Let's just hang out this afternoon. It's clear Bailey is ditching me for the rest of the day, and I've got a boat full of fuel and a bucket of worms. You did mention something about gaining experience with worms."

"I don't believe those were my exact words."

"You said for the job at the bait and tackle shop, right?"

Laughing, Charlotte covered her face. "Maybe I shouldn't leave, in case they decide to call and offer me the job."

The room felt smaller when Richard came to his feet. "C'mon," he said, extending his hand. "Let's go for a ride."

Everything about Richard screamed maturity and responsibility. The fact they'd almost kissed last night meant he was interested in her. Considering Richard was her first college crush, she wanted to dive in and spend as much time as possible with him. But Charlotte was on a mission. She needed to find Mr. Right Qualities. She'd wasted enough time with Denny, whom she realized never wanted a family. She didn't need a husband—had been there, done that—but at least she wanted a man who wanted to have a child also. Her mother had had her before she hit thirty, as did her grandmother. She owed it to herself to have a child. Richard had just raised his own child. No way he wanted to get into a relationship with someone like Charlotte. But when she cocked her head to the side and Richard offered her his signature lazy grin, who was she to deny him?

Maybe he'd be her Mr. Right for Now. Besides, it was just a ride around the lake. *What's the harm?*

Chapter 4

After an exhilarating afternoon of having her hair blown in the wind, Charlotte figured she must look like a fright. Richard was sweet enough to walk her up to her door rather than dropping her off on the dock. He didn't have to, but with her hand tucked in the palm of his, she didn't mind.

"Thanks for hanging out with me today," Richard said, helping Charlotte up the steps.

Charlotte shrugged her shoulders and shook off his gratitude but also the goofy feeling she had when they neared the top of the steps. She maneuvered herself a step up to be perfectly level with his green eyes. A five o'clock shadow had come early to his sculpted, square cheekbones. Charlotte pressed her lips together and inhaled the scent of pine needles from the wind blowing through the trees.

"You're welcome," Charlotte finally said. "I feel responsible for you guys not spending time together."

Richard shook off her response. "She woke up knowing what she wanted to do today."

A pageant was a big deal, especially if it was going to pay for college. Charlotte didn't blame Bailey for getting involved. She didn't believe Bailey would probably ever want for anything in life, but she still admired her independent steps. If only she'd stayed in school. Charlotte pushed her past mistakes aside. "I sped things along by getting her in touch with Lexi. Who, by the way, was ecstatic to start designing again."

"I can imagine." Richard placed his hands on the wood railing on either side of her.

The idle talk stalled the inevitable. They were going to kiss at some point. It was only a matter of time, she thought to herself.

"How many kids does she have now?"

"Three," Charlotte said. Three perfectly cherubic kids who smelled like baby powder and were so sweet you might get a cavity from being around them. "All back to back."

"Man," sighed Richard, raking his hand down the waves of his close-cropped hair. "I can't imagine."

"Did you want more kids after Bailey?"

A bird flew by, calling and chasing another from its nest before Richard answered. "It wasn't in the stars for me and Bailey's mom. If I had another kid still at home, I wouldn't be able to travel with work. With Bailey going off, I'm not obligated to stay at home."

For some reason her heart sank with his answer. "I'm surprised you didn't remarry."

"I never married Octavia," he answered quickly. Too quickly, and Charlotte caught the expression of disdain that passed across his face. Octavia must have been crazy to let a man like Richard go. She'd seen firsthand now dedicated he was to Bailey as a baby and now as a budding adult.

"Oh." It was all Charlotte could say. Their conversation had started taking a turn for the none-of-her-business territory. They were friends who just reconnected.

"Let me rephrase that without the animosity in my voice." Richard chuckled. "I wanted to marry Octavia. Octavia didn't want to get married."

"Why?" Charlotte blurted out loud. She didn't mean to be so forward, but anyone could see what a perfect catch he was. Smart, devastatingly handsome, sexy and clearly a loving father.

Lips pressed tight, Richard struggled before he spoke. "I don't want to speak ill of her. Octavia is Bailey's mother, but Octavia did not want the commitment of being a parent."

"I feel horrible." She wanted to hug Bailey and Richard. They were the perfect father and daughter duo. Five minutes around them and Charlotte wanted to be a part of their world. She wanted a relationship like theirs. She had her family, but they weren't close like that. There were no touchy-feely hugs or high fives.

Richard shrugged. "Don't. Bailey and I made the best of our situation."

"She is wonderful."

"She gets that from me," Richard bragged, puffing out his broad chest.

Her closed mouth threatened to burst at the seams if she didn't start laughing. Richard gave her a moment to take it in.

"I'm sorry," she said, holding up a hand. "You guys are so cute."

"Thanks," he agreed. "What about you, Charlotte. Kids?"

A stabbing pain pierced her heart. The desire to pat her flat stomach itched like hell in her palm. "No."

"I didn't peg you as a mom," Richard said with a casual tone. "I envy y'all who can take off on a whim. And now that Bailey's heading off to college for sure, I can finally join that life."

Any amount of laughter she had in her died as well as her smile. Richard's eyes grew wide as he realized his words. "I didn't mean it like it sounded."

The lump in her throat prevented her from speaking. She got she didn't live the lifestyle of a typical mother. But she was ready to start a family now. Despite his apology, Charlotte wondered if he really meant it.

Richard tried to recover. "I meant with your lifestyle. Hell. I mean, most moms I know trade in their stilettoes for a pair of Crocs."

The hideous shoes were more of an insult. Charlotte furrowed her brow together. "Just because you're a mother doesn't mean you have to give up looking good."

"But when it comes time to you putting your child's needs aside so that you look good in the latest fashion, there's an issue."

Every nerve in her body burned. Charlotte gaped. "I

don't know what you mean by that. Don't believe for a moment that every woman you meet chooses prioritize herself over her child. My cousin is a beautiful mother and has fantastic fashion sense."

"Charlotte," Richard started, "I didn't mean—"

"I'm fine. Don't worry about it," Charlotte snapped and stepped away. "It's getting hot out here, and I'm going to go inside. Thank you for a lovely afternoon."

Before he got a protest out of his open mouth, Charlotte spun on her heels and headed inside to the coolness. Why she let this stupid spat get to her was crazy. But Richard's innocent words stung. Denny had felt the same way. Denny had felt the need to ridicule Charlotte in order to get the notion of having a baby out of her head. Her ex had pointed out the things Charlotte would have to give up to be a good mother: designer clothes, travel and her beloved stilettos. Perhaps she still wore her heels now just to spite him. Today's women could have it all: a family, style and a business.

Rushing across the floor, Charlotte headed into her bathroom and pressed her back against the door. A stream of frustrated tears poured down her face. An ache of loneliness filled her heart. It sounded silly to let the words of a man she hadn't seen for years make her feel bad about pursuing all her desires. No doctor had told her she needed to change shoes in order to have a baby. But one had suggested she start considering having one sooner because she'd have a harder time conceiving the older she got.

The air-conditioning kicked through the vents, flapping a three-fold brochure she'd read in the tub this morning alongside her romance book. IVF sounded better each day. Of course, she *wanted* the experience of falling in love with a partner in life and sharing the experience of having a baby together, but she didn't think she'd ever find the right man.

The charming smile on Richard's face as he'd sat behind the wheel of the speedboat entered her mind. Why? He'd basically just told her she'd be a horrible mother. *Okay, maybe not in so many words.* Charlotte shut the recollection down before it went in that direction. He already sounded like Denny. Maybe it was a fraternity thing. Either way, his words had made it clear what he thought, and she didn't need to concern herself with his opinions. She didn't need to spend time flirting with him. What she needed to do was sit back and think about her options for her future.

Runway coaching again wasn't off the table, but the bitter taste left after the divorce settlement stopped her from starting up new. Now was the time she needed to focus on what she wanted. How bad did she want a baby? *So bad*, she answered herself. She needed that love and affection from someone who only wanted the same from her. Charlotte grew up feeling like a burden to her parents. Besides her pageantry, they barely paid attention to Charlotte. She'd already disappointed her parents by marrying Denny; they were going to freak when they found out she lost her business. After this afternoon, spending just the few moments she had with Bailey and witnessing the love Richard had for her, Charlotte craved it.

Charlotte thought about the blind date dinner going on in Southwood. After tucking the IVF brochure back into its envelope, Charlotte headed out to the back porch to retrieve her cell phone and typed a message to Lexi. If she didn't meet Mr. Right soon, she'd move on to IVF.

Go ahead and set me up with the blind date.

The so-called getaway week Richard had planned to spend with his daughter turned out to be him whiling away the last twenty-four hours without Bailey. The announcement of this new pageant—contest—now took all of Bailey's time, and of course today she'd insisted on going to a Halloween party with her friends. Richard didn't want to come across as selfish. He understood her wanting to spend time with friends and somewhat the chance to earn her own tuition. He didn't mind. At least he told himself that. The next months home without her would be hard, but Richard knew he'd have to live with the idea.

Richard needed to work out. He hit the gym and hung out with his friends for a few beers. If he stayed at the cabin, he'd end up at Charlotte's. After saying goodbye the other day, he got the feeling Charlotte was done with him—before anything had ever started. He understood when a woman said she was fine in the tone she'd used that she wasn't really fine. He felt horrible for making her feel bad. It wasn't like he was judging her, but perhaps pushing his past experiences on her wasn't fair to Charlotte.

"Why are you moping?" Julio Torres asked, pulling a clean white shirt over his head.

Last summer, when his sister Kenzie had married Ramon Torres, the Swaynes gained more family. Julio and Jose Torres often came in town to hang out with their brother and the new baby.

"I wasn't aware I was moping," answered Richard. "I'm just bummed that my time with Bailey is dwindling."

Julio scoffed, "Get out of here. You're not losing her. She's going to college, and she doesn't want you to pay for a thing."

"What my brother is trying to say," Jose said, clearing his throat, "is now is the time to start living."

"By living, I am talking about finding someone," Julio clarified with a wink. It took only a few hours of getting to know Julio to know the man's hobby was womanizing.

"He doesn't want to go through women like you," said Jose.

"He hasn't given it a try, little brother," sniped Julio.

"I'm good in the lady department," Richard clarified for them. After rolling the sleeves of his white button-down shirt, he slung his gym bag over his shoulder and followed the brothers outside. What he wanted to do was go back up to Black Wolf Creek and see what was going through Charlotte's mind. They had been having a good time, and then she froze him out just as things heated up between them. He got it—Charlotte was pissed off about losing her company and needed to find her way again, but he didn't understand why they couldn't hang out together if he apologized for his remark. First she'd have to see him. "What are you guys doing tonight? Bailey is probably going to be out late."

Julio checked his cell phone and sighed. "I was just

going to get a bite to eat before heading back to Magnolia Palace."

"Baby duty?"

Despite being a ladies' man, Julio proudly wore the badge of uncle like an honor. "Yep. But I wouldn't mind getting a bite to eat before going. Want to come?"

"I don't," said Jose. "I've got to pick up a judge in Tallahassee and bring him to protective custody."

"The life of a lawman," Julio said. He patted his brother on the back. "Nice playing tag team with you. What about you, Richard? Are you going to head back to your cabin, even though Bailey isn't there, or do you want to grab a bite?"

The only thing he'd do at the cabin was check on Charlotte. She wanted nothing to do with him and he still didn't know what he'd done wrong. "Let's eat."

"Great. I heard about this restaurant here, the Dragon Room, I think, that has the best crab Rangoon." Julio rubbed his stomach. "After that workout, I could eat at least twenty-four."

"I'd like to see," laughed Richard. While he'd eaten a tub of frosting at Charlotte's the other night, Julio was too vain to overindulge. "I'm willing to lay money on it."

Jose parted from the two of them. Since everything was within walking distance in Southwood, the men headed down Main Street. Richard knew the exact spot Julio had mentioned. As they crossed the streets, Richard watched young kids dressed in costumes ranging from princesses to superheroes and even robots. He smiled and fondly remembered trick-or-treating with Bailey and raiding her plastic pumpkin container for peanut butter and chocolate candy. It saddened him to know he'd never get the chance to do it again.

When they arrived, the long line told him they weren't the only ones in the mood for some handmade crab and cream cheese treats.

"So back to you and Bailey," Julio began. "Are you going to start dating now? Because I am in need of a new wingman. I'm running out of brothers to help me out. Every time I think I've found someone to hang out with, they go off and get married."

"I doubt you need help," said Richard. "You seem to be doing just fine." To prove his point, a couple of ladies from church slowed their walk in front of them and flirted by batting their lashes and waving their dainty fingers at them. "See?"

"That doesn't excite you? It's like being a kid in a candy shop."

"Except I am a grown-ass man," Richard clarified. "We're the eye candy with bank accounts as our wrappers."

Trying to comprehend what he said, Julio squinted his eyes. "What?"

"Can't you see these women are just after your money?"

Shrugging, Julio winked. "They can be after my money. Doesn't mean they're going to get it."

"So you don't want to settle down?"

"Not at all." Julio shivered at the idea. "Do you?"

"Not with you."

Julio flipped him off. "Cute. I'm talking about one of these ladies around here. Big country guy like yourself has to find one of these ladies worth settling down with, right? I mean, if that's what you want."

"Not here." Richard frowned. "I've dated a few of them, and trust me, I'm not looking for a relationship with a woman who only wants to spend all my money."

"Neither do I, but I'm also not going to let that make me sleep in a cold bed."

Cold beds, cold showers. They were more welcoming than a gold-digging woman. "I'm good. I'll find the one woman I can settle back down with who wants to…" He stopped what he was saying, partially because Julio's face froze with horror.

"Dude, are you about to tell me you want another kid?"

No. Do I? he thought. He wasn't about to tell him that *yeah, I wouldn't mind.* The conversation with Charlotte had gotten him thinking about Bailey leaving. If he regretted anything in life, it was not having a few more kids. The experience with Octavia had left him with a distrust in women. Any woman could change her mind at any minute and decide she no longer wanted to be a mother. Richard could never put a child through that again. It was a powerless feeling of not being able to help Bailey with certain issues. He'd dated a few women with kids but the idea of blending their families never worked. Women his age did not want to settle down with a guy with an adult daughter who—despite his many conversations with Bailey—could put them in the grandparent category. Sure, Kenzie had her babies, but Richard had to give them back. It wasn't the same as having his own.

"Man, I'm not having this conversation with a perpetual bachelor."

Julio accepted his moniker like a badge of honor.

Curling his hand, he brushed his hands against his shirt, almost polishing his nails. "No commitments, no problems."

"I think the saying is, more money, more problems," Richard corrected.

"Is it, though?"

The line moved farther in. Most of the time, when Richard came to the Dragon Room with Bailey, the dress was casual. The shirt he wore was easygoing enough, but Richard rolled down the sleeves just in case then moved along with the group.

As the line approached the entrance, Julio glanced down at himself. "Damn, I think I ought to put something else on." Julio's eyes followed another couple of well-dressed ladies passing them by.

"It's dinner, not a fashion show."

Julio backed out and held a finger in the air. "I'll be right back. Save me some Rangoons."

A tuxedo-clad man stood in the door with a clipboard in his arms glanced at his list. "Name?"

"What? Since when does Mrs. Li take names?"

"Name?"

Richard cocked his head to the side. "Cliff," he began slowly, "I coached you in youth soccer."

Cliff, now grown, had been one of the boys on the coed team with a single mother who had attended practice in leopard-print leggings, a fitted top and sky-high heels with clear bottoms. "Oh, Coach Richard, my bad." Cliff crossed a name off his list and poked his head through the air-conditioning-laden door for three seconds before facing Richard. "All right, it's all good. Go on in."

A lady, not Mrs. Li, met Richard at the door and took him by the elbow. Confused, Richard squinted his eyes. What was up tonight? Passing the folding partitions into the darkened room, Richard wondered what the hell was going on. The usual four-top tables were set up in a row with thick white cloth partitions blocking off three sides. The setup reminded Richard more of a voting booth than anything else.

Mrs. Li stood by an empty chair. "It's a pleasure to have you here," she said. "I hope you like the results."

Results? "Thanks," Richard replied with uncertainty. "I'm meeting my friend Julio. Maybe we can take these down?" He reached for the cloth, but Mrs. Li, all five feet three of her, smacked his hand away.

"Enjoy," she said, adding a coy smile.

Richard sat down and waited. Curious, he remained quiet, listening to the fryer in the back going, glasses bumping against each other. A few whispers filtered through the restaurant. Five more minutes went by and a circular spotlight shone on the black stage in the back of the restaurant. Mrs. Li stepped into the light, and a round of applause went off from the other patrons.

"Ladies and gentlemen, I've been doing this for the past few years."

Oh, so is she retiring or something? Richard thought to himself. Was he intruding on the event?

"And I've had a great time doing this. Mrs. Li is never wrong—trust me on this. I've had several marriages…"

No, she hasn't. Richard knew for a fact that Mrs. Li and her husband had just celebrated their fortieth wedding anniversary a week after she'd celebrated her sixtieth birthday. The Cupcakery did both parties and had ordered several pounds of fresh pecans for enough desserts to feed the extended Li family.

Mrs. Li raised a champagne glass in the air. "So, here's to another successful event."

With his eyes on Mrs. Li in the back on the small stage, Richard noticed the white partitions raised between the other tables so the guests were facing another guest.

It dawned on Richard what was happening. This was a blind speed-dating setup. Richard turned with dread in his bones. What woman was he about to be set up with?

"Richard?"

Richard blinked. "Charlotte?"

Chapter 5

"You've got to be kidding me," Charlotte groaned. She turned in her seat to find Mrs. Li. Did Lexi think this was a joke or something? "Why are you here?"

In truth, Richard did appear to be confused. "I came here to have dinner with a friend."

A female friend who was probably perfect for him, she thought to herself. "Of course you were."

"I mean my friend Julio. He suggested we grab a bite to eat. I had no idea you were going to be here or what is going on."

"This isn't possible. This is a blind date."

"You're on a date?" Richard leaned forward, resting his elbows on the table.

Charlotte nodded. "My cousin Lexi set this up for me."

"Wow." Richard sat back. "So, this is what she had

in mind when you were talking to her the other day. Well, I had no idea."

"Mrs. Li has been hosting these blind speed-dating events for a while now," Charlotte explained. "I've heard about them."

No mistaking the distaste for the idea. "And you wanted to give it a try?"

"Why not? I'm single."

"I suppose."

A red glass candle stood on Charlotte's side of the table. She touched it with her fingertips while Richard extracted his cell phone from his front pocket. He did look good in his button-down shirt opened right at the collar. "I don't get how this is possible. There's a questionnaire that has to be filled out in order for Mrs. Li to compile her perfect matches. You really shouldn't have been let in without being on the list."

"I know the bouncer," Richard said without looking up from his phone.

Deflated, Charlotte sank in her seat. The night was blown. She glanced around for a waiter. She needed a drink. When a young man in a black apron came over, Charlotte gave her drink order and fanned her hand toward Richard, indicating he should do the same.

Richard pushed his phone toward her and grimaced, then ordered a beer. "I just got a text from Julio."

The black letters on the screen spelled out, Sorry, man, Bailey made me do it.

Confused, Charlotte glanced up and met Richard's twinkling green eyes. "I don't get it."

"We were set up," explained Richard.

"I still don't get it. Lexi set this up for me. She filled out the questionnaire."

"And my daughter spent the afternoon with her."

Curses, Charlotte thought. "Why would she do that?"

"Because Bailey has the desire to see me dating before she goes off to school. We might as well enjoy the evening. According to this last text, the bill has been taken care of, and all we're supposed to do is eat and talk."

This wasn't the most romantic way to start a date, but considering there were only so many tubs of icing a girl could eat, Charlotte decided to stay. The waiter returned with their drinks and took their orders.

Every opportunity Charlotte had to eat something spicy, she went for it. Living with Denny, a man with a sensitive stomach, had made accommodating her cravings for the hot stuff difficult.

"Kung pao," they both said at the same time.

Richard held his hand up in apology. Since they both had the same thing in mind, Charlotte suggested they order something different and share. She needed to eat more vegetables, and the beef and broccoli looked perfect tonight, so she made the order. Richard folded his hands on the white linen tablecloth and stared. Self-conscious, Charlotte touched the white trim of her white polka-dotted blue dress. She'd thought she'd style her hair a little different tonight and had swept her black tresses into a '40s style.

"Do I have something on my face?"

"No, you're quite breathtaking tonight," he said with sincerity. "So the broccoli beef, huh? That was going to be my next choice."

Conversations began to pick up within the restaurant while Charlotte and Richard sat awkwardly together. The one thing ringing out in her mind was the questionnaire. Considering Lexi and Bailey spent the day together, she gathered they'd become fast matchmaking friends while configuring Bailey's next ball gown. Mrs. Li was supposed to be good and see through family interference and forced answers. What did she and Richard possibly have in common?

"How are you enjoying Black Wolf Creek?" Richard, the mature one, broke the silence.

Charlotte bobbed her head. "It's great. Nice and quiet now." The little dig was at him. Not so mature but at least satisfying. The tight-lipped little grin he offered told her she'd gotten to him.

"I did not ask to be here," Richard said.

"Feel free to leave." Charlotte waved her hand toward the door.

"I would, but—" Richard inhaled deeply "—my friend picked me up today."

A halfcocked laugh threatened to erupt from Charlotte's throat. "So you need a ride?"

"Are you offering?"

"Fortunately for you, I'm going in that direction," Charlotte sighed with a smile. Before they knew it, they were both laughing over the whole evening. Ease washed over her. This was better than the awkward silence between them.

"How kind of you," Richard chuckled. "I'm even willing to put in for gas."

"Of course you will," teased Charlotte. "You know the old saying about riding for free? Gas, grass or ass."

Thick brows rose in apparent amusement. "The first time I heard that from my friends was the first time I knew I needed to get my own car."

"Were you always such a Boy Scout?"

No surprise when he nodded. "Always. I think there is a reason I have only sisters and a daughter. I knew how my friends were with girls, and I didn't want that for my sisters. So it was important for me to be the example."

"I'm not mad at that."

"I never knew if you had siblings or not." Richard turned the questions on her.

"No." Charlotte frowned. "I don't think my parents even wanted to have children."

"That can't be right."

Charlotte shrugged her shoulders. "It's just something I always felt. My parents aren't the loving, picturesque duo you may see around town." Good looks ran in the family. Charlotte didn't think she was biased when it came to her father, Arthur. A basketball star back in his day, he was the most handsome man in the world, tall, with dark hair and smooth, brown skin. Iris, Charlotte's mother, was the epitome of the stereotypical southern pageant girl, always poised and popular. They'd gone to college together and naturally married and came back to Peachville to settle, far enough away from his family but close enough to celebrate holidays with them when her cousins came home from boarding school. Charlotte never saw her parents shower each other with affection or compliments. Conversations at the dinner table consisted of a few sentences composed of asking how their days went and requests to pass whatever they were having for dinner. Her mother involved herself in Charlotte's pageants and her father wrote the checks. They never debated about the cost or travel and time spent away from the house. Growing up in silence was part of why Charlotte wanted a house full of children.

Thanksgiving was around the corner. Despite not looking forward to her mother's scrutiny, Charlotte was anticipating the holidays. It had been the only time during Charlotte's beauty queen days that she was allowed to enjoy eating.

"So no siblings for me." Charlotte shifted in her seat, finally answering his question. Her French-manicured finger traced the outline of her appetizer plate. "I've always wanted a big family."

"Did you freeze me out yesterday because you thought I was talking about you not being a proper mother?"

A flash of pain gripped her heart. "Maybe. I'm sensitive."

Richard reached across the table and covered her hand with his. "That was my baggage, Charlotte. I did not mean to imply anything about you."

"I take it things between you and Bailey's mother ended on a sour note."

"To say the least."

"I can't believe you would let one woman affect your dating world," said Charlotte, not sure if she was crossing a line with him. The man had never married, even though he was a great catch.

"Are you telling me you weren't gun-shy about coming out tonight for your first date after your divorce?"

A laugh died in the back of Charlotte's throat.

"Denny and I have been over for quite some time. We fought over CEO. The only thing I'm afraid of now is starting something new." She paused, not sure if she wanted to finish her thought. At that moment she realized she didn't want to start working in the field again especially if she planned on having a child any time soon. Charlotte, unlike her parents, planned on devoting herself to motherhood full-time.

"You sound more upset over the company."

"Just like Bailey is your baby, that business was my baby." Charlotte's mouth twitched. "In saying that, I guess I understand why you've been celibate."

Clearing his throat, Richard withdrew his hand. "Don't think I haven't dated. But I realized early on that some of the women wanted to settle down with a baby as a meal ticket, and I wasn't going to go through that again. Then some of the women I met or came in contact with wanted a wealthy lifestyle."

Not being able to resist, Charlotte cracked a joke.

"The lifestyle of a farmer?" Deep inside, her heart ached. He was not the one to settle down with. He did not want any more children. When Richard laughed and flashed a genuine smile, she knew she was okay.

"Joke all you want, Charlotte. You ought to come up to the factory. Sure, we have trees, dirt and tractors. But we also have a business side with a data analysis and IT crew, accountants, marketing advisers and a cafeteria. We offer retirement and health care for our group of over a thousand employees, stretching from Southwood and Black Wolf Creek to Peachville and Samaritan."

As he spoke, Charlotte felt the pride in his voice. Chills ran up her arms. Swayne Pecans was responsible for keeping much of the region employed. Maybe he didn't wear denim, a cowboy hat and boots, but she sure as hell wouldn't mind seeing him in that attire.

The rest of the evening flowed like the water in the creek between the cabins. Richard could feel the way Charlotte relaxed around him. When dinner ended, she melted into his side, mainly by accident when a couple of preteens ran right past them, dressed as various presidents, spooky clowns and superheroes. For a moment he'd forgotten it was Halloween. Accident or not, their fingers welded together. He liked the feeling of walking out on the streets of his hometown with someone he cared for. And he did care for Charlotte. It was refreshing to be on a date with a woman who seemed genuinely interested in his business rather than the perks, like the company jet and what kind of vacation spots it could take them.

"Where did you park?" Richard asked, slipping the keys from Charlotte's free hand.

"I *can* drive, you know." Charlotte resisted.

"I know, but you already know I'm not going to let you."

"Always the Boy Scout."

Charlotte looked up at him. Under the light of the moon, with the backdrop of the lit fountain in the center of the town square, a supernatural glow came over her. Long, thick lashes extended out from her large, brown eyes. All she'd need to do was bat them at him, and he'd be willing to give her anything she asked. And he wanted more than anything to dip his head lower and capture her mouth. His heart raced. This was the first time in a while that he'd wanted so badly to taste a woman. Charlotte and Richard faced each other, both hands touching. No one had ever written a list of rules of when and where a kiss needed to happen, but right here was the time and place.

"Oh my God." The sound of a familiar, screechy voice ruined the moment. Richard pressed his forehead against Charlotte's. This couldn't be happening. Not now.

"Richard, I know that's you."

Charlotte pulled away first, her head turned toward the spot where the annoying voice came from. Richard squeezed her hand and cleared his throat. Without looking, he made the introduction. "Charlotte, meet Octavia, Bailey's—" bile rose in the back of his throat "—mother."

"Oh wow," Charlotte said under her breath.

"I'm more than Bailey's mother," Octavia said, coming closer. "Richard and I go way back."

The territorial act surprised Richard. The only person Octavia ever cared about was herself. Richard had given up a long time ago trying to force Octavia to develop her relationship with Bailey. Shoulders squared, Richard turned for the face-off. Octavia, as expected, strutted awkwardly across the cobblestone street in her heels. A man followed close behind her. Richard would have sworn he carried a jeweled purse matching Octavia's orange outfit. Charlotte gave Richard's hand a squeeze of support.

"Nice running into you," Richard said. He hadn't seen her in eight years, when she came to visit her grandmother and not Bailey.

"Yes, we were just coming from the kick-off for the Royal Regional Contest."

"Competition," the man behind her corrected, "I like to call it that. It gets the girls rowdier, don't you think?" He gave Richard an apologetic smile and extended his hand. "Her husband, Troy Davenport."

"Richard Swayne," said Richard with pity. The name of the pageant sounded all too familiar. This was the one Bailey planned to enter. Did Octavia think after eighteen years of being an absentee parent, she could show up now and offer help? "You're involved with pageantry now?"

Troy spoke up first. A proud smile spread across his face. "My daughter, Antonia, is entering."

"We're getting her the best of everything," Octavia said. "Dress, makeup artist, runway coach, dietitian, pageant hairstylist, you name it. Nothing but the best for our Antonia."

In probably what was a state of shock, Charlotte's fingers went limp. "What about your daughter, Bailey?"

Pinch faced, Octavia frowned. "Oh, is she still doing those? Isn't she too old or, like, in school?"

Beside him, Charlotte started to lunge forward. Intent on avoiding a scene, Richard tightened his fingers against hers. "Great seeing you both," he said.

Richard seethed with anger. Bailey put on a good front with her family. Even with his mother and sisters stepping into her life, a few occasions called for a mother's touch. Richard needed to find Bailey before she found out Octavia was not only back in town but supporting a rival in this upcoming pageant.

Charlotte dug her heels in the ground as they walked

toward her BMW. "Why aren't we knocking that woman down a peg or two?" It killed him to hear the sad, choked-up sound in Charlotte's voice. "I haven't even known Bailey that long and that woman—" she pointed across the street "—that so-called mother blatantly disregarded her own daughter. How dare she?"

Richard pressed Charlotte's back against the door and took the kiss he'd been waiting twenty-four hours for. His thumbs caressed her high cheekbones, wet from frustrated tears.

"Well, then." Swaying, Charlotte blinked up toward him.

"I would love to finish this," said Richard, reluctantly pulling away. The pad of his thumb pressed against the pout of her full bottom lip. "But I need to find Bailey before she runs into mother."

Back on the other side of the street, where Octavia and her husband stood, a group of people began to congregate. A stretch limousine pulled up behind them, along with three men with bright, flashing cameras, taking pictures of the Davenports. Troy must have been someone of importance, he thought with an indifferent shrug. Out of the corner of his eye he spotted Bailey and her girlfriends exiting The Cupcakery. Not sure if he could head her off in time, Richard felt his heart leap into his chest.

"Do me a favor," Richard said to Charlotte. He extracted his cell phone from his pocket. "Call Bailey— she'll answer it when she sees me calling. I just need you to distract her. I am going to try and head her off. I don't want her to see Octavia."

Richard left Charlotte's side and did a quick walk

across the street. He spotted Bailey glancing down at her phone and then putting it back in her pocket to keep walking with her friends. The group moved in slow motion, dressed like a bunch of zombies. The last he'd seen of Bailey today, she'd had an old ball gown draped over her arm and said she planned on meeting up with a few friends afterwards. Richard stopped for a moment and clutched his heart. He needed to prevent any pain headed in Bailey's direction.

"Bailey," he said in a low growl.

A friend of hers stopped walking and elbowed his daughter. "Oh my God, is that, like, your dad calling you like that?"

Curious, Bailey squinted her hazel eyes and blanched. "What are you doing here?" she said. "You're supposed to be out on a date."

"Yeah, we'll talk about that later. In the meantime, why don't you come home with me and Charlotte?" Richard inclined his head to where Charlotte waved.

"Dad," Bailey whined, "you're missing the whole point of you going out on a date with Miss Charlotte. You two are supposed to be hitting it off without me around."

They would have been, if it weren't for a certain someone arriving in town like the Queen of England. "Let's go for a ride." Richard tugged Bailey's hand, but she jerked away.

Still thinking this was a joke, Bailey wagged her finger at him. "You're getting to a certain age, young man, where it's not appropriate to bring your daughter on dates."

"Well, the date is over. Feel free to come home with us."

"Ew."

"Bailey," Richard warned.

One of Bailey's friends called her name just loud enough for Octavia to suddenly stop the ruckus she'd caused. Over the bright lights of the cameraman interviewing them, Octavia called out the moment she recognized them.

Color drained from Bailey's face. "Don't go over there, Bailey," Richard whispered.

Instead of listening to them, Bailey walked toward the commotion. Richard walked with her, eyeing her as she took in everything happening at once. She was a smart cookie. The moment a girl with a tacky tiara too big for her head and bouffant hairstyle turned from Octavia and faced them, Richard's heart broke. She looked to be about eleven. He guessed this was Antonia, the new daughter.

"What's going on?" Bailey asked her mother. "What are you doing here?"

Octavia attempted to hug Bailey, who took a step backward. "Bailey, honey, you're here. This is perfect. Maybe you can give Antonia a few tips. You did that little pageant here after all, didn't you?"

"Who is Antonia?"

The girl with the crown flashed a toothy smile. "Hi, I'm Antonia. You're Bailey."

Still confused, Bailey blinked further. "I don't get what's going on here."

The cameramen shut off their equipment and turned around to start up their own conversations. Troy ended his conversation with whoever was in the back of the limo and stretched his arm toward Bailey.

"This isn't how I wanted us to meet," said Troy. "But I'm Troy, your stepdaddy, and this is your stepsister, Antonia."

"I want to be a beauty queen just like my sister," Antonia said sweetly. "Mommy and Daddy are getting me the best of everything."

So they heard, Richard mused to himself.

"...dresses from Grits and Glam Gowns, a beauty treatment at Ravens Cosmetics and even my very own pageant coach from CEO Runways. They even hired a camera crew to catch every angle of me working and act like the paparazzi so I can get used to being a star."

Richard ground his back teeth together when the limo's back door opened up. Jesus, as if this night could get any worse...

"Richard, my boy," Denny O'Malley, with a cigar dangling between his lips, hollered, emerging from the limousine. "What in the hell are you doing here?"

"I live here, Denny." Richard pulled Bailey back to his side. "This is my daughter."

"You're..." Bailey began but Richard's hand clamped on her shoulder stopped her.

Both of them were immediately on the same page. Neither one of them wanted to bring Charlotte into this. Scanning the parking lot, Richard looked for his date. Did she leave? No, her car was still parked in the same spot.

"You guys know each other," Troy concluded, "great. We'll be one big happy family. We're here to work with the camera crew and Antonia."

"My two girls." Octavia beamed. Antonia sidled up to her mother...stepmother? Richard wasn't sure. In the eight years since he'd last seen her, Octavia had never once been to Richard's home. He doubted she knew where they lived. Antonia looked nothing like Octavia and everything like her father, Troy.

"I don't see how this is going to work."

Another voice came from the limousine. Denny opened the door. Richard spotted a pair of long fuchsia nails gripping the door as the person stepped out, her clear glass heels hitting the ground with a clunk. She didn't look much like the photograph Richard had spotted on Charlotte's computer the other night, but he was sure this was Charlotte's replacement. Not a very good one at that, he'd bet.

"Mitzi, honey, it's too humid out here for you." Denny babied the woman.

Richard took offense. The weather was perfect. As a matter of fact, a cool breeze ran between them.

"I was hired to coach just one person, not two."

"Oh no," Octavia laughed, "she's not entering." The woman had enough nerve to point at Bailey.

Offended as well, Bailey grew angry. Her friends behind her started to laugh at Octavia's obliviousness. "I'm entering, Octavia," Bailey said in a clipped tone, her hands balled into fists at her side, "and I'm getting my own custom-made dress from Lexi Pendergrass."

"Bailey, honey—" Octavia tried to reach for her, but Bailey ducked from her touch. "I had no idea you were still interested." She wrung her hands together. "We just invested in a runway coach for Antonia." Antonia's sweet smile turned to smug, satisfied her position with Octavia wasn't threatened by Bailey. "Let me see if we can work something out. Denny, Mitzi, I believe my husband and I can come to some form of agreement."

"But Bailey has her own personal runway coach as well."

Everyone in the group turned to the newest voice on the scene. Charlotte's long legs glided across the cobblestones like she floated through air. Over dinner Richard was sure she'd pinned her hair up but here her long mane was, bouncing off her shoulders, flowing in the breeze as though an imaginary fan blew in front of her.

"We weren't professionally introduced a few minutes ago," Charlotte said to Octavia. "My name is Charlotte Pendergrass, better known as the premiere runway coach extraordinaire."

And that was the exact moment when Richard knew he'd fallen in love with Charlotte Pendergrass.

Chapter 6

After Bailey and her friends promised to be safe for the rest of the Halloween night, Richard reluctantly let her stay over at her friend's house. She promised to text in the morning when they got up. Who was hc to deny her some fun after a meeting like that with her mother?

Richard then drove Charlotte to the front door of the Pendergrass cabin. He did an oversize circle in the driveway to make sure no glowing eyes in the woods glanced back at him. This wasn't called Black Wolf Creek for nothing; wolves once roamed here, and coyotes did now.

"What happens when you leave to go to your cabin?" Charlotte asked. "Aren't you afraid of being attacked by wild animals?"

They walked the wooden flooring of the wraparound porch. "I'll be okay. They're not that bad here."

"They're there," Charlotte clarified, "so it's settled. You can stay the night. We can talk about what happened tonight."

"I can't do that," protested Richard. He pressed the brass key into the hole and opened the door. Charlotte moved herself against him, lingering between him and the door frame. "I definitely don't want to talk about Octavia."

"We're adults, Richard," she said, then held her hands up. "I promise to keep my hands to myself."

But could he do the same? Richard needed time to think. Charlotte was the first person in a while about whom he'd murmured the *L* word in his head.

Electricity flowed through Richard's veins. Charlotte pressed her hand on his chest. "C'mon, I have some more cookie dough frosting from The Cupcakery."

"Now how am I supposed to say no to that?"

Satisfied with his answer, Charlotte bobbed at the knees. "You're so easy." She let two of her fingers walk the length up his chest. A few inches to the left and she would have felt his heart thump. Not letting her get too far away, Richard took hold of her fingers and pulled her back to him.

"It just takes a pretty smile, and clearly I am easy."

Charlotte's long lashes fanned against her cheeks while she glanced at his lips. Her breath quivered. "Are we about to discuss the kiss from earlier?"

"Let's just talk about the one now."

Richard didn't give Charlotte a moment to answer or ask another question. Their mouths connected. Was it possible to miss a tongue after first tasting it just a few hours ago? Could he be already addicted? Perhaps, he thought, backing her into the kitchen's island, where he lifted her up. Charlotte dropped her purse to the ground. Her fingers moved feverishly against the buttons of his shirt before she grew frustrated and ripped them off. They laughed for a moment, smiling into their kiss. Red wine lingered on her lips.

Richard's hands stroked her leg through the fabric of her dress. His hands came across the thin strip of material. Thigh highs, the original kind? Taking her by her ample backside, Richard stood her up and pulled the entire garment up over her head. She stood before him in a blue satin bra. Her breasts were like a tray of delicious food waiting to be sampled. A matching lace garter wrapped around her waist, hooking a long strip down her thigh into a pair of sheer stockings. A strappy pair of blue shoes remained as well. Richard took a step back and took in all her beauty. The dark blue and her sun-kissed golden skin worked perfectly together. Not believing this perfection stood before him, Richard dragged a hand down his face.

Charlotte bit her bottom lip and began to cover up.

"Nah," Richard whispered, "don't do that. You're too beautiful." He closed the gap between them. The palm of his hand reached for the curve of her waist. He brought his mouth down to her shoulder and kissed the tiny ridges of her collarbone. One and then the other, trailing a set of kisses against her neck. Charlotte rolled her head back and exposed her throat, another place Richard placed a set of kisses. Moaning, Charlotte caressed his chest, causing a distraction from his feeding on her delectable skin. If she didn't stop, he might embarrass himself.

Richard spun Charlotte around by the waist. She gasped, then groaned when he came behind her and took her breasts into his hands. Her back heated against his body. Kneading her skin while stroking her nipples with his thumbs, Richard pressed his lips against the nape of her neck. That soft behind of hers rolled into his hard erection. His hands snaked around her waist like an addict needing a fix. Every touch, every caress— he wanted more. Fast fingers worked her breasts, her ribs, the flat of her stomach, the span of her hips, then delved into the sweet nectar beneath the fabric of her lacy blue panties.

As his knees supported his weight, Richard kissed every inch of her vertebrae as he crouched behind her. The peach-shaped bottom filled his hands. Richard gripped the lacy material and pulled it down, pushing Charlotte's legs apart. Naked except for her heels, Charlotte looked like the sweetest dessert he'd ever laid eyes on. He leaned forward and kissed both cheeks. Still bent over, Charlotte's body offered the perfect access for his tongue to enter her wet folds. As he licked, she moaned. He could hear the sound of her palms moving across the countertop as she came, her first orgasm of the evening.

Richard waited a moment for Charlotte's quivers to stop before he spread her legs a little farther apart and unbuttoned his jeans. He could only move the denim down just enough before the desire to enter her overtook his mind. Both of them moaned in relief as he filled her to the hilt. Charlotte straightened her back; her arms snaked around to his neck and she twisted a bit to pull his mouth down to hers. Between the sweet taste of her mouth, her soft purrs, the wetness of her body and the smell of the two of them together, every sensory system in his body was wide-awake.

Charlotte broke their kiss first. "I have protection in my bedroom."

"Show me the way," Richard said, sweeping her into his arms.

Once he set her on the bed, Richard took a step back and watched her body. The quick memory of all the things he'd thought the first time he laid eyes on her came back to him. He'd imagined they'd be together like this ; never in his wildest dreams had he thought it would be this sweet. Richard protected them with a condom and joined her in bed. They made love until the early hours of the morning.

Charlotte awoke the following morning with a deep stretch. Every inch of her body felt depleted. She wouldn't change a thing.

"Coffee?"

Eyes fluttering open, she focused on the luscious sight of Richard standing in the doorway with two cups of steaming coffee; most importantly, he was shirtless. "I'd love some. Where did you find the grounds?"

"My place," he answered, coming in closer with the dark brew. "I ran over there a little while ago."

"I assume by 'ran,' you mean your morning jog?"

Richard set the blue-and-white-patterned mugs down on the nightstand next to the lamp and patted his washboard abs. "I gotta do what I gotta do."

Please keep it up, Charlotte thought to herself. She made just enough room in the bed to curve her body around his frame when he sat beside her. "Thank you."

"It is the least I can do," said Richard. "Given you're coming out of retirement and all."

Funny how she'd mentally put runway coaching out of her mind once she and Richard returned to her place. Pent-up anger flowed through her veins. Everything about what went down last night was wrong. "I still can't believe you were ever involved with that woman."

"She changed," Richard replied with a hint of sadness.

"Had she? Or was she already that way and expected you to turn out different?" For a moment she wondered if she'd crossed a line with him. Charlotte gathered that most of the women he dated wanted more than just him. They wanted the money that came along with the Swayne name. Charlotte had her own. The divorce did not wipe out her inheritance. But that wasn't what made her and Richard compatible. Last night proved why they were perfect together—explosive together. Charlotte reached out and stroked Richard's bare back with her fingertips. The muscles rippled. She shivered. "I didn't mean to get too personal."

Richard moved from her grip to face her. "We're personal, Charlotte, trust me. It's fine. I also need to let you know about Lisbeth."

Charlotte felt the corners of her mouth tug downward into a frown. "I don't want to know what my gut already tells me."

"I don't know what to say, either," said Richard, "but I don't want there to be any surprises between us if we're going to see each other. Lisbeth has a way of thinking I owe her attention when I see her in town. I've made myself clear about the past being the past. But sometimes…"

Knowing her cousin the way she did, Charlotte felt comfortable enough to finish his statement. "She doesn't know when to quit."

"Not at all. I've tried to be nice, but now it's impossible. And now that we're together, I don't want her trying to hurt you with the past."

Some of Richard's words made Charlotte's heart sing. The other half entertained her. Half laughing, Charlotte rolled her eyes. "She'll be okay, Richard. Lisbeth needs the right kind of attention. She's always been that way, since we were little. But I have another question."

"What's that?"

"Last night, was this—" she waved her hand at the bed and the rumpled sheets "—just a one-time thing? Because I must be honest with you, I went on that blind date last night because I want to be in a relationship." She held her breath and paused for a moment, not wanting to scare him off. Oh, the horror stories she'd heard from girlfriends who told men up front that they were looking to start a family. Some of her friends were left on the date; others never heard from the guys. Charlotte didn't get the abandonment vibe from Richard, but she also knew he'd just finished raising his daughter. Why would he want to go through it again?

Warmth filled her body, sending heat waves like fire the moment Richard placed a hand on her backside and blocked her from getting up. "I'm all in, Charlotte. I look forward to discovering where this will go."

"What do you think Bailey will say?"

"Well, I don't think she's going to be checking for virginal, bloodstained sheets, if that's what you're asking."

"I'm not," said Charlotte, imagining the archaic idea.

Besides, she hadn't been a virgin for a long time. "I'm going to be working with her now, Richard. I need you to trust me."

"I do."

She felt the honesty in his answer deep down in her heart. "I'm going to be tough with Bailey. And before you tell me you're fine with it, I want you to know I've coached beauty queens in Venezuela."

Richard blinked in response.

"Clearly you're not aware that Venezuela produces the most beauty queens in the world." Oh, how she loved the office in Carúpano. It hurt the most that Denny was unwilling to throw that her way. "It's not easy. I'm not easy. Bailey's going to have to wear heels all the time."

"Like you?"

"I didn't wear them in bed last night," Charlotte pointed out, licking her lips. The thought of how Richard got her out of her stilettos brought a whiplash appeal to all her senses. Her toes curled under the sheets.

Richard raised a brow. "Do you wear heels all the time?"

"Except when I'm in bed." Charlotte sat up farther and took the sheet with her to wrap around her naked breasts. Richard traced the material next to her skin.

"I should keep you here more often," he said with a playful tug at the sheet.

"You should at least let me reenergize with some coffee." In truth, Charlotte needed to rest her body. There was only so much a girl could take before she needed to go soak in the garden tub.

"And then you'll try walking without heels?"

"You're funny."

Richard reached beneath the covers toward her feet. She moved her knee to accommodate whatever it was he was trying to do. His large hands gripped the bottom of her left foot and began to massage it. Charlotte let out an involuntary moan. "It can't be good for you to wear those shoes all the time. And not in bed isn't an answer. Don't you own a pair of tennis shoes?"

"I don't play tennis," Charlotte replied drily, though her eyes rolled to the back of her head when his thumb hit a pressure point in the center of her foot.

"Who's the funny one now?"

"Oh, oh," Charlotte purred between trying to get her words out. "I'm just saying I don—*ohhh, yeah*—wear flats. I'm taller that way."

Richard continued to massage her feet, working deep circles into her heels while his fingers managed to press into the space right under her toes. Dear God, she was in heaven.

"I think your foot is permanently arched," said Richard, a scolding tone in his voice.

No way was she going to give up this awesome foot rub, but out of principle and in protest of his disapproval of the shape of her feet, Charlotte feigned tugging her leg away. A dimple sank in on his right cheek. "Are you going to make fun of my deformed feet?"

"Never." Richard lifted her heel and pressed his lips against her big toe. "You're perfect."

Charlotte spent the following two days teaching Bailey the art of pageant walking. The girl had the technique. Clearly someone had already taught her well, because it didn't take long to master Charlotte's lessons.

If Bailey was bothered by the interaction with Octavia, she didn't show it. Charlotte made sure to listen to how Bailey wanted to represent herself for the contest.

Late in the afternoon on the second day, some of Bailey's friends came over to watch and support. Some asked for advice for help with runway modeling, which was a different art all in itself. Charlotte didn't mind. She was having fun. They used the dock outside her house, and she caught glimpses of a shirtless Richard across the way working on a wood project. Around lunchtime, Bailey and her friends hurried off in the boat to pick up pizza from the marina. Richard took the opportunity to come over with a pitcher of lemonade. They sat on the wraparound porch in the rocking chairs and watched the girls drive off in the boat.

"This is the life," Charlotte sighed after a refreshing sip.

Richard cocked a glance at her. A half smile spread across his handsome face. "Country living?"

"I don't hate it," admitted Charlotte, "as long as I have air-conditioning during the day."

"And heat at night?" Richard added.

The last three nights they'd spent wrapped up in each other's arms. The first night had been when Bailey hung out with her friends. After that, Charlotte tiptoed over after Bailey went to sleep. If Bailey noticed Charlotte was there first thing in the morning for anything other than coffee and practice, she didn't let on. All this sneaking around reminded Charlotte of her dorm days. Only this time she had the most sought-after bachelor from back then—Richard.

"And the heat," Charlotte agreed, fighting the blush threatening in her cheeks.

"What about the world traveling?"

"I'm going to miss it, I can't lie. But I think I like waking up in the same place, knowing my family is close by."

"Speaking of your family," Richard began, "I was in town this morning and found your parents having brunch on the patio at Valencia's with Lexi's folks."

Charlotte pressed her lips together and nodded. She'd avoided her mother's calls. It worked better for their relationship for Iris to leave her disapproving messages. By now she was sure Iris must have learned Denny was in town. She didn't think her mother would approach him, but Charlotte wasn't sure her father wouldn't hire a team of lawyers to fight him. "My mother can't believe I was so stupid as to not pay attention to the business fine print," Charlotte admitted to Richard. He reached over and touched her hand.

"She worries."

"She worries about my stupidity looking bad for her. Who wants to invest in a bank whose owner has with a daughter who makes poor choices?"

"You were young," Richard comforted her. "I am sure you're overreacting."

"I'll just wait for you to meet her."

"We met," he said with a boyish grin. "Remember when you moved into the dorms and I had to make the promise to look out for you?"

"Yeah," Charlotte started, biting the corner of her lip. "I was a bit mortified after coming face-to-face with you after, you know, pretending to be twenty-one."

"Oh, so you admit now that you were wrong?" Richard's loud laugh scared off a family of birds from a nest in the high branches of a pine tree.

Charlotte shrugged. "I'll admit that I was there if you admit you purposely pushed Denny on me by introducing us when you thought I gave you some evil eye."

"Nah, it wasn't like you think," said Richard. "I will confess you caught my eye. But I wasn't in the space to be starting up any kind of relationship. Not with what I had going back home."

Nodding, Charlotte understood. "Okay, so fine. You were scared of me."

"I didn't say scared," Richard said quickly.

"You didn't have to, I get it." Charlotte pulled her hand away and fanned it from her toes to her head. "You couldn't handle all this woman."

"Want to test that out now?"

A shiver of pleasure washed over her. "Bailey should be back any minute. I don't want her to think her coach is flirting with her father."

"The coach she set her dear old dad up with on a not-so-blind date?" Richard cocked a brow toward her.

"You got me there," said Charlotte. She flexed her custom-made, high-heeled Timberlands.

"I can't believe every pair of shoes you own has heels."

"There is nothing I can't do in heels that I need flats for." Charlotte stood up. "I bet I can beat you to your porch and back."

Richard stayed in his chair. He folded his arms across his stomach and shook his head. "Sweetheart, I run these woods every morning. I know every inch of this terrain."

"So that's a no?" Charlotte took a step off her porch. "Or are you giving me a head start?"

"Even with a head start, I've still got you beat. All this is going to do is cause some hurt feelings and create a sore loser."

"Does that mean you want ice cream?" She took another step down off the porch. "Aww, you're so cute. How about if you win, I'll take my heels off for the afternoon? And you know the only reason why I take my heels off."

It didn't take any more taunting after that. Richard leaped out of his rocking chair. Charlotte let out a scream of excitement and started to run. Instead of taking the steps like she expected, Richard jumped over the railing and landed a few feet ahead of her.

Arms stretched out to her sides, Charlotte ran and hollered with glee at each step she took. Richard was already over the creek, waiting for her to cross. Tree vines tangled her heels. Charlotte slid a few times down the slope but never fell. As she approached, Richard's eyes were wide and he'd already stepped into the water rather than use the strategically placed stones.

"I don't need help," Charlotte said, swatting him away.

"No, seriously, Charlotte, I need you to trust me and take my hand," he said in an even-keeled tone.

"No way," Charlotte protested. She balanced herself on a smooth rock. Richard stood close enough to stretch his hand and touch her. "You're going to hold me…" Her words cut off as Richard unexpectedly swooped her up and threw her over his shoulder. "Hey!"

In the upside-down view of the pine trees, her house and the creek, Charlotte watched three coyotes descend the mountain toward the back of her cabin. Richard jogged carefully, fast and, most impressively, with her over his shoulders. Once they reached his deck, he set her down on her feet and ushered her inside.

"What are you going to do?" she asked, watching him move to a cabinet by the kitchen door.

"I'm going to warn Bailey and then scare them away." Richard pressed the buttons on a CB radio and gave Bailey an order.

"I'm here," said Bailey, her voice crackling over the intercom and the sounds of water and the engine.

"If you're close, don't panic. We have coyote visitors on Charlotte's property. I am going to scare them off."

Charlotte's heart dropped. "You're going to what?"

Richard clicked off the radio and headed to the closet by the door. It didn't take a genius to know Richard came from a family of hunters. The deer heads mounted on the walls told her everything. But to know he slept with a shotgun near frightened her.

"Are you going to kill them?"

Richard didn't answer. His face was fixed straight while loading brass-colored bullets into the barrels. Once loaded up, Richard stopped at the door and warned her to stay inside.

She didn't.

Charlotte followed Richard outside. He headed to the side of the house facing hers and aimed. She closed her eyes and plugged her ears, screaming after each blast.

When it was over, she heard a faint yelp and opened her eyes in time to watch the animals, all three of them, scurry off into the woods.

"Didn't I tell you to stay inside?" Richard spun around, anger on his face. His green eyes darkened and nostrils flared.

Charlotte's heart leaped into her throat. "I... I didn't..."

In her loss of words, Richard took the opportunity to empty the bullets and lock up the gun before he came to close the gap between them. He cupped her face with his warm hands and tilted her face toward him.

"Jesus, woman, I love you, but you're going to have to learn to trust me. I should have never given in to your silly race. And if I tell you to stay inside, stay inside. This area is not called Black *Wolf* Creek for nothing. And did I see your trash barrels not closed? You know you're inviting danger?"

Charlotte blinked several times. "You love me?"

Richard threw his hands in the air. "Oh for the love of God, you almost got killed and I'm standing here scolding you about the importance of securing your trash and that's what you hear?"

Besides the beating of her heart, yeah, she thought to herself. Charlotte opened her mouth to speak, but Richard shook his head no. Frown lines marred his handsome face.

"No, don't respond right now, Charlotte," he said, his voice at least softening. "This wasn't the way I wanted to tell you. So we're going to save the talk for another time."

Chapter 7

The Monday after Richard professed his love to her, Charlotte found herself seated in front of her mother at Lexi's Grits and Glam Gowns, feeling once again like a scolded child, after confirming the menu for the upcoming Thanksgiving meal. The long list of casseroles was confirmed; green beans, sweet potato, squash and corn were no-brainers. Lexi wanted to incorporate her husband's Puerto Rican dishes as well, and Charlotte looked forward to the mofongo stuffing. Lexi stepped away to help a customer picking up a dress from the other side of the kitchenette in Grits and Glam Gowns.

Finally alone together, Iris Pendergrass swiveled the ice in her tall glass of tea around in her hand. In her younger days, the former Miss Peachville had been the most popular girl around. Everything about Charlotte's mother was perfectly in place. Her ash-blond hair was smoothed back from her even smoother forehead in a tight chignon. While Charlotte had never known her mother to delve into the Botox world, she could never be sure. Medicated or not, Iris had always loved intimidating people with just one raised brow and a glare from her ice-blue eyes. Things weren't so different now.

Thunder sounded outside. It was as if the weather and her mother had conspired together for the rain to force Charlotte to come to Southwood and train new clients at her cousin's studio.

"You want to know what bothers me most?" Iris finally asked.

No, Charlotte thought, *but I'm sure you'll tell me.* "What is it, Mother?"

"Well, besides the fact I warned you about the lowlife you married, you let me find out what Denny did to you through social media."

Charlotte inhaled deeply. "You knew about the divorce."

Iris frowned. Her pinched nose sniffled. "I'm not speaking about that. I mean, thank God for small miracles. Now you're no longer tied to that creature."

No one had ever been good enough for Iris's daughter. As the daughter of a peach farmer, Iris never wanted Charlotte to date a farmer, regardless of wealth. She wanted her to marry a business-minded man, preferably one from old money. Charlotte did not want her mother finding out about Richard. He checked off every negative box in her materialistic mother's mind.

"I can't believe you're not going to fight Denny on

the company. You are the one who built it with your hard work, not his."

"It was his money." Charlotte shrugged. It was easier to accept the loss when defending it to her mother. "I didn't read. I can't get mad at anyone but myself."

"I cannot get over your naivete."

"Thanks, Mother. Are you done belittling me?"

Stiffening, Iris brushed at inconspicuous piece of lint off her dark blue blazer. "I am trying to help."

"By making me feel bad about the choice I made twelve years ago?"

"Well, hopefully you're rebuilding, with all these girls following you around like lost puppy dogs."

It was more like Charlotte followed Bailey around. They went out for breakfast, just the two of them, dished on their favorite celebrities and shows. Bailey told her about *Riverdale* while Charlotte informed her about the hunks she crushed on back in the day. She'd never had this type of connection with her own mother.

Charlotte cast a glance over her shoulder into the studio, where earlier today she and Bailey went over examples of random contestant questions for when Bailey made it to the top three. A half dozen girls practiced on the mock runway while the others walked the hardwood floors in front of the mirror and pageant pivoted. At the center of it all was Bailey, having fun hanging out with her friends and helping them. The girl didn't mind sharing the pageant or her coach. It was like she was secure that Charlotte was still hers. She liked that feeling…being wanted. Charlotte didn't mind, either, as the crowds grew.

"Are you guys talking about the crowd in there?"

Lexi asked, reentering the kitchenette. "If so, I've got some great news for you, Char."

Not now. Charlotte shot a glance at her cousin. "That your husband and brother-in-law aren't going to attempt to make the macaroni salad?" Charlotte asked as she and her mother shared a bonding moment and shivered simultaneously. Neither Reyes man could cook.

"You guys are real cute," Lexi said with a grin filled with snark. "I was going to tell you that the mothers have already paid for your services."

"I didn't set up anything," said Charlotte.

"Don't worry about it," Iris said, patting Charlotte's hand. "I'm going to handle this."

"Mother," Charlotte warned, but it was too late. Iris scooted away from the table and headed into the other room. Lexi blocked Charlotte from getting up.

"Sit down, little cousin," she said. "Maybe you need to let your mom help."

"Help or take over?"

"Help," Lexi clarified in a clipped tone. "I'm a mom now, so I get the need to want to help."

And what a great mother she was. Lexi and Iris were two different species. "You're not like her," said Charlotte.

"No two moms are the same. But when our kids hurt, we will do anything to make the pain go away."

Charlotte grabbed her own glass of tea and took a sip of the sweet brew. "I am not in pain. I have accepted what has happened."

"All five stages of grief," Lexi said. "Without the help of Idris, eh?"

Smiling, Charlotte nodded. "I don't need him."

Lexi pretended to faint. She grabbed hold of the back of the chair before coming around to sit down. "Say what?"

Charlotte turned to face the window to avoid her cousin's questioning stare. She made eye contact with Richard, who was standing outside with the other parents on the sidewalk, spying on their girls while shielding themselves from the rain with umbrellas. He flashed a heart-fluttering smile.

He loved her.

Though the words hadn't left her lips, Charlotte knew she loved him. Was it even possible in such a short amount of time? Charlotte looked away but only caught her cousin staring at her.

"I stand corrected. Say who?"

"What?" Charlotte blinked innocently.

"What's going on with you and Richard Swayne?"

He loves me, Charlotte wanted to say in a giddy outburst, as if that answer explained everything. What she felt for Richard was unlike anything she'd ever experienced before in her life. She couldn't wait to spend more time with him and Bailey.

"I don't know what you're talking about."

"Right," said Lexi. "I've never seen Richard flirt with another woman like what I've just seen. Not even with…"

Even though she stopped herself, Charlotte knew who Lexi thought of. "I know about him and Lisbeth."

"There really isn't a 'them,'" explained Lexi. "I know Lisbeth had a cougar thing for him. She was a year ahead of him in school. He never took her up on it, to my knowledge. I do know Richard's been the number one bachelor around here. He went for quite the pretty penny in last fall's bachelor auction."

No doubt, Charlotte thought to herself. "We're old friends."

"That's right. He did go to FAMU with you. Wasn't he your RA?"

Charlotte nodded. "Yes, and one of the main people who tried to talk me out of quitting school." She twisted her lips at the memory of sitting in his dorm room, pictures of baby Bailey tacked to his corkboard.

"And now his daughter is off to college," Lexi commented with her elbows propped on the table. "He's finally an empty nester. I can't imagine."

Charlotte knew Lexi had a long time before she and her husband, Stephen, would be home alone. "The kids are getting so big," she noted. "Don't rush it."

"I guess," sighed Lexi, giving Charlotte a wink. "Hopefully next Thanksgiving we'll have a new addition."

She doubted it. The phrase *empty nester* rang in Charlotte's mind. She remembered that Richard was her Mr. Right for Now. He might feel like he was falling in love with her, and that could very well be true, but would it still stand when Charlotte decided what road she was going to take to become a mother? In all reality, why would he want to start over with a new baby? She'd heard the jokes he made with Bailey about turning her room into a man cave or tearing down walls to create a loft in their home, and of course the amount of traveling he would be able to do now that he didn't have another mouth to feed. The jokes were in good fun, but a part of Charlotte worried at any hint of the truth.

Outside, Richard was carrying on a deep conversation with Mrs. Vonna Carres, owner of The Cupcakery. *Probably begging her not to sell me any more icing.*

"Hey, now that you're back," Lexi said, tapping the table, "are you still working on your options envelope?"

The envelope containing her IVF pamphlet remained in Charlotte's romance novel as a bookmark. With the fun she had had these last few days with Richard, she hadn't thought about it.

"Not really," Charlotte admitted.

"What about finishing school? And before you protest about your age, the last time we visited Kimber, there was a whole track dedicated to nontraditional students wanting to go back to school."

Charlotte thought about the idea of leaving Richard just as they'd reconnected. She didn't want to, but what lesson would she have learned from her divorce: to stay behind because of a man? Her heart sank at the idea. But Lexi was right. Charlotte knew she'd never feel complete until she finished college. She certainly had a lot to consider.

For most of the week she had left staying at the cabin, Charlotte and Richard were careful with their routine. At night, Richard came and collected Charlotte when he went outside to secure the trash barrels. They giggled like teenagers during their tryst, all the while thinking Bailey hadn't noticed a thing and had just accepted that Charlotte was over at the house before the sun rose in order catch the first cup of coffee.

A night of sensual interludes with Richard caused her to need several water breaks. On one of those trips,

Charlotte tiptoed into the kitchen, and when she closed the door, she saw Bailey standing there with a flashlight under her face. The incident caused Charlotte to scream and Richard to come running out of his bedroom. Thank God this was a time when she'd thrown on Richard's NBA Black Wolves basketball jersey. The material came down to her knees. Richard wore a pair of black baller shorts and rushed into the kitchen.

Busted, as Bailey liked to say. She sat the adults on the couch and paced back and forth in her yellow, footed pajama set. "How long has this been going on?"

"Bailey, we're adults," said Richard. Though he sat down, he placed his hands on his knees and kept his back straight. As he manspread, his thick thigh grazed Charlotte's leg.

Charlotte tried to sink into the cushions of the sofa. She covered her face with sheer embarrassment.

"I understand the two of you are adults, and let me be the first to say—" Bailey stopped pacing and stood in front of them. Her long red hair was piled on top of her head in a messy bun, which bobbed back and forth as she moved. "—I knew there was something between you guys."

"Which is why you set us up on the blind date?" Charlotte asked. Richard sat there with his hand over his mouth, not making a sound.

Bailey held her two fingers in the air. "Scout's honor, I just filled out Dad's questionnaire. Miss Lexi did yours. When I filled out yours, Dad, I just wanted you to meet someone nice. I saw how you and Miss Charlotte were getting along and how she made you smile, so I wanted to see more. I told Miss Lexi and she suggested I sign you up and fill it out to the best of my abilities and let the Fates take over. I guess Mrs. Li really does know what she's doing."

"Why would you interfere?" Richard asked.

Bailey wrung her hands as she stood in front of them. Charlotte felt sorry for the girl. Richard wasn't being cruel. His tone was of concern. That certain hint of disappointment in his voice reminded her of listening to her own parents. Charlotte wondered if she should leave. This was a private matter. She inched her way to the edge of the couch, but Richard wrapped his arm around her waist and pulled her close.

"We're grateful for your attempt, Bailey," Richard finally said. He turned to Charlotte and nudged her. "Aren't we?"

Charlotte blinked. "Yes, we are. Do you have any questions for us? Any concerns?"

"Would you have tried to talk my dad into sending me off to boarding school?"

"What? No, of course not," Charlotte said.

"What about taking my dad on a trip around the world and leaving me home with a babysitter when I was little?"

What kind of women had Richard dated? "After this pageant with you, my job as a runway coach is completely over. If I have to go out of the country, it will be on a trip with your father and hopefully you."

The grip around Charlotte's waist tightened. "Do you have any other questions?" Richard asked.

"Do we need to have the talk about the birds and the bees?"

Charlotte blanched. Richard grabbed her hand and

stood up, shaking his head. He tugged Charlotte with him. "Good night, Bailey."

"Wait," Bailey called out, giggling, "I wasn't going to give you guys the protection talk. I actually want a little brother or sister."

Two days after Bailey found out about them, the rain finally gave up, Richard went back to installing a platform to place over the dock at the Swayne cabin. The pageant and its prizes were great but also coming up soon. If Bailey needed a better place to concentrate on her walk without having to go into town every day, then he'd build her one. The Pendergrass dock was not a viable place for stiletto heels. He winced the few times Bailey and her friends got wedged in spaces between the boards. Charlotte made runway walking an art form. She glided like an angel, never missing a beat.

Speaking of missing. Richard glanced at the time on his cell phone. Charlotte and Bailey had gone into town for a dress fitting, apparently something that couldn't be done yesterday when they were in Southwood.

He didn't like the idea of them driving around in the woods at dark. The coyotes from the other day hadn't been back. After scaring them off, Richard had made sure Charlotte learned to wash off her frosting containers before leaving them in the trash.

Like clockwork, Bailey pulled his truck up the hill and circled the driveway.

"Hey, Dad," Bailey said, hopping out of the driver's side. "Bye, Dad."

Richard shook his head. "It gets worse each greeting." He chuckled and made his way to the passenger's side.

The door opened and Charlotte extended one red heel first, and then the next. She wore a pair of black-and-white-checkered pants that seemed to be airbrushed on.

"Let me help," he said hurrying his steps.

"I can manage to get out of a car, Richard." On that note, a twig twisted beneath the tire of the car and wedged under Charlotte's foot. Richard made it to her in time before she fell.

"You were saying?"

Charlotte rolled her dark eyes. "A gentleman wouldn't gloat."

"Introduce me to one when you see him." Richard nestled his mouth against her throat. She smelled like mocha. His mouth watered. Charlotte stiffened in his arms. He already knew what she was protesting. "Bailey already knows about us."

"She knows about us but she doesn't need to witness our public display," Charlotte said, untangling herself from his arms.

The fact Bailey knew about them and approved was great but it felt even better to see how Charlotte and Bailey got along. They were almost inseparable and that made him happy beyond his expectations. Charlotte clearly meant to be more than a close friend to Bailey. She gave his daughter advice and that warmed his soul. Bailey clung to every word Charlotte said and took it to heart.

Richard glanced up to the balcony, where he found Bailey staring down at them. Had she heard?

"She's right," Bailey called out. "I'm glad you two are hooking up, but it isn't really something I want to see."

Richard dragged a hand down his face and groaned. It was on the tip of his tongue to tell her to go off with her friends, but he remembered the reason they were at the cabin. He winced, feeling a flicker of guilt. They were supposed to spend quality time before she went off to college, and here he was, fondling the girl next door. He cast a glance at Charlotte, who straightened out her frame.

In truth, they were spending time together. The three of them were. The great thing about it was no one seemed to mind. Could life get any better?

"Richard," Charlotte said, "we need to talk."

Those four words never meant things were going to get better. They usually meant life-altering things, such as the time Octavia came to him after study hall and told him she was pregnant, or when he graduated college and she'd come to tell him she'd met someone else. And of course there were the women he dated who'd ended their relationships because they did not want to raise another woman's child.

"What's up?" Richard bit the inside of his cheek to control his emotions. "Let's not talk here. Maybe after dinner?"

Charlotte half smiled and nodded her head. "Sounds like a plan to me. I'm going to change out of these clothes."

"Into a more comfortable pair of stilettos?"

"It never gets old," Charlotte said over her shoulder.

Richard remained outside until Charlotte disappeared through her door before heading inside himself.

The kitchen counter was filled with things for tonight's dinner. Marinated chicken for the grill and a dozen vegetable kabobs. Was this a dinner suited for a breakup?

When he needed to end things with a woman, Richard liked to take them out for one nice, fancy meal, either at DuVernay's or Valencia's in Southwood, where she wouldn't dare to make a fuss in front of her peers.

"You okay, Dad?"

Richard blinked out of his daze. Bailey stood in front of him with her hands on her hips. She wore a pair of pink shorts, a pink-and-white-striped shirt and sparkly stiletto heels. She almost reached the same height as him. Unprepared for how grown-up she looked, Richard leaned against the counter. He knew she was eighteen, and dressed like this she looked like an adult. He wasn't ready.

"What is wrong with you, old man?"

"I think I need you to go upstairs and change into one of those little pony dresses you used to love."

Bailey laughed and waltzed over to the fridge for a bottled water. She had Charlotte's grace down pat. "You're nuts. Did Charlotte tell you the news?"

Charlotte had shared the breakup with Bailey already? Well, probably because they were going to continue working together. Weren't they? At least he prayed Charlotte wasn't the type of person who would cut off ties with Bailey just because she and her father weren't working out. "No," Richard replied evenly, despite the rapid beat of his heart.

"That Mitzi chick who took Charlotte's job away from her fell and hit her head. I know I shouldn't laugh." Despite that, Bailey continued to laugh, a defense mechanism he assumed she used to cover the hurt over her birth mother's preference. "All that money Octavia and what's his face…"

"Troy," Richard provided.

"Yeah, Troy, threw at them, and the coach fell off a stage."

"Is it serious? She's okay, right?"

Bailey's eyes rolled upward. "She'll be fine.

"So speaking of hands," Bailey began, "what are your intentions with my runway coach?"

"I don't know what you mean."

"Sure you don't." Bailey faced her father to make sure he saw her give him an epic eye roll. "I don't want you to screw this up."

Neither did he, but if he questioned himself, what did Bailey think he was going to do? "Did Charlotte say something to you?"

"Did you know Charlotte was a beauty queen in Peachville?"

"I knew she and Kenzie ran in the same circles."

"And did you notice how we have animal heads on our walls while her place is covered with tiaras?"

Richard nodded. "That place has been shelter for many beauty queens."

"I'm just trying to point out the different worlds you two come from," said Bailey.

Something about his daughter's tone reminded him of the disappointed smile on Charlotte's face when he first said he was a farmer. Sure, they'd hashed out what was going on with them at the time, but it had been a while since Richard had felt not good enough. The family was several generations deep with money, yet because Richard still worked the farm, he sometimes felt like he didn't measure up to other people. Even in his recent business proposals, Richard went in with a feeling he didn't deserve to be there. He gulped down the self-pity.

"Dad, I'm going to need you to take Charlotte out on a date, a night on the town. Spruce yourself up a bit." Bailey pointed her long, manicured fingernail at his face. "Shave, even."

"So you don't think the grill is right tonight?"

Bailey gave her head a vigorous shake. "Go clean yourself up and surprise her with some flowers or something."

"But we have this food."

"I'll take care of the food here," said Bailey. "Go."

On the advice of an eighteen-year-old, Richard showered off the grime from today's work and shaved. It was slim pickings in his closet since he hadn't expected to use this quality time with his daughter to go on a date. But nevertheless, Richard cleaned up into a pair of tan slacks and a green, button-down shirt. There were a few nice places in Black Wolf Creek he could take her to.

Not wanting Charlotte to come over in the dark, Richard drove over to her place and knocked on the door. The floor-to-ceiling windows gave him enough of an view of the inside of the place. He didn't like how open it was for anyone to see inside. His heart flounced a bit at the sight of her through the glass. Where he was decked out in something Friday casual-ish, Charlotte wore a white Black Wolves T-shirt knotted at her belly button, formfitting jeans to hug her delicious curves and a pair of bright white tennis shoes. He did a double take at her footwear and grinned.

"Don't you dare laugh," Charlotte warned, opening the door. "Hey, why are you dressed? Aren't we grilling?"

"Change of plans. We're going out to eat."

Charlotte glanced down at her attire. Her face became a little ashen at the thought. Richard reached for her hand. "Don't worry, you look beautiful in and out of heels."

The family-owned Italian restaurant Richard took her to was fancy enough for Charlotte to feel underdressed but secluded enough that once at their private table, no one noticed. They sat at a table in the back by a partition made up from a rack filled with vintage wine bottles.

"We didn't have to go anywhere," said Charlotte after Richard made a delicious wine choice for the two of them: Toast of the Tiara.

A carefree shrug accompanied a lopsided grin that sent bubbles through Charlotte's belly as he raised a brow to ask. "And be under the watchful eye of Bailey?"

"Bailey has practice to do," said Charlotte, then pressed her lips together. Not like Bailey needed much coaching—just more time getting comfortable being in the heels all the time. The last orders Charlotte gave her runway crew was they were eventually going to be able to run a mile in heels.

Richard reached across the red tablecloth. The antique silverware caught the light of the candle fixed in a chianti bottle. Charlotte's lips parted. She wished they were back at her cabin exploring more of one another. Judging from the grin across his face, Richard wished the same thing.

"We'll stop by your place after dinner," he said.

Would they last that long? The back of Richard's pickup truck might have to make do. And she didn't mind at all. Charlotte swore the pent-up desire she had for him oozed from her pores. "I can't believe my time at the cabin is coming to an end."

"Did your furniture arrive at Lexi's?"

With an exhale of relief, Charlotte nodded. "Yeah, just the basic things I can't live without."

"Like a curio filled with tiaras?"

Charlotte bit the corner of her bottom lip. "You've been spying?"

"I had to drive through town to get to my office," explained Richard. "And you know how small-town gossip spreads. Everyone on the street admired your belongings from afar."

A groan escaped her throat. "Great. Well, at least I can be grateful my bureau of personal lingerie didn't fall out."

"Now that I'd like to see." Richard perked up.

The idea of being in her own place again excited Charlotte. She'd felt the freedom for a brief semester when she started college. By her second semester she was married and living with Denny. Staying at Lexi's gave Charlotte plenty of time to find her perfect home. How many quaint, two-story houses with a wraparound porch would she find down here? Thankfully, Lexi's husband, Stephen, owned the number-one local real estate agency and had a knack for finding the perfect home.

"You had something you wanted to talk about with me?" Richard asked, his thumb stroking her hand. The intimate touch made her forget what she wanted to stay. The way the pad of his thumb circled her skin was just like the way his tongue caressed her nipples. Charlotte shivered and shook her head, remembering they needed to talk.

"What exactly is Antonia to Bailey? She doesn't look anything like her."

"Bailey is a Swayne through and through," Richard said in a clipped voice. Hard lines appeared on his face.

Charlotte studied the frown marring him. "That she is. It shows in her pageantry that she's a Swayne and a Hairston. We worked together on her pageant questions, gown changes and her walk today, and I'm telling you, she's got talent."

"I couldn't tell you," answered Richard with a heavy sigh, the corners of his mouth softened. "You'd think we would know if Octavia had another child, but we didn't even know she got married. When she left us, the guy she then married was not Troy."

"That's so sad." Charlotte realized she shouldn't complain about her own mother's coolness. At least, in her own way, Iris cared. To not tell your own flesh and blood what went on in your life was beyond her. "I don't get her."

"Neither do I," sighed Richard, withdrawing his hand to lean back in his seat. "I gave up trying to figure her out a long time ago."

"What about forcing her to have a relationship with Bailey?"

"Octavia gave up all parental rights to my daughter."

"Legally?"

Richard gave a slow nod. "Not in the courts, but in a letter she wrote to me and my family. I never filed it because I'd hoped she would come to her senses one day and have some form of remorse for leaving Bailey."

"Vile," Charlotte hissed; all the while her heart broke. "What does Bailey think?"

"Bailey doesn't know about the letter's existence. She gave up considering Octavia her mother."

Charlotte felt her brows raise automatically.

"What if she finds out?" Charlotte nibbled on her bottom lip. "Bailey is strong and independent, I get that, but she is still a human with feelings."

Richard reached out again and recaptured Charlotte's hand. "I love that you care so much about Bailey, but she will be okay. Now why are you asking about their relationship?"

"Mitzi injured herself yesterday, falling off the stage." She watched the way Richard pressed his lips together to try not to laugh. "I told you pageantry is a sport."

"I know it's wrong to smirk, but I don't feel bad. Why do you sound so concerned?"

"As much as I hate Mitzi for what she's done, she is still a human."

"I swear, before the night is through you're going to be inducted into sainthood."

Charlotte laughed. "I'm not sure that's how it works. But either way, it doesn't matter what I wanted to talk about."

"Tell me anyway," Richard pressed.

"Octavia offered me a blank check to train her step-daughter."

Charlotte studied the contours on Richard's face. Deep lines played at his forehead. She reached across the table and tapped his hand. "But after what you just told me, I can't wait to rip it up in her face."

Chapter 8

Richard took the dangling key ring with the tiny sparkling silver tiara to Charlotte's place of residence, Lexi's place, from her dainty fingers. After their date on Friday, they spent the rest of the weekend rearranging the furniture that arrived into place and then enjoyed their last few nights in Black Wolf Creek.

On Monday, it was time for her to start her new life in Southwood. Watching her behind wiggle as she walked in front of him down the hall drove him nuts. If he didn't get her inside the place right now, he might take her right here. With one gust he swooped her into his arms. Charlotte squealed in delight and wrapped her arms around his shoulders.

"Quiet now." Richard hushed her with a quick kiss on her strawberry-tinted lips. "You don't want your neighbors knowing what you're doing."

"What is it we're about to do, Richard?" Charlotte asked as she nibbled on his collarbone through his green pullover.

Any other Veterans Day, Richard would be at work on the receiving docks at the farm, should a package be delivered, so that the employees could attend Southwood's parade to honor the vets. Today, Swayne Pecans was receiving an equipment drop-off for the pecan trees, but Richard was supposed to leave things alone—according to his father. Mitchell Swayne was taking care of everything. This gave Richard time to help Charlotte get settled into Lexi's place and reacquainted with downtown Southwood. Richard and Bailey lived on the other side of Southwood in a two-story, four-bedroom home. He couldn't wait to have her over to his place for dinner, perhaps this Sunday evening for a home-cooked meal from a stove, not a grill.

"I'm about to strip you out of these tight jeans you're wearing and get you out of these heels." Though he loved her heels, Charlotte got better traction in bed without them. His hands fumbled with the keyhole. Thoughts of taking her right in the foyer entered his mind. These last days in Black Wolf Creek had been filled with bonding time with Charlotte and Bailey. But adding Charlotte into the mix, sweet as it was, had been sexually frustrating. The ladies stayed up for long hours, Charlotte filling Bailey's head with beauty pageant stories from other countries. As fascinating as the tales were, the time prevented Richard from having his way with Charlotte. She didn't help matters, either, wiggling around in leggings, heels and tied-up T-shirts.

Richard's body was so rock hard right now he might crack the door open if the lock didn't work fast enough.

The pent-up sexual frustration had clearly boiled over to the Charlotte as well. Her long fingers were already stretching his shirt over his head. The moment Richard entered the apartment, his steel-toed boot hit the luggage on the floor by the door. "I thought we put everything in your room."

"We...did..." Charlotte said between kisses against his jawline. She drove him crazy with her mouth.

"Then whose stuff is this?"

They both stopped what they were doing to look at the brown-and-gold luggage by his feet. Though it bore the same LV initials as Charlotte's bags, these weren't hers. "Wh-what the hell?" Charlotte stuttered.

To answer them, a young woman with black hair and hazel eyes stepped out of the bathroom, wiping her hands on the back of her jeans; she stopped walking and stood right by the shelf of Charlotte's accolades. Tiaras on the top shelf, plaques on the bottom.

"Kimber?" Charlotte asked.

"Uh-oh," Kimber said. "I take it you didn't hear from Lexi today."

Richard set Charlotte down on her heels and kissed his afternoon of play away. Charlotte pushed her way in front of him and crossed the room to hug Lexi's niece by marriage. He followed them into the living room, where a stack of books was strewn across the glass-top coffee table. Papers, pens, erasers and a giant green-and-orange thermos sat on the corner. Someone was cramming.

"No, she didn't," said Charlotte. "Is everything okay?"

"Oh, probably because I didn't hit Send on the last one I came up with." Kimber extracted a bedazzled pink cell phone from her bra and offered an apologetic smile in Richard's direction. "I keep saying after I study one more page I'll let her know, and then I was afraid if I let my uncles know that I'm here they'll start to worry and want to come over, and then of course there's Philly."

The sounds of a college senior on the verge of hyperventilating were all too familiar. Richard strode into the kitchen in search of a brown paper bag. He found most of the drawers empty, reminding him to take Charlotte out to the grocery store at some point. Finally, after searching in the empty cupboards, he found the bags in a thin drawer by the stove. As an RA he'd kept them by his front door. When he returned into the living room, he found the two ladies seated on the black leather couch.

"I am so sorry about intruding," Kimber wept. "I can go see if Dario is downstairs and stay with him."

The father in him panicked. "No," he blurted out. Stephen and Nate Reyes would string him up if they knew their niece had wound up at Dario Crowne's apartment. Dario was a nice kid and all, but he had a reputation with the ladies in town.

Charlotte raised her brows at him. He hated the idea of not being able to have some alone time with her, but he understood the importance of peace and quiet for Kimber.

"I'll gather all this stuff up and get out of your way," said Kimber.

"It's okay." Charlotte inclined her head at Richard.

The inevitable was coming. This was the one of the

rare times Richard hated being the mature and responsible one. Nodding, he headed toward the door. Charlotte met him in the foyer at the same spot where less than five minutes ago he'd wanted to take her.

"I'm sorry," Charlotte whispered. "I didn't know, but there's no way I can tell her…"

Richard shushed her with a quick kiss. "It's okay. You're now a citizen of Southwood. We'll do this," he said, wagging his finger between the two them, his touch lingering at the collar of her gold sweater, "another time."

It killed him to see her lashes fan against her high cheekbones in the same fashion they did when she closed her eyes right at the brink of an orgasm.

"You're too sweet, Richard Swayne."

"You say that now." Richard forced himself to smile. "But a moment ago I was about to rip off your clothes…"

"Hey, guys," Kimber's voice called out, acting like a bucket of cold water. "I forgot to tell you that I did order some pizza. Maybe that will help with the idea of me crashing here for a few days."

Just a few days more, Richard told himself. He inhaled deeply and gave one straight-armed wave. "I'm good, Kimber. I'll see you around."

Charlotte's fingers curled around his collar. She brought him down for a deep kiss. Richard savored the sweetness of her mouth. "I'm going to hold you to that promise."

"Don't worry, Bailey will be off at school soon, and we'll have all the time in the world to be alone together," Richard replied.

Once the apartment door closed behind him, Richard took a moment to catch his breath and gather his bearings. He wasn't some lovesick boy. He was just a man in love. The fact they hadn't spoken the *L* word since the first time he'd blurted it out wasn't lost on Richard. He wanted there to be a special moment between them. The last time he'd said the words to a woman, it was to Octavia, nineteen years ago, in the back seat of his father's car out at Bayou Besos, a local spot for teenagers back in the day. The other time had been when she was huddled in the girls' bathroom at Southwood High School cradling the toilet, crying over what they found out was morning sickness. Neither time was romantic. Richard couldn't explain what it was with Octavia. All he knew was that, with Charlotte, this was something new. It was pure. And he couldn't wait to set up an evening alone with her.

Finally able to walk, Richard extracted his phone and decided the best thing to get his mind off his desire for Charlotte was to talk about work. The new equipment, aptly called the a tree shaker, cost a pretty penny but promised to keep the majority of the pecans in the bin for transfer, thus lessening the backbreaking job of raking the orchard forest for fallen nuts. The job was tedious, and yes, kept people employed, but this machine offered a cutback and advancement for those who wanted to learn the business.

Swayne Pecans had been in business for decades. The enthusiasm to continue the legacy took dedication. Richard was the last in the line for his father. Kenzie and Maggie had no desire to work in agriculture. Given the way things were going with Bailey, it looked like there would be another beauty queen in the family. What a shame he never had anyone interested enough to pass the business on to.

"Mitchell here."

The sound of his father's voice made Richard smile. "Hey, Dad."

"Son," Mitchell Swayne said cheerfully. "I was about to call you and tell you about the successful delivery."

Richard listened to his father go on about the morning at the orchard all the way down the stairwell of the apartment complex until he got out to the garage and behind the wheel of his SUV. "Sounds like everything went off without a hitch."

"Don't act like I'm a retired old man," joked Mitchell. "I've got plenty of farming left in me, especially now since you've switched sides and gone corporate on me."

A suit and tie didn't take the farmer out of Richard. "I'll stop by sometime this week."

"So you've ended your vacation with Bailey at Black Wolf Creek, huh?"

"Beauty queen duty called," Richard said.

"How proud your mother and sisters will be. Speaking of them," Mitchell went on. "There's been a change in things this year for Thanksgiving."

"Is Mom cooking?" Both men shared a laugh at his mother's expense.

"Right. I doubt that. Kenzie wants to have Thanksgiving at Magnolia Palace. Erin offered to cook a turkey. I may deep-fry one. Are you and Bailey up for that?"

A part of him wanted to spend the holidays with just Bailey. Bailey and Charlotte. But considering this would be her first holiday back, he was sure Charlotte had plans with her family. He would have to settle for seeing her after Thanksgiving, if he could wait that long. The idea of them being apart didn't sit well with him. It made him miss her already. She was their family.

Richard's parting words—about Bailey's imminent departure—didn't go unnoticed for Charlotte. He looked forward to his empty nest, and who was she to begrudge him for it? Charlotte knew she needed to distance herself from him.

It wasn't too hard. The first week of settling into Lexi's apartment, now with a roommate, Charlotte grew used her routine in Southwood. Lexi talked her into helping out some of her clients from a youth program and Charlotte couldn't turn her down. She woke up in the mornings and headed down to the studio without having to use a car. Charlotte didn't mind the walk. In some of the places she'd lived in, girls walked miles to work with her. This was nothing. This was quaint.

Southwood was the perfect spot to settle down. Lexi's apartment overlooked the town square. She loved the way the shops of various sizes were lined up. It wasn't hard to imagine this place in the olden days with dirt streets lined with horses and buggies.

Charlotte waved to Miss Gwen from Osborne Books and trotted over to the purple shop to help her pull out a glass-topped table, whose lavender-and-ivory umbrella protected Charlotte's eyes from the bright sun. The temperature had dropped, but the brightness remained. A touristy couple sat down at the table they just set up. It didn't take long for Charlotte to realize most people used the bookstore as a place to stop and enjoy their pastry or cupcake from The Cupcakery next door. Miss Gwen thanked Charlotte and told her to come back in a few weeks, that she had a book for her.

Though not sure what she meant by that, Charlotte promised to come by then. Before heading over to the studio, Charlotte stopped in and picked up a couple of cupcakes for the moms waiting with their daughters. Saturdays were set aside for free runway lessons for young girls in the toddler range from the Four Points area. Kids from Peachville, Black Wolf Creek and Samaritan came over. The cuteness overload increased Charlotte's desire to have a child…one way or another. This morning she'd taken out her options envelope from her nightstand and reviewed adoption. Some of the girls in the troupe today were in need of permanent homes. Charlotte just lacked the home right now. On numerous occasions Richard had made it clear about how much he looked forward to being done raising kids. Until she had her own life and home situated, she'd put starting her own family on a back burner. Maybe she'd revisit it after the New Year and enjoy her time with Richard for now.

Pushing the mental obstacles out of her mind, Charlotte persevered on and enjoyed the excitement of her runway lessons today and then get into a bit of dance practice. It gave Charlotte a chance to don the sneakers Bailey had gotten her. Out of habit, Charlotte checked her reflection in the glass of the door, fluffed the ends of her feathered hair and let her tresses fall to her thin sweater in rich gold, burgundy and orange. Her burgundy heels clicked on the black-and-white tiles of The

Cupcakery and shoved her oversize bag containing her comfortable shoes farther back on her shoulder.

At this time of day, she'd already beat The Cupcakery's morning rush. Charlotte learned quickly if she timed her schedule out just right, she'd miss the foot traffic but still come in when a fresh batch of cupcakes were brought out.

"Charlotte!" Tiffani Carres greeted her.

She waved Charlotte over to the front counter. The delicious smell of decadent chocolate filled the air.

"I swear, if you guys were able to bottle up the scent in here you could make a fortune," said Charlotte. Two elderly ladies seated at a hot-pink table nodded. Like most people, they shared an oversize cupcake— caramel, Charlotte guessed—and each had their own steaming cup of coffee.

"I'll keep that in mind next time British Ravens comes into the shop."

A former local beauty queen, British had fallen in love with Donovan Ravens of Ravens Cosmetics and relocated here.

"What's on the menu today?" Charlotte asked, her eyes spanning what was in the display case. Crunched up red-and-white peppermint candies sprinkled the top of a white-iced chocolate cake with a red wrapper. "Christmas already?"

Tiffani put her fingers to her lips to shush her. "Don't tell anyone. You know Southwood likes to hold off rushing the seasons. It's Halloween, Thanksgiving and then everything Christmas."

Charlotte gave her head a slow nod. "I think I did notice no one had decorations up just yet. A lot of the streets in the cities I've traveled to in the States were already lined with Salvation Army Santas, Christmas trees and holiday music before Halloween."

"Don't fret," said Tiffani. "The minute the last bit of turkey is sealed up in a Tupperware container, all Christmas hell will break out."

"Really?" Charlotte giggled at the thought of a big red, white and green explosion of elves running up and down Southwood's cobblestone streets, decorating everything.

She wondered if by next year at this time she'd be in her own place with Richard. Or would she and Richard want to decorate? The thought made her hiccup. Tiffani raised a brow in seeming amusement, but any question she had went away when the bells above the door jingled. A couple walked in together, arm and arm. Charlotte wondered if the two were an actual couple but decided they reminded her more of Richard and Bailey. The man stood next to Charlotte, confirming her suspicions as she noticed the gray in his beard. Beside him, the girl untangled herself from his grip so she could press her fingers against the glass display, despite the red sign asking customers to refrain from doing so. Glitter spelled out the word *please*.

"Welcome to The Cupcakery," Tiffani sang out to them. "I haven't seen you guys around here before."

"Daddy and I are here for the Royal Regional Contest." The girl turned her back to the display case, her arms still spread out across the glass for dramatic effect.

Used to entitled girls like this, Charlotte rolled her eyes and inhaled. The rumbling sound from under her sweater reminded her why she was here. She stepped forward toward the register.

"Tiffani, I'll just get a dozen assorted."

"Sure," Tiffani said, taking her eyes off the newcomers. "I'll even throw in a few minis for the little FBITs."

"What does that stand for?" the young woman asked.

Tiffani's lips clamped into a tight smile. Her shoulders rose with what could be controlled annoyance. "It stands for Future Beauty Queens in Training. There's a session going on in a few minutes at Grits and Glam," she said, casting a glance at the dad and then back at the girl, "and an age limit."

Charlotte hid her smile behind a faux cough. The two ladies at their table, however, had no shame. They burst out laughing. One even pointed toward an empty chair near them. "Y'all, c'mon over here and have a seat with the geriatric gang."

Pink box in hand and the threat of laughter bubbling, Charlotte took her package and headed out the door.

Chapter 9

A week before Thanksgiving, Richard called Charlotte and invited her to his family's company Thanksgiving luncheon. They'd been an official couple for a while now and Charlotte was anxious to re-meet the rest of Richard's family. This meant something to her. He cared. This budding relationship was unlike anything she'd ever experienced before. Denny's parents had never concerned themselves with him or her. She remembered how disappointed she'd felt because she always wanted to have that big, loving, extended family with her in-laws. This inclusion made her feel wanted. Loved. The plan for him to pick her up from her apartment changed when an out-of-town business emergency called him away. Instead of Richard showing up, his sister Kenzie surprised her. It wasn't the first time business had called him away in the weeks they'd been seeing each other. She thought she understood. But tonight she felt a pinch of resentment.

Charlotte loved catching up with her old beauty queen friend. Kenzie gave Charlotte the tour of the headquarters and a detailed history of the Swaynes and their importance in the development of Southwood. Charlotte understood. She was a Pendergrass. Her family, too, was part of the founding fathers. The Pendergrass family lore stated that her great-great something grandfather had started a bank and offered loans to people of all colors in town. She felt proud, knowing his actions helped other people set up roots in Southwood and raise their families. Thinking about it reenergized Charlotte's desire to have a baby. She decided to speak with Richard and let him know where her mind was at.

Everyone attending the luncheon spoke fondly of Richard. The secretaries made it no secret they missed seeing him come in every day when he was away. A few of them recalled how jealous they were of Richard's personal secretary. Considering how blind she'd been to Mitzi becoming close with Denny, Charlotte wondered if she needed to be worried. A slight wave of nausea washed over her, but she sipped on her clear cup of cola and tossed the idea out of her mind. Sure, Richard spent a lot of time away from Southwood. But this was what she wanted, right? Richard wasn't staying late at his office; he was traveling down to Florida for business. He'd promised to meet Charlotte at the party today.

"Charlotte."

Charlotte turned at the sound of her name. The fluttering of her heartbeat reached her ears at the sight of Richard heading over toward her with the world's cutest baby perched on his shoulders. If it were scientifically possible, her womb would leap out of her body right now and attach itself to Richard in a bear hug.

"Hi there," Charlotte breathed.

The baby, roughly ten months old, looked like he might have a future as a bongo player, considering the way he banged on Richard's head. The baby with loose, red curls squealed in delight at the woman standing next to Charlotte.

"There's mama's baby," Kenzie cooed while stretching out her arms. "Charlotte, this is my son, Maverick."

Richard lifted his nephew over his head. "What have you guys been feeding this monster?" He leaned over and kissed Charlotte's cheek. "I've missed you."

"You were missed here, too," Charlotte answered honestly. She pressed her hand against the green checkered shirt he wore under a dark blazer, right where she could feel his heart thumping in her palm.

"Wow," Kenzie said. "Don't you feel bad for never coming to any of my pageants, Richard?"

Richard took his eyes off Charlotte for a moment. "What?"

"I was just thinking about how much time you two would have had together if you met back in the day."

If that were true, Charlotte thought with reluctance, there wouldn't be a Bailey in the picture. "I think we've made up for lost time," she said.

"We need to make up for some more lost time," Richard growled softly into her ear.

The warmth of his breath against her earlobe made

her knees weak. Richard wrapped his arm around her waist to secure him against his side. The daggering stares from the secretary pool felt all too familiar from back in Charlotte's beauty queen days.

"You're just the traveling man," Kenzie went on.

"Bailey's been gone picking out her dorm stuff with her roommates," Richard said with a shrug, "so I finally get to do adult things." The span of his fingers reached down to Charlotte's lower back. Any farther and he'd pull up her cream-colored sweaterdress.

Perhaps she had some sort of torture fetish. One moment Charlotte wanted to tuck a baby into bed with Richard and the next she just wanted to get into bed with him. *Knowing good and well he does not want to revisit changing diapers again*, an inner voice scolded her.

"Hey." Richard nudged Charlotte's side. "Want a tour?"

"I already gave her one," answered Kenzie.

"A tour from the girl who doesn't work here?" Richard laughed. Charlotte shook her head at the sibling banter.

Baby Maverick leaned out of his mother's arms into Charlotte's. Her heart melted.

"He's trying to make me jealous," Richard said, pinching Maverick's toes through his adorable little black sneakers.

The baby turned and rested his head against Charlotte's shoulder.

Kenzie clucked the roof of her mouth and let out a laugh. "Wow, he usually only goes to family."

"Well you need to be careful, li'l man," Richard said

to Maverick. "This lady's mine. You can't steal her with your cute, chubby cheeks."

"I don't know," sighed Charlotte, "this hug is everything right now."

"Tell me about it," Kenzie went on. "I can have a bad day at work and Maverick can cure everything."

"Congratulations, Kenzie," said Charlotte. "Maverick is beautiful."

Beaming, Kenzie nodded.

Charlotte lingered a little while longer, absorbing that baby scent. She reluctantly handed him back once Maverick became fussy.

"And this is why I'm glad I don't have more," Richard teased his sister.

Hands free, Richard led Charlotte back through the building and to the mail room, where he'd started out. He'd eventually worked his way up to his own corner office that overlooked the orchards. Charlotte understood Richard's devotion to the company and keeping up the tradition of the business. Hundreds of employees attended the luncheon with their families. Charlotte had heard the love and appreciation from the families.

As they walked and talked, Richard held on to Charlotte's hand. Her mind was preoccupied with her future. She loved and hated the way he made her feel but she also wanted to raise a child. It wasn't fair of her to ask Richard to start all over again. Excitement dripped with every syllable he spoke about going out of town without having to worry about who would look after Bailey or about her coming home late, or finally being able to do all the things he missed out on due to being a teenage parent. Walk around naked, not have to worry about making sure someone else had dinner, and even eating ice cream for dinner if he wanted without feeling guilty for being a bad role model. How could she be mad at him for finally living his dreams? She knew she was being selfish, but when Richard touched her, she felt a wholeness come over her. Did she want to give up her dreams of being a mother just to be near him? No, she thought sadly. She wasn't getting any younger.

The pageant was a week from today. After that, things would go back to her new normal. The Christmas break and New Year rapidly approached. Bailey would head off to school, and Richard would remain busy and away with his new career. He made it clear he did not want to do it all over again. Until she decided to tell him her plans, Charlotte intended on enjoying the time they had together.

The sun dipped below the tops of the trees, sending a dusty gold glow over the farm.

"This view is fantastic," said Charlotte.

"Isn't it?" Richard sat beside her with two glasses of wine in his hands.

Full from the buffet earlier, Charlotte shook her head. "I can't believe you've left this office view."

"This will still be my place," he said, "but you ought to see my office."

Charlotte stood closer to him. "I can't wait."

"Neither can I." Richard set the glasses on the desk to free his hands so he could stroke her shoulders. "Come with me."

A flash of mystery twinkled in Richard's eyes. "We are not going to be cliché," Charlotte warned him, "and christen your office."

Richard took Charlotte's face in his hands. His mouth neared hers for a sensual kiss. His lips were soft and demanding at the same time. Charlotte interlaced his large fingers with hers. It was as if her feet floated just above the floor. "I just wanted to take a moment to show you how much I've missed you these last few days," said Richard, breaking the kiss.

"I've missed you, too," said Charlotte. "How was your work trip? You were so busy showing me all the ins and outs of the business."

Richard rested his hip against the desk. Charlotte found herself drawn to stand in between his thick thighs. "It was great. You'll have to come with me next time. You'd like traveling with me," he said.

Charlotte's heart cracked, knowing her decision about her future. "I've traveled enough in my lifetime, Richard, remember."

A tight smile showed his displeasure about her answer. "I'm trying here, Charlotte. Is there something going on?"

Not wanting to mar the situation between them, Charlotte offered a sweet smile that she felt didn't reach her eyes. "It's been a long day, I'm sorry. Maybe I'm not good company tonight."

"C'mon and watch something with me." Richard rose and led Charlotte outside. "I know something that's worth watching." Richard brought Charlotte out to the balcony where two chaise lounges sat with a small round table. A bottle of champagne perched in of an ice-filled bucket, two long-stemmed crystal glasses on the table beside it. Richard motioned toward a chair for her to take, while he sat at the other. They sat in silence as the sun slipped between the branches of the miles of pecan trees. A cool nip filled the breeze in the moonless evening air.

"This is beautiful," Charlotte gasped.

"Yeah," he responded. "I know."

Thanksgiving Thursday, the smell of roasted turkey made Charlotte's stomach growl each time she walked into the kitchen. Every time she tried to help, however, Iris and Aunt Mary shoed her out. The mother takeover kept everyone at bay. Charlotte headed outside, where she found Lexi seated on the porch swing, wrapped in an oversize shawl. Lexi opened the orange plaid material and patted the seat beside her.

"I'm going to go crazy if I stand inside my house listening to my mother," said Lexi.

"It has to be better than the silent treatment, though, right?" Charlotte remembered the rough patch Lexi and her mother had gone through when Mary did not agree with her life choices. At least Iris always spoke to Charlotte, even if her tone was laced with ridicule. Even today, her mother silently disapproved of Charlotte's outfit. Charlotte had gone with a short, blue plaid skirt and a white cable-knit sweater and her favorite pair of heeled Timberlands.

The scuffle on the lawn drew Charlotte's attention. Stephen, his brother Nate and their cousins, Julio, Ramon and Jose all chased a black-and-white soccer ball across the lush green lawn of the suburban neighborhood. Like those of most homes today, the driveway was packed with cars, and so were the curbsides. The soccer ball hit one of windows of a sleek black car.

"Time," shouted Julio, rushing to inspect the damage. "The dent will only help it look better."

Lexi turned to face Charlotte. "I can't complain about things. I wanted to do Thanksgiving here at the house."

The home had belonged to Stephen and Nate's older brother, Ken, before he and his wife had passed away, leaving behind their two girls, Kimber and Philly. Philly, now eleven, ran back and forth with the grown men. Kimber hid upstairs in her old bedroom, studying. Last night would have been a perfect night for Richard to come over, Charlotte thought, but his own Thanksgiving celebration had kept him busy. They'd tried to coordinate a time to meet up today, but Charlotte doubted that would happen.

"Are we going to see Richard today?" Lexi asked, nudging Charlotte's shoulder. "I see Ramon is already here. He said they ate around noon."

Biting her lip, Charlotte shook her head no. "Ramon said he got a pass to come over early because his brothers are here. As for Richard…" Charlotte paused to shrug her shoulders. "He's got his family thing going on. This is his last Thanksgiving with Bailey before she goes to college."

"You don't sound so happy. Have you admitted you love him yet?"

The word *love* shocked Charlotte's heart with an ache. "He knows I love him."

"Why do you sound so sad?"

"Because I want something Richard can't give me right now."

"A baby?"

Charlotte nodded. "I don't even have to physically give birth." After this last week working with the toddler beauty queens and holding Maverick, the desire to be a mom overwhelmed her.

"Hang on," Lexi said, tapping her chin. "Isn't one of the options adoption?"

Charlotte nodded. "Yep. And don't think I haven't thought about the group from Samaritan that come into the studios on Saturdays. Some of them live in a foster home."

"Raising a preteen and a toddler isn't as glamorous as I make it," said Lexi with a joking smile.

"Kimber and Philly think of you as their savior," said Charlotte. "Kimber told me about how you made sure they had a hot meal that didn't come to the table as a combo or a pizza box."

Lexi cringed with a shiver. "Don't remind me. I swear if Amelia were here, we'd have a debate over who was the worst cook, Stephen or Nate."

Amelia Marlow Reyes was Nate Reyes's wife, a local business owner and producer for Multi-Ethnic TV.

"You and Amelia debate," Charlotte began with suspicion, "but y'all allowed them to make the potato salad?"

"How could they mess that up?"

"I don't know, cuz," Charlotte said. "I've seen some pretty out-there recipes online. I may not be the best cook in the world, but even I know raisins don't go in the potato salad."

"That box belongs to Philly," Lexi said quickly. "She loves them in her oatmeal."

"We'll see," Charlotte teased.

"Let's get back to you and Richard Swayne—you know, the man you're in love with."

"It doesn't matter if I'm in love or not. This is a no-win relationship."

"So, what's the plan?"

Charlotte took a deep breath, hoping the idea would stop the pounding in her heart. "After the pageant, I'm going to end things with Richard."

There, the words were out there in the universe, rather than written on a piece of paper and shoved in her options envelope. The idea pained Charlotte, but she knew it was for the best. Charlotte knew she would need to focus on mending her heart, and what better way than with a new house she could prepare for a new child who needed a home? She couldn't stay at Lexi's forever. She needed a home of her own.

Lexi rocked the swing with her foot on the porch. "I can't say I agree with handling things like that. You haven't told Richard about your desire to have a baby, have you?"

"No." Charlotte shook her head from side to side. "Every time he talks about being able to travel and come home to a house and not have responsibilities, what am I supposed to do? Richard deserves the father of the century award for stepping up and taking care of Bailey on his own. It was his responsibility, but he did it. I can't really ask him to go through that again," said Charlotte.

"Yes, you absolutely can," countered Lexi.

"I don't know." Charlotte frowned.

"I'll support you in whatever you decide," said Lexi.

"I know." Charlotte nodded. "You giving me a job

at Grits and Glam Studios has been wonderful. I can't thank you enough."

"I didn't *give* it to you," declared Lexi. "It is all you. You're in high demand around here. That paycheck you got today was one hundred percent of the money from the parents for working with the girls. I can't help but reap the benefits in my shop for your presence."

Charlotte fought the blush threatening to accompany the smile she tried to suppress. This was getting too mushy. She sighed and stood up from the swinging bench. The motion made her woozy. Her eyes moved around the neighborhood. A wide variety of single-family and two-story brick homes stretched down the street. The underground power lines helped seal in the quaintness of the neighborhood. A couple of small children raced down the sidewalks, and teenagers played at the end of the driveways with their basketball hoops. There were a few for-sale signs in the front of the neighborhood. Maybe she'd get Stephen to show her some.

The silver bells tied to the door with a giant red bow jingled as the front door squeaked open. Arthur and David Pendergrass pushed the screen door open and stepped into the cool air. The brothers wore matching red-and-gray throwback jerseys from their days at Southwood High School.

"Daddy," Lexi warned.

"Dad?" Charlotte shook her head before her father got the chance to explain.

"Relax, niece of mine," said Uncle David. "We're going to teach my son-in-law and his family a few lessons in American football before we eat."

The only thing Charlotte could do was sit back, hold

hands with Lexi and pray no would need to call the paramedics. A few neighbors joined the impromptu game against the Reyes and Torres men. Each time a car came through, the men stood off to the side like teenagers and politely waited for a clearing to play two-hand touch in the streets. Her stomach still bothering her, Charlotte headed inside to get a carbonated drink. Her mother warned her not to ruin her appetite. Through the glass of the front door Charlotte saw pulling into the driveway the one thing that would ruin her appetite.

A gaudy white limousine awkwardly tried to park in the driveway already filled with the guests' cars. Instead of coming back around the block, the driver remained in the middle of the road, stopping the game. The men complained but Charlotte couldn't help but wonder if her dad secretly was thankful for the forced break, since it gave them a chance to catch their breath.

Without waiting for the driver to open his door, Denny stepped out of the back. Irritation washed over Charlotte. Her ex-husband, dressed in a green Florida A&M tracksuit, rushed across the driveway toward the house. "Charlotte," he said in an unusually frantic voice. "I've found you."

Arthur stepped in front of his former son-in-law with his hands up in warning. "This isn't the place for you, Denny."

"But I need to speak with Charlotte, Dad."

"No." Arthur shook his head from side to side. Charlotte rarely saw her father angry. If he ever was, it was during tax season when he worked on his partnership at the Pendergrass Bank with his brother. "I'm Mr. Pendergrass to you. I have always been that to you."

Denny, at six feet tall, crossed his over his chest. "C'mon, don't be like that."

"Arthur," Iris scolded from the screen door. "I swear I don't know where all this testosterone is coming from, but you come in here right now. I allowed Denny to come over here."

Charlotte's hair bounced off her shoulders as she turned her head from left to right, wondering what had gotten into her parents. They were not this type of family. They did their own things and minded their own business. The nerve of her mother to invite someone here! This wasn't even her house. Charlotte cast a side eye at her cousin. Lexi shrugged her shoulders.

"I'm not going against your mom," Lexi whispered.

Determined to find out why Denny was here, Charlotte wrapped her arms around herself and leaned against the pillar of porch. "What's going on, Denny?"

Stephen corralled everyone outside to the backyard where there'd be more room. "You gonna be okay?" Stephen asked Charlotte.

"Of course, thank you."

"I fail to understand why we have go to the back of the house when there's just one of him," said Julio.

Despite the bickering and resentment at the intruder, the men all went to resume their game. Charlotte waited until she heard the front door close before she stepped off the front step to the walkway. Numbness rolled through her. Denny stretched his arms for a hug. Charlotte thought she'd be sick.

"What do you want?" she snapped at him, not sure how long she'd be able to handle the strong stench of his cologne. Charlotte was sure it was the same brand he always wore but now, after months apart and of course the takeover of her company, Charlotte wondered why she ever stood him.

"I need you, Charly."

"It's Charlotte." Charlotte cringed at the nickname. There'd been a time in her life she'd allowed him to say and do whatever he wanted. It was him who made her see CEO Runways as a business. When he'd put up the collateral to get things started, she was blinded by his faith and believed they were in love. Had she waited and stayed in school like her parents had begged, she might not have failed.

Denny nodded his head. "Okay, I'm sorry."

Aside from running into him with Mitzi a few weeks ago, she hadn't seen Denny in months. Their lawyers had worked everything out on their own in their divorce. The time apart was welcome. Common sense was no longer clouded. "I'll repeat it again, Denny. Why are you here?"

"I came to strike a deal with you."

If he'd been wearing a clown nose and wig, the statement would have worked better. Charlotte offered a slight laugh. "Cute."

"You know I'm all about my business."

"You mean *our* business," asked Charlotte, "or at least the one you fooled me into believing I had a part in creating."

"You did," said Denny. "You had a lot to do with CEO."

"I *was* CEO," Charlotte screeched through her teeth. Her hands balled into fists by her side. "You lied to me from day one of us meeting."

Denny pressed his head to his heart. "I didn't have a backup plan, Charlotte. You did."

"A what?" Charlotte scrunched up her face and shook her head. "You know what, I don't want to hear whatever your reasons were for deceiving me."

"Charly—Charlotte, I am willing to make a deal with you."

Never.

"I've never failed a thing in my life."

Funny, Charlotte thought, miffed, placing her hands on her hips. She considered a divorce a big failure. This just went to show that Denny never took their marriage seriously. Why did she waste her time with him? Waste her life?

"Charlotte, these people are offering an obscene amount of money. I can't turn down this deal, and I can't do it with your help. You're the face of CEO Runways."

He was never going to do it with Mitzi by his side, but Charlotte was never going to tell him that. Bailey had this pageant on lock. To be sure Bailey knew how to handle herself inside and out, the two of them practiced every morning at the studio, timing her walk across the stage, to perfecting the *Hamilton* number "Satisfied." Bailey's voice was up there with the wonderful Renée Elise Goldsberry.

Charlotte researched all types of pageant questions and asked them of Bailey at random times of the day to keep her on her feet. They watched all the news channels to study everything going on in the world, just in case the judges wanted to throw in a curveball question. Bailey even gave up hanging out with her friends in order to practice harder. There was no way Charlotte planned on filling him in on that. The audacity of this jerk, thinking he could waltz back into her life. She moved on autopilot to shorten the distance between them. The only thing he needed was a hard slap across his face. Charlotte raised her hand. Never in a million years would she...

Denny flinched from her blow. "I'm offering you a million dollars on signing just to become full partner with me. Fifty-fifty from here on out. You know the clientele."

Charlotte stopped in her tracks. "What?"

"The office in Venezuela is also yours if you sign with me."

The window from the living room opened with a clang. A smoke alarm went off, echoing down the street.

"We're okay," Nate Reyes hollered. A billow of smoke filled the afternoon air followed by a few choice words from the women cooking in the kitchen.

The small interruption came at the perfect time. Charlotte had a moment to think about Denny's ridiculous offer. Judging from the smirk on Denny's face, he didn't find his offer so ridiculous. *Carúpano.* There were children there who needed to be adopted. She could start the road to her instant family and regain a successful business: the two things she'd wanted all along. Breath began to fill Charlotte's lungs. Cold air whipped through her hair and face.

"Judging from the way you're nibbling on your bottom lip, I can see you're contemplating it."

A Ludacris song came blaring from down the street. A half a beat later an old-fashioned red sports car skidded to a stop before hitting the limousine. The wheels cut hard and screeched on the pavement.

"What you need to see is that your car is in the way and you're causing a traffic jam."

"I'll leave once you give me an answer," said Denny. Irritation returned. "You need to go."

"But your mom said…" Denny pleaded.

"I'll deal with my mother." Charlotte curled her fingers into fists.

Nodding his dark head, Denny turned on his tennis shoes. "All right, we'll talk later." He whirled his finger in the air. The limousine's engine came to life. "But I will need an answer the morning of the pageant, Charlotte, in order for this deal to go through." Denny stepped closer to Charlotte. He took her hands in his and brought them to his lips. "This new venture can heal things between us."

The last person she wanted to heal with was Denny. He could rot in hell for all she cared. But this offered a promise of what she'd been wanting. Still twisted from the idea, Charlotte paused a second too long, rather than push him away.

"Hey, roomie."

The voice from the red car brought Charlotte back to reality. "Kimber." Charlotte snatched her hand back then stepped away from Denny. She caught a glimpse of Kimber being helped out of the passenger's side of the muscle car by what Charlotte would describe as a muscle head. Dario Crowne lived on the other side of their apartment complex and clearly had crush on Kimber. The limousine backed up. Once the vehicle moved closer to where Denny stood in the driveway, the other side of the road became clear. There, his hip perched on the hood of his SUV, wearing a dark pea coat with a beige sweater, was Richard, arms folded across his broad chest and an amused but quizzical expression on his face. Judging from his face, he'd witnessed the awkward moment.

"Rich," Denny called out with a wave.

Charlotte rolled her eyes at Denny's annoying way of shortening everyone's name. Out the corner of her eye, she spotted Iris tiptoeing onto the porch. She'd deal with her later.

Richard walked over to the two of them while Bailey parallel-parked his car. The last time they were all together, Halloween, there'd been no time for pleasantries. Charlotte didn't expect any now.

"Denny," Richard returned with a curt nod. "What brings you here?"

"Oh, I just came to see my girl."

Charlotte snarled, but Richard draped his heavy arm around her shoulder. Denny's brows rose. His body leaned back. "Whoa, when did this happen?"

"Happy Thanksgiving, Denny," Richard dismissed the man.

Tight-lipped, Denny nodded and turned to the limousine. "Think about my offer, Charly. I can still give you everything you ever dreamed of."

Chapter 10

The Swaynes always woke up early to cook and eat by noon on Thanksgiving Day. This gave them plenty of time to rest, watch a few games and either make rounds to other family members' homes or volunteer—and of course eat again. The only thing different about today for Richard was that he'd woken up at Magnolia Palace, the boutique hotel run by Kenzie and Ramon. Ramon then popped over to the suburbs to meet up with his brothers and cousins for an afternoon workout.

When Bailey, Richard and Kenzie turned into the neighborhood where the Pendergrasses lived, he briefly forgot Charlotte would be here. But why wouldn't she? This was her family as well. What he didn't expect was to find her ex-husband's mouth on her hands. He hated the fact he needed to be the responsible person and not haul off and punch Denny O'Malley in his smug face.

"Richard," Lexi greeted, coming through the front door. "What a pleasure to see you."

"Thanks, I hope we're not intruding. We were just dropping Kenzie off," Richard explained. His sister had already disappeared inside the house. She had a habit of making herself comfortable wherever she went.

Lexi offered a kiss on his cheek and squeezed his arm. Lexi was good people. "Not at all, come on in." She waved him into the sunken living room. Photographs of the two Reyes girls, Kimber and Philly, cluttered the wall. A football game played on an oversize television. Whistles blew, and the Pendergrass men cursed. "I'd hoped with you here my husband might actually come inside and act like a grown-up, but clearly my father and uncle need some guidance, too."

A young girl walked into the room and extended her hands. "I'll take your coat."

"Thank you," Richard said, shrugging out of the heavy material. Philly was Ken Reyes's youngest daughter. Richard could remember when she was born and was not shocked to see she was blossoming into a polite young lady. Kimber was around here somewhere. She'd arrived a few seconds earlier in a hot rod car driven by a family friend.

"That's Philly," said Charlotte. "And I'm not sure if you've met my father, Arthur Pendergrass."

Her father, a six-foot-plus man close to his own father's age, rose from his section of the couch and extended his hand. Living in a small town, Richard knew exactly who the Pendergrasses were. Anyone from any of the four towns knew them.

"Richard Swayne," said Richard. "Pleased to meet you, Mr. Pendergrass."

"Mitchell's boy," Arthur's deep voice boomed. "I know your daddy's a few years older than me, so you should just call me Arthur."

While he wasn't sure it was respectful to do so, Richard did as he asked. "All right, Arthur. Is this the Cowboys-Lions game?"

"Cowboys," clarified David Swayne in his red and gray sweatshirt. "C'mon and have a seat."

The sliding glass door opened, and the rest of the members of the Reyes family came in, all visibly pleased to see Richard there.

Nate Reyes followed close behind, rubbing his shoulder. "When did Dario start chauffeuring Kimber around?"

"You worry too much," said Charlotte.

"I need to." Nate balked at the idea of his niece and Dario. "I was going for a pass, and the dude tackled me."

"That was his job," Ramon clarified. "Next time throw the ball quicker."

Charlotte slipped from his side, which was okay. Richard welcomed the comradery with the men and being able to watch the game.

Bailey had woken him up first thing this morning to get him to go down to the gates and pick up the morning paper for the local Black Friday ads. He wondered if Charlotte planned on going. Would she want to go with him? Would she wake up in his bed again? It had been a week since they'd been together. Richard craved her love.

Charlotte returned a few moments later with a tray of appetizers. The other men swarmed her. Richard held on to Charlotte's back to brace her. When the tray was empty, she returned to the kitchen.

"So, who are you here to see, Richard?" Arthur asked, tossing a shelled pecan in the air and catching it in his hand.

Stephen and Julio chuckled. Thankfully Charlotte's mother then waltzed into the room to let everyone know they'd be eating in a moment. The seated men rose, everyone elbowing each other to get into a line. Richard followed suit. He glanced around for Bailey and found her helping the smaller children get settled at the cornucopia-decorated table. She would have made a great big sister. Richard tried talking himself into all the reasons he looked forward to being having an empty home. He joked, he teased and he came up with outrageous things he'd do but deep down inside, the idea of the void Bailey's departure would leave scared the hell out of him. He'd cheated her out of siblings and created a monster in himself by being a dependent father.

"All right, everyone," Mary Pendergrass said, clapping her hands. "We're going to do this buffet style. You're welcome to sit at the grown-ups' table or go back into the family room and finish the game."

Richard wondered how Lexi and Stephen felt at the takeover of their house, but it was none of his concern. He thought he'd be used to it by now, with his sisters always doing the same at his house. Charlotte came into view at the table up ahead and tucked her hair behind her pearl-studded ears. His heart lurched against his rib cage. The line moved. Then he remembered the wine he'd left in the back seat of the car. Richard excused himself and trotted back out into the cool weather. Bailey's parking job wasn't great and the back passenger door opened into the curb, but he didn't care. He wanted to hurry back inside to get the food and Charlotte.

How he was hungry again was beyond him, Richard chastised himself as he walked back inside. If he went left into the living room, he would now be at the very end of the line. If he cut right toward the kitchen area he might get his spot, but he wouldn't feel right, so he got to the back. Behind him he heard a set of voices.

"I believe they're dating." The voice came from Arthur.

"Are you sure?" The question came from Iris Pendergrass, no doubt. "Well, I guess that couldn't be a bad thing. He comes from a good family."

"By good you mean wealthy, don't you?"

"It always helps," said Iris.

Not wanting to eavesdrop, Richard stepped forward, but Iris's voice got higher, freezing him in his place. "If I had my druthers, she'd take Denny's offer."

"We do not like Denny," Arthur said sternly. "Let her work things out with Mitchell's kid."

"He's got a ready-made family. Is that something Charlotte really wants?"

This is different, Richard thought to himself. Most of the time his wealth drew women to him. For a second, it appeared to be a selling point for Iris. But as always, the fact he had a child or in this case a step-grandchild, was a deal breaker for her. Then again, Richard thought, raking his hand over his face, he wasn't dating Iris Pendergrass. He knew Charlotte and her parents weren't as close as she wanted them to be. Marrying Denny had not helped. Was Charlotte going to listen to her mother now? Richard didn't want to be a reason to come between them, not when it seemed they were mending their relationship. It was clear he and Charlotte were going to have to have a talk tonight after all.

"Do you want to talk about today?" Charlotte asked him the moment she entered her apartment. Richard passed her house keys back to her, and she slipped them into the bowl on the table braced against the couch facing the balcony and the late evening's view of the town square.

She'd thought he might want to chat right away after seeing Denny. Instead of making things uncomfortable, Richard had melded into the family fold. At one point he'd played ball with the rest of the men—her father, too. She had a feeling everyone was going to hit up the aspirin bottle the next day. Black Friday shopping might end up being just the ladies.

Instead of talking, Richard took hold of her hands. She figured his silence on the car ride back to her place meant he was bothered by Denny showing up. Hell, Charlotte was still mad herself. If it weren't for a house full of nonimmediate family members, she would have given her mother a piece of her mind. Who did Iris think she was, discussing her life with, of all people, Denny?

"I don't want to talk about Denny," Richard said into the darkness.

Charlotte flipped on the light in the living room. "Okay, did you have a fun time?"

Richard sat on the couch and nodded. "I did. The food was delicious. I didn't mean to stay so long."

"How else would I have gotten home?" Charlotte asked, offering a coy smile.

The pageant was in a few days. She knew she needed to end things with Richard. But she still had time. That whole evening had proved Richard wasn't ready to settle down with a family. Julio Torres kept going on about the guys' trips they were going to take to Puerto Rico now that he no longer had a kid to raise. Richard at the cabin was sweet and attentive. Richard around his friends was a total frat boy, high-fiving every idiotic adventure the guys suggested, then celebrating each idea with a swig of beer. Fortunately, Charlotte thought, Bailey had been outside with Kenzie's son, Maverick, and Lexi's three kids, Kenny, Angel and Vic.

Richard faced Charlotte. The streetlights below spilled into the room. "I have a feeling someone would have offered you a ride."

"All right," she said with a nod, "are we going to get into the Denny thing?"

"Really, no. Denny left and I stayed. That's really what matters to me."

Charlotte chewed her lip. Why did he have to be so damn sweet? "I didn't know he was coming."

"We're not talking about him." Richard held Charlotte's hands. "I do want to ask you something."

Lowering her lashes, Charlotte took a deep breath. The image of him getting down on one knee entered her mind. She imagined an heirloom ring perched in the center of an open black velvet box. "Sure."

"Can I kiss you?"

Heart fluttering she nodded. "Of course you can." Before she finished her permission, Richard lowered his mouth to hers. His tongue took hers with slightly more aggression than she'd remembered him doing before, but her pulse raced with excitement.

He held on to Charlotte's hand until they returned to her apartment. Bailey had wanted to stay behind a little longer, so Kimber had offered to bring her back to the apartment when they were done cleaning up.

There was no need for an explanation about Denny's presence but Richard saw on Charlotte's face that she wanted to explain. Richard didn't need one. He really did not want one. Charlotte's libido was on fire. Once their mouths met in the right rhythm, Richard began peeling off her clothes. His hands snaked over her hips, lifting one leg and propping it on the coffee table. The idea of Kimber coming home and interrupting them made things more exciting. Richard dropped to his knees. Kisses and nips trailed along her inner thigh.

Desire poured through her veins. She quivered for him. Richard's hands snaked around to her backside, and goose bumps ran wild down her spine and leg. Charlotte lifted her foot for him to pull her panties down. Richard gently nipped her calf and back up her leg. Charlotte positioned herself for anticipated pleasure. Richard had the magic touch and tongue. Charlotte closed her eyes while her fingers stroked the top of his head. With his mouth on her bud, Charlotte gripped his cheeks as she rode the first wave of orgasm. While she was still in throes of passion, Richard lifted her by her butt cheeks and carried her into her bedroom.

The light to her walk-in closet remained from when she'd rushed out of her place earlier today. Now it provided enough of a glow in the room for a preview of what was to come. Excitement raced as her blood pressure rose. The sight of him standing at the foot of her bed while she positioned herself just right made her gasp. Richard stretched his sweater over his head. Heart leaping in her throat, Charlotte committed to memory the way his broad chest tapered down to a narrow waist with cut, washboard abs. He undid his pants and kicked out of his shoes. She propped herself up on her elbows and bit her lip.

"Do you know how long I've waited to do this?" he asked, standing before her in all his magnificent, naked power.

Pulling her right leg up onto the mattress, she nodded. "I may have an idea."

Richard stepped in front of her, extended his hand and helped her to sit upright. Doing as he bade, Charlotte allowed him to lift her sweater up over her head. But for a thin white camisole, she'd gone braless this afternoon. Richard lifted the weight of her breasts in both hands and knelt, bracing his elbows on the edge of the bed. Every bone crackled in her hands when Charlotte gripped the comforter as Richard pushed her breasts together and flicked his tongue over both nipples before suckling them. Charlotte arched her back. Her legs wrapped around his waist, and with a little coaxing, she drew him in to her, filling her to the hilt. Both gasped at the same time. Their eyes locked. Their rhythms matched one another. She started to bite her lip again, but Richard captured her mouth, then her neck, and feasted once again on her breast. Charlotte tossed her head back and rode the second wave of orgasm.

Still breathing heavily, Charlotte used the power of her legs and urged Richard on to his back. Skirt wrapped around her waist and shoes still on, she straddled his waist. She let her hair fall to one side while she leaned across him for the nightstand. Richard pulled the curtain of tresses to the side and began to kiss her collarbone. Giggling, Charlotte jumped, accidently pulling the drawer out of the frame but not before her fingers gripped the foil package of the condom.

"All right now," Charlotte said into the darkness of the room, "this is my turn."

"Turn for what?" Richard played dumb.

Charlotte pulled herself back on top of him, her thighs resting on his. With the closet behind his head, she knew he could see what she was about to do. Charlotte lowered her head to his steel-hard erection. First, she kissed the tip, evoking a quizzical groan from his throat. When she slipped her mouth over his entire shaft, his stomach muscles tightened. And when she bobbed her head up and down, she heard the familiar sound of his knuckles cracking and felt the bedsheets move beneath them as he gripped them for stability. Finally, apparently not able to take it, Richard planted his hands in her hair and guided her head up and down. His hips lifted off the bed, but Charlotte didn't plan on stopping until she sent him over the edge the way he'd done to her this evening. But just as his breathing became labored, Richard pulled Charlotte off him, flipped her on her backside. If she'd wanted to protest, there was no time. Richard pulled the condom out of her hand, tore it open with his teeth and put it on so quickly she didn't have an opportunity to see just how hard he was. But she felt the deep passion from each stroke as he drove into her, sending her into submission. There was no way she planned on letting Richard go.

At some point in the middle of the night, Richard got up to use Charlotte's private bathroom. Charlotte slept peacefully on one side of the bed with one hand tucked under her cheek. Heart swelling with love, Richard shook his head. He loved this woman with all his heart.

Whatever her mother's fears were, Richard knew he and Charlotte would work things out. It did disturb him to know Iris Pendergrass wouldn't accept Bailey. Sure, Bailey was grown now and connecting with her college friends, but she still was part of the family.

Richard washed his face in the bathroom's sink and stared at his reflection. Over his shoulder he watched Charlotte turn and take the covers with her, exposing her bare behind. He licked his lips and contemplated waking her up again and showing her just how thankful he was.

In a few hours, most of Southwood's residents and those who came to the charming town would be ready for Black Friday shopping. The only thing on his mind was figuring out how he could find out Charlotte's ring size. She needed to be his wife. He recalled the painful rejection when he'd proposed to Octavia. While Richard doubted Charlotte would laugh at the notion, a part of him did worry about her answer. She loved him—his body, mind and soul told him so. He wanted to wake her now and ask her to marry him. How many kids did she want? Did she even want them? He'd do whatever she desired.

The drawer beside the bed remained on the ground. Richard turned off the bathroom's light and sat down on the edge of Charlotte's bed, careful not to make the mattress squeak and wake her. When she didn't stir, Richard leaned over and picked up the drawer and the contents spilled around it: a pack of condoms, a flashlight, a romance book and an opened envelope, spilling out strips of paper, brochures and pamphlets. In black, the word *options* was spelled out on the front of the envelope. One document had an estimate for starting up a new business and the pros and cons. On the list of cons was the fact that she had no credit. Her pro, if he did agree, was her decade of experience and the list of crowned beauty queens she'd worked with. The last few weeks Charlotte had helped at her cousin's studio. He felt a sense of pride in her, knowing she wanted to start her own place.

Another sheet of folded paper contained her options for new careers, including the position as cashier at the bait and tackle shop back in Black Wolf Creek. He smiled at the memory of her confidence when she'd told him about it. There was no doubt Charlotte could handle touching bait all day. The next option she had for a career was cashier at The Cupcakery. Somehow Richard figured she'd asked to be paid in frosting.

Richard started to tuck the papers back into her envelope. But when he read another one of them, he felt sudden confusion. The in-vitro fertilization one made him scratch his head. Maybe Charlotte had picked that up for a friend. But the next pamphlet came from the Children's Home Society in Samaritan. The next piece of paper on the ground was another question to herself in her own bubbly handwriting: New Company or New Baby.

In the last month of knowing Charlotte, he'd never once heard her mention of wanting to become a mother or even getting pregnant and having a baby. They'd talked about everything under the sun from politics to favorite television shows. Richard had poured his heart out about Octavia to her. He empathized with Charlotte over the loss of her company. But a baby? Nope, he never recalled conversation like that. He felt betrayed. Why didn't she tell him about this? This was big. This changed the direction of their relationship.

A lump formed in his throat. Was he not good enough as an option? Picking up the last piece of paper gave Richard his answer. After pageant, end things with Richard. At least she put a frowny face beside it. Richard placed everything in the envelope and then back in the drawer. He decided what he could do was give Charlotte a head start on her plans.

Waking up and finding Richard gone did bother Charlotte a little bit. She wasn't going to lie about that. Last night she realized she'd be ridiculous to let someone like Richard out of her life on a notion he might not want a child. He might. The only way to find out was to ask him.

She left the first message before showering. Then she dried off and sent a text. After dressing in a pair of comfy, candy-cane pajama pants and a white camisole, she left a third message on his machine. Charlotte headed out of the bedroom and found Kimber stretched out on the couch with an ice pack on her forehead.

Kimber opened one eye. "Are you in a Christmas outfit twenty-four hours after Thanksgiving?"

"'Tis the season," Charlotte replied cheerfully.

"I should have asked for your Christmas credentials before deciding to crash here," Kimber bellowed.

Laughing, Charlotte paused at the couch with her hands on her hips. "Are saying you're not kicking off the Christmas countdown with me?"

"Exactly," Kimber said with a playful smile. She winced and laid her head back down on the pillow.

A pot of coffee already brewed in the kitchen. Over the counter Charlotte spied the coffee table and a cup by Kimber. Pink packages of sweetener cluttered the counter. These were the little things Charlotte did not miss about having a roommate. When she shared a dorm room in college, she'd hated having to clean up after others. At least with Kimber, Charlotte didn't have to worry about her clothes being worn without permission. Kimber not only was finishing up school but also took care of beauty queen duties as Miss Florida A&M International. Her major in broadcast journalism took her all over the States and in front of several designers. She had her own wardrobe.

"Do you need a refill?" Charlotte lifted the pot in the air.

Kimber lifted her head long enough to see over the counter. "No, thanks. I still have some here. I'd drink it, but the sound it made when I set it down just about killed my head."

"A little hair of the dog, then?" Charlotte grabbed a bottle of Torres rum and shook its contents—or at least what was left.

The answer Kimber gave came out as a groan of misery. "Remind me to never open the door for Dario Crowne anymore."

Charlotte finished fixing her coffee and headed back to her room.

"Oh yeah," Kimber called out, "if you get hungry, Lexi and Amelia sent over some leftovers for us. We have enough to last until Christmas."

The idea of eating didn't go over well with Charlotte. She glanced down at her phone, expecting to find a response to her text or see her phone lighting up with Richard on the other end of the line. Neither happened. An uneasy queasiness hit her. Was he ghosting her?

Chapter 11

There was one thing Charlotte knew was going to happen today: she was going to see Richard, one way or another after two full days of radio silence. Today was the Royal Regional Contest. Charlotte arrived first thing in the morning. Since a few of Bailey's friends were in attendance for a shot at the free tuition, Charlotte didn't want to play favorites.

The Royal Regional Contest was held on neutral ground, equidistant between all four towns, at Brutti Hotel in the center of Four Points Park. Sponsoring the event was a social media mogul, Natalia Ruiz. Natalia and Charlotte had mutual friends, though they hadn't seen each other in a while, but Charlotte felt comfortable knowing Natalia was in charge.

Like most pageants, there were three portions leading to the main event. Instead of walk-throughs in ball gowns and swimsuits, this pageant offered a choice of wardrobe style, which meant they could select business attire or fitness. They'd practiced her talent and job interview questions since they left Black Wolf Creek.

Each event was going to be held at a different time of the day. By the evening a new beauty queen would be named. Charlotte smoothed her hands over the front of her black capri pants.

Heading to the next room, Charlotte put her weight against the silver bar of the door to open it. The door silently opened, and she stepped out into the hallway. None of the contestants were supposed to be here, let alone cornering one of the judges. She knew for a fact they were off-limits. The judges were already listed in the pageant agenda. She'd met two of them first thing this morning. Two were ladies from north Georgia, one of whom had pageanted with Charlotte back in the day, and the other was a buyer at a department store. The judge in question was one she hadn't met, but she had seen his picture. He owned a chain of luxury car dealerships all over the state of Georgia. Talking to him was the man she'd met a few weeks ago at The Cupcakery. She might have mistaken him and his daughter's attitude that day, but certainly she didn't mistake the man counting out several green bills to the judge.

Charlotte snapped photos on her phone—the same phone that Richard still hadn't used to communicate with her. Her pulse raced with a combination of excitement and shock. She'd captured someone cheating at a pageant. Seriously? Charlotte headed off to find the Natalia's event coordinator.

How appalling for this to happen! The integrity of the pageant was at stake here. Did they truly think they could buy the title? This angered Charlotte. Not just for Bailey's sake, but for all the young girls who had worked so hard. Charlotte rounded the corner toward the front desk but stopped in her tracks when she spotted the event coordinator of the pageant embracing Octavia and Troy Davenport at the same time. Troy gave the woman a slow handshake and while Charlotte knew she couldn't prove what ended up in her palm, she was sure it was money. The fix was in, not once but twice. No one could be trusted. The pageant needed to be called off.

Why were these people blessed with becoming parents? Octavia had had the chance twice and she still blew it. What on earth did Richard ever see in her? Here she was, being ghosted for whatever reason, yet he still allowed that woman the chance to be in Bailey's life? Balling her fists, she started to leave.

Charlotte spun around in her heels before they saw her. Families were beginning to walk through the lobby. With the first run-through in a few hours, she was sure everyone wanted to get a good seat. There was nothing Charlotte could do other than warn Bailey. Despite being hurt from Richard's decision to give Charlotte the silent treatment, she still tried his cell. It went directly to voice mail, as did Bailey's number. There was nothing Charlotte could do to warn them. It bothered her that Richard chose now to clearly end things with her. She just wished she knew what had happened. They could have ended as friends. Hell, she'd planned on ending things soon anyways. It was this attitude, though, she thought with irritation. It was good to know about this child behavior of his now.

"Not now, Richard," Charlotte mumbled. She could only imagine Bailey seated next to Richard in their truck and him telling her not to answer.

Feelings hurt, she still needed to pull herself together. If the pageant was already fixed, there was no reason for a show. But how was she supposed to stop this? Tickets were purchased, gowns bought, and then there was the funding parents had invested into Charlotte's services. The best thing for her to do was go outside and try to head off the Swaynes.

Outside, the sun rose over the tops of the tall pine trees surrounding the hotel. Young ladies, waltzing through the valet station and the parking lot in sweatpants with their hair in rollers, were beginning to fill the lobby.

Finally, she spotted the top of Bailey's messy bun. Thank God for her red hair. Bailey appeared to be in the company of her friends to the left and the right of her. Charlotte breathed a sigh of relief that Bailey wasn't ignoring her at the request of her father but rather having fun with her friends on the way over here.

"Bailey," Charlotte hollered out. She waved her arms above her head to get her attention. "Oh, thank God I found you," said Charlotte once she reached her.

Bailey opened her arms to hug Charlotte. She smelled like cotton candy. "Hey!"

Bailey was bubbly as ever. Charlotte felt bad for having to break the news to her.

"Can we go somewhere and talk?" Charlotte asked and took hold of Bailey's elbow. Like the rest of the contestants, Bailey was dressed down to come to the hotel. A lavender garment bag was slung over her arm, and she hung on to the hanger for her.

"Is this about you and Dad?"

You *and Dad*, not you and *my dad*. A mother passing by, shared a knowing smile, as if she were part of the parent club. Charlotte's lungs filled with pride. The response made her Charlotte's heart race. Did she know something? No, she wasn't going to involve Bailey in this whatever fight she was in with Richard. "It is more complicated than that."

Concerned, Bailey excused herself from her friends. One of them offered to take her bag up to her room.

"So what's up?"

"I don't really know how to say this, Bailey," Charlotte began. "I know all the hard work you've put in to this pageant, and you have every chance of winning."

"But?" Bailey turned slowly toward her. The sun shone through her hair, creating a golden halo.

Charlotte but her bottom lip. "I don't think this venue is right for you."

"I don't understand," said Bailey. "You don't think I can win?"

"Oh no, sweetie," Charlotte cried. "I think you can beat everyone here hands down, if it weren't…"

"You don't believe in me?"

"Bailey?" A deep voice boomed, catching both their attention.

People passed by, and in the clearing stood Richard. He wore jeans with a pair of cowboy boots underneath. His arms were folded across a faded blue V-neck shirt. And a frown marred his handsome face. "Why do you think she wouldn't win?" Richard asked while standing in front of his daughter.

The human shield made Charlotte feel left out, the three of them had been so close this last month. A piece of Charlotte's heart cracked. Not sure how much she wanted to divulge about Octavia's possible deception with Bailey around, Charlotte sighed heavily. This was beyond the ultimate betrayal and while Bailey was a strong young lady, this act was deplorable. In all honesty, she'd thought Bailey would take her word for it and leave things at that. This was turning into a "because I said so" moment.

"I believe in Bailey," said Charlotte, then she peered around Richard's frame. "I believe in you," she reiterated, making eye contact with Bailey's tearful hazel gaze. "I'm just having some reservations. Can we leave it at that?"

Richard folded his arms across his chest. Now was not the time to notice the way his shirt fit so snugly against his hard muscles. "No."

Shocked, Charlotte blinked several times, trying to make his deep refusal somehow sound positive.

"Bailey's worked hard for this," Richard went on. "Why are you trying to stomp on her goal?"

"I—I'm not." Charlotte was typically always poised and ready with an answer, which she'd learned as a beauty queen and passed on to her young followers. Now here she was stammering away to find something to say.

"Why don't you share your options with us?" Richard's clipped words emphasized on the word *options*.

The crack Charlotte had felt a few seconds ago transitioned into a shattering in the pit of her stomach. "Why are you being like this with me, Richard?" She reached out to touch his arm, praying skin-on-skin contact might bring him back to his senses. Instead, Richard wrapped his arm around Bailey's shoulder.

"Charly."

Charlotte cringed. "Oh good grief," she groaned. Not now. Of all people to walk through the crowd right now, she did not need it to be Denny. Given the flat lines of his mouth and flared nostrils, neither did Richard.

"There you are," Denny went on without a care for whom she was standing with.

"The team is all here waiting for you."

"Team?" Bailey and Richard chorused.

"Not now, Denny," Charlotte said through gritted teeth. There was no team, and she'd given no answer to his ludicrous offer. She thought no response was enough for him. She'd be a fool to work with him again. "There is no team."

"If you're working with him, that means you're working with Octavia and Antonia." Giant tears filled Bailey's eyes.

"Bailey, I'm not working with them. Not now, not ever. There is something I need to check on first with the sponsor and then I will tell you everything," Charlotte said softly. People were staring. She wanted more than anything to blurt out what was going on, what she'd seen earlier, but she also knew prying eyes stirred up curiosity and spread rumors. Natalia would never conduct business this way. Charlotte needed to find Natalia and find out what was going on. Charlotte didn't want to cause a riot. But was she willing to break Bailey's heart over it?

"Charly, let's go." Denny reached out to take hold of Charlotte's arm.

Richard intervened and blocked Denny from making contact. "Hey," he warned.

Did it make her morbid for her heart to start racing with excitement when Richard still acted possessive of her? "Bailey, I don't want you to enter, because I believe..." Charlotte took a deep breath and glanced around. To be safe, she whispered her response. "I saw one dad paying off a judge, and I saw with my own eyes, Octavia stepping out of the director's office hugging someone. I believe they fixed the pageant. I want to talk to the sponsor. She's a friend of mine."

Bailey's tears dried. Eyes still red, she narrowed them on Charlotte. "So they paid off a coordinator."

"And I saw another parent paying off a judge," said Charlotte. "This pageant is tainted."

"One judge? I could beat that. Why would you work with me and make me believe I could win when you don't have any faith in me?"

Upon realizing there were other people in the fray, Denny snapped his hands in their direction. "Little girl..."

Richard grabbed Denny's fingers and bent them back. "We're not going to do that, either."

A gurgled cry escaped Denny's throat. He buckled at his knees and put his free hand over Richard's. "Damn it, Richard."

"Go away, Denny," Charlotte said with her hands on her hips.

"Don't worry, *Charly*," Bailey spat out. "We're going."

As his daughter took off in tears through the crowd, Richard scratched the back of his head, not sure what the hell had just happened. All he did know was his daughter was upset and he needed to make it better. Before going after Bailey, Richard turned once more for a glance at the woman he thought he'd fallen in love with, but she'd left, leaving him and Denny eyeing each other.

"What are you doing here, Denny?" Richard asked. "Beauty pageants?"

"It's a competition, Rich," said Denny, still nursing his hand. "I can't walk away from a good one."

"The money, you mean?"

At least Denny was honest. He shrugged his shoulders and smoothed his uninjured hand over his slick black hair. "There's quite a bit of coins being made, and not just from this interview—" He used air quotes when saying the word *coins*. "I get that you've always had a soft spot when it comes to my wife."

"*Ex*-wife," Richard clarified through gritted teeth. He shoved his hands in his pockets to keep from punching the smug man before him. Whatever he felt for Charlotte right now was between them. Finding out Charlotte had plans to leave him without talking to him now hurt worse than ever. She'd lied to him. While he wasn't sure if he wanted to confront her on the matter, he wasn't going to stand here and listen to Denny try to lay claim to her.

Denny's face lit up. "That's right." He snapped his good fingers. "You had a thing for her until I came along. And wow, here I am again, taking her away from you."

Even though he knew better, Richard still had to inquire. "What are you talking about?"

"She didn't tell you?"

"About you yanking her company out from under her?"

"Water under the bridge," said Denny. "She and I spoke. We're moving beyond that. I know when I've made a mistake, and I know how to make up for it. I've offered Charlotte a partnership. Her mother and I've gone over the paperwork together. Charlotte's about to become a very rich woman again, with a lot of power in Venezuela."

The country she loved, Richard thought for a moment. Somewhere in their many conversations, she mentioned enjoying it there. They'd talked about everything, or so he thought. In turn, Richard knew he'd cut Charlotte off with not asking what she wanted.

"Oh, she didn't tell you?" Denny smirked.

Richard hated the fact they were in a public setting. He disliked this man, this frat brother of his. And what he couldn't stand most was Denny having the upper hand, or thinking he had the upper hand at knowing what Charlotte wanted.

A maniacal chuckle came out of Denny's throat. "Besides running her own studio, the only thing Charlotte ever wanted was to be a mother. She can adopt as many kids as she wants once she's there."

"And you knew this all along and you never gave it to her?" Richard would have given Charlotte the world, including the opportunity to be a mother. He'd never hated the idea of becoming a father again; in fact, he'd never met anyone he thought he could trust to share the experience of being a parent with, not until Charlotte.

The way Denny's shoulders bobbed up and down as if he hadn't a care in the world made Richard want to strangle the man. "Because Charlotte is too talented to settle down. She is used to a fast-paced life. What we were doing, constantly moving around, that was no way to stop and have a baby, let alone go through pregnancy. I've seen pregnant women, swollen ankles, bloated bellies. Charlotte can be pretty vain. Have you ever seen the woman without makeup?"

Actually, Richard thought to himself with a raised brow.

"Forget I asked," Denny said with a bitter frown. "Look, as long as you can put a job in Charlotte's face, she forgets about having a kid."

Since there were too many witnesses, it was best for Richard to remain still. "You don't deserve her."

"You're probably right there," agreed Denny, "and I'm not trying to win her back. I'm trying to protect my business interest. I can see where I failed when it came to taking the company from Charlotte. Call me bitter."

"You're broke," Richard realized.

"*Broke* is a harsh word. I prefer to believe my investments are frozen. I need this job to free up some money, and as much faith as I have in my partner in crime, Mitzi, who even though is unfortunately injured, doesn't have the same reputation as Charlotte. Hurt or not, I need Charlotte, and this deal is something Charlotte needs as well. Are you telling me you can offer her something more?"

Even if he had the right answer, Richard wasn't going to share it with Denny. If what Denny said was true, Richard understood where Charlotte was coming from, or at least he got her dilemma. She wanted to be a mother even if she had to walk away from what they'd started. Why didn't she open up about it instead of making plans to end things with him after the holidays? Whether or not Charlotte agreed to work with Denny in the future, Charlotte took his offer, that would be an act of betrayal in Bailey's eyes. Was Charlotte willing to risk Bailey's feelings just so she could obtain her goal of motherhood? This situation gutted him. It reminded him of Octavia's ultimate deception.

"I see you need to think things over," Denny said, interrupting Richard's thoughts. "And I need to find my former business partner."

Richard turned to leave. Unless Bailey wanted to stay and participate, there was no point of sticking around. He refused to stand here and watch everything unfold.

Since Charlotte couldn't get a hold of Natalia, she called Lexi, who in turned called Amelia. The sisters-in-law told Charlotte to sit tight while they headed over. According to the time on her cell, the pageant started in forty minutes. Stomach in knots, Charlotte waited outside the hotel by the fountain to get some fresh air.

The parking lot was still littered with guests. A few contestants practiced their talents outside. Charlotte winced when a baton went flying up in the air, only to come down on someone's windshield. An alarm pierced through the crisp air. Charlotte closed her eyes and absorbed the sun's warm rays. The temperature was typical for this time of year, cool in the morning and warm in the afternoon. Charlotte contributed her overheatedness to the story she was about to break to the world.

This morning's events played in her mind. Her heart ached recalling the hurt look on Bailey's face. How would she ever make it up to her? She still hadn't seen

Bailey since she walked away. Charlotte felt keeping Bailey out was best. Octavia had already fixed the competition for her other child. What kind of horrible woman would do that to her own flesh and blood? If she ever became a mother, she'd do everything in her power to ensure her child always felt safe and loved. She loved Bailey as if she were her own and thought she'd been protecting her.

A chilly breeze whipped through the air. Charlotte's eyes snapped open at the sound of a familiar deep voice. "She's not doing it." Richard's long, lean frame stopped just to her left. He shifted his cell phone into his right hand. "I don't know, Kenzie. I can't talk her into doing it."

Charlotte wasn't sure if she should speak up or leave. Instead, she tried to step back into the bushes behind her, blend in. Maybe he would keep walking.

"I don't care what Charlotte thought or said," Richard snapped. "No, there's nothing to say to her. We're done... Stay out of my business, Kenzie."

Charlotte's heart lurched into her ribs. His entire tone dripped with loathing. How had things gone so wrong so quickly? She was only looking out for Bailey's best interest.

"Hey, Miss Charlotte!"

At the sound of one of the toddler girls nearby calling her name, Charlotte had no choice but to stand up wave. "Hi, sweetie."

Phone in hand, Richard turned. He at least waited until the coast was clear before going in on Charlotte. "So now you're spying on me?"

Was it possible to die from the heartache vibrating against her rib cage? "I was here first, Richard."

"But you didn't leave when I came out."

Charlotte's spine straightened. "Now hold on a minute. Why should I be the one to leave?"

"Hasn't that been your plan all along?" he stated rather than asked.

"What?"

"Whatever, Charlotte," Richard said before he walked away. He got three steps ahead and stopped again. "You know, I always shielded Bailey from women who wanted nothing to do with her. I stayed away from money-hungry women who made no future plans to include my daughter. I'm just not sure which is worse—them, or me allowing you to come into our lives, only for you to plan on leaving us."

"What?" Charlotte choked out. Her hands went to the collar of her blouse. "What did Denny say?"

"Denny didn't have to say much," Richard snorted. "You already had your designs to leave. There isn't any point of denying it. I found your options list and the note telling you to leave me."

"Now who's spying?" Charlotte asked, her hands on her hips. Her mind raked over all the things she had in her envelope. Was he also angry because she wanted to have a baby? "Richard," she began softly. "Do you want to talk about this or do you just want to be mad?"

"You hurt my kid, Charlotte," Richard said evenly. "Even if there was something to talk about before, there isn't now."

The lack of emotion in his voice scared her even worse. He was done with her. They stood there, both composed and staring at each other. Charlotte's insides were dying. She fought down the lump in her throat. Thankfully a muscle car pulled up in front of them. The horn sounded off, capturing Charlotte's full attention.

"Kimber?"

"Hey," said Kimber, getting out of the passenger's seat. "I was on the way here when Aunt Amelia called. You've got to tell me what's going on—this is totally going to help my article." Kimber spoke a mile a minute and paused to look back at the spot, where Richard had once stood and now was empty. "I'm sorry, did I interrupt anything?"

"No, we're finished," Charlotte said with a deep exhale.

"Okay, good," said Kimber, pulling a pair of black suspenders up on her shoulders. She wore baggy khaki pants and a white T-shirt knotted at her waist. "As you know, I'm majoring in journalism and linguistics." Kimber reached into the driver's side of the car. Dario huffed, almost annoyed at being drawn into this, and handed her a fedora hat with a handwritten sticky note in the strip that read *Pageant Press Gazette*.

"I'm leaving, Kimber," said Dario. "You good?"

"Yeah, thanks for the ride. I'll get one of the aunts to bring me back."

Both ladies stood there for a moment while the car peeled out of the lot. "All right, let's get started," Kimber said, taking hold of Charlotte's arm. "There were over two hundred girls who registered for the event. And you think the fix is in for one particular winner?"

Charlotte's eyes were glued to Kimber's hat. "You

don't think that's going to get people to talk to you, do you?"

"You'd be surprised at how many people are willing to open up if it gives them a bit of the spotlight. I learned that from Aunt Amelia. You know she used to get reality stars to open up easily on her old shows. And she is gung-ho about this top story. You know, Amelia used to produce Natalia's reality show on MET."

Charlotte nodded. "I know. And I haven't seen Natalia here. So I don't want to point any fingers, but I do have this." Charlotte showed Kimber the photos she'd snapped.

"Oh crap," Kimber gasped. "This dude, this is Mr. Laing. He's Vera Laing's father. She's Lexi's former student. If he's paying off a judge, I totally believe in the shady business now. I guess this is Vera's last chance at trying to win a crown. Wait until Lexi finds out about this."

It hadn't been Charlotte's intent to ruin everyone's day today, but clearly by the end of the pageant, several people weren't going to be happy.

Chapter 12

Sunday morning, the day after the pageant, Charlotte found herself curled up on the couch wrapped in a soft red-and-green Christmas-themed Berkshire blanket, watching Kimber on the cable news along with Lexi and Amelia. The stress of the pageant drama had taken its toll on Charlotte. Kimber feared the flu was upon her.

On the other side of the sliding glass doors, Kimber leaned against their apartment balcony railing with downtown Southwood as her background while being interviewed by Marion Strickland from *Pageant Press Gazette* for a virtual blog. Ever since Kimber's breaking exposé on the fraud at the Royal Regional Contest had gone live last night, network stations kept calling their house line. With connections to MET, Amelia had called her team in for a professional job to speak to contestants, parents and judges. Amelia had tried to get an interview with the Davenports and the Laings, since both parties were supposedly involved in controversial bribery, but those families left the Brutti Hotel through the back doors. The judge bribed by the Laings took off as well. Gianni Brutti, owner of the hotel chain, threated to call his lawyers to sue the contest until the namesake on the marquee, Natalia Ruiz, showed up. Amelia uncovered that Natalia's aunt Yadira, the coordinator, had been the one to set up the event after thinking putting together a pageant would be easy. She hadn't expected the number of contestants nor the bribes thrown her way or the judges she'd chosen to be corrupt as well. Yadira admitted the Davenports offered her top dollar to name Antonia as the winner.

Natalia had flown in to town late last night and did a piece with Amelia and now followed up with legendary reporter Marion and the budding one, Kimber. Natalia offered full refunds for every entrant and wanted to investigate getting charges pressed against everyone involved, including her aunt.

"I can't believe the turn of events," Amelia said, crossing one leg over the other after reaching for her big mug of coffee. "Poor Natalia."

Poor Bailey. When the story broke last night, Charlotte sent Bailey a text asking her if she wanted to talk but she never responded. Charlotte feared the damage was done. She was sure she had her confirmation when she sent Richard a text to let him know she'd never taken Denny's offer and had received no response. Richard hated her and had probably warned his daughter to stay away. Charlotte tossed and turned with heartbreak.

When she'd written down the option to end things with him after the pageant, Charlotte had thought she was doing the right thing. Richard had already raised his family. A clear break was perfect for them. At least she'd planned on talking to him about it first, not cutting him off like he did her. Charlotte shivered under her blanket at the memory of the cold way he'd turned his back on her. And here she was, thinking Richard was the mature one.

"I was thinking the same thing about Bailey and all the girls who have come through Grits and Glam Studios," said Lexi, setting her mug of coffee on the table and pushing a box of tissues toward Charlotte. "Have you heard from her?"

Taking a tissue, Charlotte blew her nose. "No. But I don't expect to, either." She guessed whatever illness she was going through didn't plan to stay long. The strong, peppermint-chocolate scent of the hand sanitizer she used filtered through her nose. Typically, she enjoyed the combination, but not today. Her stomach rolled.

"You poor thing," Amelia said. "The last time I was around a crowd of people like that last year, I got the flu, too."

"And then you got the flu shot this year," Lexi reminded her.

The two women high-fived each other, making Charlotte roll her eyes. "I'll get wise with age, too."

"Hey now," they chorused.

Charlotte began to laugh, but the sound came out more like a groan. She had an appointment with the doctor tomorrow. "Sorry, I couldn't help myself."

"Well, at least you're smiling now." Amelia set her cup down on the coffee table. "I know you're not feeling good about the pageant, either," she said. "I'm not sure if you're aware of it, but when I was in high school, I wrote an exposé on the migrant workers at the peach farms in Peachville and practically bankrupted the town."

"My grandfather mentioned it," said Charlotte, "but your story helped turn the city on the right path."

"And you blowing the whistle on the pageant is going to be for the greater good, too."

"Technically," began Lexi, snapping her fingers, "since they decided to call themselves a contest rather than a pageant, should you really feel bad?"

As if considering that side of the story, Amelia tapped her chin with her index finger. "You know, you're right. That's how I'm going to spin it from here on out. Thanks to Charlotte's hot tip, I'm the one who saved the town this time," she joked.

The doorbell rang. "Slow your roll, Norma Rae," Lexi said as she popped up to get the front door.

Kimber, Marion and Natalia entered through the sliding glass doors into the living room from the balcony.

"How's it going?" Charlotte asked the ladies.

Natalia, who'd lived half her adult life on camera, spoke first. "It was great."

"I'm really sorry for having to blow the whistle," said Charlotte.

"Don't be," said Natalia. She crossed the room and sat on the coffee table. "I am done with my aunt Yadira always butting into my business. She almost ruined my reputation by concocting this scheme and slapping my name on the event. I owe you my life, Charlotte. I just don't know how to repay you."

"Just keep my name out of the papers," said Charlotte. "I may have to work in the field again one day." Though she had no plans to work with her ex ever, Charlotte needed to keep her options open.

"So, you're taking the job with Denny?"

Charlotte and everyone else in the living room turned around. Bailey stood against the open door, her arms wrapped around her waist. Her hazel eyes fixed on Charlotte, pleading with her. "Oh, sweetheart, no, not with Denny, I turned him down," Charlotte said. "I may still coach but never with him." She thought Bailey hated her. Bailey looked lost. Every fiber in Charlotte's being wanted to get up and hug her, let her know everything would be all right. Lexi closed the door behind her. The heavy sound appeared to snap Bailey out of her zone. She glanced around the room with wide, saucerlike eyes.

"Wow, so, like, talk about one of my nightmares coming true."

"What's that, sweetie?" Lexi asked, wrapping her arm around Bailey's shoulder and leading her into the living room.

"I'm standing in the room with legendary beauty queen legends—Miss Lexi as Miss FAMU, Charlotte as Miss Gillum Hall and queen of the runway, Miss Natalia the reality star—"

"I was also second runner-up to Miss Puerto Rico," Natalia interjected.

"Oh yes," Bailey agreed, "how could I forget? Miss Amelia, the producer of a reality show and I do believe a onetime contestant for Miss Southwood, and Kimber, the current Miss Florida Sweetheart, and the best reporter in the pageant world."

Marion curtseyed. "Why, thank you. Were you one of the contestants?"

"This is Octavia Davenport's daughter," Amelia explained.

"Oh?" Marion covered her mouth and blinked.

"I prefer to be known as Richard Swayne's daughter," Bailey countered.

Eyes wide, Marion snapped her fingers. "The red hair," she said making the connection. "Kenzie Swayne's niece."

"That would be the one." Bailey beamed and extended her hand. "It is a pleasure to meet you."

"Same here, and I'm pretty sure I'll be interviewing you at a crowning soon, too."

By the way Bailey blushed, Charlotte knew the pageant bug was still in her. "Everyone was just finishing up here. Would you like something to eat?"

"Oh, that's right," Kimber said, "we have a lot of leftovers."

"Thanksgiving leftovers?" Marion asked.

Kimber nodded and linked her arm with Marion's. "Come with me, let me hook you up with some southern delicacies. Have you had fried turkey before?"

Amelia, Natalia and Lexi followed the ladies into the kitchen. Charlotte patted the empty end of the couch for Bailey to sit. "I don't want you to get too close. I'm trying to fight a cold here."

"I don't mind." Bailey sat down right next to Charlotte and hugged her.

Happiness filled Charlotte's heart. "Bailey, I'm so sorry about the way things went down yesterday."

"Don't be," said Bailey. She turned on the couch so she faced Charlotte better. "I should have just taken your word for it."

"I didn't give you enough reason to trust me." Charlotte took ownership of her part.

Bailey shook her head. "No. I was so hell-bent on beating Antonia, that was all I saw."

"I didn't want you to find out about just how far Octavia would go to back her."

"Eh." Bailey shrugged her shoulders. "I should have expected something like that from her."

"I don't see how a mother could be that way," said Charlotte. "I'm sorry."

"I don't consider Octavia my mother. I mean, I get she did give birth to me, but she never wanted me."

Charlotte's heart cracked again as Bailey gulped. "She was young."

"She didn't want me," Bailey said again. "I know this for a fact. I read it in a letter she wrote my dad when I was a baby."

The letter. Richard had told her about it over their dinner in Black Wolf Creek. "Does your father know you know?"

"Of course not. Daddy's spent my whole life looking after me. He never took a job out of town. If the company needed him to travel, he took me or just didn't go. I know we have a weird bond, but you gotta admit, he's a pretty lovable guy with a kind heart. But you know that already, don't you?"

For a moment Charlotte thought Bailey had described Richard as cold. Kind? Sure, when he wanted to be. Charlotte did not answer the question, just as Richard didn't respond to her text.

Bailey patted her lap. "C'mon, now. I know I'm not supposed to meddle in grown folks' business, but I know Daddy loves you. He's spent so much time with these women around here wanting him for his money, Octavia included. None of them ever wanted anything to do with me."

"That can't be true," Charlotte started to argue, but Bailey continued.

"I can admit I am a daddy's girl. Women are threatened by it. I know a few women he took out on a few dates thought they could plan out my future and send me off to boarding school. I'm glad he found you. You love him. You least come from your own money."

"You sound like my mother," Charlotte chuckled.

"Not all women who are independently wealthy were perfect peaches for Daddy, either. Some of them still found me as competition for his affection."

"You would have always come first," Charlotte said softly.

The corners of Bailey's mouth turned down. "You said 'would have.'"

This was the part of the grown folks' business Bailey mentioned. The bond between the father-daughter duo was impenetrable. Charlotte had learned this firsthand, and she never wanted to breach it again. She reached out and patted Bailey's shoulder. "I don't know what's going to happen between your father and me. I don't think he wants to see me, and quite frankly, I'm not ready to see him."

It took a minute for Bailey to respond. "He's been moping around the house since last night. I know he's miserable. He loves you. Do you still love him?"

"I do," Charlotte answered honestly. The reality was, they had different goals in life. "But sometimes love isn't enough. And I just need you to know that no matter what goes on between your father and me, you and I have a bond. I know I'm not your birth mother but I will always think of you as mine. I'm always going to be here for you. Do you understand that?"

Bailey smiled sweetly with a threat of tears in her eyes. "I do."

"Okay, good." Charlotte reached over and hugged Bailey, kissing the top of her head.

"All right," Lexi called out, "everything good in there?"

"We're good," Charlotte and Bailey both responded then hugged once more.

Lexi and the rest of the ladies stepped out of the kitchen. Everyone carried a dish over to the table by the balcony. "Let's break bread, then."

The two-story house where Richard had raised Bailey sat on a hill with a long driveway at the end of a gated community. Richard had chosen this home years ago when he'd graduated from Florida A&M with his degrees and gotten his promotion at the company; he put down the deposit and never looked back. In the living room, Richard picked up an old photo of Bailey when she was first born. It was the only photo taken right after Bailey's birth of himself with Bailey and Octavia. Even then the smile on Octavia's face was forced. He saw it now. How different the lack of genuine smiles there, compared to the happy grins on a group photo of himself, Bailey and Charlotte on their last day at the cabin.

The grandfather clock in the living room struck five. Bailey had left early this morning and hadn't been back. Richard slid the volume up on his phone, remembering he'd shut all communications off yesterday. When Bailey walked away from the contest yesterday, he knew there'd be a thousand questions from his mom and sisters. He had no answers for them or himself. Since he didn't know how to process Charlotte's plans about ending things with him, he'd beat her to the punch. Not talking to her, though, killed him. He was an idiot for trying to do that. But what else was he supposed to do? The woman he thought he'd fallen in love with didn't trust him enough to tell him her about her dream to be a mother. He hated having to hear it from Denny, just as he hated Denny, rather than him, knowing Charlotte's desires.

Early this morning Richard had thought picking out a tree to decorate would cheer up the mood around the house. Since coming home yesterday after the fiasco with Charlotte, Bailey wasn't in the mood for anything, not even eating the cupcakes from The Cupcakery, the peppermint-chocolate ones. He figured she didn't want to eat them because they were the ones she and Charlotte ate together, and they'd just remind her of the betrayal.

Richard headed into the kitchen. The cold tiles cooled his bare feet. The weather outside was perfect enough to keep all the windows open. In the breakfast nook in the kitchen, a cross breeze came in through the front yard to the screened-in pool. The neighbor's kids used the dip of Richard's driveway as part of a ramp into their yard. The squeals of delight filled the air. He smiled and helped himself to another cup of coffee. It was close to dinnertime, and he wasn't sure if he needed to go ahead and get dinner ready. There was enough Thanksgiving leftovers from Kenzie for two more meals. And the Reyes family had sent him and Bailey home with a few sweet potato pies and some *pernil*. He couldn't wait to get into the roasted pork again.

Out of the blue, the doorbell rang. Since he'd turned off all social media since yesterday, he figured Kenzie was about to bust a gut to find out what happened. Heading to the door, he yanked it open, surprised to not find his sister. Instead, here was a stranger who'd never set foot in this house.

Octavia Davenport.

Richard stood in at the doorway, refusing to budge. Octavia had never bothered to come here before; why start now? Christmases, birthdays, graduations all came and went and she'd never responded to one invitation.

"Can't I come in and explain?" Octavia pulled down a pair of oversize dark sunglasses and batted her eyelashes. She wore a tan raincoat wrapped tight around her waist and the collar pulled up by her cheeks.

He wanted to laugh but didn't. "You have nothing to say. Bailey isn't even here, anyway."

"Well, that's good. I wanted to talk to you before I reach out to Bailey." Octavia looked off to the side at the driveway. A breeze filtered through her false lashes, causing her to dip her head and adjust the glue.

Mad at himself for knowing the difference, Richard sighed. The tricks of the beauty queen world were a part of growing up in his household. The emphasis on a good-quality glue-on falsies was important. Richard saw why now, thanks to the lectures Charlotte had given her students.

"We." He pressed his fingers to his chest and then pointed at her. "We have nothing to talk about."

"But I wanted to apologize," whined Octavia.

"It is whatever."

"Don't be like that. We once had something." Octavia playfully tugged at his shirt.

"Sure, until you decided you didn't want to be tied down with a family," Richard countered with a chuckle and smoothed her hand away from his shirt. "Anything you thought we had was done and over with when you decided walk away."

"I was sixteen, Richard. Up until we had the ultrasound, I thought I just had the month-long flu."

The memory of her naivete made him laugh out loud. The first month of her pregnancy Octavia just didn't feel well. For two months more she started getting sick.

Octavia smiled sweetly. When she was genuine, her beauty surpassed her flaws—almost.

"I wasn't much older," he reminded her.

"Yeah, but you were born with an old soul, from how you always did your homework right after it was assigned to your choice of music, and even your taste in food. How many kids from Southwood were eating sushi in high school? You were studying other countries for pleasure instead of assigned reading."

"And somehow you found that to be a character flaw?"

Octavia nodded along with a quick shrug of her shoulders. "To a stupid girl like me, hell yes." She stepped back on the front porch. "I wasn't ready."

"And you are now?" Richard snorted.

Holding her left hand in the air, Octavia snorted back at him. "I'm already married now, with a child."

"I wasn't proposing."

"Maybe not to me, but you will one day," she said. "I thought you might have found the perfect person in Charlotte."

Richard thought of Charlotte. The idea of settling down with her seemed so out of reach now. As pissed off as he was with her, he still wanted to see her one last time. Not comfortable having this discussion about his current ex-girlfriend with his old girlfriend, Richard frowned. "What do you know about my life?"

"I know you stayed in Southwood to give Bailey a stable home. But I know you put your life on hold for her. Everyone knows about it. I used to think you didn't date much because of me, but I learned that you've since dated several women."

Holding up his hand to stop her, Richard shook his head. "I don't need a recap of my past."

"You sure?" Octavia asked with a raised brow. "Because it seems to me you passed up on a lot of potential relationships."

"A lot of women who wanted access to the family money—sound familiar?" Richard reminded her. "At least they wanted the family money. You didn't want to stick around to see how things would pan out. Got yourself attached to the richest guy you could for your fast cash and dumped your daughter without batting an eye."

At least Octavia had the decency to hang her head in shame. "Look, you don't have to invite me in. I just wanted to come by and apologize face-to-face."

"Now, there something I didn't expect to hear from you, ever."

"I never thought I would see an exposé of myself and my behavior."

What was she talking about?

"Yeah, Grandma is pretty embarrassed by me as well. She came to my hotel room and dragged me to morning service."

The same grandmother, he had no doubt, who'd met him at at Four Points General with a shotgun to tell Richard he was going to do right by her granddaughter. Still with no idea of what Octavia was talking about, he just listened.

"People from my past are coming out of the woodwork, letting me know what a horrible mother I was to Bailey. And until I had it displayed for me on TV, I always thought I did the right thing by walking away."

"Let me get this straight…whatever story is on television is what made you realize you have been wrong? You're a grown-ass woman now. Your behavior last month with your other daughter…"

"Step," Octavia interjected. "She's Troy's daughter. I was trying to bond with her and even prove to you and Bailey that I'm not bothered by your bond."

He'd had enough of listening to her. Richard grabbed the doorknob. "You need help."

"Wait," she shrieked. "I've already said how stupid

my behavior is. Like I said, I wanted to prove my devotion to Antonia."

"Doesn't help your cause right now. You were disgusting and careless with my daughter's feelings."

Instead of arguing back, Octavia nodded and took his scolding. "Tell me about it. I'm not trying to justify it, just acknowledge it. I got death threats when people found out I paid off the director to favor Antonia."

Richard folded his arms across his chest and leaned forward. "I'm sorry, what?"

"I wouldn't have realized what a jerk I was if it weren't for Charlotte and her connections."

His Charlotte?

"Even though no one said she was the source, I know she saw me leaving the office. She was walking away, but she does have a distinct walk. She wasn't a runway coach for nothing."

"All right, so you've made your apologies," said Richard, clearing his throat. His pulse raced. What the hell had happened after they left the hotel? "Tell your grandma we're good. I have to go."

Before she could answer, Richard closed the front door and headed to his office on the second floor, taking three steps at a time. Charlotte's Facebook page was quiet. He grabbed his phone and dialed Kenzie's line. It went straight to voice mail. Richard went to Charlotte's other social media pages. He sat back in his office chair and covered his mouth in disbelief. Now he understood why Charlotte had wanted Bailey far away from yesterday's event. Damn, he didn't realize just how serious it was. Parents and contestants were accused of infractions between judges. What he knew about pageants told him that it didn't take much to ruin a beauty queen's credibility. If he hadn't shut Charlotte out, he might have understood her.

"What have I done?" Richard asked himself out loud. He thought of Charlotte's options list. All roads led to her wanting to have a baby. Then he thought about Octavia's words. With Bailey going off for good, he did brag more and tease about all the traveling he was going to be able to do now. He was an ass. The way he presented himself, his future life did not fit into Charlotte's plans. But that couldn't be further from the truth. He was so sorry he didn't stop ask her. And he for damn sure wanted to kick himself for the silent treatment. She didn't deserve it. If she wanted a baby with him, he'd be honored. The cell phone vibrated on the desk.

Maggie Swayne's face appeared on the screen. "My God, big brother," she gasped in her typical overdramatic fashion.

"What's up? Have you spoken to Kenzie or Bailey today?"

Her voice sounded off, like she was in a tunnel. "Did you see the news?"

"I have. I don't understand it. Where are you?"

"I'm heading to Atlanta for a conference of the Georgia pageantries," said Maggie. "All directors have to meet and figure out how to stop fraud happening ever again. I was trying to reach you to find out if you heard from Kenzie."

The wind sounded again. "Are you driving?"

"No, Caden is. Hang on, I have another call."

Maggie clicked back over.

"Hey, big brother, I need you to remain calm, but

uh, I also need you to get over to Four Points General Hospital. Bailey and Charlotte have just been brought into the emergency room."

Chapter 13

It always amazed Richard that no matter how long it'd been since his last visit, the hospital still smelled like strong antiseptic. This felt like the cleanest place on earth, yet it kept his stomach in knots. He was at his weakest at the idea of something happening to Bailey. He hated her to be in pain. Colds, tonsils, anything, it killed him. Richard worried just the same for Charlotte. Though he'd ghosted her for the last few days, he never wanted anything bad to happen to her. He loved her. She needed to know this. Footsteps pounded the freshly buffed floors to the beat of his racing heart. The waiting room at the end of the corridor seemed miles away. Richard paced his breath and willed himself to keep walking.

The furniture of the waiting room hadn't changed

much. A few rows of black leather seats attached at the armrest filled the back of the room. A couple of sets of maroon plaid love seats were pushed back to back. Strangers from the neighboring counties sporadically filled in the spaces. Richard found Kenzie, his parents, Stephen Reyes and the Pendergrasses surrounding a doctor in a white lab coat. Kenzie spotted him first. She ran to him and threw her arms around his shoulders.

"What happened?" Richard tried to remain calm. He ground his back teeth together. His hands, while hugging his sister, were balled into fists. Was she in an accident? Charlotte's parents glared at him.

Mary Pendergrass swatted Stephen's chest and arm. "This is all your fault."

"Hey, ouch, I'm sorry." Stephen held on to his arm to shy away from her.

Richard cleared his throat. "Can someone please tell me what is going on?"

Mitchell turned and faced his son. "Easy now, everything is going to be okay. It appears the girls have a bit of food poisoning."

"What?" Richard bellowed. "From what?" As far as he knew, Bailey didn't eat at the house this morning. How did she even get mixed up with these folks?

Clearing his throat, Stephen raised his hand. "I don't know how it is possible, but I think the potato salad I made was the source of this."

Richard mentally scanned all the dishes he'd seen on the buffet table. Fried turkey, corn-bread dressing, cooked-to-death green beans, greens, ham, five different casseroles. Out of everything, he didn't recall potato salad.

"It was the dish with the raisins in it," Iris Pendergrass said with a frown. The coloring in her alabaster skin drained further.

Lips curled, Richard shook his head. "Are you telling me that my daughter willingly ate potato salad with raisins in it?"

"Not on purpose," said the doctor. The name on the badge read Dr. Marvin. Richard didn't know if that was a first or last name, but he knew the guy looked young. "I've spoken with one of the ladies who had a mild case. It appears she used the same spoon she used to scoop the leftover potato salad onto the plate with the Thanksgiving leftovers."

Richard pinched the bridge of his nose. "Who all is affected?"

"Bailey went over to Charlotte and Kimber's place," said Kenzie, "so there was them and Lexi, Amelia and two other friends."

"Jesus," breathed Richard. "Where are they? Can we visit with them yet?"

"Two members at a time," said the doctor.

Not giving a crap what anyone else wanted, Richard stepped forward. No one argued with him. Bailey was the youngest out of the group of ladies. She needed her father. He'd see her and then check on Charlotte. Dr. Marvin led Richard down another corridor. His footsteps sounded off the walls. Black frames hung on the walls with photographs of former directors and donors to the hospital from all the counties. Knowing Bailey's condition wasn't as bad as he anticipated, Richard relaxed more. Heeled footsteps followed behind him.

"Mr. Swayne, is it?" Charlotte's mother said, following him and the doctor.

"Richard," he corrected and stopped walking for her to catch up with him. "I bet you're relieved, huh, Mrs. Pendergrass?"

Both parents shared a smile of understanding. He recalled Charlotte mentioning how everyone thought she favored Lexi, but Richard saw the strong resemblance to her mother. They shared the same large, expressive eyes. It was evident Mrs. Pendergrass was worried about her daughter.

"Iris," she offered. "It is a relief she'll be okay for now."

"That's right," he said. "She's probably going to leave again. I guess you're going to miss her, aren't you?"

Iris's blue eyes expressed sadness—tears touched the rims of her lashes before she blinked and looked away. "You haven't heard?"

Richard pressed his lips together. "No. I mean, she's been offered a job in Venezuela. Denny told me so."

"Charlotte turned down the job," said Iris.

"I'm confused."

"Charlotte did not appreciate me going behind her back and speaking with Denny."

Given the conversation he overheard at Thanksgiving, it didn't surprise Richard. He shoved his hands in his pocket and nodded. Relief washed over him. If Charlotte stayed, he still had a shot of proving his love. His heart filled with excitement. There was a chance. "Okay?"

"I don't want you to take it personally," Iris explained. "It is clear she had feelings for you and struggled with whether or not she wanted to move away. I didn't think you were ready to offer Charlotte what she's been wanting. Even though working with Denny was a deal with the devil, she would get what she legally deserved."

"Her business?" Richard asked. "I know nothing about the pageant world. I can't give her that."

"Bless your heart, you're very handsome," said Iris, reaching out and patting Richard's arm. "Go see your daughter."

Dr. Marvin nodded toward at an open door, ushering Iris inside before pointing toward another closed door. Richard's eyes were already scanning the chart with Bailey's name. Inside the room, a heart monitor beeped steadily. Bailey's golden-red hair spread on the pillow behind her while her face was turned as she gazed toward the window. Richard's heart swelled with pride and relief again.

"Hey, baby," he said softly.

"Hey, Daddy." Bailey looked over at him and offered a weak smile. "This has to be the worst thing ever." She lifted her left hand. A long tube held in place by a needle in her arm rocked back and forth. "The doc says I need to stay hydrated but that I can go home."

"I'll let him be the one to tell me that." Richard dragged the hard plastic maroon chair by the window over to the side of her bed. "Tell me something."

"Huh?"

"What did potato salad with raisins taste like?"

Bailey groaned and moaned at the same time. "I only had what was on the spoon and it was exactly like it sounds. Who does that?"

"I believe the person who did it is sorry," said Richard. "Hey, speaking of sorry, you had a visitor today."

"Oh yeah?" Bailey struggled to sit up with the help of the remote control on the side of the bed. "Was it Idris Elba?"

"What?" Richard narrowed his eyes. "The man is way too old for you."

"It's a joke, Dad." She sat up, and automatically Richard stood to help her with her pillows. "Stop, I've got it."

Richard sat down. "Smothering again?" he asked her.

"Smathering," she said. "Now if Idris didn't come to visit me, who did?"

"Octavia came to apologize."

Bailey's big eyes grew wide. "Say what now? Let me guess, she is ashamed at how she was portrayed in the exposé by Kimber."

"I heard Charlotte had a lot to do with it," he said.

"She did. I was wrong for not listening to her," said Bailey, looking down at her hand. "I was mad because she told me no and then even more upset that she was going to work with Antonia."

Richard nodded. "I understand, sweetie. I was mad for the same reasons."

"It was like she was sending me away, like the ladies you used to date wanted to do," Bailey confessed.

Not being able to help himself, Richard took her hand in his. "I would never let that happen."

"I know," Bailey sniffled. "I realized she was trying to spare my feelings. She didn't want me to see Octavia root for her daughter."

"Step," Richard corrected with a raised brow. At his daughter's raised brows, he explained Octavia's visit.

Bailey sat and listened, rolling her eyes the majority of the time. "Well, that's all I can say for her."

"It is whatever," said Bailey. "Legal or not, she gave up the right to be my mother."

"Did Charlotte tell you this?" Richard asked.

"I told Charlotte that this morning." Bailey explained why she'd gone over to the apartment. He adored her for taking the responsible route and apologizing for her behavior, but he wished he'd known. He would have been a part of that apology. Bailey went on about being in the room with all the beauty queens and how she couldn't wait to sign up for the next pageant. He reminded her there would be contests in college just the same.

After an hour of talking, Bailey's nurse came in and took off the saline IV bag and brought in the wheelchair to discharge her. She was going to need to stay hydrated this evening and monitored, which Richard didn't mind at all.

In the hallway the antiseptic smell greeted him again. This time, the other doors to rooms containing the other patients from the incident were opened as well. Stephen pushed Lexi. Nate hung on to Amelia's chair. A couple of interns held on to two ladies Richard recalled seeing on the pageant exposé. Dario, from downstairs, pushed Kimber first. Richard glanced around. Charlotte was missing. Had she left early, or was she staying overnight? He pushed Bailey's chair past the room he'd seen Iris enter. The room stood empty—even the bed was stripped of its sheets.

"Did they release Charlotte?" Richard asked, catching up to Lexi.

Pale faced, Lexi nodded. "She left a while ago."

"Lucky," Amelia groaned.

"She must not have eaten," said Stephen.

Kimber shook her head. "You know, I don't think she ate at all. She's been sick already."

"Oh," said Dario. "I thought you said she was in the bathroom getting sick."

"She was," answered Kimber, looking up at her driver.

The men in the hallway glared at Dario. He chuckled sheepishly. "Kimber came over to my place and said everyone was getting sick. I just gave a number to the emergency operator of how many ambulances to send." He held his hands in the air and let the chair coast for a moment.

"Dude," Stephen warned.

"My bad." Dario grabbed the handles again.

Richard scratched the back of his head. "Excuse me, Nurse," he said to a woman wearing a pair of pink scrubs. "What happened to Charlotte Pendergrass?"

The young lady looked nervously at him. "She was discharged."

"I'm her cousin," Lexi said, taking hold of the nurse's hand before she got the chance to turn and leave. "I need to know where she went."

"I believe her mother said she was taking her home, to Black Wolf Creek."

"How weird," said Kimber. "She's been sick to her stomach for the last few days, didn't eat any of the food to get food poisoning and now she's going home to her parents' cabin in Black Wolf Creek?"

No mistaking the way Lexi and Amelia shared a look. Their eyes cut over to the other two women Richard didn't know, and they all shared a smile. Slowly the revelation started to make sense to Richard, given the symptoms and the timing. His heart raced with bewilderment. Charlotte was pregnant.

"Are you sure you want to be there alone?"

After recovering from a wave of nausea, Charlotte sat down on the edge of the couch in her cabin. It seemed the moment her pregnancy had been confirmed, morning sickness kicked in. "There's kind of no other place for me to be," said Charlotte into the speaker of her phone.

Charlotte frowned at the idea of being single, unwed and pregnant in her childhood bedroom. Being back at the apartment with Kimber would have been fine, but she knew it was crunch season and Kimber needed to buckle down and study. The best place for peace and quiet was here, back in Black Wolf Creek.

"No, Mama, I'm fine where I am."

"Can I bring you food?"

"No," she gasped while her stomach quivered. "I just want to eat my sleeve of crackers and drink my apple juice."

The other end of the line went silent for a moment. "Well, okay. If you insist on me not being there tonight, I'll check on you tomorrow."

Charlotte slid her finger to the red button to disconnect the line. All she wanted to do was be alone and cry. She wasn't sure why. She'd wanted a baby and finally her wish was coming true. Unfortunately, it meant she was going to have a child with a man who wanted nothing to do with her. Ironic how when she first arrived at Black Wolf Creek over a month ago she'd wanted to have a baby without necessarily having a husband to go along with it. Now, she was having a baby and the father did not want to have anything to do with her. Charlotte had never been more afraid in her life.

The garbage cans behind the house rattled. Charlotte's heart thumped against her chest. How could the coyotes come so fast? She hadn't thrown anything away. Then she realized, she had gotten a little sick out back. The gross idea of a coyote… She frowned and closed her eyes. Deep, steady breaths helped her control some of the nausea. The problem was, each time she closed her eyes she imagined Richard's face. She'd spotted him yesterday evening when her mother came into her hospital room. His eyes were focused on Bailey's door, of course. The worried lines on his face reminded her even more how she didn't belong in their circle. Bailey had given her a glimmer of hope, but it fizzed when Richard never came to check on her. He'd said they were done. They were done.

Charlotte opened her eyes. From her position in the living room, she screamed at the figure at the door. The motion detector light delayed, and just as Charlotte was sure there was a masked murderer at her door, the light shined on Richard's face.

"What the—?" She scampered off the couch and ran through the kitchen to unlock the doors.

"You didn't cover your trash cans properly," Richard warned her.

Blinking in disbelief, Charlotte shook her head. "Thanks for making the trip to tell me."

Richard stepped farther into the kitchen. A bubble

caught in Charlotte's throat, preventing her from speaking. She craned her neck up at him. A thick layer of red beard grew on his chiseled cheeks. Richard took a black skullcap off his head and smoothed his hand over the closely cropped hair.

"I didn't come here for just that, Charlotte."

"Why are you here, then?" she managed to say, folding her arms across her chest for a distance she knew she didn't want but had to create.

Richard stepped closer. She lowered her arms. He took her cheeks in his hands and tilted her face to his.

"I'm an ass, Charlotte."

"Agreed," she said curtly.

"I first need to apologize for slipping into my over-protectiveness with Bailey the other day. I didn't realize—"

Charlotte cut him off. "You didn't realize that I cared so much about her that I didn't want her to get hurt? That I'd risk my reputation as a pageant coach and the future of being hired by any other client just to make sure her feelings were spared?"

Richard licked his lips. Charlotte wanted to share in the tasting of his mouth, but she was still hurt. "Why did you?" he asked of her.

"I didn't want either of you hurt," she said, gulping.

"Why?"

"Because I love Bailey," Charlotte said. "I love you."

Richard lowered his lips to capture hers. The coldness of touch immediately warmed once their tongues greeted each other's. Charlotte pressed her hand against the fabric of his long-sleeved black shirt, where his heart beat against her palm.

"I love you, too, Charlotte," Richard admitted. He pulled her into a hug and kissed her chin, her neck, and pulled her hands up to his mouth. "These last twenty-four hours have taught me one thing."

"Richard." She tried to stop him. She was about to break the news to him that was going to change his future plans.

Her protests didn't matter. Richard continued. He lifted Charlotte by the hips and set her on the island bar in the kitchen, where their heights were better matched. "Charlotte, I may have given you the wrong impression about myself. I love my life in Southwood. I loved being a father. I'm still going to love being a father to Bailey when she needs me. Yes, she's moving, which gives me the opportunity to do more traveling, but it doesn't take me away from Southwood, Bailey or, more importantly, you."

Charlotte's heart thumped. Richard stood where they were eye level. "The only traveling I want to do—whether it's out of the country, here to Black Wolf Creek or even to the grocery store—is with you. I want to marry you, Charlotte."

Hot salty tears streamed down her cheeks. "Richard, you need to know something."

"The only thing I need to know first is that you want to marry me, too." Richard pressed his forehead against hers.

"I'd love to marry you, Richard," she began. "But we…"

Richard silenced her with a deep kiss. Had she not been sitting down, her knees would have buckled beneath her. Everything about his kiss told her things were going to be all right. At least until they heard a loud boom from next door. Both broke contact and glanced out the large floor-to-ceiling windows. An orange glow grew from the fire pit next door.

"What the hell?" Richard said, taking Charlotte by hand. "I don't want to leave you here. Come with me. I think I see Bailey's friends' cars out there."

Really? Because Charlotte didn't see a thing. Her eyes were still adjusting from the blinding fire down below. "She's probably having a bonfire before she heads off for school, you know."

"If we're going to be married, we've got to face these parenting moments together."

Richard held on to Charlotte's hand as they crossed the creek into his property. *Parenting*, she thought with a grin. She'd break the news to the both of them at the same time. Through the clearing Charlotte noticed Bailey's friends, who turned out to be Kenzie, Lexi and Amelia, all seated in the lounge chairs and holding mugs in their hands. Lexi and Amelia looked a lot better now than when she last saw them in the ambulances. The sliding glass door to the Swayne home opened, and Charlotte's father and uncle came out carrying a tray that looked like it contained burgers.

"You guys," Stephen called out after them, "Nate and I brought the salad."

"No," everyone chorused.

"That's cold," said Nate. "It came from a bag from the store."

Charlotte stopped at the edge of the fire pit. "What is going on?"

Bailey poked her head out of the door. "Is she here? Oh, hey, Charlotte."

"Hey, Bailey," Charlotte called out, a little confused why she didn't come over and hug her. "You feeling better?"

"I am now." Bailey bounced down the steps, holding something behind her back.

Everyone gathered around. Everyone included Richard's family, his mother and father and his sisters. Charlotte wasn't sure she wanted to tell his entire family about her pregnancy.

"This is for you," said Bailey. She pulled a banner out from behind her back that read, Welcome to the Family.

Tearfully Charlotte looked up at Richard. He smiled before he spoke. "Your father and I already spoke."

"We did," said Arthur. "I gave him permission to ask for your hand."

Charlotte raised a brow. Her father knew she was pregnant. Did he greet Richard with a shotgun? "Daddy?"

"Oh wait," said Mary Pendergrass. She handed something rolled up for Paula Swayne and Iris to hold from each end.

"Congratulations on the future baby beauty queen."

"Could be a boy," one of the men hollered out.

In the time she'd found out she was pregnant, Charlotte hadn't thought about the gender. Charlotte's heart jumped to her stomach. Eyes wide, she turned to glance up at Richard's smiling face. "You know?"

"I figured it out," he said with a cocky grin.

"You made it abundantly clear you didn't want any more children," Charlotte replied.

"And you never gave me the chance to see if I wanted to have children with you, Charlotte," he said gently.

He was right. She hadn't confided in him. Charlotte looked away for a moment. "I don't want you to feel obligated. Having a baby is my dream."

"And now it's ours, and I can't wait to start this journey with you."

Her heart soared. Was it possible to be so happy? "I feel I need to warn you that I plan on working at the studios."

Richard wrapped his arm around her shoulder. The touch warmed her soul. "I support whatever career you want to do, Charlotte. Just as long as you'll marry me."

"You know I will."

"Charlotte. I love you." He wrapped his arm around her shoulder and drew her close while their mingling families blended together.

"I love you, too," Charlotte said before sealing her declaration with a kiss.

* * * * *

SPECIAL EXCERPT FROM

*Despite her family's billions, Samira Ansah is climbing
the corporate ladder on her own. She needs to buy
a lucrative property owned by bestselling author
Emerson Lance Millner. The sexy recluse isn't selling,
but when he assumes she's his new assistant, Samira plays
along to get closer. There's nothing fake about the sizzling
attraction between these two opposites. But revealing the
truth could close the book on their future...*

Read on for a sneak peek at
Christmas with the Billionaire,
the next exciting installment in the
Passion Grove series by Niobia Bryant!

She took another step closer. "Mr. Millner—"

"I'm sure Annalise explained to you that I need an assistant for the weekends only. Your main priority would be typing my handwritten book, updating my social media accounts and running errands," he said, turning to stride across the room to stand next to the lit fireplace.

"You write by hand?" she asked, unable to hide her amazement and forgetting the reason for her visit.

"Yes," he said, his voice deep.

"And you've finished your new book in the Mayhem series?" she asked.

"So, you're familiar with my books?" he asked, his attention locked on the crackling fire.

Samira wished she could see his face. She felt almost like he was hiding it from her intentionally. "Yes," she finally answered. "My favorite is *Vengeance.*"

He grunted.

She eyed him. There was something so powerful but still sad about his stance. The way he moved. The way his stare was downcast. She was surprised at how strongly she needed to know what gave him such a demeanor. It, plus the dark interior of the home and neglected exterior, was all so mysterious—maybe even more so than one of his novels.

The man was an enigma. How could someone so abrupt and insolent write with such emotion and rhythm that she was forever transformed by his words? The two did not match.

"I assume since you're here you made Annalise's round of cuts," he said.

Annalise? As in Annalise Ray?

"Absolutely," she lied, completing winging this unexpected interaction.

"I like that you don't talk much."

She pressed her lips together.

"Do you want the job?" he asked, crossing his strong arms over his chest.

She didn't miss the way the thin material stretched with the move. "Wait. What?" she asked, forcing her attention from his fit form framed by the light of the fire and on to his words.

A billionaire heiress working as an author's weekend assistant. The thought actually made her smile.

The smile widened.

And maybe a better chance to get to know him and just what his reservations are about selling the land.

She contemplated all the pluses and minuses of the ruse. Some work related.

Samira eyed the fine lines of his taut body and her body instantly responded to him.

Some not.

"Yes or no?" he asked, his tone brusque.

Is this crazy? Am I?

"Yes, Mr. Millner, and thank you," she said.

Will this work?

"Good. Ms.…"

She opened her mouth but closed it as she almost supplied him her real name. He might very well know the Ansah name. "Samantha Aston," she lied, pulling the name out of the air.

Ding-dong.

She briefly looked over her shoulder to the front door at the sound of the doorbell.

"Your first duty is sending away all the other applicants," he said, turning and leaving the room with long strides.

What the hell have I gotten myself into?

Don't miss Christmas with the Billionaire
*by Niobia Bryant, available November 2019
wherever Harlequin® Kimani Romance™
books and ebooks are sold.*

Want to give in to temptation with
steamy tales of irresistible desire?

Check out **Harlequin® Presents®**,
Harlequin® Desire and
Harlequin® Kimani™ Romance books!

New books available every month!

CONNECT WITH US AT:

Facebook.com/groups/HarlequinConnection

Facebook.com/HarlequinBooks

Twitter.com/HarlequinBooks

Instagram.com/HarlequinBooks

Pinterest.com/HarlequinBooks

ReaderService.com

**ROMANCE WHEN
YOU NEED IT**

PGENRE2018

Looking for more satisfying love stories
with community and family at their core?

Check out **Harlequin®** Special Edition
and **Love Inspired®** books!

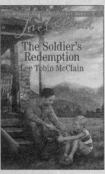

New books available every month!

CONNECT WITH US AT:

Facebook.com/groups/HarlequinConnection

 Facebook.com/HarlequinBooks

 Twitter.com/HarlequinBooks

 Instagram.com/HarlequinBooks

 Pinterest.com/HarlequinBooks

ReaderService.com

**ROMANCE WHEN
YOU NEED IT**

HFGENRE2018

Love Harlequin romance?

DISCOVER.

Be the first to find out about promotions, news and exclusive content!

Facebook.com/HarlequinBooks

Twitter.com/HarlequinBooks

Instagram.com/HarlequinBooks

Pinterest.com/HarlequinBooks

ReaderService.com

EXPLORE.

Sign up for the Harlequin e-newsletter and download a free book from any series at **TryHarlequin.com.**

CONNECT.

Join our Harlequin community to share your thoughts and connect with other romance readers!
Facebook.com/groups/HarlequinConnection

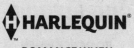

HARLEQUIN®

ROMANCE WHEN YOU NEED IT

HSOCIAL2018

lover in you!

Earn points on your purchase of new Harlequin books from participating retailers.

Turn your points into **FREE BOOKS** of your choice!

Join for FREE today at **www.HarlequinMyRewards.com.**

Harlequin My Rewards is a free program (no fees) without any commitments or obligations.